Liza Marklund is an ... columnist, and goodw... ~~ed to any branch of the~~
~~Her crim~~ ... ~~n or before the date~~
Annika Bengtzon instantly became an international
hit, and Marklund's books have sold 13 million copies
in 30 languages to date. She has achieved the unique
feat of being a number one bestseller in all five Nordic
countries, as well as the USA, and she has been awarded
numerous prizes, including a nomination for the Glass
Key for best Scandinavian crime novel.

The Annika Bengtzon series is currently being adapted
into film, and will launch with the movie of this novel,
under the title *Nobel's Last Will*.

Neil Smith studied Scandinavian Studies at University
College London, and lived in Stockholm for several
years. He now lives in Norfolk.

Also by Liza Marklund

VANISHED
THE BOMBER
EXPOSED
RED WOLF

By Liza Marklund and James Patterson

POSTCARD KILLERS

LAST WILL

Liza Marklund

Translated by Neil Smith

CORGI BOOKS

TRANSWORLD PUBLISHERS
61–63 Uxbridge Road, London W5 5SA
A Random House Group Company
www.transworldbooks.co.uk

LAST WILL
A CORGI BOOK: 9780552160940
9780552167499

Originally published by Piratförlarget in Swedish
in 2006 as *Nobels Testamente*
First publication in Great Britain 2012

Addresses for Random House Group Ltd companies outside the UK
can be found at: www.randomhouse.co.uk
The Random House Group Ltd Reg. No. 954009

The Random House Group Limited supports the Forest Stewardship
Council (FSC®), the leading international forest-certification organization.
Our books carrying the FSC label are printed on FSC®-certified paper.
FSC is th   g
environmenta   rement
policy

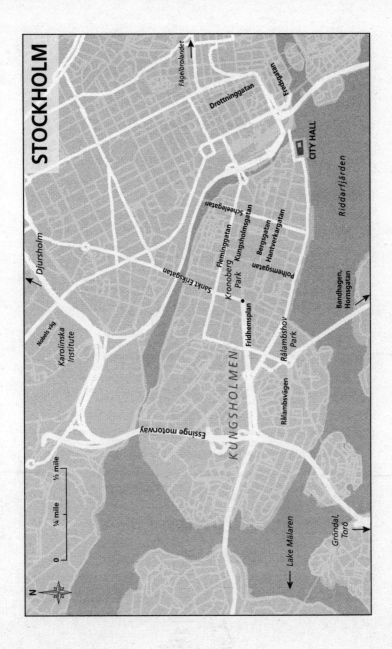

STOCKHOLM

N

0   ¼ mile   ½ mile

Lake Mälaren

Essinge motorway

KUNGSHOLMEN

Grøndal,
Torö

Rålambsvägen

Rålambshov
Park

Fridhemsplan

Kronoberg
Park

Flemingatan
Kungsholmsgatan
Scheelegatan

Sankt Eriksgatan

Bergsgatan
Hantverkargatan

Polhemsgatan

Bandhagen,
Hornsgatan

Riddarfjärden

CITY HALL

Fredsgatan

Drottninggatan

Fågelbrolandet

Djursholm

Nobels väg

Karolinska
Institute

A Note on the Currency

Calculated at a rate of 10.3 Swedish Krona to the British pound, the monetary figures in this book would convert approximately as follows:

10kr = 97p	500kr = £48.50
50kr = £4.85	1000kr = £97
100kr = £9.70	2000kr = £194
200kr = £19.40	3000kr = £291

Part 1
DECEMBER

Thursday, 10 December

Nobel Day

1

The woman known as the Kitten felt the weight of the weapon dangling under her right arm. She tossed the cigarette to the ground, lifted her skirt and crushed the butt with the underside of her stiletto.

Find any DNA on that if you can.

The Nobel festivities had been going on inside the banqueting rooms of the City Hall for three hours and thirty-nine minutes now. The dancing was under way, and she could make out the sound of music as she stood outside in the freezing street. The target had left the table in the Blue Hall and was walking up the flight of steps towards the Golden Hall. The text message she had just received had given her the target's position.

She sighed, realizing how irritated she felt, and gave herself a mental slap. This job required concentration: there was no room for aimless worrying or thinking about alternative careers. This was all about basic survival.

She forced herself to focus on the immediate future, on the sequence of events she had memorized by going over it again and again, until she was bored stiff by it, but certain the job would be carried out successfully.

She set off with light, measured steps, the salt and

gravel rough under the thin soles of her shoes. The temperature had fallen below zero, forming patches of ice on the ground – a scenario she had hoped for, since she'd look colder and more vulnerable, but hadn't been able to assume. She hunched over, the chill making her skin pale and her eyes water. If they looked red it would be no bad thing.

The uniformed police officers were positioned exactly where they should be: two on each side of the archway that formed the entrance to Stockholm City Hall. She braced herself.

Time for mark number one: pale and beautiful, frozen and cold, mobile phone in her hand. Showtime!

She stepped into the archway just as a group of happy revellers appeared from the other direction. Their voices broke through the cold air, their laughter echoing. The bright lights from the building threw contrasting shadows over their cheerful faces and styled hair.

She looked down as she walked, and reached the first police officer at the same time as the raucous men started yelling for a taxi. When the cop made an attempt to talk to her she threw out her arms and pretended to slip. The policeman reacted instinctively, the way men often do, and caught her flailing arm. She muttered something in incomprehensible English, withdrew her hand and glided towards the main entrance, thirty-three measured steps.

So fucking easy, she thought. I could be doing better things than this.

The flagged courtyard of the City Hall was full of limousines with tinted windows, and she spotted the security guards out of the corner of her eye. People were streaming out of the building, alcohol breath pluming from their mouths, the feeble light of the torches giving their faces grotesque shadows. Straight ahead, beyond the cars and the garden, lay the glittering black waters of Lake Mälaren.

She approached mark number two: the entrance to the Blue Hall. An elderly man was blocking the doorway and she had to stop. He stood to one side to let out a group of blue-haired ladies, who were following him, and she had to bite her tongue and stand there, shivering, while they creaked out into the courtyard. One intoxicated gentleman said something impertinent as she slipped into the cloakroom with her mobile in her hand but she ignored him, left him behind and moved towards mark number three.

Annika Bengtzon stood up from table fifty as her dinner partner, the managing editor of *Science*, pulled back her chair for her. She felt a little unsteady. Her shawl – it had belonged to her grandmother – was slipping and she clutched it more tightly round her. There were so many people, so many swirling colours everywhere. Out of the corner of her eye she saw the permanent secretary of the Swedish Academy hurry past her table. God, he was handsome, she thought.

'It's been a pleasure,' the editor said, kissing her hand before vanishing into the crowd. Annika smiled politely. Maybe he had been a bit upset when she had turned down his invitation to dance.

She fiddled with her shawl and checked the time. She didn't have to get back to the newsroom just yet. Anders Wall, the financier, slid past with his wife, as the head of Swedish Television headed in the opposite direction. She felt someone stop right behind her, and looked round to see Bosse, a reporter for the other main evening paper.

'How many stars do you give the starter?' he said quietly, his lips far too close to her ear.

'Four skulls-and-crossbones,' Annika said, standing still, her bare shoulder against the front of his jacket. 'How many points does Princess Madeleine's neckline get?'

'Two melons,' Bosse said. 'The speech by the fellow who got the prize for medicine?'

'Eight sleeping-pills . . .'

'May I?' he asked, bowing with a flourish.

Annika glanced round quickly to make sure the man from *Science* wasn't nearby. She nodded, pushing her elegant clutch inside her larger bag and hoisting it on to her shoulder. Her shawl was draped over her forearms, her skirt creased. Bosse took her hand and walked with her towards the steps leading to the Golden Hall. They sailed between the tables, past the flowers and crystal glasses. Annika had skipped most of the wine, just tasting it so she could include it in her article about the evening, which was, frankly, an insult to the readers: she didn't know a thing about wine. Even so, she still felt a bit giddy. She took Bosse's arm as they ascended the staircase, holding up her skirt with her other hand.

'I'm going to trip,' she mumbled. 'I'll fall on my arse and roll all the way down and knock the legs out from under some important politician.'

'No one's ever fallen down these stairs,' Bosse said. 'When they were building the City Hall the architect, Ragnar Östberg, made his wife walk up and down them in an evening gown for a whole week, while he adjusted the steps to make sure you could glide up and down them and never fall. The staircase has worked beautifully ever since, but his wife divorced him.'

Annika laughed, a bit too loud and for a bit too long.

Soon she would have to leave the party and go back to the newsroom to write about it. Soon the spell would be broken – her long, flowing dress would turn into a top from H&M and a polyester skirt. 'It's completely crazy, really, being part of something like this,' she said.

Bosse put his hand on her arm and guided her up the last steps, just as the winner of the chemistry prize had done with the Queen.

They emerged on to the long balcony overlooking the Blue Hall, then had to fight their way through the crowd surrounding a drinks table outside the doors to the Golden Hall.

'One for the road?' Bosse asked, and she shook her head.

'One dance,' she said, 'and then I have to go.'

They stepped into the Golden Hall, the impressive banqueting room. The walls were covered with artworks and mosaics made with real gold, and the orchestra was playing, but Annika paid little attention to the tune. All that mattered was that she was here and Bosse was holding her, and she was spinning round and round, the golden mosaics swirling.

Observing the vaulted ceiling and limestone floors, the woman known as the Kitten was inside the building. Silk creased and stretched across full stomachs; ties rubbed against red necks. She slid unnoticed among the other evening-gowns, no need to look around. In the past few months she had been on a number of guided tours, in three different languages, through the halls and galleries of the City Hall. She had taken pictures and carefully studied the whole building; she had been on test-runs, even test-slips. She knew the exact length of her stride and where she could catch her breath.

17

It was a pretty spectacular building, she had to admit. The chance to admire the architecture was the best thing about this job.

Twelve steps into the Blue Hall.

She stopped under the pillared walkway and composed herself before entering: 1,526 slightly asymmetrical square metres, the aftermath of the meal, people crowding on to the marble floor, light sparkling from thousands of glasses. The royal couple had gone, the security staff with them. She allowed herself a brief moment of contemplation, and realized that she would rather have taken part in the dinner than do her job. These events always seemed to have a pretentious theme – this year it was Nordic winds. She thought it sounded rather revolting, but she liked the way the meal had been set out.

Damn, she thought. I really need a different job.

Oh, well. Mark number four. Turn right, a quick glance.

She stepped out from the paired granite pillars and set off towards the staircase, ten steps in her high heels. She could hear the music from the Golden Hall clearly now, and it mustn't stop.

A moment later a man was standing in front of her, saying something. She stopped and took a step to the side, then another. The bastard wasn't letting her through, and she was forced to push past him and hurry up the forty-two steps, each one thirteen centimetres high, thirty-nine centimetres across.

Then the long balcony of the Blue Hall, seven doorways into the Golden Hall, seven doorways leading to the great works of art in there, portraits of the Queen of Lake Mälaren and St Erik.

The text: *Dancing close to St Erik.*

She pressed on, pushing her way through efficiently and quickly, past doorway after doorway until she reached the last. The music was louder. There was a key-change – it was getting close to the end of the piece. She walked into the crowd of dancing guests. Now she really had to focus.

For the first time during this job she felt the familiar tickling sensation, the adrenalin rush that sharpened her senses, the satisfaction. The millions of mosaic pieces shimmered in her eyes. She looked around: the musicians on the far side by the ugly Queen of Lake Mälaren painting were building up to the crescendo. She scanned the clothes, the people. She had to locate the target *now*.

And there it was.

Right there, on a direct line from mark number five to mark number six, dancing. Bullseye.

Ninety seconds. She fired off a text to her wingman, raised her right arm, opened her evening-bag to drop in her mobile, then felt for the pistol.

At that moment she was jolted by a laughing figure moving just to the left of her –what the fuck? The floor slid, she lost her balance and took another unplanned step, feeling her heel sink into something soft and her elbow jab someone's ribs. She heard a yelp.

The sound was so unexpected that she looked up and stared into a pair of heavily made-up eyes that reflected both annoyance and pain.

Shit!

She looked away quickly and took the final steps.

The weapon was heavy and solid in her hand, and the concentration that finally filled her made every sound around her fade away. She was calm and clear. She raised the bag towards the dancing couple, aiming at the man's leg: the first shot. The sound was scarcely audible, the recoil manageable. The man sank to his knees, leaving the woman unshielded. She raised the bag, aimed at the woman's heart and fired the second shot.

She let go of the weapon, the bag with its bullet hole dangling from its strap. She refocused her gaze on the door, eight steps to the oak door that symbolized the next mark: one . . . two . . . three . . . four . . . five . . . six (now the screaming started) . . . seven . . . eight. She had made it, and pulled it open with no problem. It closed silently behind her; four steps to the service lift, two floors down and then three steps along the slope to the goods entrance.

She relaxed slightly, the adrenalin rush starting to fade.

Not yet, for fuck's sake, she said angrily to herself. *This is the tricky bit.*

The cold was paralysing as she stepped outside. Ninety-eight slippery cold steps towards the water, a hundred-metre dash.

The guards in the courtyard stiffened and in unison raised one hand to their ears. *Shit.* She'd expected to get a bit further before they found out what had happened. She pulled the gun from her bag as she let the door of the goods entrance close behind her. Three men were guarding the side of the building facing the water, just as planned, and she shot them one by one, intending to immobilize them, not necessarily to kill.

Sorry, guys, she thought, *nothing personal.*

A bullet fired from somewhere behind her hit the granite pillar beside her, chipping off a shard of stone that hit her cheek. She flinched, then crouched down, pulled off her shoes and ran.

Her sense of hearing was coming back and she could make out the roar of the powerful outboard motor.

She left the shadows and turned sharply to the right through the garden. The frozen grass crunched beneath her bare feet, pricking like needles. Shots were being fired from somewhere behind her, and she was darting and flying, the pistol and shoes in her hands as she tried to hold up her skirt.

The engine noise cut out as the boat swung in alongside the City Hall.

The icy wind stung her face as she threw herself down the granite steps. The waves of Lake Mälaren were hitting the hull and splashing over the sides as she landed awkwardly in the stern. The feeling of triumph vanished almost immediately and was replaced by a restless irritation. She felt her cheek. Damn, it was bleeding. As long as it didn't leave a scar. And it was cold as fuck too.

Only when the tower of the City Hall had disappeared behind them and she was taking off her evening-gown did she realize she had lost one of her shoes.

2

Detective Inspector Anton Abrahamsson's baby was three months old and had colic. The child had been screaming day and night for eight weeks now and the detective and his wife were at their wits' end. He was able to go off to work and get a break sometimes, but it was worse for his wife. He tried vainly to comfort her over the phone: 'It has to stop some time, darling? Has he burped? Have you tried Minifom?'

The emergency call to the communications office of the Security Police came through just as his wife started to sob with exhaustion.

'I'll be home as soon as I can,' he said, putting the phone down on her and angrily snatching up the emergency call. It hadn't come from either the bodyguard unit or any of their own units, but from the regular police. Which meant that the regular police force, whose primary duties were to look after the traffic and keep curious bystanders away from crime scenes, had a better grasp on the security situation than the Security Police. That was Anton Abrahamsson's first conclusion.

The second dawned on him a moment later. Someone's going to end up in serious shit because of this.

The third made the hairs on his arms stand up as

he realized the threat they might be faced with. Shit. They're here now.

I have to call the paper, Annika thought.

She had ended up lying face-down on the dance-floor, the marble ice cold against her bare arms. A man was throwing up in front of her, another was standing on her hand. She pulled it away without any sense of pain. A woman was shrieking somewhere to her right. The orchestra had stopped playing in the middle of a note, and in the silence the screams echoed around the Blue Hall and throughout the City Hall.

Where's my bag? she thought, and tried to get up, but was knocked on the head and found herself back on the floor.

A moment later the people around her vanished and she was being lifted, a man in a dark-grey suit sitting her down with her back to the rest of the hall. She found herself staring at an oak door. I have to get hold of Jansson, she thought, and looked round for her bag. She'd left it by the copper doors leading to the Three Crowns Chamber, but all she could see now was a mass of people milling about and men dressed in dark grey rushing in.

Her knees started to tremble and she felt the familiar rush of anxiety but managed to keep it at bay. This isn't dangerous. She forced herself to take deep breaths and see the situation rationally. There was nothing she could do.

The mosaic figure on the far wall stared at her encouragingly, its snake-hair floating around its face. A fat woman in a black lace dress beside her rolled her eyes up to the ceiling and fainted. A young man was moaning so loudly that the veins on his neck were standing out, like rubber bands. A drunken older man dropped his beer glass on the floor with a crash.

I wonder where Bosse has got to, she thought.

Her pulse slowed, the blurred noises in her head began slowly to clear, and she could make out words and phrases again. She could hear calls and orders, mostly from the dark-grey suits. They were talking in steely voices into wires that snaked from their ears towards their mouths, then down into inside pockets and trouser-linings.

'The service lift is too small – the trolley won't go in. We'll have to take it out through the ceremonial entrance in the tower.'

She could make out the words, but not who was saying them.

'The building's secure, over . . . Yes, we've separated the witnesses and are in the process of emptying the banqueting halls.'

I have to get my bag. 'I have to get my bag,' she said out loud, but no one heard her. 'Can I get my bag? I need my mobile.'

The mass of people was moving slowly now. A white-clad woman came running in from the Three Crowns Chamber, pushing a trolley in front of her, followed by a man with another, then several men with stethoscopes, oxygen masks and drips. Medical teams. Further away in the Golden Hall the Nobel banquet guests stood like a wall, faces white, mouths agape. The screaming had stopped and the silence was deafening. Annika listened to the quiet conversation between the white coats. The bodies were loaded on to the trolleys. Only then did she notice the man – the man who had fallen on the dance-floor: he was conscious, moaning. The woman was lying completely still.

A moment later they were gone.

The noise rose again and Annika took her chance. She slunk past two suits and managed to reach her bag. One grabbed her just as she was fishing out her mobile. 'You're not going anywhere,' he said, with unnecessary force, but she shook herself free.

She rang Jansson's direct line in the newsroom and got three short bleeps in response.

Engaged.

What the . . . ?

She tried twice more and then looked about for help. No one noticed her.

'Your name?' A man in jeans was standing in front of her, holding a pad and pen.

'Sorry?' Annika said.

'Criminal Investigation Department. Can I have your name? We're trying to figure out exactly what happened. Did you see anything?'

'I don't know,' Annika said, looking at the blood on the marble floor, already dark and congealing. She shivered and realized she had dropped her shawl, her grandmother's best shawl, which she had worn when she was a housekeeper at Harpsund, the prime minister's country estate. It was in a heap on the floor next to the pool of blood.

That'll have to go to the dry-cleaner's, Annika thought. *I hope it's okay.*

'My name's Annika Bengtzon,' she said to the police officer. 'I'm covering the Nobel banquet for the *Evening Post*. What happened?'

'Did you hear the shots?'

Shots? Annika shook her head.

'Did you notice anyone suspicious in connection with the shots?'

'I was dancing,' she said. 'It was crowded. Someone pushed into me, but nothing suspicious, no . . .'

'Pushed? Who was doing the pushing?'

'A woman. She was trying to get through and stood on my foot.'

'Okay,' the policeman said, writing something in his pad. 'Wait here and someone will come and take you for questioning.'

'I can't,' Annika said. 'I've got an article to write. What's your name? Can I quote you?'

The man in jeans stepped closer to her and pressed her up against the wall so hard that she couldn't breathe. 'You're going to wait right here,' he said, 'until I get back.'

'Not on your life,' Annika said shakily.

The police officer groaned and dragged her into the Three Crowns Chamber.

My deadline, Annika thought. How the hell am I going to get out of this?

Editor-in-chief Anders Schyman had just settled on the sofa in his living room with his wife and an Almodóvar film when the night editor rang. 'There's been shooting at the Nobel banquet,' Jansson said. 'At least five people have been shot. We don't know if they're alive or dead.'

Schyman looked at his wife, who was pressing the remote in a vain search for the right subtitles. 'It's the round button,' he said, at the same time as the night editor's words registered in his head.

'Annika Bengtzon and Ulf Olsson from Pictures are there,' Jansson said. 'I haven't been able to contact them because the mobile network's jammed. Too much traffic.'

26

'Tell me again,' Schyman said, signalling to his wife to pause the film.

'Too much traffic on the mobile network – thirteen hundred people trying to make calls from the City Hall at the same time so it's gone down.'

'Who's been shot? At the Nobel banquet?'

His wife opened her eyes wide and dropped the remote on the floor.

'Some were security guards, but we don't know about the others. The ambulances headed off, sirens blaring, towards Sankt Göran Hospital a few minutes ago.'

'Bloody hell!' Schyman said, sitting up straight. 'When did this happen?'

He glanced at his watch – 22.57.

'Ten minutes ago, fifteen at most.'

'Is anyone dead?' his wife asked, but he hushed her.

'This is mad,' he said. 'What are the police doing? Have they arrested anyone? Where were the shots fired? Inside the Blue Hall? Where were the King and Queen? Haven't they got any fucking security in that building?'

His wife laid a calming hand on his back.

'The police have sealed off the City Hall,' Jansson said, 'so no one can get in or out. They're questioning everyone and will start to let them out in half an hour or so. We've got people on their way to get eye-witness accounts. We don't know if they've arrested anyone.'

'What do things look like in the rest of the city?'

'They've stopped all the trains, and the main roads out are blocked off, but planes are still taking off from Arlanda. There aren't many flights left this evening. We've got people heading for the Central Station, the motorways, pretty much everywhere.'

His wife gave him a quick kiss on the cheek, then got up and left the room. Pedro Almodóvar's women disappeared into an indeterminate future, their impending nervous breakdowns on hold.

'Have the police said anything?' Schyman asked. 'Terrorism, extremists, any suggestion of a threat?'

'They've announced a press conference, but not until one a.m.'

Someone shouted in the background and Jansson disappeared for a moment. 'Well,' he said, when he was back on the line, 'things are pretty hectic here. I need some quick decisions. How many extra pages can we add? Can we hold back some of the adverts? And who do you think we should get in to do the lead article?'

The darkness hung heavily outside the editor-in-chief's living room. He could see his own reflection in the glass and heard his wife running a tap in the kitchen. I'm starting to get old, he thought. I'd rather spend the evening on the sofa with a DVD. 'I'm on my way,' he said.

Jansson hung up without reply.

His wife was standing at the counter making a cup of tea. She turned round and kissed him when she felt his hands on her shoulders. 'Who's been killed?' she asked.

'Don't know,' he whispered.

'Wake me up when you get home,' she said. 'You don't have to deal with this alone.'

He nodded, his lips touching the back of her neck.

The Kitten changed gear and accelerated cautiously. The little motorbike growled encouragingly, its headlight dancing on the gravelled tarmac.

This really was too damn easy.

She knew that being overly confident wasn't good: it increased the risk of carelessness. But in this case there were no more obstacles ahead. The rest was just a walk in the park.

The job itself had been presented to her as a challenge, and that was what had interested her. She had soon seen how simple it would be, but she had had no intention of saying so to her employer. Negotiations had taken place on the understanding that the job was extremely dangerous and difficult, which had obviously affected the size of her fee.

Ah, well, she thought. You wanted it to be spectacular. Hope you liked it.

She swung into a narrow cycle-path as a branch struck her helmet. Stockholm was usually described as a major city – a metropolis with glittering nightlife and an efficient security service. That was a laughable exaggeration. Everything outside the city centre seemed to consist of scrappy patches of woodland. There was a chance that a couple walking their dog had seen her and her wingman head off in different directions on their bikes, but since then she hadn't seen a soul.

A major city indeed, she thought scornfully, as she rode past a deserted campsite.

She rolled her shoulders – she was still freezing. The thick jacket wasn't helping, and the boat trip chilled her to the bone. The silk evening-gown was at the bottom of the lake, with her bag and eight bricks. The sack holding them was made of netting, so the water would soak through the material and wash away any biological evidence within a few hours. She still had the gun, as well as the one remaining shoe and her mobile. She was planning to get rid of them somewhere in the middle of the Baltic.

The thought of the other shoe troubled her. It had her fingerprints on it, she was sure. The shoes had been clean of evidence when she'd set out on the job, but before that last sprint she had taken it off and held it. God knew where she'd dropped it.

There was light ahead of her and she realized she had reached the only inhabited road along the shore. She forced the shoe out of her mind, changed down a gear and turned off the path and up on to the road. Street-lamps shone on the tightly packed houses and she let the motorbike roll down the slope, following the shoreline. A few youngsters were hanging about by a jetty. They glanced at her idly, then went on laughing and kicking at the gravel. She knew that all they saw was a single person of uncertain gender on a small motorbike, wearing dark jeans and a helmet with a visor. There was nothing to stick in their minds.

The street came to an end and she rolled on into thin forest again, glancing at her watch. She was slightly behind schedule, by a minute or so, because of the frost. It had been raining on the evening she had timed the journey, but the road hadn't been slippery.

She accelerated gently, and a moment later it happened.

The tyres lost their grip and she felt the bike disappear from beneath her. Her left leg took the first blow and snapped like a matchstick just below the knee. Her shoulder hit the tarmac next, then her head, as she thought, I haven't got time for this.

When she came to she was lying face-down on the ground.

What the hell had happened?

Pain was pulsing through her left side. The motorcycle was still growling somewhere behind her, its headlamp shining into the trees.

She groaned. Fuck. What was she going to do now?

She pulled off her helmet and laid her cheek against the frozen ground for a few seconds, forcing her brain to clear.

At least the bike's engine was still running: she could feel its vibrations through the ground. But she herself wasn't in great shape. Her leg was broken and her shoulder was buggered. Carefully she flexed the right side of her body.

It seemed okay.

She sat up with her left arm hanging uselessly by her side. The joint was dislocated: she'd seen it happen to other people but had never before experienced it herself. Her leg was excruciatingly painful – she could feel the shaft of the bone pressing against the skin just below her left knee.

She shuffled backwards until she felt a narrow tree-trunk behind her, and groaned again. The list of possible options she had to choose from was shrinking fast.

Using her right side she dragged herself upright and, with a well-judged motion, threw herself forward, letting her left shoulder hit the tree-trunk.

Holy fucking shit! The pain as the joint popped back into place was almost unbearable, and she clung to the tree with her fit arm to stop herself fainting.

When she had pulled herself together, she flexed the fingers of her left hand, and gently moved her arm. It was fine. But there was nothing she could do about her leg.

She leaned down and picked up the helmet. Carefully she hopped over to the motorbike, pulled it upright and, with a great deal of effort, hauled herself on to it. She had to bite her lip as she put her left foot on the pedal. The pain brought her out in a sweat as she adjusted her position on the seat.

For a moment she wasn't sure which direction she should be going in. The forest looked the same both ways and she couldn't tell where she had come from.

Shit!

She checked the time. Thirteen minutes behind schedule.

Her wingman would wait for half an hour in the boat out at Torö. She had given him orders to set off for Ventspils after that.

Fear hit her like a dagger in the chest. Would this crappy job up in what felt like the bloody North Pole turn out to be her last?

She put the helmet on, dropped the visor and put the bike in gear. She turned it and rode in what she hoped was a southerly direction, with her left knee jutting out at an indescribably wrong angle.

3

Annika trudged behind the police officer through the winding passageways of the City Hall until they reached a long corridor. In the distance she could make out chandeliers hanging from heavy roof-beams, but here there was nothing but gloom, shadows and silence.

Irritated, she speeded up and walked past the police officer. 'How long is this going to take?' she asked, looking at her watch.

'I'll see if this is where he meant,' the officer said, stopping. He took hold of her upper arm as if she were a suspect, likely to make a break for it.

She pulled free as he knocked on a door bearing a sign that stated this was the Bråvalla Room. 'If I'd wanted to get away I'd already have gone,' she said.

Inside sat two officers in plain clothes, along with a reporter Annika recognized from television news. The reporter was crying so much that her shoulders were shaking. One of the officers let out such an angry yell that the man with Annika jumped as he hurried to shut the door. 'Not that room,' he said, the tips of his ears starting to glow.

They carried on walking in an awkward silence, passing grey doors in grey walls, until they came to an office where another round of questioning had just begun with a member of the Swedish Academy. Annika couldn't hear what was being said, but she saw the police officer making notes and the man nervously fingering the leg of his chair.

I have to remember everything, she thought. I have to be able to describe it later. She noted that the scene was also being observed by the architect of the City Hall, Ragnar Östberg, whose bronze bust watched over the events with a concerned expression. *Did you have any idea that something like this could ever happen in your building?* Annika wondered, before her thoughts were interrupted by the police officer's clammy hand.

'Can you wait here a moment?'

'Do I have any choice?' Annika said, turning away.

It was brighter in this room. She could make out the details more clearly: marble busts above the doors, bronze hinges and door-handles, ostentatious chandeliers.

'Look, I need time to write up my story,' she said, but the officer had already disappeared down the corridor.

A door opened and someone was calling her name. She went in.

'Close the door behind you.'

The voice made her stop. 'I might have guessed you'd be here,' she said.

Detective Inspector Q was unshaven, his features more drawn than usual. 'I asked to take care of you myself,' he said, from a chair at a heavy oak table. 'Sit down.' He gestured for Annika to take a seat on his left, turned on a tape-recorder and poured himself a glass of water. 'Interview with Annika Bengtzon, reporter on the *Evening Post* newspaper, date of birth and full name to be noted later, conducted by Q in the Small Common Room of Stockholm City Hall, on Thursday, the tenth of December, at . . .' He paused for breath and ran a hand through his hair.

Annika settled carefully into a black-framed chair with red-leather upholstery, glancing up at the sombre gentlemen in the oil paintings staring down at her from their heavy frames.

'. . . at twenty-three twenty-one,' he concluded. 'You saw someone acting suspiciously in the Blue Hall at approximately twenty-two forty-five this evening. Is that correct?'

Annika put her bag on the floor and clasped her hands in her lap, listening to the traffic of central Stockholm rumbling in the distance. 'I don't know that she was acting suspiciously,' she said.

'Can you describe what happened?' the detective inspector said.

'It was nothing significant,' Annika replied, her voice slightly shrill. 'I haven't got time to sit here making small-talk. I didn't see anything out of the ordinary. I was dancing and a girl pushed me. You can't expect me to sit here when the whole newsroom is waiting for me and my article.'

The detective inspector leaned forward and turned off the tape-recorder with a little click. 'Now, listen, you headline-chasing bitch,' he said, leaning towards her. 'This isn't the time to be arrogant. You're going to tell me what you saw, exactly as you remember it, right here, right now. It was only half an hour ago, and you were one of the people standing closest to what happened.'

She stared back at him for a moment, then looked away, her gaze sliding over the heavy leather-bound books on the dark oak shelves. Did he really just call her a *headline-chasing bitch*?

'We'll question you more thoroughly later,' Q said

quietly, sounding tired and friendlier. 'Right now we need a description. Take it chronologically, from the moment you saw this person, and leave us to work out what's important.' He started the tape-recorder again.

Annika cleared her throat and tried to relax her shoulders. 'A woman,' she said, 'it was a woman who pushed me, with her elbow, then she stood on my foot.'

'What did she look like?'

Annika felt as if the room was collapsing on top of her. She began to feel claustrophobic and put her hands over her eyes, gasping for breath in a long, tremulous sob. 'I don't know,' she whispered.

Her mobile started to ring. She dropped her hands to her lap and sat up. They waited for it to stop.

'Okay, let's try it a different way,' Q said, when it had finally fallen silent. 'Where were you when she pushed you?'

She recalled the music playing, the glamour, the happiness, the darkness, the crush.

'On the dance-floor. I was dancing. At one end of the Golden Hall, not the one with the orchestra, the other.'

'Who were you with?'

Confusion and shame washed over her and she looked down at her hands. 'His name's Bosse. He's a reporter for the opposition.'

'Blond, quite well-built?'

Annika nodded, her cheeks hot.

'Can you answer verbally, please?'

'Yes,' she said, slightly too loudly, and straightened her back. 'Yes, that's right.'

'Might he have seen anything?'

'Yes, obviously, although I don't think she trod on him as well.'

'And then what happened?'

36

Then what had happened? Nothing. Nothing at all. That was all she had seen. 'I don't know,' she said. 'I turned my back to her and didn't see anything else.'

'And you didn't hear anything?'

People chatting? The music? Her own breathing?

'Only a couple of muffled noises.'

'Can you explain?'

'Like puffs of air. I turned round and saw a man slump to his knees. He was dancing with a woman and she was surprised when he just collapsed like that. She looked up and saw me and then she looked down at her chest. Then I saw she was bleeding – blood was sort of pumping out – and she looked up again at me and slumped to the floor and everyone started screaming . . .'

'When did the second noise come?'

Annika glanced at Q. 'The second?'

'You said "a couple of muffled noises".'

'Did I? I don't know. There was one and then the woman was looking at me and then there was another. Yes, two, I think . . .'

'How far away were you from the couple when they fell?'

She thought for several seconds. 'Two metres, two and a half, maybe.'

'The woman who pushed you, did you see her as they fell?'

Had she? Had she seen a woman?

'Shoulder-straps,' Annika said. 'She had narrow shoulder-straps. Or a bag with a narrow strap.'

Q nodded and made a note in his pad.

Annika pressed her fingertips to her eyelids and tried to remember. Bosse's hand had been scorching through the fabric on her back, holding her so tightly to him that she could feel his cock against her stomach, her own hand behind his neck. That was what she remembered. The music had been like an apron, dull, neatly ironed, but it was only there to conceal them, so they could hold each other in the glittering golden light. 'I was elbowed in the side,' she said hesitantly. 'And someone stood on my foot. I don't know which came first.'

Her mobile started to ring again.

'Turn it off,' Q said, and she clicked to cut off the incoming call.

It was Jansson, of course.

'Was it done on purpose, you being trodden on?'

She put down her mobile, now on silent. 'Definitely not,' she said. 'There was a big fat man dancing right next to us. He knocked into the woman and she bumped into me.'

Something happened in Q's eyes, a little flicker of interest. 'Did she say anything when she bumped into you?'

Annika looked down the bookcase to a leather-bound volume of council protocols from 1964, in the same way that she had looked down at the woman with the shoulder-straps. 'She was fishing for something in her bag,' she said. 'The strap was quite short so she had to lift her arm up a bit to get it out – like this.' She raised her right arm and showed how she might look for something in an imaginary evening-bag.

'What colour was the bag?'

'Silver,' she said, to her surprise and without hesitation. 'It was matt silver. In the shape of an envelope.'

'What did she take out of it?'

Annika looked away from the bookshelf. She could remember nothing, just the pain in her foot. 'It hurt,' Annika said. 'I let out a yelp. She looked up at me.' She nodded hesitantly, as something occurred to her. 'Yes,' she said, convincing herself. 'She looked up at me, right at me.'

'Did she say anything?'

Annika gazed out across the polished table. 'She had yellow eyes,' she said. 'Completely cold yellow eyes, almost golden.'

'Yellow?'

'Yes, golden yellow.'

'And how was she dressed?'

She shut her eyes again and heard the throb of the music, seeing the shoulder-strap before her. It was blood-red, red like liver, unless it was the bleeding woman's dress that was red. Or the blood. Unless the shoulder-strap was white, maybe, white as snow against brown skin, unless the shoulder was white and the strap black? 'I don't know,' she said, perplexed. 'I really don't know . . .'

'Yellow eyes – could they have been lenses?'

Lenses? Yes, of course they could, unless they weren't actually yellow but green.

Q's mobile phone started to vibrate, and a Eurovision song rang out, 'My Number One', the Greek number that had won a few years ago. Unless it was this year. The detective inspector glanced at the display and muttered, 'I have to take this.' He switched off the tape-recorder and turned towards the closed door as he spoke.

He went on, his voice rising and falling. Annika had to get up and move away, drawn by the sound of traffic outside. Slowly she breathed out on to the cold window-pane, and the view vanished for a moment. When it returned she could see Hantverkargatan, the street she lived on, and beyond that the Klara district of Stockholm, trains thundering past, and the old Serafen health centre over to the left.

Her health centre! Her doctors, where she had been with Kalle only that morning, another ear infection. So close, just four blocks from home, but it felt like another world now. Her throat constricted.

'The victims have been identified,' Q said, returning her to the room. 'Did you recognize them?'

She went back to the chair, her legs shaking, and perched on the edge, clearing her throat. 'The man was one of the prize-winners,' she said. 'Medicine, I think. I don't remember his name off the top of my head, but I've got it in my notes.' She reached for her bag to indicate that she could find out, just an arm's length away, but stopped mid-gesture.

'Aaron Wiesel,' the detective said. 'An Israeli, he shared the prize with an American, Charles Watson. The woman?'

Annika shook her head. 'I'd never seen her before.'

Q rubbed a hand over his eyes. 'Wiesel's in surgery in Sankt Göran right now. The woman was Caroline von Behring, chair of the Karolinska Institute's Nobel Committee. She died on the dance-floor, pretty much instantly.'

All warmth vanished from her hands and her fingers turned numb. With an effort she pulled up the shawl that had fallen behind her and draped it over her shoulders again.

Her eyes as she was dying. *She was looking at me when she died.* 'I have to go now,' she said. 'I'm really sorry, but I've got an awful lot to do.'

'You can't write about this,' Q said, leaning back heavily in his chair. 'Your observations about the woman who pushed you match the description of the fleeing killer. You're one of our key witnesses so I'm imposing a ban on disclosure, effective as of now.'

Annika was halfway out of her chair, but sank down again. 'Am I under arrest?' she asked.

'Don't be stupid,' Q said, as he got up, clutching his mobile.

'Disclosure bans only happen during arrest procedures,' Annika said. 'If I'm not under arrest, and no one else has been arrested, how can you impose a ban on disclosure?'

'You're not as smart as you think,' Q said. 'There's another form of disclosure ban, according to chapter twenty-three, paragraph ten, final clause of the Judicial Procedure Act. It concerns the accounts of key witnesses and can be imposed by the head of an investigation where a serious crime is suspected.'

'Freedom of speech is protected by the constitution,' Annika said, 'and that carries more weight. And you're not the head of the investigation. In a case like this that would have to be a public prosecutor.'

'You're wrong there as well. A head of this investigation hasn't been appointed yet, so I'm acting head right now.'

Annika stood up angrily and leaned over the table. 'You can't stop me saying what I saw. I've got the whole article in my head – I can write a fucking brilliant eyewitness account, three double pages easily, maybe four. I saw the murderer in the act of killing, I saw the victim die—'

Q spun round towards her, pressed his face right up to hers. 'For God's sake!' he shouted. 'You'll get a fine so big you won't know what hit you if you do. Sit down!'

Annika sat down with a thump, hunching her shoulders. Q turned his back on her and dialled a number on his mobile. She sat in silence beneath the huge portraits as he made his call and gave angry orders.

'You're putting me in an impossible position if I can't write anything,' Annika said.

'My heart bleeds,' Q said.

'What are my bosses going to say?' Annika went on. 'What would your bosses say if you refused to investigate a crime because I said you couldn't, because I had to write about you?'

Q sat down again with a deep sigh. 'Sorry,' he said, and gave her a slightly guilty look. 'Ask me something, and I might be able to give you an answer.'

'Why?' Annika said.

'Because you can't write about it anyway,' he said, smiling for the first time.

She thought for a moment. 'Why didn't anyone hear the shots?' she asked.

'You did. You said so.'

'But only as little puffs of air.'

'A pistol with a silencer would fit into the sort of bag you described. And you don't remember anything else about her appearance? Her hair, or her clothes?'

Eyes, just eyes, and the shoulder-straps. 'She must have had long hair. I'd have remembered a short style – they're more striking. But I don't think there was anything special about it. Dark. I don't think it was loose – maybe it was tied up somehow. And her dress . . . she must have been wearing an evening-dress. I didn't notice anything odd, so I suppose she must have looked like everyone else. How did she get into the Golden Hall, do you know?'

Q flipped through his notes. 'We're checking to see if she could have been on the guest-list, but we don't really know. There are other witness statements saying she could have been a man dressed as a woman. What do you think about that?'

A man? Annika snorted. 'It was a girl,' she said.

'How can you be sure?'

Annika's eyes slid back to the protocols from 1964. 'She looked up at me, so she must have been shorter than me. How many men are that short? And she moved quickly, easily.'

'And men don't?'

'Not in those shoes. It takes a lot of practice to move as easily as she did.'

'And you saw her heels?'

Annika stood up and hoisted her bag on to her shoulder. 'No, but I've got the bruise one of them made on my right foot. Please, can I call you later tonight?'

'And where do you think you're going?'

She stopped. 'The newsroom. I have to go and talk to them. Unless you can stop me working as well?'

'You have to go down to the profiling unit of National Crime and put together a Photofit of the killer.'

Annika threw out her arms. 'Are you mad? I've got a deadline in a couple of hours. Jansson will be tearing his hair out by now.'

Q walked up to her, clearly desperate. 'Please,' he said.

The door opened and a uniformed officer came in. For a moment she thought it was the man who had escorted her to the interview, but it wasn't. He was similar, though, a stereotypical example of a broad-shouldered, thoroughly Swedish graduate from the police training course.

She stopped in the doorway and turned back to the detective inspector. 'Did you really call me a *headline-chasing bitch*?' she said.

He waved her out of the room.

*

She pushed past the stereotype, fished out the wire of her ear-piece and dug out her mobile from the depths of her bag. The young police officer seemed about to protest, but she fixed her eyes on the end of the corridor and swept away from him without deigning to look at him.

'Where the hell have you been?' Jansson snarled, before she had a chance to say anything.

'Questioning,' she said quietly, holding the microphone a millimetre from her mouth. 'I had a sort of close encounter with the killer – they reckon she trod on my foot.' It hurt each time she took a step.

'Great, the eight and nine spread. What else have you got?'

'Hey,' the police officer behind her said, 'who are you talking to?'

She speeded up, but stumbled over the hem of her dress and dropped her ear-piece. Her shawl slipped to the floor and the draught of the corridor swept over her, settling on her bare shoulders like a damp towel. She shivered. The Academy member had been replaced by two stewards in white jackets with their backs to her.

'Annika?' Jansson said, as soon as she popped the ear-piece back in.

'I can't write anything. Q has imposed a disclosure ban. I could probably be charged just for talking to you about the killer. I have to go over to Kungsholmsgatan for further questioning.'

'Okay, put your phone away,' her police officer said.

Annika spun round. 'Listen,' she said, 'I'm going to talk as much as I damn well want to on this mobile. If you don't like it you can arrest me.'

She turned and carried on walking.

'The term "arrest" doesn't apply in a situation like

44

this within the Swedish judicial system,' the policeman said.

'Call the paper's lawyers and find out exactly what I can and can't say,' Annika said into the microphone. 'How's it looking? Is there anything particular you're missing?'

Jansson sighed. She shared his frustration and wished she could do something to ease it. 'Everything. Everyone else has already got text and pictures up on their websites, and we've only got the stuff from the main news agency. When will you be back here?'

'Don't know, but as soon as I can. How much did Olsson manage to get?'

Jansson groaned quietly. 'Nothing. He thought the angle was wrong and the light too poor, so he didn't take any pictures.'

'You're kidding?' Annika said.

The policeman held open a door for Annika and she emerged on to the balcony overlooking the Blue Hall, beside the first doorway to the Golden Hall.

'Not really. We've got no pictures, basically.'

Annika's heart sank. It wouldn't be the photographer who took the blame: it was always the reporter, especially if it was her, and especially right now. It was only three weeks since she had forced the editor-in-chief to publish an article that showed the family who owned most of the paper in an extremely bad light. 'What do you need?' she asked.

'Anything with blood and policemen.'

Annika ended the call and turned sharply to the left. She was inside the Golden Hall before the policeman had time to react. The whole of the banqueting room was bathed in light from the powerful lamps of the forensics team. The artwork of the woman with bulging eyes stared down at her. In the far distance, beneath a headless St Erik – the result of confusion over the height of the ceiling when the hall was built – two men were crouching at the spot where the woman had died.

Annika raised her mobile, activated the camera function and snapped a picture. She moved two steps forward, and took another, five more steps, and got one more. The police officer grabbed her arm but she shook him off. She jogged ten paces and managed to get two more as the forensics officers noticed her.

'Okay, you're leaving right now,' the police officer said. He picked her up and carried her out on to the balcony. He put her down by the staircase on the stone floor. She realized she was standing on the very spot where members of the royal family and the Nobel Prize-winners always had their pictures taken before their long glide down one of the most famous staircases in the world.

How different it was for them, she thought, looking out over the remains of the dinner for thirteen hundred guests. Earlier that evening the prize-winners had gazed out across meticulously laid tables and immaculately dressed guests, sparkling crystal and porcelain with real gold rims, flowers and trumpets.

The Blue Hall, with its mute brick walls, was desolate now. The top table had been cleared, but the rest of the plates were still there, food congealing on soiled table-cloths. Napkins lay scattered across plates as well as on the floor, and the chairs were all over the place, some of them tipped over. At 22.45 all activity in the Blue Hall had ceased, time had stopped and the moment when the next tables should have been cleared had never arrived.

'How long will the City Hall be closed off?' Annika asked.

'As long as necessary. Where are your outdoor clothes?'

There was a uniformed officer in the cloakroom. He handed over Annika's padded jacket with an expression of deep disappointment at the role he had been allocated.

'I had a bag with my shoes in it as well,' Annika said. 'Black boots.'

Annoyed, the policeman went back to look for it. Annika took out her mobile. While the officer was searching the racks, she brought up the pictures of the Golden Hall and pressed *send*.

She stared fixedly at the shell-shaped bronze lamps of the hallway as the message floated through the pitch-black winter night and landed in Jansson's inbox at the *Evening Post*'s offices.

Friday, 11 December

4

Anders Schyman was standing in his corner office, staring down at the Russian Embassy. The whole area lay in darkness, except for a circle of light around the weak lamp by the entrance and the light creeping out of the security hut with its frozen soldier. Sometimes the soldier walked a few steps along the inside of the iron gate, then back again, moving his arms to warm himself.

How surprised he would be if something actually happened, the editor-in-chief thought. How astonished he would be if someone drove up in a car and started shooting towards the embassy building, or clambered over the wall and landed right in front of him. He wouldn't have a chance because the intruder would have everything on his side: surprise, determination and knowledge of the next step in the chain of events.

We're so vulnerable, Schyman thought. It's completely impossible to be on your guard the whole time, never miss a single detail about your own safety. The whole world faced the same dilemma, not just the West: everyone was affected.

Money, power and influence, he mused. The world has never been safe from people who are prepared to take short-cuts in order to acquire them, but it feels as though everything is getting worse.

There were rumours that the Nobel killer was a woman. At the press conference the police had neither confirmed nor denied anything: they didn't want to talk about threats received, or about the security arrangements. Security had been good, and they weren't aware of where it had broken down. Everything seemed to have gone to plan, and it wasn't yet possible to say why it had failed.

It had started to snow, lonely flakes drifting hesitantly towards the ground. Schyman's eyes stung with tiredness. He blinked a few times and went to sit down at his desk. He checked his watch. Maybe this isn't what I ought to be doing after all, he thought. If this is how things are going to be, if terrorism has arrived here and security is to be the main focus from now on, maybe I should let someone else take over. Security will be used as an argument to justify more restrictions, more surveillance, and the principle of freedom of information will be completely undermined. Maybe a new type of journalist is needed to keep watch on this new age, and they'll probably need a new sort of leader.

For a moment he succumbed to self-pity. The paper's owners had no confidence in him, and his future prospects seemed bleak.

'Annika's here now,' Jansson said, over the intercom.

He pressed the button and leaned forward to reply. 'Good. Bring her in.'

What *does* she look like? he thought, as she entered the room. Cowboy boots, a black quilted jacket, a huge, filthy bag, and a pink tulle skirt. She had piled her hair into a heap on top of her head and stuck a pen through it to hold it up.

'The lawyer's confirmed that she can't write about the actual shootings, or anything that happened immediately before or after,' Jansson said, tumbling into one of the chairs. 'And she can't be interviewed or convey her observations of the event in any other way either. Breaking a ban on disclosure isn't punishable according to statute, but there'd be big fines, apparently, however the hell they justify that . . .'

'What did you see?' Schyman asked.

'I thought you'd already heard,' Annika said, sinking into a chair as well, looking pale.

The editor-in-chief waved away her reluctance and she seemed to shrink under his gaze, lacking the energy to protest. 'I got a pretty good look at the person they think is the killer,' she said. 'Evidently there weren't many people who did.' She ran her hand through her hair, dislodging the pen. Her hair fell, like a heavy curtain, over her face. 'I've spent three and a half hours in National Crime Headquarters, trying to put together a picture of the girl. It didn't exactly turn out well, but the police say it's better than a written description.'

'So you saw the killer?' the editor-in-chief said, noticing to his embarrassment that he sounded excited. 'The shots were fired by a woman? Did you see the actual murder as well?'

She gazed down at her hands. 'She was looking at me,' Annika said, raising her head to meet his gaze. 'She was looking at me when she died.'

'Caroline von Behring? You saw her get shot?'

Without thinking, she pushed her hair up again and fixed it with the pen. Her eyes were staring at a point somewhere above the roof of the Russian Embassy when she answered. 'There was something in the way she looked at me,' she said, still staring out of the window, her hands in her lap now.

'And you've got nothing to contribute? To us, I mean, your employers.'

She looked at him, and something dark crossed her eyes. 'I don't know anything about what the police are doing, apart from what I've experienced personally. You're far better informed about that than I am. I presume that the colour of Queen Silvia's dress is no longer particularly important.'

Schyman suppressed his annoyance and turned towards the night editor instead. 'Is there any way of getting round this?'

'Not according to the lawyer.'

The editor-in-chief stood up, unable to sit still. 'This is what I was afraid of,' he said, throwing out his arms in frustration. 'We've got a unique first-hand account and our hands are tied by the police who are forbidding us to report one of the most spectacular crimes ever, and on what grounds? For fuck's sake, we live in a democracy!'

Jansson glanced at his watch, disconcerted, as always, by emotional outbursts of this sort.

'Chapter twenty-three of the Judicial Procedure Act,' Annika said, 'paragraph ten, final section. The accounts of key witnesses can be protected by the head of an investigation where a serious crime is suspected. It's a very old law, mainly there to make sure investigations can't be sabotaged.'

'There are always good reasons to impose limits on freedom of speech,' Schyman said, waving a finger at his employees. 'Anyway, how the hell could they let something like this happen? Wasn't there any sort of security in the City Hall?'

Annika rubbed her eyes with the palm of her hand. 'Of course there was, but the Nobel banquet has always been regarded as a fairly average security risk. The level of security has been the same for years now. The police work with the security forces, the organizers and City Hall management. There's nothing unusual about it.'

'The police man the doors, and the security forces take care of individual protection,' Schyman summarized.

'Exactly,' Annika said wearily. 'The cordons around the City Hall have never been especially comprehensive. It's a much bigger job to secure the Concert House for the actual awards ceremony. They shut off all of Hötorget and parts of Kungsgatan . . .'

'What about bodyguards?' Schyman said. 'Where the hell were they?'

'The security police never comment on personal protection,' Annika said, 'but the escort regulations determine how and in what ways the police are to transport and guard the government, the royal family, guests on state visits and so on. There's a certain number of functions . . .'

Schyman raised his hands to stop her. 'I'm talking about the complete failure of the police,' he said. 'How could this happen? I want to focus on that. Focus! The police aren't going to get away with this by whining about needing new legislation.'

'Do you want a quick run-through of the morning editions?' Jansson asked, shifting uncomfortably on his chair.

Schyman sat down again, his face red after his outburst. He gestured to the night editor to go ahead.

'We haven't got much in the way of pictures of the crime scene,' Jansson said. 'Ulf Olsson, you know, that idiot who loves celebrity events, he had five hundred shots of Princess Madeleine and not a single one of the attack. He didn't manage to set the aperture or sort out the focus, and is blaming the resolution of his digital camera for why he has no pictures. Annika got a few shots of the Golden Hall when the City Hall was cordoned off, no one else has got anything like that, but they were taken on a mobile phone and the technical quality leaves a lot to be desired. We're running one on page eight, and another on nine, two forensics officers by a pool of blood. They're pretty strong images.'

'What else have we got?' Schyman asked.

'We're keeping an eye on Swedish Television, to see if they release any of the material they didn't broadcast. They had a camera inside the Golden Hall when the shots were fired, but it looks like it was positioned next to the orchestra at the wrong end of the room. The question is, how much the film shows, and whether they're going to release anything anyway.'

'Of course they won't,' Schyman said. 'Why on earth would they?'

'Well, this is a pretty special case,' Jansson said.

Anger flashed through the editor-in-chief. 'Why?' he said. 'What really makes this murder so special, other than the fact that it was unusually public?'

'Triple murder,' Jansson said. 'The second guard just died, and the third's still critical. And, no, I don't think anyone sees this as a normal murder.'

'The dead guards must have families and children,' Annika said.

The editor-in-chief stood up again. 'So, these murders are so unusual that we need new legislation?' he said. 'So special that we suddenly need a completely new set of ethical rules?'

Annika looked at her watch and glanced at the night editor. 'What else have we got?' she asked.

'There were freelance photographers outside the City Hall so there's more material from out there. The whole damn city's cordoned off, so we've got masses of pictures of stern-faced cops and big cars. Pages ten and eleven, police hunt last night.'

Schyman walked over to the window, where he stood with his back to the Russian Embassy. 'Are the police expecting to make any arrests in the foreseeable future?' he asked.

'The boat the girl escaped on has been found in Gröndal, and they think she got away south by car, towards Södertälje. She must have had help, someone driving the boat, and probably someone else on the inside as well.'

Schyman picked up a ballpoint pen and drummed it against his thumbnail. 'Why south?'

'The police are saying that they were prepared for something of this sort and set up road-blocks more or less at once. If she'd headed north or east she would have been caught, and there's nothing but water to the west. We've got a map of the escape route with some pretty accurate timings. The police reckon she was south of Skärholmen before twenty-three oh-five because that's when the road-block went up.'

He saw that Annika was staring at the pen and tossed it aside. 'What about pictures of the victims?' Since the driving-licence authority and the passport register had both closed their archives to the public, getting hold of pictures of victims was a recurring problem, another consequence of the fallout from 11 September, the new age.

'Both von Behring and Wiesel were very public people,

so there are plenty of images of them. Pelle in Pictures has pulled out a frame from the live broadcast in the Blue Hall as well, where they're sitting next to each other at the table, laughing and raising their glasses. The quality's not great, but it's on six and seven. Then we've got the royal couple and their reaction. Of course, they didn't see a thing but Berit's managed to make it sound pretty dramatic. They were sitting in the Prince's Gallery talking to some of the prize-winners when the shots were fired. If you measure the distance between the killer and the royal couple, it's actually no more than a few dozen metres, even if half of that is thick stone walls—'

'What about the cover of the first editions?' the editor-in-chief interrupted.

'We're waiting for the Photofit picture. The headline will be "Face of the Killer", or something like that.'

Schyman thought his tired brain might implode. 'We're waiting for a Photofit that our reporter helped produce but which we can't print because a fucking police-state says we can't do our fucking job, informing the public.' He slumped on to his chair again and flapped a hand. 'Out you go, get the paper finished,' he said. 'But I want to see the front page before it goes to print.'

As his two colleagues gathered their things and left the room he got up and went back to the window to see what the Russian soldier was doing.

The shack was empty. The soldier had gone.

Annika went into her room and wrote down everything she could remember. She noted exactly what had happened, including dancing with Bosse. All the details, what the police had said, everything she had seen and how she had felt.

She ended up with a poor, rather confused account, but it would never be published. She wanted it as a prop for her memory – she'd sat through enough trials to know that witnesses forget. Their memories change over time, and she wanted access to her original experiences. So that no traces of the text were left on the newspaper's server, she wrote it directly as a draft on her personal email account. That was where she usually left texts that she needed to access from other computers, or anything she wanted to keep secret from the paper.

She sat for several minutes after switching off her computer, looking out over the newsroom. She was exhausted, but it was doubtful that she'd be able to sleep tonight.

She saw Jansson heading to the smoking shed with a cigarette and a cup of coffee, grabbed her outdoor clothes and hurried after him.

'Well, he was in a bloody awful mood,' Jansson said, glancing at Annika, who sat down beside him with a cup.

'He gets like that when I'm around,' Annika said, peering at her coffee. 'He's furious because of what I wrote about our proprietors and TV Scandinavia. You heard he didn't get to be chair of the Newspaper Publishers' Association?'

Jansson lit his hundredth cigarette of the night and blew the smoke on to his coffee. 'I think you're taking it too personally. He's a grown-up, after all, with a whole load of different responsibilities. If he spent his time worrying about things like that he'd never get anything done.'

Annika could feel the heat of the liquid through the thin plastic and moved her fingers to stop them getting burned. 'I know Schyman,' she said quietly. 'Better than a lot of people realize. Trust me, this is the sort of thing he takes seriously. It'll pass, but not until the chairman of the board has forgiven him. Give him six months, then maybe I'll be let back in from the cold.'

'What sort of nonsense is that?' Jansson said, after he'd taken a sip. 'Out in the cold? Covering the Nobel banquet is a prestigious job!'

'With Olsson trailing behind me? You're joking. And in this get-up?' She tugged at her pink skirt, which now had a tear in the hem. She could feel Jansson looking at her in the way he sometimes did, as if he was studying an unusual plant or bird. Not maliciously, more in wonder.

'What was it really like?' he asked, taking a deep drag on his cigarette.

She shut her eyes, trying to remember her impressions of the Blue Hall. 'Overwhelming, to start with. A lot of light, a lot of people. Pretty horrible food – the starter was inedible. But it was warm, not stone-cold like everyone always says about those meals . . .'

She had ended up on the same table as Bosse. They'd met before, not least when they were covering the murder of Michelle Carlsson out at Yxtaholm Castle. They'd chatted and laughed, nudging each other and drinking toasts.

'Is it true they always put journalists behind a pillar so they can't see anything?'

Annika nodded. 'Completely true. Three and a half hours and we didn't have a clue what was going on up at the top table. You probably saw more on television. Is there anything you're missing?'

'Did you really see the murders?'

She took a deep breath and collected her thoughts.

'Only the one up in the Golden Hall. Von Behring was the only one who died there.' She fell quiet, remembering the look in the woman's eyes, her body lying absolutely still. 'I saw her get shot, then fell to the floor beside her . . .' She heard her voice break, and an odd sound bubbled up from her throat, which she masked by drinking some coffee. 'But I didn't see the killer at that precise moment, and I didn't see her fire the shots.'

Jansson lit another cigarette. 'So how could you help produce the Photofit?'

'I bumped into her a few moments before she fired – she stood on my foot.' Annika put the plastic cup on the floor and pulled off her boot. A violet swelling, the size of a five-kronor coin, was visible through her tights.

'Bloody hell,' Jansson said.

'They'll release the Photofit in the morning – I'd put money on it. They need to check with some other witnesses first.'

'How do they go about it? Is someone there drawing?'

Annika felt her shoulders relax for the first time all night. 'It's digital. You sit inside the old police head-quarters on Kungsholmen, in a normal office with three computers. They start working with the person who has the best information, the one they think saw most. When you've told them all you know you go through it again, but back to front this time, and that dredges up other details. When you talk about something chrono-logically you're looking for things that fit together, in order to make the narrative go forward . . .' She knew she was babbling, but she couldn't help it: the words were tumbling out of her as if they'd been bottled up all night. Jansson listened and nodded and smoked, and she felt that it was doing her some good.

'I had to go out and have a cup of coffee for fifteen

minutes, and when I came back in the technician had come up with a picture on the computer. Then I had to say what was most wrong about it. The hairstyle, I said. He laughed and said that nine out of ten women always start by saying that the hairstyle is wrong. And the whole time I could see things that didn't fit with my memory. I had to stay while they made the changes, which is why it took so long.'

'Did he sit there drawing different noses?'

Annika took a sip of the now cold coffee and shook her head. 'The computer program has several hundred that can be moved around, made bigger or smaller. Then eyes and lips and so on . . .'

'Wow,' Jansson said.

She crushed the plastic cup and knew that he was asking because he cared about *her*, not the Photofit. 'Thank you,' she said quietly.

Suddenly he stubbed out his cigarette in the ashtray and got up with a little jerk. 'Well,' he said, 'back to the grind.'

She was left alone in the smoking shed, looking out through the nicotine-stained glass as the news team gathered for their second wind, another edition, a new day.

All of a sudden Thomas was aware of the streetlamps making patterns on his bedroom ceiling. He lay still for a few seconds, trying to work out what had woken him.

Something was rattling outside, a bus or a car. All these city sounds, all these constant stress factors. The engines and noises from the street filled his home. He was so fed up with it that he wanted to scream. How wonderful it would be to get away from here.

He rolled over to face Annika's side of the bed.

It was empty. She hadn't come home.

Anxiety kicked in. What could have happened? Why did she have to put herself in harm's way all the time? Covering the Nobel banquet shouldn't have taken all night, should it? What was there to write about, apart from the guests' outfits?

He looked up at the ceiling again and gulped.

He recognized this feeling all too well. Irritation crept up on him more often, these days. She never seemed to take into account that she was married and had children.

At that moment he heard the front door open in the hall. 'Annika?'

She turned the light on and came into the bedroom, standing on tiptoe. 'Hello,' she whispered. 'Did I wake you?'

He pushed himself into the mattress, pulled up the covers and did his best to smile. Not her fault. 'No,' he said. 'Where have you been?'

She sat down on his side of the bed, still wearing her ugly jacket. She looked very odd. 'You didn't hear the news last night?'

Thomas plumped up the pillows and pulled himself up a bit. 'I was watching the sport on Three.'

'There was a shooting at the Nobel banquet. I was standing alongside and saw it happen. I've been with the police all night.'

He looked at her as if she were far away, not sitting with him. He felt that if he stretched out his hand he wouldn't be able to reach her. 'How could something like that happen?' he asked feebly.

She pulled a newspaper out of her dreadful old bag. The smell of fresh newsprint hit him as he turned on the light.

Speechless, he took the paper and stared at the picture of people drinking a toast: a dark-haired woman and an almost completely bald man, both smiling, both dressed up to the nines.

'They shot the winner of the prize for medicine?'

She leaned over him and pointed at the woman. 'She was killed, Caroline von Behring. She was chair of the Nobel Committee at the Karolinska Institute. I saw her die.' She pulled off her coat and sighed quietly, then sat there with her head hanging and her back bent. It sounded like she was sniffing.

All of a sudden she was there with him, and he had an opportunity to comfort her. 'Anki,' he said, drawing her to him, her dress rustling as she ended up on top of him. 'It's all right now, you're here with me.'

She pulled away, reaching for her jacket, then got up and went out into the hall. The distance she imposed between them made him annoyed again, and disappointed, and bitter. 'I've got my meeting with Per Cramne at the department today,' he called after her, unnecessarily loudly. 'This is a big day for me.'

He thought he heard her open the fridge and pour herself a drink. She didn't answer.

Subject: In the Shadow of Death
To: Andrietta Ahlsell

Emil, Emil, the youngest and the blondest of the Nobel brothers, the one who dances and laughs most.

How Alfred loves him.

64

Emil, who has just passed his school-leaving exams, Emil, who is looking forward to starting his course at the Institute of Technology, Emil, who wants to be like his big brother, who wants to be like Alfred.

In his free time he helps his big brother with his work, oh, how he works – and he's smart! He's so good that he has responsibility for the production of the nitroglycerine that's going to be used in the construction of the main rail line north of Stockholm, the new railway, part of the new age.

It's the morning of Saturday, 3 September 1864, and he's standing out in the fenced-off yard outside Alfred's laboratory, distilling glycerine with C. E. Hertzman, a fellow student; you can almost hear their voices in the clear air, a hint of autumn on the wind.

Perhaps Alfred hears them. Perhaps big brother listens to their laughter and chat as he stands by his open window on the ground floor of the main building, talking to Blom, the engineer.

Then, at half past ten, Södermalm shakes, foundations crumble, windows break on Kungsholmen, on the other side of Riddarfjärden. A great yellow flame is visible throughout the capital, a flame that quickly becomes an enormous pillar of smoke.

Alfred is hit by the shockwave in his window. He is thrown to the floor with facial injuries. A carpenter, Nyman, who happens to be passing on the street outside, is blown to pieces. A thirteen-year-old messenger boy, Herman Nord, and nineteen-year-old Maria Nordqvist are also killed. The bodies of Emil and his friend Hertzman are in such a bad state that at first it was impossible to say how many people had died.

The destruction of the laboratory complex is immense. The *Postal Paper* writes laconically: 'Of the factory nothing remained other than a few blackened remnants, scattered hither and thither. In all the buildings in the vicinity, and even in those on the other side of the sound, not only were all the windowpanes broken, but also the lintels of their frames.'

Stockholmers spoke about the Nobel explosion for several decades.

Alfred himself goes back to work the next day.

He never speaks about the accident. He writes hundreds of letters, but he never mentions it.

And he never marries. He never has any children. He leaves his life's work to those who carry humanity forward, through peace, inventions and literature.

In his correspondence he describes his great loneliness, his deep sense of meaninglessness, his gnawing restlessness.

Never home, always travelling.

5

Annika was walking down a long corridor with no end in sight. Large crystal chandeliers hung above her head, the glass tinkling and rattling even though there was no obvious breeze.

Far away, she could just make out a faint source of light.

She knew what it was.

Caroline was there. Caroline von Behring, the dead woman: she was waiting for Annika. But Annika had to hurry, she had to run: it was important. And suddenly a wind blew and made the chandeliers crash back and forth above her, clattering above her head.

I'm coming, Annika tried to shout, but the wind muffled her voice.

You've got to hurry, the wind whispered, because I'm dying.

No! Annika cried. Wait!

At the next moment, Caroline was lying in front of her on the marble floor and looking up at Annika. Annika was so relieved that she fell to her knees beside the woman and leaned over towards her mouth to listen, and that was when Annika realized that the woman's chest had been torn open: she could see the rhythmic *contractions of her heart and the blood gushing out with every pulse.*

No! she screamed in panic, trying to get up, but she was stuck: her hands were heavy as lead, impossible to lift. I didn't mean to get here too late – that wasn't what I wanted!

But then she realized that it wasn't Caroline von Behring lying there before her. It was Sophia Grenborg, her husband's former colleague, with whom he'd had an affair, and the horror switched to jubilation.

Now you die, she thought triumphantly.

Then Thomas was kneeling beside Sophia, taking her in his arms, as the blood poured out of her.

She woke up with a start. The light in the room was grey. She could still hear Sophia Grenborg's tinkling laughter, fragile and cold as shards of ice. She's gone now, Annika thought. She'll never bother us again.

Thomas had taken the children to nursery, and she reached down to the floor for her mobile to see what the time was – 10.46. She'd been asleep for three and a half hours.

The dream followed her like an uncomfortable shadow as she showered and got dressed. She skipped breakfast, calling Berit and arranging to have an early lunch with her instead.

More snow had fallen during the morning, muffling the city. The number 62 bus glided up to the stop, shapeless and soundless. The driver didn't look at her as she got on, showing her season ticket. The vague sense of unease from the dream followed her down the aisle as she passed the other passengers, none of them paying her any attention.

I don't exist, she thought. I'm invisible.

Twelve minutes later she got off outside the Russian Embassy where Berit was waiting. They made their way to the office canteen with the latest editions tucked under her arm.

They picked at their food as they read.

There were the victims: the prize-winner, the chair of the Nobel Committee, and the three guards. The information about the last three was sketchy: their full names hadn't been known until the early hours so no one had had time to contact their families yet.

'We'll have to divide that between us this afternoon,' Berit said, and Annika made a note on the edge of the page.

The prize-winner had been moved from the intensive care unit to a normal ward.

'I don't suppose he'll be sharing a room with Dodgy Hip Helga,' Annika said, turning the page.

'He's got half of Mossad guarding him,' Berit said, and ate the last piece of her crispbread. 'They're having quite a time explaining how he came to be shot. They knew there were loads of threats against him.'

Charles Watson and the injured Aaron Wiesel, the two prize-winners, were stem-cell researchers and vocal advocates of therapeutic cloning. The decision to award them the Nobel Prize for Medicine had been controversial. It had unleashed a wave of protests from Catholic and radical Protestant groups.

'Did you follow the debate when the prize was announced?' Berit asked.

'I can't say I did,' Annika said. She cut a piece of stuffed cabbage. 'They want to grow embryos for their stem-cells?'

'Yes, they want to transplant cell nuclei in their research, and that's a way of producing embryos purely

69

for experimentation. George Bush was trying to stop this sort of research in the US with every means at his disposal. It's still controversial in Europe as well.'

'And the religious nutters in the US are saying that the intention is to create some sort of Frankenstein's monster, and that the scientists are playing God?'

'Not just the nutters. A lot of people share that view but express it in slightly milder terms. These aren't easy questions.'

Annika tapped her fork on her plate. 'So what have they done with Watson, the other prize-winner?'

'He was flown out to the US in a private plane last night. I think they'll be flying Wiesel out, too, as soon as he can be moved.'

Caroline von Behring's life and career had been quickly summarized during the night by a reporter they had never heard of before.

'Must be someone on the online edition,' Annika said.

The article was flat and badly written. It revealed that the chair of the Nobel Committee had been fifty-four years old when she died. She was related to the first winner of the Nobel Prize for Medicine, 'the German military physician Emil Adolf von Behring from Germany'. Emil Adolf von Behring had been behind the theory of immunization, and discovered modern vaccination in the form of a serum against diphtheria. For this he was awarded the Nobel Prize for Medicine in 1901. Young Caroline had followed in her ancestor's footsteps and become an expert in immunology. She had made her breakthrough at a young age, and gone on to have a prestigious career at the Karolinska Institute. She had become a professor at the age of thirty-eight, when she was also voted on to the Nobel Assembly. Three years later she was one of only six members of the

Nobel Committee, the board responsible for making the final decision on the allocation of the medicine prize. At the age of fifty-two she was appointed chair of the committee, a position she held for three years.

She had been married to her second husband, and had no children.

The palace had conveyed the royal couple's condolences, which was probably all the media would get from that quarter now.

'There's practically no private information about the Israeli – Aaron Wiesel,' Annika said. 'What do we know about him?'

'Single, childless, works in Brussels with the American. Fairly secular, if you ask me.'

'Gay?' Annika asked, wiping a piece of bread round her plate to mop up the last of the dressing.

'Probably. I think he and Watson are a couple. They look quite cute together.'

A large part of the paper was taken up with the unsuccessful police hunt for the killer. There were pictures of police officers on bridges, in tunnels, beside various stretches of water. The Photofit was on the front page and took up another whole page inside the paper. The caption stated that the picture had been produced with the help of 'witnesses at the crime scene', no mention of Annika. Practically every article about the police hunt had been written by the reporter Patrik Nilsson, who, with Berit, now made up the crime desk.

'Have you seen the competition?' Berit asked.

Annika picked up the other paper and quickly leafed through it. They had roughly the same selection of articles and pictures, with one exception: Bosse's article.

Annika felt herself blushing as she skimmed through his text. It covered three whole pages and described the course of events in the Golden Hall from a personal perspective. It was both unnerving and very focused. He evidently hadn't seen the killer, or noticed the couple fall after they had been shot, or seen the killer leave the hall. Even so he had managed to pull it together: the hall and the lights, the dancing, the heat, the blood and the screaming.

And she's dancing with me, we're dancing in the Golden Hall beneath the gaze of the Queen of the Mälaren. She's light in my arms and I want to be here for ever . . .

Annika read that sentence three times and felt her pulse quicken.

'Do you want coffee?'

Annika nodded.

They moved to the sofas with their mugs and papers.

'What was security like at the entrance?' Berit asked, putting down her mug on a white napkin. 'Metal detectors? Bags through a scanner? Pat-downs?'

Annika folded the other paper with a snort. 'Nothing like that. Everyone went in through the main entrance – you know, the gateway on Hantverkargatan – then over the courtyard and up to the doors that lead straight into the Blue Hall. We had to queue there for a couple of minutes, show our invitations, and then we were in.'

'Really?' Berit said sceptically. 'Please tell me that the invitation had some sort of electronic tag.'

Annika took a sip of her coffee and shook her head. 'Printed black type on cream card. You know, I still don't think that's right,' she said, examining the Photofit on the front of the paper. 'But I can't work out what's wrong with it.'

'You must have got a good look at her.'

'For about two seconds,' Annika said. 'To start with

72

I didn't think I remembered anything, but the police officer in the profiling unit was pretty good. He dragged out details that I hadn't even thought I knew.'

'It must have been a very unnerving experience,' Berit said.

Annika slumped a little in the sofa, staring blindly at a large tapestry hanging on the wall. 'To begin with I almost had to laugh,' she said, her voice suddenly weaker. 'It looked so funny, the old guy tumbling over like that – I thought he was drunk. Then there was a scream, sort of off to the right, and it just got worse until everyone was screaming and the orchestra stopped playing. Then the screaming carried into all the other rooms, like a big wave . . .'

Berit waited for a few seconds after Annika had stopped talking. Then she said, 'What were the security people doing?'

'During dinner they were spaced across the balcony outside the Golden Hall and along the pillared walkway down towards the courtyard. When the dancing started they spread out – there were a lot of them in the Prince's Gallery with the royal couple. There were more down by the entrance, I suppose, hardly any by the dance-floor. But once Caroline had fallen they came running from all directions, getting hold of those of us who had been standing closest. We weren't allowed to leave until we'd been questioned.'

'So you saw when the man was shot . . . Did you see her get hit as well?'

Annika ran her fingers through her hair, pushing it back. 'I don't know,' she said. 'But I was looking at her when she realized she'd been shot. Blood was jetting out of her chest. And then I fell over – someone knocked into me and I ended up on the floor right next to Caroline.

There was a man beside her with his hands over her heart and blood was pumping up between his fingers. It was bright red, with air bubbles in it . . .' She put her hands over her eyes.

'God, how horrible,' Berit said. 'Don't you think you ought to talk to someone about it?'

'What – like therapy?' Annika said, straightening up. 'I don't think so.'

'Why not? A lot of people find it helpful.'

'Not me,' Annika said, and a moment later her mobile rang.

It was Spike, the head of News. 'Were you thinking of coming in today, or are you on holiday?'

'I'm sitting here working,' Annika said.

'Good. Then you already know what's happened.'

Annika went completely cold. 'What?'

'The terrorist group Neue Jihad have claimed responsibility for the Nobel killings.'

The newsroom was almost empty. Annika Bengtzon and Berit Hamrin came running in from the staff canteen, clutching their bags and coats. Patrik Nilsson was reading at the main news desk, and Spike was talking animatedly on the phone as he gestured simultaneously to Pelle at the picture desk. Anders Schyman brushed some snow from his shoulders, before pulling off his duffel-coat and tossing it on to an empty office chair. 'Shall we go through all of this one more time?' he said, hearing how tired he sounded. 'This attack is a type of crime we haven't seen in Sweden before. Which means that we have to be extremely conscious of where the ethical boundaries lie, and very careful to see that Swedish law is upheld.'

He glanced quickly across the open-plan office.

None of his colleagues had slept more than a couple of hours so he was hardly in a position to complain. This is a new age, he thought, sitting down heavily on the sofa.

Spike slammed the phone down and grabbed a pile of printouts. 'Neue Jihad,' he said. 'A Muslim terrorist group based in Germany. The security police have been waiting for something like this. Half an hour ago the terrorists released a statement through a server in Berlin in which they claimed responsibility for "the murder of the Jewish Fascist and Zionist Aaron Wiesel, an infidel who deserved to die". They seem to be a fairly creative bunch, and considering what they've managed to do so far they'll probably be a force to reckon with in the future. Patrik's been in touch with Ranstorp, the terrorism expert – we're trying to put together an outline of the group's previous attacks, and see if they can be linked to al-Qaeda.'

'There's one thing wrong, though,' Annika said.

Annika and Berit had put their coats on top of his wet duffel-coat and had sat down in a couple of empty chairs at the end of the news desk.

'What?' Patrik said.

'Wiesel didn't die,' Berit said.

Spike lost his train of thought and looked at them with a mixture of surprise and resentment. 'For God's sake,' he said, 'that's just a detail.'

'Not for Wiesel,' Annika said. 'I can guarantee you that.'

Schyman was watching them from the corner of his eye, and decided not to get involved.

Spike made a sweeping gesture. 'What do I know? Maybe they wrote the message before the attack took place, then couldn't change it. And they did actually

75

manage to carry out their plan, to get in and shoot him during the Nobel banquet.'

'*Before*,' Berit said. '"Before the attack took place"?'

Spike looked smug. 'Precisely. The police are holding a press conference at fourteen hundred hours. I thought Patrik could take it – if you're not doing anything else, Patrik?'

Patrik Nilsson clicked to close the news-agency website and yawned loudly. 'Well,' he said, 'I was going to concentrate on Ranstorp, and check my sources at the National Defence College.'

'Okay. Annika, you take the press conference,' Spike said, getting ready to move on.

'Well,' Annika mimicked, 'I was going to concentrate on von Behring, and check my sources at the Karolinska Institute.'

Berit started to giggle, and Schyman felt himself getting annoyed. 'Are we going to cover the press conference or not?' he said.

'I can take it,' Berit said, swallowing her laughter.

'Are we going to talk to the family?' Schyman asked. 'Caroline von Behring must have some sort of background. Husband, children, parents?'

'I haven't been able to find that out yet,' Patrik said.

Spike did his best to share out the rest of the work, but as usual it was the reporters themselves who decided what they were going to do.

This newspaper needs a bit more discipline, Schyman thought. The organization doesn't work any more. It needs an overhaul. Nothing's going to be the same in the future. 'Think of the online edition when you're out in the field,' he said, as his colleagues were getting ready to go. 'There are no deadlines any more, just continual updates. This is about teamwork, remember. Annika, can I have a word?'

She stopped, her arms full of clothes, papers and notes. 'What?' she said.

He walked up close to her so the others wouldn't hear. 'Do you still maintain that you can't write about what you saw?'

She was pale, with dark rings under her eyes. 'I'm not the one maintaining anything,' she said. 'The paper's lawyer is. He seems to think that Swedish law is worth upholding.' She headed off towards her office, a mess of uncombed hair down her slender back.

Annoyance rose from his gut and burned in his throat. The thought ran through his brain before he had time to stop it: I've got to get rid of her.

6

Annika shut the door of her glass office with a soft thud. Schyman had become unbearable. Last night he had seemed unbalanced, and now he was handing over all responsibility to Spike, the man with the worst judgement in Sweden. Thank God Spike was so easy to manipulate. I've got to keep out of this, she thought, switching on her computer.

Berit had gone to the press conference at the police headquarters, and was planning to visit the wounded security guard in hospital. He'd regained consciousness and was keen to tell his story. Another wannabe celebrity, Annika thought, then felt cruel.

The families of the other two guards had declined to co-operate with the paper. Berit had already taken flowers and passed on their condolences, but neither of them had been interested. The paper's medical correspondent was going to try to track down Wiesel, who was still in a pretty poor way. Sjölander was looking into the right-wing Christian nutters in the US with their radical views on medical research, while Patrik and a couple of the web-edition staff were keeping in touch with the police and the investigating team.

She went into the paper's archive, then on to the Net,

looking for information about Caroline von Behring. Considering she was such an influential woman, she was extremely anonymous, Annika thought. She'd never worked anywhere apart from the Karolinska Institute and never appeared in the media, other than in connection with her work: short reports about promotions, little quotes whenever the winners of the medicine prize were announced.

Only in the past few weeks had her name been linked to any form of controversy: the fact that Wiesel and Watson had been awarded that year's prize.

She looked up some of the contributions to the debate about Wiesel and Watson's stem-cell research. Some suggested that the Karolinska Institute was the devil's work, corrupt and biased and completely immoral. On one American site she found a caricature of von Behring with horns and a tail, and on another Alfred Nobel appeared as Frankenstein's monster with the caption: *Is this what the Committee wants?*

There were also impassioned articles defending the decision from other researchers, self-proclaimed heroes who were fighting to wipe out all human sickness.

The question was whether it was acceptable to use eggs left over from artificial insemination, to adapt their stem-cells and use them for research. That was the technique, known as therapeutic cloning, that scientists had used to come up with Dolly the Sheep.

The most famous advocate for stem-cell research in the US was the now deceased film star Christopher Reeve – Superman – who had broken his neck in a riding accident. With seven scientists he had sued President George W. Bush for putting a stop to stem-cell research. Right up to the end, Reeve had hoped that the new technique could help him walk again.

Annika clicked on through the mass of information on various websites. How on earth had she ever found out anything before the Internet existed?

She found a feature article about a book entitled *Ethics and Genetic Technology: Philosophical and Religious Perspectives on Genetic Technology, Stem-cell Research and Cloning*, which clarified that the most obstinate resistance to the research came from Catholic and Protestant groups. Western culture had become so individualized that single-cell eggs were regarded as having human rights.

Judaism, on the other hand, didn't seem to have any great problem with the modification of human embryos. The possibility of saving lives was seen as more important than the embryo's human rights. Human beings acted as God's assistants to improve creation; our duty was to be fruitful and multiply and replenish the earth. And if genetic research could help us do that, so much the better.

Even Islam seemed to think that stem-cell research was entirely reasonable. Most religious experts would allow such research if it benefited humanity. In their world, the embryo only becomes a complete human being when it gains a soul, which happens one hundred and twenty days after conception.

So if al-Qaeda was involved, the motivation wasn't what Wiesel had in his test-tubes, Annika thought, going back to Caroline von Behring.

The dead woman was in the telephone directory, with three different numbers. She was listed alongside her husband, Knut Hjalmarsson. Their home address was in Lärkstan, in the Östermalm district of Stockholm. A pretty smart part of town.

Annika tried all three numbers. The first redirected

her to a switched-off mobile. The second reached a fax-machine. The third rang twenty times without anyone answering. She put the phone down and sighed. She wasn't going to get an article out of this. She looked at her watch: twelve thirty. She was due to pick the children up by five o'clock at the latest. And she had to go shopping: it was her turn to cook. And it was Friday, which meant that everything had to be a bit more special than on other days. She sighed again, picked up the phone and ordered a taxi.

It had got colder. The snow didn't seem to be falling as heavily because the flakes were smaller. Instead they swirled on the increasing wind, making people shiver and turn up their collars. Like a grey-black mass, they slid onwards through the slush on the pavements. Annika leaned back in her seat and shut her eyes.

Reality faded and she let it slip away, dozing against the seat's headrest as the car zigzagged through the city traffic. She slept, mouth open, all the way along Sankt Eriksgatan and Torsgatan, out to the Karolinska Institute in Solna, just beyond the city boundary.

The sharp turn into the university campus woke her with a start. She paid, slightly groggily, and found herself standing outside a squat two-storey building of brownish-red bricks with oblong windows. The Nobel Forum, at number one Nobels Väg.

She walked over and pressed the button on the intercom.

The building seemed cool and deserted, as if in mourning. Annika made her way to the Nobel office and was about to knock when a dishevelled woman, her eyes red, pulled the door open. 'What do you want?' She was short and round, her hair henna-red, dressed in a white blouse and pale trousers.

Annika had the same uncomfortable feeling she always had when approaching the relatives and colleagues of people who had met an untimely death. 'I'd like to ask some questions about Caroline von Behring,' she said, suddenly not sure what to do with her hands.

The woman sniffed and gave her a sceptical look. 'Why? What sort of questions?'

Annika put her bag down on the floor and held out her hand. 'Annika Bengtzon,' she said. 'From the *Evening Post* newspaper. Naturally we have to cover the events at the Nobel banquet last night, and that's why we'd like to write about Caroline von Behring.'

The woman shook her hand. 'I see,' she said. 'What sort of thing are you thinking of writing?'

'Caroline von Behring seems to have been fairly withdrawn in her private life,' Annika said. 'Obviously we'll respect that. But she did have a very public professional role and I'd like to ask a few questions about her work and position as the chair of the Nobel Committee.'

'How did you know to ask for me?' the woman said.

Annika pointed at the sign on the door that read 'Nobel Office'.

'No, no,' the woman said, taking out a handkerchief from her trouser pocket and blowing her nose. 'I don't work in there.'

She took Annika's hand again. 'Birgitta,' she said, 'Birgitta Larsén. I'm part of Caroline's network. Or was . . . I suppose. The network's still there, of course, it's just not Carrie's any more. I don't know how to put it but I dare say you'll – you work with words, don't you?'

Annika considered how best to reply, but Birgitta Larsén wasn't really interested.

'This is where the office staff work,' the woman said, gesturing over her shoulder, then started walking down the corridor. 'The assembly and committee consist of professionally active professors spread out across the campus. What do you want to know?'

She stopped and looked at Annika, as if she had only just noticed her.

'I'd just like to talk to someone who knew Caroline,' Annika said. 'Someone who could tell me a bit about what she was like as a person, and as a colleague.'

Birgitta Larsén turned on her heel. 'Well, then,' she said. 'Let's find somewhere to sit down.'

She swept away down the corridor on noisy heels, and Annika followed her, feeling oddly clumsy. She couldn't seem to wake up properly from her nap in the taxi.

Close to the entrance Birgitta Larsén turned left into a bland conference room, with an overhead projector and a little television set on wheels. 'This room is used for small meetings, such as when the Nobel Committee meets. That piece of art's called *The Mirror*,' she said, pointing at some black and white squares on the east wall.

Annika glanced round the room. Her attention was taken by a window oddly positioned in one corner. It was getting dark already, the light outside a deep graphite-grey. 'So you work here at the Karolinska Institute as well?' Annika asked, sitting down at the circular conference table.

'I'm a professor in the Department of Physiology and Biophysics,' she explained. 'Carrie worked with immunology at the Department of Medical Epidemiology and Molecular Biology.'

'How well did you know Caroline?' Annika asked, holding her notebook in front of her.

The professor stopped at the window beside the television and stared out at the snow as it gradually melted away. 'We took our doctorates at the same time,' she said. 'There were several of us, quite a few women, who got them the same month. That was pretty unusual in those days, even though it was only twenty-five years ago.' She turned to Annika again. 'It's crazy how time passes so quickly, isn't it?'

Annika nodded without saying anything.

'Caroline was the youngest, of course,' Birgitta Larsén said. 'She always was.'

'From what I understand, she was very successful,' Annika said.

Birgitta Larsén sank on to a small side table. 'Successful, yes, that's one way of putting it,' she said, sounding tired. 'Caroline has been one of the foremost immunologists in Europe since the late 1980s, even if people didn't always recognize that here in Sweden.'

'What sort of research did she do?'

'She made her breakthrough with an article in *Science* in October 1986, to great acclaim from the entire scientific community. What she did was to develop Hood and Tonegawa's discovery of the identification of immunoglobulin genes.' Birgitta Larsén looked at Annika, checking for some sign that she was keeping up. Annika was unable to oblige. 'T-cell receptors,' the woman said, 'for which Tonegawa was awarded the Nobel Prize.'

Annika nodded again, even though she really had no idea, and scribbled frantically in her notebook. 'And you stayed good friends?'

Birgitta Larsén looked up at *The Mirror*, and Annika noticed that her eyes were filling with fresh tears.

'Always,' she said, pulling out her handkerchief again. 'I think perhaps I knew her better than anyone except her husband.'

Annika looked down at her notebook and knew she couldn't back away now: she had to get as much information as she could out of this shocked woman. 'What was she like as a person?'

Birgitta Larsén laughed suddenly. 'Vain,' she said. 'Caroline was born Andersson. She got the von Behring from her first husband. She kept the name when she remarried. A name like Hjalmarsson won't open any doors for you in the medical world. Whereas von Behring, ha! She was very happy for people to think she was related to old Emil. You know about his discovery of serum and vaccines?'

Annika nodded. Yes, she knew about that.

'No children, of course, but you know that,' the woman went on. 'Not that Carrie had anything against children, she'd have been happy if any had come along, but it never happened and I don't think she minded. Does that sound strange?'

Annika took a deep breath before answering, but the professor went on: 'Carrie lived for her work, and she was a true feminist. She always made sure that women were promoted around her, even if it wasn't something she boasted about. If she had, she'd never have been appointed chair of the committee, as I'm sure you can understand.'

Annika carried on nodding.

'Obviously it was tough sometimes, always trying to stand up for women but never being able to fight openly for them. If she had, her position would have been at risk and she couldn't let that happen. She was worth more as an example to women in this industry than as a fighter for them. I think most people would agree with that.'

Birgitta Larsén fell silent and looked out of the window again. It was now completely dark.

'How did Caroline take the criticism of the decision to award the prize to Wiesel and Watson?'

The woman replied, expressionless, 'Carrie was the one who pushed through the award for their work. She knew that the whole assembly would end up in hot water, but she went ahead anyway.'

'Do you think the attack could have had anything to do with the prize?'

Birgitta Larsén stared at Annika as if she'd never seen her before. 'What did you say?' she said, her face hardening.

Annika gulped. 'Or do you think it was purely an accident? That Wiesel was the target and Caroline just happened to be in the wrong place at the wrong time?'

The professor stood up with a little jerk. 'I don't think I like what you're insinuating,' she said sharply, more tears in her eyes. 'Would you go now, please?'

'What did I say wrong?' Annika asked, astonished. 'Have I upset you?'

'Will you please leave this building?'

Annika gathered her things. 'Thanks for taking the time to talk to me,' she said, but the woman had turned back to the window.

The snow had stopped falling and a sharp frost had taken its place. Annika's thighs were on the point of freezing solid by the time her taxi turned up.

'The *Evening Post* newspaper,' the driver said, when she had told him the address. 'You know, you write a load of crap in your paper. It's reality television and naked exposés and dodgy politicians all the time. I never read it.'

'So how do you know what's in it?' Annika wondered, pulling her mobile out of her bag.

'I just know, and there's a load of crap about Muslims as well, raping people and blowing things up.' The man was an immigrant, his accent very strong.

'Yesterday we had an article saying that most Muslim scholars want to permit stem-cell research because the Koran says that research is beneficial to humanity,' Annika lied. 'Can you turn the radio off so I can make a call?'

The taxi-driver switched off the noise and didn't say another word.

'How was the press conference?' Annika asked, when Berit answered.

'The police are working with their colleagues in Germany and are hinting that they're close to making an arrest,' Berit said. 'Spike was right about them waiting for something to happen. But at the same time they're saying they're not dropping other lines of inquiry. How about you? How are you getting on?'

'Okay. I spoke to an upset work colleague of Caroline's. It'll make a short piece. So what are these "other lines of inquiry"?'

'As far as I understand it, they're only looking at groups close to al-Qaeda. They think the Israeli was the target and Caroline's death was an accident.'

The taxi was heading along the Solna road, across the Essinge motorway. Annika saw that the traffic in both directions was at a standstill and checked her watch. A quarter past three: the Friday rush had started. 'I don't believe this al-Qaeda stuff for a minute,' Annika said. 'If they'd wanted to attack the Nobel banquet they'd have blown the City Hall sky-high. They've never gone for attacks focused on individuals, then run off after shooting the *wrong* person.'

Berit sighed. 'I know,' she said, 'but what can we do? This is what they're working on so that's what we have to write about in the paper.'

'We can find someone who thinks it's ridiculous,' Annika said. 'Someone who can draw parallels with Hans Holmér and the whole stupid focus on the Kurds after Olof Palme was shot.'

It was no secret that the assassination of the Swedish prime minister had never been solved largely because the head of the investigation had spent the first year sitting in his room dreaming up different conspiracy theories involving the PKK, the Kurdish independence movement.

'And how likely is it that we'd get an article like that published?' Berit asked, and Annika knew she was right. The paper would never publish an article that was genuinely critical of the police at a time like this: the police would simply talk to their competitors, freezing them out.

'Shall we meet up in the office?' Annika said.

'I'll probably be a while. I'm on my way to see the security guard now. Are you working this weekend?'

'No one's asked me to,' Annika said.

'Good. Stay away,' Berit said, about to hang up.

'One more thing,' Annika said. 'Why would anyone want to murder Caroline von Behring?'

'Let's just hope that the police's "lines of inquiry" are broad enough to include that question.'

Annika picked Ellen up from nursery, only a quarter of an hour late. The little girl had had a nap that afternoon, which meant she'd be up half the night.

Kalle was at pre-school in the next building. He collapsed in a little heap on the floor when he had to put his coat on. 'I wish I was dead!' he wailed, and Annika dropped her bag, sat on a bench and pulled him on to her lap. 'You know I love my special boy,' she whispered, rocking him. 'You know you're the most important thing in the world to me. Have you had a nice day?'

'Everyone's stupid,' he yelled. 'Everyone's stupid, and you're stupidest, and I wish I was *dead*!'

The first time he had said this, Annika had been shocked into silence. A chat with a nurse at the childcare clinic had calmed her down: six-year-olds go through a mini-puberty, with raging mood-swings that often take an extremely dramatic form.

Now four-year-old Ellen was standing there silently, staring wide-eyed at her brother. Annika pulled her daughter to her. 'Do you want to come shopping with me? Then you can choose some crisps and sweets.'

Kalle wiped his tears and wriggled like a worm. '*I'm* going to choose the sweets!' he shouted. 'And I want a *fizzy drink*!'

Annika took hold of him again firmly. 'Stop shouting now,' she said. 'You can choose your sweets, and Ellen can choose hers. But there'll be no fizzy drink today.'

'I want a fizzy drink!' he screamed, struggling to free himself.

'Kalle,' Annika said, forcing herself not to shout. 'Kalle, you have to calm down now or there won't be any sweets at all. Are you listening? Do you remember what happened last time?'

He stiffened in her arms and his breathing slowed a bit. 'I didn't get any sweets,' he said, and his lower lip started to tremble.

'That's right,' Annika said. 'But today you can have some because you've stopped shouting and you're not going to make a fuss about fizzy drinks. Okay?'

The child nodded, and Annika turned to her daughter. 'What sort of a day have you had, darling?' she asked, kissing her forehead.

'I did a drawing for you, Mummy,' she said, wrapping her arms round Annika's neck.

'How lovely,' Annika murmured, as tears of exhaustion welled in her eyes.

They did their shopping in the Co-op at the corner of Kungsholmsgatan and Scheelegatan under slightly chaotic circumstances. Ellen dropped her sweets on the floor, where they were promptly run over by a pushchair, and Kalle had another little outburst about them not buying any fizzy drinks.

Annika's forehead was beaded with sweat as she hauled the last bag of groceries into the hall from the lift.

'If you put the television on, the kids' programmes will be on in a little while,' she called after the children. She hung up their outdoor clothes and lined up their boots under the bench in the hall, then carried the shopping into the kitchen and unpacked it on the worktop.

Damn, she'd forgotten to get any salt.

She peeled the potatoes, chopped some onions and cut the pork chops into strips. As the potatoes came to the boil she fried the onions until they were transparent, then put them at the bottom of an ovenproof dish. Then she fried the pork with some bacon, as she had no salt, then added cream to the juices in the pan, poured it over the meat and put the dish into the oven.

She'd just laid the table and lit the candles when

Thomas got home. He came into the kitchen, jacket flapping, as he loosened his tie. 'I think I'm halfway there,' he said, giving Annika a quick kiss on the hair. 'This job's made for me. My CV is perfect, and with my personal contacts in the department, I can't see how anyone could beat me to it. Haven't you made any salad?' He was standing by the table, looking at what she had done. 'I thought we'd agreed to have something green with every meal,' he said, turning towards her.

'We did,' Annika said. My day's been absolutely great as well, she thought. I've been out to the Karolinska Institute and talked to a murder victim's work colleague. The police are about to arrest a group of German terrorists and I went shopping and made dinner. Aloud, she said: 'Can you get the kids while I chop up some salad?' She went to the fridge with a lump in her throat.

Saturday, 12 December

7

Jemal Ali Ahmed was wrenched from sleep and found himself at the centre of ear-splitting noise and blinding light. He knew at once what had happened: his whole being was shouting it at him. This was a direct hit. The war had come and his house was exploding, unless it was his parents' place, his childhood home in the mountains above al-Azraq ash Shamali – he could hear the goats screaming and the beams collapsing.

The children, he thought, stretching his hands into the burning light. Allah, protect my girls, look after my daughters . . . He got to his feet and tumbled helplessly out of the truckle-bed on to the floor before he realized where he was. Thank heaven: of course he was in the flat.

His surprise loosened the grip that panic had had on his heart. But what on earth was happening to his home? And where was his wife?

'Fatima,' he called, but the smoke muffled his voice.

He was surrounded by the terrible, blinding light. The noise rumbled in constant waves round the room, his nose hurt and his eyes were streaming.

'Jemal!' his wife cried, somewhere to the left of him. 'The house is burning! It's on fire!'

This isn't a fire, he thought. This is something else.

'Jemal!' she screamed. 'Dilan, Sabrina, the girls, Jemal! Save the girls!'

He shut his eyes against the light and crawled in his pyjamas towards the living-room door. Whatever this was he had to get the girls out, as long as he wasn't already too late. It was so difficult to move, like being in a nightmare. He tried calling for his daughters but his voice caught in his throat and no sound came out. He started to sob, and reached out to the doorframe for support.

'Sabrina,' he cried, 'Daddy's coming,' and a moment later he realized that it wasn't the doorframe, just a faceless dark shape aiming an automatic rifle at him. He screamed, until his bowels emptied into his pyjama trousers.

Thomas was sitting with the sports section of the morning paper held up as a shield against the rest of the world, as the children squabbled over a sandwich. Annika was trying to read the news, but gave up when Ellen spilled her chocolate milk across the floor.

'Do you know what?' Annika said. 'You can clear that up together, then go and get washed and dressed.'

'Why should I do it?' Kalle said. 'She was the one who knocked it over.'

'Paper,' Annika said, passing him several sheets of kitchen-roll. 'Wipe it up. Ellen, paper. Wipe it up.'

'Have you remembered we're going for mulled wine today?' Thomas said, from behind the paper.

The children mopped up the mess and threw the paper into the bin. Annika took her sandwich, her coffee and the morning paper into the living room. She spread the paper out on the coffee-table and switched on the television.

An army of police in riot gear rushed into a flat. The picture shook and there was a lot of noise. Then the screen went completely white. In the top-left corner stood the text: 'BANDHAGEN THIS MORNING'. 'What the hell?' Annika said, putting down her sandwich. 'Thomas! Have you seen this?'

In response she heard the shower start.

An impersonal voice announced that the police national response unit had broken down the door of a rented property in Bandhagen at six eighteen on Saturday morning. Officers in riot gear had stormed the flat and found the suspected terrorists asleep inside. The head of the cell had been caught on a truckle-bed in the living room, while his teenage daughters had been asleep in their respective bedrooms. The screen showed footage of a woman in a nightdress being led off to a police van.

'Bloody hell,' Annika said, staring at the screen. 'They've gone mad. Look at that woman – she's got nothing on her feet. Thomas!'

The newsreader was back on the screen again and explained that that morning's arrests were directly linked to the attack on the Nobel banquet, although the police hadn't yet said precisely what the link was. The Security Police had said very little. They had evidently videotaped their successful operation and distributed the tape to Swedish Television and TV4 in time for it to be shown on the late-morning bulletins.

Thomas came into the living room, still brushing his teeth. 'Wot'sh habbened?' he asked.

'Go and spit that out,' Annika said, and Thomas disappeared into the bathroom.

A pre-recorded item came on, someone from the Security Police explaining that the operation was being carried out fully in accordance with the national police regulations that governed such situations. 'Any police authority must immediately inform the National Police Service through the national communications centre if a terrorist act has been committed or is believed to be imminent within that authority's jurisdiction,' the man from the Security Police said.

'So there was no doubt in this instance?' an unseen reporter asked respectfully.

'None whatsoever,' the officer said. 'Because a terrorist act was feared, and because paragraph three of the regulations states that the principal duty of the national emergency unit is "to combat acts of terrorism within national boundaries", there was no doubt at all.' He concluded by pointing out that the operation had been judged one hundred per cent successful.

Then the dramatic footage was shown in full once more.

To begin with, the building lay in complete darkness, hardly visible against the black night sky. Then the shock grenade detonated on the second floor, a gigantic explosion that flared in the lens and turned the screen white briefly. Shadows moved in the windows, and the camera shook. A row of armoured police vans drove up at speed and braked sharply outside the door, and police in riot gear poured out of various doors, automatic weapons at the ready.

Kalle came into the room and crept up next to Annika. She put her arms round him without looking away from the screen.

'What are they doing, Mummy?' he asked.

'The police have picked up a family to ask them some questions,' Annika said.

'Is the family dangerous, Mummy?'

Annika sighed. 'I don't know, darling, but I don't think so. Not the girls, anyway. What do you think? Do you think they look dangerous?'

Two half-naked teenagers in handcuffs were being pushed into separate police vans.

He shook his head. 'I think they look scared.'

The phone rang and Kalle took that as his signal to run off.

It was Berit. 'Have you heard about Bandhagen?' she asked.

'It's on television now,' Annika replied. 'What's this link to the Nobel murders that they're going on about?'

'That's why I'm calling,' Berit said. 'You haven't heard anything?'

'Me?' Annika said, surprised. 'I've only just got up. What are the police saying?'

'"Internal surveillance".'

'Oh, no.' Annika groaned. 'Someone's put the squeeze on them to come up with results.'

'Probably,' Berit said, 'unless the mother just happens to look exactly like the Photofit picture you helped them with. The footage is pretty poor quality, but maybe you can see her face.'

Annika drew breath to reply, but stopped herself. What could she say? How much was she allowed to confirm or deny? 'The Photofit has been made public, and you can see it doesn't look at all like her,' she said carefully. 'And I don't know if I'm allowed to say anything.'

Berit sighed. 'This is really tricky,' she said. 'I can see you're in an impossible position, but it's making things difficult for the rest of us. We're having to tiptoe around you, trying to find out things that you already know.'

'Look,' Annika said, sitting up on the sofa, 'I don't really know anything except that a woman stood on my foot when I was dancing in the Golden Hall. The police haven't said anything to me about Bandhagen or Berlin. I've got no idea what they've managed to cook up. The fact that I just happened to be there doesn't stop me working on the story.'

She could hear Berit rustling something at the other end of the line.

'I know,' Berit said quietly. 'But I think you might as well take it a bit easy this weekend. Patrik's covering the police and I'm doing the rest, so shall we say we'll see you on Monday?'

A shocked silence vibrated between them.

'Sure,' Annika said. 'Fine.' She hung up with an indefinable feeling of emptiness. When had anyone ever called to say that she *didn't* have to work?

'Who was that?' Thomas said, from the doorway, drying his freshly shaven chin with a towel.

'Berit from the paper. She—'

'That's bloody typical,' Thomas exclaimed, dropping his towel on the floor. 'Because we agree to go and have mulled wine with my parents today, naturally you have to work. I *knew* it!'

'Actually I don't,' Annika said, getting up. She picked up Thomas's towel and held it out to him. He'd left some blood on it from where he'd cut himself shaving. He turned away without taking it, and she watched his broad shoulders disappear into the bathroom again. She stood there for a few moments as a jumble of contradictory feelings churned in her gut. She wanted to reach out to him so much, but she hated his arrogance. And she hated the thought of him with that little blonde whore from the county council, Sophia Grenborg. Annika had managed to put a stop to their affair without letting Thomas realize that she knew about it. It's over, she thought. Everything's all right again.

Mulled wine with her parents-in-law in Vaxholm was as strained as she had feared it would be. Their turn-of-the-century villa was full to bursting with enthusiastic city types in blazers and well-polished shoes. Annika went round the gathering, holding her children's hands. Ellen and Kalle were dressed up, neatly combed and subdued. The crush at each doorway was so great that blockages soon built up. She felt sweat break out under her breasts and the children's hands would soon be too slippery to hold.

A lot of the guests came from the suburb's active business association. Thomas's father had been on the board for more than thirty years. There was talk of tourists, how many, how to attract more. There was grumbling about businesses that only opened during the summer months, taking customers from those who stayed open all year round. There was talk of the Christmas market, which was on at the moment and would be for another week.

And, just for once, there was talk of current affairs.

'It's a good job they've caught those Nobel terrorists,' a blue-haired woman was saying to a white-haired one as Annika walked past on a mission to find something for the children to eat.

'Imagine, al-Qaeda in Stockholm!' one man was saying. 'They could even be here in Vaxholm!'

She carried on, steering the children towards the kitchen.

'Yes, but I have to say, those Nobel banquets are seriously overrated. The food is always stone-cold by the time you get it.' That had come from one of the younger guests, an overweight man who worked in the same bank as Thomas's first wife. 'No, it isn't,' Annika said, stopping. 'That's a myth spread by people who've never been invited.'

The conversation around her died and a group of men stared at her in surprise.

'I see,' the overweight man said, looking hard at her black jeans and the jacket that was too big for her. 'So you know better?'

'The food's warm. Inedible, but warm,' Annika said, then pulled the children into the kitchen. It, too, was full of people, mostly women in sensible shoes and neat dresses. They were chatting and laughing, waving their wine glasses, now filled with Burgundy after the obligatory mulled wine.

'Annika,' Doris, her mother-in-law, said, 'can you give me a hand to carry out these trays? I'd do it myself, but you know what my hip's like.' Beside her stood Eleonor, Thomas's former wife. Eleonor and her mother-in-law had kept in touch after the divorce, exacerbating Annika's sense of inadequacy.

'The children need something to eat first,' Annika said, pretending not to see Eleonor. 'Then I'll be happy to pass round the snacks. Can I make some sandwiches?'

Doris's thin lips grew even paler. 'But, my dear,' she said flatly, 'there's plenty of food here.'

Annika looked down at the trays on the worktops, herring canapés, prawn canapés, mussel canapés. She bent down to Kalle. 'Have you seen Daddy?' she asked quietly, and her son shook his head. She took the children's hands again and set off once more into the sea of people.

When she finally found Thomas in the wine cellar, her back was sticky with sweat. He was talking to Martin,

Eleonor's new husband. Martin looked amused, but Thomas seemed ill-at-ease and slightly drunk. 'The problem isn't that the police are bugging criminal groups,' he said, spilling some of his mulled wine as he tried to emphasize the importance of his argument. 'The problem is that their activities aren't regulated, and can't be controlled, and we have no legislation governing how they should handle the mass of surplus information they get these days.'

'Thomas,' Annika said, 'the kids have to eat. I'm going out to buy something for them.'

'Pretending we don't need new legislation is just sticking our heads in the sand . . .'

'Thomas!' Annika said. 'I'm going to take the children home now. Do you think you'll be able to get a lift back into town with someone later?'

He turned to look at her, annoyed at the interruption. 'Why? Where are you going?'

'The children have to eat. They don't like herring and mussels.'

Martin followed the exchange, grinning, crossing his arms, the wealthy entrepreneur enjoying the paltry concerns of the middle classes.

'Can't you make them a sandwich or something?'

Thomas was evidently embarrassed by her presence in the cellar. Annika swallowed her anger and the sense that she was not good enough. 'Do as you like,' she said.

She walked away, the children trailing after her.

Annika stopped at McDonald's on the E18 on her way into Stockholm. The children got a Happy Meal each. After they had eaten most of their hamburgers and pulled their plastic toys apart, she sent them off to play in the ball-pool. She bought a coffee and sat down with the evening papers next to the play area.

Their rival had managed to put together a special supplement, and had a picture of the arrest of the family in Bandhagen on the front page. Bosse had written the article. She traced his name with a fingertip, then glanced up to check that no one had seen her.

The *Evening Post* had nothing – at least, not in the early edition she'd got hold of. She had no illusions that her paper would have shown any better judgement or held any other opinion of the main news of the day: they just hadn't had time to do anything about it.

Apart from that, the papers were fairly similar, more or less as you might have expected. They had both bought the German terrorism angle and were identifying al-Qaeda as having been behind the attack. And they had both identified Aaron Wiesel as the intended target; Caroline von Behring was an unfortunate woman who had just happened to be standing in the way. Bosse's picture byline stood at the top of an article about Caroline's life.

He's writing about the same things as me, she thought.

His paper claimed that the search in Germany had been close to reaching a conclusion during the early hours of the morning, and the *Evening Post* quoted three anonymous sources claiming that three men had been arrested in Berlin the previous evening.

The wounded security guard spoke in both papers about the shooting by the water, and looked exactly the same in both pictures. Wiesel was said to have flown out of the country, but no one could say where to.

Annika's short piece about Caroline von Behring appeared as a two-column item at the end of the coverage.

The other paper had two more spreads of graphics, with comment and analysis that added nothing.

The *Evening Post* had one thing that the other paper didn't: on the comment pages a Professor Lars-Henry Svensson from the Karolinska Institute claimed that the Nobel Committee was unethical and corrupt, but his argument was unstructured and somewhat confused.

The activities of the Karolinska Institute are today governed by a number of profit-seeking companies [he wrote]. *The Nobel Committee chooses to prioritize questionable research into the origins of life. Using the Nobel Prize for profit is reprehensible for many reasons, but primarily because it goes against Alfred Nobel's last will and testament . . .*

'Mummy, he's throwing balls at me,' Ellen yelled from the sea of balls.

'Throw them back,' Annika said, and went on reading:

The fact that Watson and Wiesel were awarded the Nobel Prize for Medicine is nothing but scandalous. Caroline von Behring was a great advocate of controversial stem-cell research, and her efforts were also pivotal in making sure that Watson and Wiesel were awarded this year's prize. One might wonder at her motivation. We can't lose sight of the debate about the future consequences of therapeutic cloning. The discussion of ethics and the value of human life must not be allowed to die with Caroline von Behring.

Who had accepted this peculiar article? Annika wondered. It came perilously close to libel of the deceased.

In all likelihood the professor had tried to get it into the more prestigious morning paper, the other evening paper, then several more publications before he had come to them, and there were very good reasons why the others had rejected it.

'Mummy!' Kalle shouted. 'She's hitting me!'

Annika rolled up the papers and pushed them into her bag. 'Okay,' she said, getting up. 'Do you know what we're going to do now? We're going to look at a house!'

8

It was already getting dark as she steered the car slowly along Vinterviksvägen in Djursholm. The road was narrow, with sandy pavements along the edge of the tarmac.

She pulled up by the kerb. 'What do you think, then, kids?' she said, turning to the back seat. 'Is it going to be fun living here?'

The children looked up from their Gameboys and gazed distractedly at the white villa swimming in the encroaching darkness. 'Are there swings?' Ellen asked.

'You'll have your own swing,' Annika said. 'Do you want to go and have a look?'

'Can we go in?' Kalle asked.

Annika peered out through the windscreen. 'Not today,' she said, her gaze on the modern building. A sea view, she thought. A large garden with apple trees, oak parquet flooring throughout, open-plan kitchen and dining area, Mediterranean-blue tiles in both bathrooms, four bedrooms. She recalled the pictures in the advertisement on the Internet, the light, airy bedroom, the open spaces.

'Why can't we go in?' Kalle said. 'The people who used to live here have moved, haven't they?'

'We haven't bought the house yet, Kalle,' Annika said, 'so we don't have our own keys. We can only go inside when the estate agent's here.'

'Where's Daddy?' Ellen said, suddenly realizing that Thomas wasn't in the car.

'He's coming later. He stayed at Grandma and Grandad's for a bit longer.' She switched off the engine and darkness swallowed them.

'Mummy, put the lights on!' Ellen was afraid of the dark, and Annika quickly switched on the lamp in the roof.

'I'm getting out to have a look,' she said. 'Do you want to come?'

The children ignored her, focusing on their computer games again.

Annika opened the door and stepped carefully out on to the frozen tarmac. The wind was blowing from the sea – she could feel its dampness even if she couldn't see the water. The 'sea view' in the advertisement was actually restricted to a little glimpse from one bedroom on the top floor, but that didn't matter.

She shut the door and walked over to the fence. It was only three weeks since she had uncovered an old Maoist network in Luleå, and along the way she had found a large bag of euro notes, worth 128 million kronor, in an old junction-box. At the end of April next year, she would get a tenth of that sum as her reward for handing it in. In other words, 12.8 million kronor.

She had found the house in Djursholm before the money had landed in her lap, practically newly built, quiet and peaceful, only 6.9 million. She had got it for six and a half. No one else had offered more than that.

The contracts would be exchanged on 1 May, once the reward had been paid out. They'd be selling their flat on Hantverkargatan in the spring; she'd already been in touch with an estate agent and had it valued. They stood to get up to three and a half million for it.

'Maybe you could buy a boat,' Annika had said, curling up in Thomas's lap.

He had kissed her hair, then pinched her nipple. 'Shall we go and have a little lie-down?' he had whispered, and she had pulled away.

Couldn't, didn't want to. Every time he wanted to have sex she saw him with Sophia Grenborg, kissing in public outside the NK department store. She kept imagining their bodies wet with sweat, their ecstatic faces.

'Mummy,' Ellen said, through a crack in the car door. 'I need a wee-wee.'

Annika turned and went back to the car. 'Come on, I'll help you,' she said, getting the little girl out of her child-seat.

She looked round to find a suitable spot, past the treetops and buildings. The sky was clear, stars lighting up one by one. The silence around them was dense and black. The house, her house, sat on a corner plot beside a crossroads. It was surrounded by others in various styles, patrician villas from the turn of the last century and large brick buildings from the fifties, with huge windows and basements. Lights had started to come on, making the windows shine like cat's eyes. She could make out the house next door through the bare trees; the plots were all large, divided by hedges and fences.

A thought struck her: her house was the only new one. It was also one of the smallest in the area, with its 190 square metres.

'Where shall I do my wee-wee, Mummy?'

Annika walked round the car. 'Here. No one will see.'

As her daughter was pulling down her tights and

109

squatting at the side of the road Annika heard a car approaching. It got louder – the car was going fast. Then its headlights broke through the darkness and swept over her. It was a dark Mercedes with its lights full on. Instinctively she raised a hand to shield her eyes, but the car turned into what was going to be *her* drive, carried on past the house and across the lawn to the next plot.

'What the hell . . . ?' Annika took a couple of steps towards the fence.

'Mummy, I've finished,' her daughter said behind her.

'Get into the car and I'll be right back,' Annika said, heading up the drive.

It was rutted with wheel-marks, all heading towards the house then going off in different directions.

She took a few steps out on to the frozen lawn, following the tracks.

The deepest ones led to where the Merc had just disappeared. She saw the car's brake-lights behind the bushes and heard the engine die. A tall, thickset man in a cap got out and locked the car. Then he seemed to stare straight at her, and she stepped back instinctively into the shadows.

He's just taking a short-cut across the garden while the house is empty. How lazy.

The man carefully scraped the snow from his shoes and went inside one of the other houses, a rambling villa from the turn of the last century, all towers and pinnacles.

She studied the grass again, trying to follow the other tracks in the darkness. They disappeared into other plots, other houses.

'Mummy, when are we going?'

The urgency in Kalle's voice distracted her from the obvious conclusion about the tracks before it had

110

finished developing. 'Now,' she called, and turned back towards the road.

A woman walking a dog was approaching as Annika got closer to the car. 'Hello,' the woman said, with a faint smile.

'Hello,' Annika said, realizing she was freezing.

'Do you know if it's been sold yet?' the woman said, nodding towards the house.

'Yes,' Annika said. 'I've bought it.'

The woman stopped, somewhat surprised, as the dog tugged at its leash. 'How lovely,' she said, removing a glove and holding out her hand. 'Ebba Romanova. I live over there.' She gestured with the hand holding the leash to a house a short distance away. Annika glimpsed another grand villa with a veranda and a summerhouse in the garden. 'And this is Francesco,' she said, patting the dog.

'We won't be moving in until May,' Annika said, as she opened the driver's door.

'Oh,' Ebba Romanova said. 'How wonderful. May is so lovely out here. I do hope you'll be happy.'

Annika took a step towards her and pointed towards the house that the Merc had driven up to. 'Do you happen to know who lives there?'

Ebba Romanova followed the direction of her finger. 'That's Wilhelm Hopkins, chairman of the villa-owners' association.' She pulled a face. 'He's a little eccentric,' she said, with a laugh.

Annika couldn't help joining in.

'Well, I'll see you again soon,' Ebba said, easing her glove back on and setting off along the road once more.

Annika raised a hand to stop her: there was one more thing, something she was wondering. But the woman opened her gate and disappeared before

Annika could ask her question: why is my garden full of tyre-tracks?

The traffic heading into the city was sluggish. She couldn't find anywhere to park near Hantverkargatan and ended up down by the City Hall before she found a more or less legal space. The children were tired and cold, so she decided to take the number three bus the two stops to the flat.

She looked at the sky – there were never any stars visible in the city. Never any real silence, and never any real darkness either. I like this, she thought. It's nice, never being alone.

Her eyes settled on the main entrance to the City Hall, some twenty metres away. The heavy gates were closed. There hadn't been any word yet on how long the banqueting halls would be closed off.

Only two days ago, she thought, with a shudder.

They were home just in time for the daily instalment of the television advent calendar for children.

Annika went into the kitchen and dialled Thomas's mobile, but he didn't answer. She laid the table and pulled out some leftovers from the fridge, pork from yesterday and a bit of sausage Stroganoff from Thursday.

Just as she had put the sausage into the microwave the doorbell rang.

Thomas forgot to take his keys, she thought, as she went to answer it.

But it was Anne Snapphane, her best friend. 'God, I hate moving,' Anne said, slumping on the bench in the hall. 'I can't believe I've got so much stuff. I mean, I'm such an anti-materialist.'

'Hmm,' Annika said, glancing at her friend's Armani jeans and Donna Karan top.

'Don't you "hmm" me,' Anne said. 'I've almost unpacked now. I've got eight cheese-slicers. Isn't that ridiculous? And boxes full of old vinyl records. Which reminds me, I don't suppose you want to see if there's anything you'd like?' She sighed as Annika held up her hands defensively. 'No, you've never been one for music, really, have you?'

'Is Miranda with Mehmet?' Annika asked, heading back into the kitchen where the microwave was bleeping.

Anne didn't answer straight away. She followed Annika and leaned back against the dishwasher with her arms folded. 'Playing happy families with him and his pregnant fiancée, yes,' she said quietly.

Annika poked at the sausage. 'Do you want anything to eat?' she asked.

'No, but I'll have a bloody huge bottle of red,' she said.

When she saw Annika stiffen, she laughed. 'Only joking,' she said. 'I'm not going to do that any more. I did promise.'

'Do you like the flat?' Annika asked instead, filling a jug with water.

'I don't know about "like",' Anne said. 'Obviously it's good being able to live next to Mehmet, it's closer for Miranda, but I'm not sure that art nouveau is really my style.'

Annika emptied the jug and refilled it with fresh, colder water. Her cheeks were glowing and for some reason she felt stupid. Anne had moved into the city so her daughter could be closer to her dad, and stay at the same school with the same friends. When Annika had found herself suddenly awash with money, she had offered Anne an interest-free loan so she could sort her life out. When it turned out that she wouldn't have the money before April, Anne had hit the roof. She had to move *now*, her dream flat was for sale *right now*, she couldn't live *anywhere* else.

Annika had stood as guarantor of a short-term loan until her reward was paid out. But now Anne seemed to think that the whole move had been nothing but a nuisance.

'Have you heard anything from TV Scandinavia?' Annika asked, to change the subject.

Anne snorted. 'My former employers have announced that they won't be paying any redundancy money, and that's all I've heard from them. If I have any objections to this decision I'm welcome to put in a claim against them through the New Jersey courts. So, hey, I wonder what I should do. Maybe I'll get into my private plane and nip over . . .' She sighed loudly. 'I have enough trouble scraping together the money for my monthly season ticket here . . .'

'Kids,' Annika called towards the living room. 'Food!'

'I've been thinking about doing some lecturing,' Anne said, hoisting herself up on to the kitchen worktop. 'I think I'd be able to put together something good on how to sort your life out and all that. There's a market in developing leadership skills, self-realization, all that sort of rubbish. What do you think?'

'Did you say you wanted some food?' Annika asked. 'We're about to eat.'

'Sausage? No, thanks.'

'I can do you a salad, if you like?' Annika offered.

Anne shuffled on the worktop, irritated. 'Just tell me what you think of my idea!'

'Come on, you two, before it gets cold,' Annika

114

called, towards the living room. 'Well, lecturing would be good, but what would you talk about?'

'Myself, of course!' Anne said. 'How I overcame my drink problem, how I got out of the gutter when I lost my job as head of a TV station, how I manage to maintain a close and rewarding relationship with my ex-husband while he's busy building a new family.'

The children came into the kitchen and scrambled on to their chairs.

'Sausage Frog-enough, yum,' Ellen said.

'It's called Stroganoff,' Kalle said. 'And it's just as good as the Nobel banquet, isn't it, Mummy?'

Annika smiled at him and Anne raised her eyebrows. 'Of course, you got caught up in all that, didn't you?' she said. 'Poor you, having to cover that sort of nonsense. Couldn't you have refused?'

'It wasn't too bad,' Annika said. 'Until . . . well, you know.' She fell silent and gestured at the children with her fork.

'So,' Anne said, 'do you think I'd be able to earn a living?'

'Sure,' Annika said. 'It's pretty specialized, but you'd be really good at lecturing. It's great listening to you tell your stories. I think a lot of people would come out stronger after a session with you.'

Anne smiled broadly and jumped down from the worktop. 'That's exactly what I think,' she said. 'Listen, you haven't got a spare five hundred I could borrow, have you? The move and everything cost so much, and I've a feeling I really need to go to the cinema.'

'The cinema?' Annika said.

'Yes. I can't go and have a drink now, so what else am I supposed to do?'

Annika got up. 'Hang on, I'll go and get it.' She pulled

her last five hundred from her purse and gave it to Anne:
Thomas would be furious that she had no cash left just
twelve days before Christmas.

'Oh, you're a darling,' Anne said, and danced out into
the hall.

Annika heard the door close behind her friend as an
unfamiliar, unwelcome chill ran through her.

And Thomas wasn't answering his mobile.

Monday, 14 December

9

The plane landed at Bromma Airport at 05.32. It was a
Raytheon Hawker 800XP, registration number N168BF,
a small business jet that usually carried between six
and eight passengers. On this cold, star-lit morning the
plane would be carrying just one passenger. His name
was Jemal Ali Ahmed, a forty-seven-year-old father of
two, living in Bandhagen to the south of Stockholm.

Anton Abrahamsson, an officer with the Swedish
Security Police, and two of his staff were in place to
oversee the extradition of the suspected terrorist on
behalf of the Swedish authorities. They had bundled the
prisoner into a room inside the airport terminal. He had
been cooperative and was extremely tired.

Abrahamsson had gone out to wait for the plane.
I'm heading off to talk to the Yanks, he had told his
subordinates. This was the first time he had led a group
on this sort of operation. It's not surprising they picked
me, he thought, stamping his feet to keep his circulation
going. He had been involved from the first call-out to the
City Hall through to the raid on the flat. It was entirely
logical, really, that he should see it through to the end.

He felt strangely agitated by the situation, even though
there was no reason why he should. The Swedish police

cooperated with foreign police authorities every day. It was entirely routine. The government had decided on extradition the previous evening, and everything was in order. Admittedly, the decision had been taken very quickly. That sort of thing was usually dealt with during routine cabinet meetings on Thursday mornings, but there was nothing to stop such decisions being taken at any other time. It was the whole set-up that was getting to him.

He liked the dark airport, the ungodly hour, his clear task. The Americans had promised to pick up the terrorist and take him back to Jordan, and no one had protested – the Yanks had been on their way already and it saved tax-payers' money. Besides, it was thought that the prisoner might try to escape, although he hadn't been told how, which helped make this a matter of urgency.

It was possible that his memories of the terrorist's capture were contributing to his general sense of satisfaction. Abrahamsson had been standing in the stairwell when the attack team had broken down the front door and thrown in the grenade, and he himself had been paralysed by the shock, even though he had been a long way from the explosion. The terrorist had evidently managed to find his way out of the room in spite of the grenade, which indicated a degree of professional training as well as extreme motivation. A real tough nut, in other words.

It'll be good to get shot of him, Abrahamsson thought, and for a fleeting second the image of his colicky baby son was in his mind.

The plane taxied in and stopped in front of the weakly lit terminal building. Instinctively Abrahamsson backed against the wall. The jet engines were roaring so loudly that the windows were rattling.

The air was icy and smelt of aviation fuel. He stamped his feet a bit harder. All of a sudden he felt very alone. The airport had just opened, but routine flights wouldn't start for another couple of hours.

Then a man was coming towards him, heavily built and clean-shaven, wearing a thick parka and sturdy boots. 'Howdy,' the man shouted, reaching out his hand.

The engines powered down, making conversation possible.

The man introduced himself as George and explained that he worked in the service of the United States. His eyes were clear and friendly. 'We really appreciate that we can collaborate on this and solve this issue in such an efficient way,' the man said, in his American drawl.

Abrahamsson smiled broadly and said something similar.

'This isn't like transporting any sort of freight, of course,' the American said. 'We've got a few guys from the CIA with us to keep an eye on the prisoner during the flight. We don't want to risk anything while we're in the air.'

Abrahamsson blinked against the cold a few times and nodded. It was like that, then. Well, in the air the captain and international aviation regulations were in charge, so whatever happened inside the plane was none of his business.

'Our guys will have hoods on, for their own security, naturally.'

Abrahamsson nodded again.

'And of course we need to conduct our own security check of the prisoner, as I hope you'll appreciate.'

Abrahamsson was starting to find the conversation troubling, in spite of the American's reassuring manner.

'Well,' he said, 'we've already had our doctors examine the man, and I can assure you that—'

'It's like this,' the American said calmly. 'We'd really appreciate the opportunity to build our own picture, okay?'

Abrahamsson opened, then closed his mouth. Eventually he said, 'I see. In that case, I will have to be present throughout the examination.'

'No,' the American said amiably. 'As soon as the plane landed we took over responsibility. I thought that was clear.'

Now he felt obliged to protest. 'I represent the Swedish police,' he said. 'We are on Swedish territory now, and Swedish police are responsible for the exercise of all official authority here.'

The American looked ever so slightly shocked. 'But of course,' he said, 'of course. Naturally, everything will be conducted legally and correctly, because I live in the finest democracy in the world.' He took a step forward and nudged Abrahamsson's shoulder. 'This is going to be just fine,' he said. 'Shall we go?'

Abrahamsson lumbered after the American towards the terminal, unable to shake off his sense of unease.

They walked into the terminal through one of the gates and went quickly to the room that had been placed at the disposal of the Security Police. Inside they were holding Jemal Ali Ahmed prisoner, hands and feet bound. He had been there most of the night and his face was completely grey. Abrahamsson's two colleagues were dozing on their seats just inside the door.

'Okay,' George said. 'Check him out.'

Behind Abrahamsson a row of hooded men stepped inside the room. They were wearing overalls, had masks over their faces and were carrying various types of equipment.

Abrahamsson opened his mouth to protest, but George propelled him gently to one side. 'This will only take a minute,' the American said, with a smile.

Abrahamsson's colleagues were jostled into the corner with their boss. Speechless, they watched as two masked men stepped up and pulled the prisoner to his feet. Jemal Ali Ahmed, who hadn't seen them coming, threw himself backwards against the wall, screaming.

'On the floor,' George ordered.

'Aren't you going to do anything?' one of his officers said to Abrahamsson.

'Like what, exactly?' he replied.

The prisoner was pushed to the floor, and his terrified eyes met Abrahamsson's. 'Help me!' the man cried in Swedish. 'Please, help me!'

Abrahamsson stared at him, unable to move. The CIA agents pulled off the prisoner's shoes as he kicked and screamed. Three agents held him down as he squirmed. They cut his clothes off him, socks and trousers, underwear, jacket and shirt.

'Check the cavities,' George said, and the men pulled the prisoner upright again. His eyes were bloodshot, saliva running down his chin. The agents pulled off the last remnants of his clothes until he was completely naked in the cold room, his hands and feet still bound. He sobbed and snorted as they forced his mouth open, his whole skinny body shaking. They poked about in his mouth, shone lights, stuck things into his ears and examined his genitals.

When a man drove a finger inside his anus he roared.

Abrahamsson turned to his colleagues. 'I think it's time to go home and make our report,' he said.

The Swedish Security Police left the room together.

The echo of the prisoner's screams was cut off as soon they closed the door.

Annika walked through the gates of the nursery with her children, carrying bags of tinsel for the annual St Lucia festivities, elf outfits, and saffron Lucia buns. The celebrations weren't due to start until the afternoon, a day late, but what did such details matter? The children had been practising for weeks and now there was going to be some serious singing.

It was hot and crowded in the main nursery room. Ellen slowly and carefully pulled out Poppy and Ludde, her favourite dolls, as well as her electric crown of candles, and put them on her shelf. Annika glanced at her watch. An inflexible timetable meant that she'd have to leave work at a quarter to four at the latest if she was going to catch the Lucia procession. Thomas had already announced that he wouldn't be able to make it. He had yet another meeting with Per Cramne from the department that afternoon, and wasn't to be disturbed.

Finally Ellen had finished sorting her things and could be handed over to the nursery staff, who were just laying out breakfast.

'She's already eaten,' Annika said, then took Kalle to the pre-school next door.

As soon as he got inside the building, he collapsed into a roaring heap of arms and legs with the other boys, as usual. He had spent the morning complaining noisily about having to be an elf, demanding instead to be a vampire. Annika had explained that that wouldn't really work in a Lucia procession, and after a lot of whimpering he had finally agreed.

Sunday had been calm and peaceful. Thomas, who

124

had got home from Vaxholm in the early hours, had been hung-over and spent most of the day sitting at his computer. Annika had been getting ready for Christmas with the children, but had managed to do the washing and a bit of research into Professor Lars-Henry Svensson and his connection to the Karolinska Institute. They'd ordered in pizza for dinner.

Now she left the children and fled.

When the nursery door closed behind her she always felt a huge sense of relief. Hours of unbroken concentration lay ahead and she could take possession of her brain until a quarter to four. The sun was coming up; it looked like it was going to be a cold, clear day.

She pulled her mobile out of her bag and called Spike's direct line at the news desk. He answered with his usual grunt.

'In half an hour there's a press conference in the Wallenberg Room of the Nobel Forum out at the Karolinska Institute,' Annika said. 'Do you think we ought to cover it?'

Spike groaned. 'We don't really care, do we?'

'They'll probably make some sort of announcement,' Annika said. 'I thought Nobel and the Karolinska Institute were fairly interesting at the moment, but what do I know?'

Spike rustled some paper. '"Fairly interesting" won't do today,' he said. 'Go and make sure we aren't missing anything, but don't think you're going to get a novel out of it.' He hung up without waiting for a reply.

Annika caught the number one bus on Fleminggatan from the corner of Scheelegatan, took it as far as Sankt Eriksgatan and changed to the number three, which went all the way to the Karolinska Hospital, next to the Institute.

The entrance to Nobels Väg was thick with cars and people.

God, so many people, Annika thought. Masses of dark-grey suits, today covered with dark overcoats, were wandering about and talking into their collars. Annika zigzagged her way to number one Nobels Väg, the same building she had visited on Friday.

'Accreditation, please.'

A dark-grey figure was standing in front of her, with a wire in his ear, holding out his hand.

'Er . . .' Annika said. She hadn't known that accreditation was necessary.

'She's with me,' she heard a voice say behind her, and spun round.

Bosse was standing there with his press-card and his filled-in documentation. He had a woolly hat pulled down over his forehead and a knitted scarf wound round his neck. His eyes were dazzlingly blue. Annika felt a shiver in her stomach and gave him an awkward smile.

And she's dancing with me, we're dancing in the Golden Hall beneath the gaze of the Queen of the Mälaren. She's light in my arms and I want to be here for ever . . .

'Getting a bit sloppy with the groundwork?' Bosse whispered, blond hair sticking out round his ears.

Annika had to laugh even though there was nothing amusing in the situation.

'Shall we go in?' Bosse said, offering her his arm.

They walked down a long, pillared corridor, the windows stretching to the floor, letting in the morning glow. A thin trickle of academics and journalists was heading in the same direction.

On the opposite wall dark doors concealed unknown rooms.

'You haven't written anything about the banquet,' Bosse said, glancing at her.

'I have my reasons,' she said.

He stopped in front of her and looked at her hard. 'Is it true that you helped them come up with the Photofit?'

She was aware that her eyes were wide, and she paused for breath.

'I won't write anything about it,' he said. 'I'm just worried about you. Have you got anyone you can talk to?'

She nodded.

He took a step to the side and they walked on. 'You can always talk to me,' he said. 'I never reveal my sources.'

They reached another security check, and had to pass through a scanner before being waved through to the auditorium.

The Wallenberg Room was at the far end of the ground floor. They were funnelled through a disproportionately small doorway, and found themselves in a red hall containing twenty or so curved rows of seats, with a small stage at the front. The room had swallowed a couple of hundred people; it wasn't going to be anywhere near full.

Annika and Bosse sat slightly behind most of the others. Their legs were rather too close together, but neither of them moved. Annika felt the contact as a crackling warmth running through her body. 'Have you heard anything about the investigation?' she whispered, leaning even closer to him.

'The boat they escaped in was stolen in Nacka in August,' he whispered back, his hand sliding along her arm.

She was unnerved by his touch. Bloody hell! She'd jump into bed with him right this minute if she could.

She moved her leg and focused on the people in the room, trying to work out who the other journalists were. She recognized the science editor of the prestigious morning paper, and presumed that the others had similar interests. Up on the stage a group who definitely weren't journalists was gathering. There's something impenetrable about reporters at a press conference: they never whisper and chat, as these people were doing, never reveal any emotion.

'Who are that lot?' Bosse muttered, pointing without touching her, and at that moment Annika recognized Birgitta Larsén's henna-red hair in the crowd.

'Scientists,' she whispered back, 'maybe members of the Nobel Assembly or the committee. The woman in the striped jacket is a professor here, Birgitta Larsén. I've met her before.'

Some of the scientists were conferring, heads close together. Annika noted that the others moved away from them and kept their distance. She wondered what they were saying.

The rows of seats were gradually filling, with a mix of media people, staff and students. The room was approximately half full when the doors were closed and the press conference could begin.

On the stage stood a large portrait of a smiling Caroline von Behring, with a floral wreath next to it. Annika looked into the dead woman's eyes, recognizing her gaze all too well from her research. Beside the portrait there was a conference table with chairs, microphones, nameplates and three men seated behind it.

'Yes, well,' the first said, tapping his microphone gently, 'if we could all settle down, then we'll begin.' He was a thickset man, dressed in a black suit and bright-red tie. The sign in front of him said he was the vice chair of the Nobel Committee, Professor Sören Hammarsten. His hands were small and unusually white, as if he were suffering from the pigmentation disorder that Michael Jackson was supposed to have had.

'I would like to welcome you all to this press conference. We have something extremely exciting to announce,' Hammarsten said. 'But first I would like to say a few words in memory of our recently deceased chairperson.' He turned towards the portrait. The man beside him, whose sign said he was Ernst Ericsson, head of MEM, pulled out a handkerchief and blew his nose quietly.

MEM, Annika thought. That's the Department of Medical Epidemiology and Molecular Biology. The department where Caroline von Behring worked.

'Dear Caroline,' Hammarsten said, his voice filled with emotion. 'You will always be with us in our hearts, in our research and in our history. You guided the institute towards greater recognition, and you worked magnificently as the custodian of Alfred Nobel's last will and testament.'

'Sacrilege!' a man in the front row shouted, and the whole room tried to see who it was.

Hammarsten pretended not to have heard him. 'No matter how difficult it might feel today,' he said, 'it is our duty to look ahead. That is what Caroline would have wanted. For that reason we must all continue working for the future, for Caroline's sake, and in the spirit of Alfred Nobel.'

'You're betraying Nobel's memory!' the man in the front row shouted. 'You're playing God and exploiting Nobel's testament to justify your own egotistical ambitions.'

129

Hammarsten leaned towards the microphone, his bald patch glinting under a spotlight. 'Lars-Henry,' he said, 'if you can't keep your objections to yourself, I shall have to ask you to leave.'

The man responded by standing up. He shook his fist towards the podium, his voice rising to a falsetto pitch. 'Nemesis!' he shouted. 'You ought to watch out! Nemesis has already struck, and she will strike again!'

'And who do we have here?' Bosse asked.

'I think his name is Lars-Henry Svensson,' Annika told him. 'He's a professor and a member of the Nobel Assembly. He wrote a rather confused opinion piece for us on Saturday.'

'Divine retribution!' Svensson cried. 'Nemesis! You have truly challenged her!'

'Security,' Hammarsten said, into the microphone. 'Can we have Security to the Wallenberg Room.'

The narrow door flew open and a group of dark suits streamed in.

The third man along the table on the stage leaned back in his chair, unable to conceal an amused smile. He was, apparently, Bernhard Thorell, MD of Medi-Tec Group Ltd, and he was considerably younger than the other men. He might have been in his forties, and looked completely different: suntanned, in good shape, wearing a dark Italian suit.

'Nobel's testament is inviolable!' Svensson bellowed. 'Yet we still break it, over and over again. And Nemesis, his final wish, we keep that well hidden . . .'

Everyone in the room watched as the suits surrounded the professor and dragged him out of the room. After the door had closed the silence was as dense as cotton-wool.

'I must apologize,' a perspiring Hammarsten finally

said, knotting his small white hands on the desk in front of him. 'Caroline's death has affected all of us in different ways.'

'What on earth did he mean?' Annika whispered, staring at the door through which the man had vanished.

'I haven't the foggiest,' Bosse whispered back.

'It is with great pleasure that I can present one of the global pharmaceutical industry's most influential figures: Dr Bernhard Thorell, managing director of the pharmaceutical company Medi-Tec, all the way from its headquarters in Los Angeles, California,' Hammarsten said.

The man next to him, Ernst Ericsson, leaned back and folded his arms over his chest. Thorell nodded benevolently at the gathering, and Hammarsten was almost purring.

'Today we are delighted to be able to announce that Medi-Tec has just entered into a research partnership with the Karolinska Institute,' Hammarsten said. 'This is an extremely significant and rewarding programme that will stretch across several years. Bernhard?'

The professor leaned back and indicated that it was the younger man's turn to speak.

'I would like to start by pointing out,' Thorell said, in a deep, melodic voice, 'that I have been deeply affected by Caroline's death.' The air of amusement had left him now. 'Caroline was my first adviser in the academic world, and I couldn't have wished for a better start to my working life. I will always be deeply grateful to the Karolinska Institute for providing the basis of my scientific career.'

Hammarsten appeared very moved by this, but Ericsson looked so uncomfortable that his skin seemed to crawl.

'What are they up to?' Bosse whispered.

'My own background and personal recommendation have obviously contributed to the fact that Medi-Tec has chosen the institute for this particular research project, but it was in no way the decisive factor,' Thorell said, and paused.

A dense silence fell on the hall. Thorell whispered something to Hammarsten, and all of the journalists seemed to lean closer to the podium.

'One hundred million dollars,' Thorell went on, in a neutral tone. 'Medi-Tec has decided to put one hundred million dollars at the disposal of the Karolinska Institute. One hundred million dollars to be used for future research into the immune system, its interleukins, signal pathways and other structures . . .'

Feverish activity broke out among the students around them, as well as among the two groups of researchers in the front rows. The murmuring grew to an almost unbearable level, and people were standing up from their seats. Only the reporters failed to show any response.

'Three quarters of a billion kronor,' Annika whispered to Bosse. 'Is that a lot or a little in this sort of context?'

'I'm guessing it's quite a lot,' Bosse said quietly.

Hammarsten appealed for silence, then said, 'As head of MEM, it will fall largely to Ernst Ericsson to administer this project over the next five years,' he said. 'Ernst?'

Ericsson was a thin, grey-clad man, his eyes puffed and red. His suit hung limply from his thin frame. He leaned towards the microphone. 'It is part of our articles of association,' he said, 'to accept any project-funding we are offered.'

He fell silent and looked round the room, shuffled in his seat and moved even closer to the microphone. Annika could see his chin trembling.

'I would like to take this opportunity,' he said, 'to protest against the commercialization and profit-motive that have come to characterize the activities of the Karolinska Institute—'

'Ernst!' Hammarsten said sternly. 'This is neither the time nor the place—'

'Be quiet!' the grey man interrupted, his voice surprisingly forceful. 'You know perfectly well that we can't pretend this debate doesn't exist. Not only does it throw into doubt the independence of our research, but also opens us up to charges of bias where the Nobel Prize is concerned.'

Two men at the front stood up again and started shouting at him.

'Security!' Hammarsten called into the microphone once more. 'Security to the Wallenberg Room!'

Ericsson, too, stood up now, and the two groups of scientists at the front got to their feet. Everyone was talking and shouting and gesticulating wildly.

'What a bloody circus,' Bosse said. 'Have you ever seen anything like it?'

The suits poured into the room for the second time, but this time they never reached the platform. Birgitta Larsén got up, in her striped jacket, and spoke to the suit in charge, pointing and explaining. They turned and left.

'They're twitchy as greyhounds,' Annika said. 'Pretty much anything's making them jumpy.'

'It's Nemesis,' Bosse said. 'Nemesis is after them.'

'They ought to be afraid,' Annika said. 'One of them's already dead.'

10

The Kitten stuffed the rag into her mouth and bit down so hard her jaw almost locked. The pain of breaking her leg on that bastard path up at the North Pole was nothing compared to this. The break had started to heal in completely the wrong way, and the alcoholic doctor her wingman had dug up had been forced to break it again.

'Now I'm going to stretch the leg and put it in the right position before I plaster it,' he said, sounding apologetic. 'I'm so sorry I haven't got any painkillers.'

She was lying on the table in his filthy kitchen on the outskirts of Jurmala, forty-seven kilometres from Riga airport. The whole house was disgusting. She had never been able to understand why these bastard Eastern Europeans were too stupid to look after their homes. And it was draughty too, so cold. Great frosted patterns had spread across the inside of the kitchen window.

'Here we go,' the doctor said, and the Kitten roared into the rag. *Holy fucking shit!*

Sweat was pouring down her neck, and she was breathing so hard that her nostrils stuck together inside.

Her wingman wiped her forehead with a dirty cloth and she twisted her face away. Bloody amateur, she thought, hanging around waiting for an hour and a half at Torö when I'd expressly told him to get going after thirty minutes. She couldn't work with amateurs. It was out of the fucking question.

'I'm going to go and mix the plaster,' the doctor said, reaching for the same cloth that her wingman had used to wipe her face. Fucking Communist amateurs.

'The worst is over now,' her wingman said sympathetically, taking her hand, but she pulled it away and spat out the rag.

Yes. For me, she thought.

'The car's waiting outside,' he said. 'Automatic gearbox, just as you said. I used the Latvian credit card.'

'Idiot,' the Kitten snarled. 'I told you to pay in cash.'

'I know,' he said, 'but then I'd have to hand the car back here in Jurmala, and paying with a credit card means we can leave it at the airport.'

'Idiotic fucking Communist rules,' the Kitten said. 'Where are the keys?'

'Here,' he said, patting the right pocket of his trousers. 'But you can't leave tonight, not until the plaster has set. There's a pair of crutches by the door.'

The quack came back in with a rusty bucket. 'I'll try to be careful,' he said, and set to work plastering her swollen, bruised leg.

Jesus *fucking* Christ, he was slow! He fiddled and wrapped and fussed, and every time he touched her leg she groaned.

She shut her eyes – everything around her was still swaying. The crossing in the little boat had been terrible. They had had snow and rain and wind, one after another. The waves had splashed over the prow until the Kitten had thought they were going to sink, but she hadn't had the energy to feel scared. She had

135

been drifting in and out of consciousness with the pain in her leg.

She couldn't remember how she had made her way out to Torö on the motorbike, the only thing in the whole sorry affair she was happy about.

She had worked as she always did. She had allocated numbered posts to the locations where the events had taken place and rehearsed until they were second nature, even when she was semi-conscious.

'There,' the doctor said, gathering his tools together. 'Now it just needs to set.'

Her wingman was good with boats, which was why she had picked him. That was probably why they had made it across the Baltic without drowning, she had to admit, but he was useless at finding decent doctors prepared to do a bit of private work. This one would start blabbing the moment he got out of the door.

'How long before it sets?' she asked, unhappy that her voice sounded so weak.

'It depends,' the doctor said, wiping his hands on the towel. 'Heat and humidity will affect it, but you can rest here until it's firm.'

'Can you help me up?' she said to her wingman, who rushed over at once and supported her as she got into a sitting position. 'Can I have my bag, please?' She held out her right arm (her beautiful strong right arm), caught her Chanel bag by the shoulder-strap and felt the weight of the weapon swing in her hand.

'And some water, please?' she said. The two men turned towards the sink.

She slid out the gun, still with its silencer on, and shot the doctor in the spine. He slumped forward with his head in the sink.

Her wingman swung towards her with a look of

136

surprise and she shot him between the eyes. 'Fucking amateur,' she said.

It was a stroke of luck that she'd changed her mind about throwing the gun into the sea. She put it back into the bag.

She felt the plaster. It was completely soft. How long would she have to sit here with these two corpses?

'Oh what the hell?' She heaved herself to her feet, hopped over to her wingman, dug about in his trouser pocket and pulled out the car keys with his mobile phone. She checked his other pockets. He had just a wallet containing his passport and credit cards in his jacket. False, of course, but never mind.

She put the wallet and phone in her Chanel bag and hopped out to the front door. It hurt like hell, and the plaster was already deformed. She grabbed the crutches, opened the door and went out.

The bag vibrated. She was confused. What was going on?

Halfway out of the door she stopped, balancing unsteadily on her good leg as she took out the phone and looked at the display. *You have 1 new message.*

Before she even pressed *read* she knew what it meant. Complications.

Anders Schyman was seriously worried. Whenever a big news story broke, the strengths and weaknesses of every form of media stood out all the more clearly. He took a stroll round his desk, chewing a biro.

As far as the Nobel killings were concerned, the *Evening Post* had handled the story relatively well from a journalistic point of view, even if they could have done with Annika Bengtzon's eye-witness account of events in the Golden Hall. But technically they had been left behind by pretty much all other media. Of course, the *Evening Post* had a website and even some online video-footage, and they occasionally put audio files on the net, but no one was listening to them. No one cared. Schyman wasn't naïve, but he had underestimated the Internet's significance, as the Nobel killings had made clear. An opinion poll had revealed that 56 per cent of Swedes had got their news about them online.

He sorted the papers on his desk, then walked nervously to the window to look at the guard on the embassy gate. As usual, one soldier was standing there. Maybe it was always the same one. At any rate, this guy was confusingly similar to all the others, with the same fur hat and bored expression, squinting in the sunlight as he inspected the limousine that was slowly pulling up at the main entrance of the *Evening Post* building.

'He's arrived downstairs,' his secretary announced over the intercom.

I know, the editor-in-chief thought. I can see him.

The chairman of the board, Herman Wennergren, was climbing carefully out of the car, concerned about his well-polished shoes.

He'd better go for my proposal, Schyman thought, or I'm going to have to learn to play golf.

Some minutes later the chairman looked extremely focused as he stepped into the office. 'What a wretched business,' he said. 'The Nobel banquet is one of the few decent parties we have in this country. Have you found the killer yet?'

'We're working on it,' Schyman said, and had to stop himself running over to take the man's coat. Instead he picked up his bundle of papers and invited the chairman to sit down at the conference table.

'I don't understand what's so important,' Wennergren

said, putting his leather briefcase and silk scarf on the sofa. 'Why couldn't it wait until the next board meeting?'

'I've sketched out a proposal for how our news-gathering operation should be developed in light of the challenges and opportunities of the digital age,' Schyman said, sitting down.

He left a pause as Wennergren sat opposite him.

'This is a far-reaching proposal covering everything from technology and personnel to attitudes and infra-structure,' Schyman went on.

Wennergren said nothing, but looked sceptical as Schyman put the first sheet of paper in front of him.

'Let's be honest,' he said. His hands were clammy. 'Since we brought forward publication from the afternoon to the morning, the paper's deadline is several hours earlier. The television news has far more broadcasts, which means that the same reporters have to come up with more items in less time. And the Internet means that information can be published moment by moment. That hasn't resulted in an expansion of choice, but the exact opposite. Less time for reflection means that everyone coalesces around a consensus. Because all the media are covering the same things, in the end it's only their different approaches that set them apart from each other.'

'Hmm,' Wennergren said, glancing at his watch.

Schyman forced himself to slow down: he was sounding too frenetic. 'The *serious* media,' he went on, 'have always focused on technology, law, the economy and politics, which have traditionally been seen as typically male subject areas. The positions they adopt have always been part of the public arena, and are regarded as respectable and, well, serious. This is where

139

we find the finer end of the media: the morning papers, Swedish Television news, and national radio news.'

He leaned back and tried to relax his shoulders.

'*Tabloid* journalism, which of course we represent, is found principally in the evening papers in Sweden. In them we are pretty much content to focus on personal, private matters, which are generally regarded as female subject areas. A single individual is positioned at the centre of a story, and the news is reflected through their feelings and experiences.'

'What does this have to do with anything?' the chairman of the board asked, now looking confused.

'With any crime or catastrophe,' Schyman said, 'it's vital for people to be able to empathize with those involved. They have to feel the despair of relatives, confront the destructive motivations of those responsible. In the foreign media it has largely been up to television to focus on "personal" journalism of this sort, but here in Sweden the news broadcasters have chosen a "more respectable" direction. And this is where our new ventures come in.'

'I don't quite follow you,' Wennergren said, his eyelids fluttering anxiously. 'Do you mean that we have to become more female?'

Schyman lowered his voice. 'This is the only untapped media space in Sweden today,' he said, underlining his words by tapping his pen on his printouts. 'Tabloid news television, with a personal angle.'

'Television?' Wennergren echoed.

'Precisely,' Schyman said. 'Television is a useless medium for conveying facts, but wonderful for emotion, drama, people, closeness, everything the evening papers have long had a monopoly on. The day that someone sets about making tabloid television for a broad audience, they'll wipe the floor with their competitors.'

Wennergren wore an expression of amazement. 'But our principal shareholders, the family, have loads of television channels. Why hasn't anyone done this already?' he asked.

'Up to now there have been technological limitations and broadcast licences to worry about,' the editor-in-chief said. 'It's always been too expensive, and outside the regulations. But now any resistance is mainly a question of prejudice and mere tradition – they'd never touch tabloid news.'

Here he handed over the second sheet of paper. 'Today there's nothing to stop it happening,' he said. 'It's all about getting in there first and seizing the initiative. Then we can deal with the exact shape and priorities.'

'This all sounds extremely visionary,' Wennergren said, 'but not very realistic. Where exactly would there be the physical space for something like this?'

Schyman felt the tension in his shoulders ease and couldn't help smiling. 'That's where infrastructure and technology come in,' he said.

'A move is out of the question,' Wennergren said. 'We can't afford it.'

Schyman's smile grew even broader. 'I've done a lot of thinking about that,' he said, 'and I've got a suggestion.'

Spike was eating a banana when Annika arrived in the newsroom. 'Was it worth covering?' he wondered, as she passed the news desk.

'You actually eat something apart from pizza!' Annika said, staring at the piece of fruit.

The head of news beamed. 'Did the King show up? Anyone from the competition?'

She composed her features and managed to sound

nonchalant. 'Bosse was there,' she said, 'but the King couldn't make it. It was pretty chaotic. The Karolinska Institute has got hold of a hundred million dollars for research, but they seemed to disagree about everything else. And they're all upset that their Nobel chairperson is dead.'

'Good,' Spike said. 'Let it go. We've got so many four-colour adverts that I doubt we'd have room for the King even if he died.'

Annika went into her office and closed the door, tossed her outdoor clothes in a heap and switched on her computer. As the programs loaded, she hunted about for anything edible in her desk drawers, to no avail.

What had got into her? She was flirting with a man from their main competitor, the least suitable person she could have picked, quite apart from the fact that she was married with two kids and on the point of buying a house in Djursholm. Thoughts aren't unfaithful, she thought. I can feel whatever I like as long as I don't do anything about it. I'm not going to emulate Thomas.

And once again she saw the woman before her, Sophia Grenborg, blonde and smartly dressed, a younger version of his ice-cold ex-wife Eleonor.

Without thinking, she Googled Sophia Grenborg and came up with some interesting results. *New Challenges* was the title of one section of the County Council's website; it covered internal matters. Annika read the final item carefully:

The new administrator in the traffic safety department is to be former project leader Sophia Grenborg. Most recently Sophia worked as co-ordinator of the congress group.

'This feels like an exciting challenge,' Sophia

142

says. 'I've always been keen to experience new things, and I'm very grateful for the confidence management have shown in me.'

She read the piece twice. Was the woman being ironic or did she always rely on cliché? A small photograph showed her false smile. Burn in hell, bitch, she thought.

She clicked away from the picture and called up information about how much money the academic world had at its disposal.

I get too angry, Annika thought. I ought to do something about that. I don't want her to go on poisoning my life. She's gone, and she isn't going to bother us again.

It turned out that Swedish universities and colleges had received in total 1.6 billion kronor for what was called commissioned research last year. Spread over five years, Medi-Tec's grant came to something like a hundred and fifty million a year, which was a sizeable amount but not sensational. From the archives it was apparent that the Karolinska Institute had received a hundred and fifty million in donations from private individuals.

The fact that a single company was granting them money wasn't particularly odd either: 43 per cent of all their research grants came from both Swedish and foreign businesses, she read. It isn't something for the *Evening Post*, she concluded.

'Have you eaten?' Berit said, over the intercom, and Annika was so relieved to hear her voice that she leaped up from her desk.

They settled down in the staffroom with cheese sandwiches and coffee.

'There's something not right about Neue Jihad,' Berit

143

said, pouring milk into her plastic cup. 'The day before yesterday a reliable source told me that the German security police had arrested three young men as early as Friday, but I can't get official confirmation of that anywhere. I've just spoken to the sister of one of the boys, and she's adamant that the police broke in and dragged her brother away at four o'clock on Friday afternoon.'

Annika stirred her coffee. 'What's so odd about that?' she asked.

'No one's prepared to admit there were actually any arrests,' Berit said. 'The police say they don't know anything about it. The men haven't been charged, or remanded in custody, in either Stockholm or Berlin. They've just disappeared into thin air.'

'They must be somewhere,' Annika said, taking a bite of her sandwich. 'And what's the connection to Band-hagen that the police were on about?'

Berit leaned forward. 'Ah,' she said. 'You've put your finger on something really nasty there. The father has disappeared, just like the lads in Berlin. The mother and girls have been released, but there's been no sign of the father since he was dragged out of the flat.'

'Have you spoken to the mother?'

Berit shook her head, chewing. She swallowed, then said, 'They've gone somewhere else. I got hold of the youngest girl's teacher, who turned out to be very talkative. The girl is in year nine, and is captain of the basketball team. Her elder sister is in the second or third year of a sixth-form science course at some college in the city. She's practically a genius.'

'Where are they from?' Annika asked.

'Jordan, the teacher thinks, or maybe Syria. They arrived here when the older girl was small, and the basketball captain was born here. The mother's got permanent residency, but for some reason the father hasn't. They've lived in the same two-room apartment out in Bandhagen for thirteen years. The parents run a key-cutting and shoe-repair business in an underground station.'

'They sound pretty dangerous,' Annika said.

'Don't they just?' Berit said. 'I've put a note through their letterbox and left a message on their answer-machines, at home and at the shop, so we'll see if they get in touch.'

They sat in silence for a while, munching their sand-wiches. Annika thought the silence was a bit oppressive, but wasn't sure if she was imagining it. Was Berit still upset that she was sitting on information no one else had?

'I haven't heard a thing from the murder investiga-tion,' she said. 'Have you got any idea of how they're getting on? Do they know how the girl got into the ban-quet?'

'Well, she wasn't on the guest-list, that much is certain. They don't think she spent long in either the Blue Hall or the Golden Hall before the killings. So she must have got into the building after half past ten that evening, but they don't know how.'

Annika finished off her coffee. 'Do they know how she got out?'

'A service lift and then a goods entrance. The lift isn't supposed to work without a card and a code, but on a stressful evening, like the Nobel banquet, several of the lifts are left open or the event would grind to a halt. I'm writing a piece about that for tomorrow.'

'Is there a scapegoat yet?'

'Not yet,' Berit said. 'They're all shielding each other so far.'

Annika got up, fetched the coffee-pot and refilled their cups. 'I heard that the getaway boat was stolen in Nacka in August,' she said. 'Do you know any more about that?'

Berit nodded thoughtfully. 'There's one thing I don't get,' she said. 'They found the boat in Gröndal, and they think the killer headed south by car.'

'And?' Annika said.

'There's no junction on to the southbound carriageway from Gröndal. You have to go all the way down to the Nyboda junction to get on to the motorway if you're heading south, and that's a really messy route. It would take at least five minutes longer.'

Annika emptied her second cup of coffee. 'If the alternative was heading north, surely the Nyboda junction makes more sense?' she said.

Berit pushed the remains of her sandwich away. 'But if she was heading south by car, why not leave the boat at Stora Essingen instead? It would have been a shorter trip by boat, and she could have got straight on to the motorway. I don't get it. Anyway, what have you been doing today?'

'I was out at Karolinska,' Annika replied. 'I didn't get anything. Which reminds me, have you ever heard of a Bernhard Thorell?' She wondered if she should say anything about Bosse, but decided to keep quiet.

Berit gave the sandwich another chance, took a bite, chewed and swallowed with some effort. 'God, this wasn't made in the past couple of days,' she said. 'Thorell? Related to Simon Thorell?'

Annika shrugged and gave up on her own sandwich.

'Simon Thorell,' Berit said. 'You don't recognize the name? He was a venture capitalist, big in the seventies, pretty much the first to make a killing from it. He and his wife died in a car-crash in the Alps, if I remember rightly. A tragic story.'

'This guy's the head of a pharmaceutical company in the States,' Annika said.

Berit wiped her fingers on a napkin. 'Are you writing anything for tomorrow?' she said, getting up.

'Spike wasn't interested,' Annika said, following her out.

'Have you seen the amount of space we've got?' Berit said. 'Christmas sales in the shops are going to hit a new record, if the number of adverts in the *Evening Post* is anything to go by.'

'One more thing,' Annika said. 'Do you know what Nemesis is?'

Berit tossed her cup, sandwich and napkin into the bin. 'Nemesis,' she said. 'The Greek god of revenge and retribution. Why do you ask?'

'No reason,' Annika said.

Subject: The Price of Love
To: Andrietta Ahlsell

Bertha Kinsky arrives in Paris in early May 1876 to work as Alfred's secretary. She's thirty-two years old when they meet, an Austrian countess. She's beautiful, unmarried, extremely intelligent – and very poor.

Alfred meets her off the morning train and they take his cab to breakfast at the Grand Hotel. Bertha, who went on to become an internationally famous author, describes the journey: *The rays of sunlight played with the shimmering fountains of the Rond Point, and made the lanterns and harnesses of the countless vehicles sparkle.*

147

They talk about the world and about people, current affairs and philosophical problems. Alfred is even able to talk about his experiments and she understands. They talk about art and life, and they talk about peace.

Alfred is concerned about what his inventions might do. He isn't a violent man, quite the contrary! He believes that the art of war is in its very early stages, that an arms race is imminent. His conclusions are many decades ahead of their time: when destructive weaponry has finally reached its apex, fear will *force* people to live in peace with one another.

They have one week together. One week at the Grand Hotel in Paris. Alfred has found something he will never find again. He realizes almost at once that this is unique: here she is! And he asks her openly: is her heart free?

She replies honestly: there is a man, a young nobleman, whom she is not permitted to marry. She is too poor and too old, but her heart is his.

So Alfred leaves the Grand Hotel in Paris and when he returns she is gone. She has sold her last diamond necklace to pay her hotel bill.

She has fled to Russia with the young man. She marries Arthur von Suttner on 12 June 1876 and spends nine years in exile, living in the Caucasus mountains in a place called Mingrelia. She becomes an author and peace activist, but she never forgets. Bertha stays in touch with Alfred Nobel for the rest of his life, but mainly by letter. They meet on a few occasions after the summer of 1876 – the terrible summer of 1876.

Alfred, Alfred, how he suffers in his apartment

in Paris! How he grieves in his grand house on the Avenue Malakoff, painfully aware of the emptiness in his life.

During the summer of 1876, when he is stumbling blind, worse than ever before, he reaches out his hand and there stands a young woman in a florist's in Baden bei Wien. Her name is Sofie Hess, she is young (only twenty years old), she is an orphan and *alone* (just like him). She is pretty and she reminds him, at least superficially, of Bertha.

Perhaps she could become like *her*. Perhaps Alfred could turn Sofie into a *dame du monde*. Perhaps she could become a countess with the ability to discuss the great issues of life.

How Alfred tries! He educates, informs, equips her. Perhaps he loves her, because he gives Sofie a villa in Ischl and a large apartment in Paris (not far from his own). Or perhaps he merely possesses, buying something that he cannot have.

But Sofie isn't so young. She isn't twenty: she's almost thirty. She isn't an orphan, her father Heinrich is alive. She is merely alone, alone in her large apartment in Paris on the Avenue d'Eylau, alone and bored. Alfred is so *dull*. He does nothing but make new demands. He travels around his factories and writes long letters, about projects and experiments and legal problems and dynamite companies, and Sofie yawns. She replies in her childish handwriting, telling him gossip and asking for more money.

Dearest Alfred, when do you realize that you have been deceived?

When do you find out that father Heinrich is alive? When Sofie returns to Vienna and calls herself Frau Nobel? When she admits that she is expecting another man's child?

Her coquettish begging echoes through the years:

My dearest Alfred!
I haven't heard from you for a long time. I am also extremely concerned because I myself am very poorly and have no peace . . . I have no money to live on and must today pawn my last brooch. I have never experienced anything so bad before. And the poor child – what do the fates have in store for it?
Fondest wishes and kisses from your
Sofie

What must the industrial magnate have thought when he read this text in its big, round hand? What strings is she plucking, the girl who never became a lady? What is it in her ingratiating tone that persuades him to send money, again and again and again?

Alfred, why do you allow yourself to be exploited?

My dearest Alfred!
I can find no apartment for they are all too dear . . . I am wretched. It is depressing to spend the winter living in a hotel room with a small child, with nothing but terrible food . . . Will you give me permission to use your surname? Can you send some money? You are all I have in the world.
Now I send you heartfelt kisses.
From your eternally beloved
Sofie

Three million kronor. That is how much he sends, every year, three million kronor!

How incredibly starved he must have been, how incredibly alone and abandoned.

He pays so much, and gets so little in return.

Tuesday, 15 December

11

Anders Schyman knocked on Annika's door. She looked up in surprise from the paper she was reading and gestured for him to come in. 'What do you want?' she asked, getting up to move the clothes she'd tossed over the only other chair in the room.

Schyman closed the door behind him and adopted what he hoped was an open, neutral expression. 'I wanted to know what was happening with the disclosure ban and your job,' he said, managing to sound both authoritative and friendly. 'How do you think it's working? Is there much of a clash?'

Annika sat down again, sighed heavily and threw a half-eaten Lucia bun into the bin. She had brushed her hair and looked as if she'd actually slept for once. 'I can't see any problems,' she said, 'but I get the impression that Berit and the others are finding it a nuisance. They think I'm holding back a load of information I don't actually have, and they're tiptoeing round me even though there's no need.'

The editor-in-chief sat on the other chair. 'Yes, that's my impression too,' he said, 'and I think it's an unfortunate situation. I know you can't tell me, but I'm going to ask anyway. Do you know anything besides

155

what you've told us? Anything that could be of the slightest interest?'

The young woman looked at him with her heavily made-up eyes. There was something in her that always unsettled him, as if she knew something about him that she shouldn't. Now she stared at him in silence for several seconds. 'Two things,' she said at last. 'As far as I can see, they wouldn't add anything of value to our reporting, but they haven't been released publicly yet, I presume for reasons connected to the inquiry.'

'I'm not going to ask what they are,' Schyman said, 'but as long as there's anything you haven't told us, it complicates matters.'

'Her eyes,' Annika said. 'They were yellow. I'm absolutely sure of it, because I'd never seen anyone with such unusual eyes before. But that hasn't been mentioned anywhere. They even changed the colour in the Photofit – she's got green eyes in it.'

The editor-in-chief nodded, surprised by the confidence. He decided to wait for the second fact without prompting her.

'And her bag,' the reporter said. 'She had an oblong, silver evening-bag with a narrow shoulder-strap. Inspector Q told me that a small gun with a silencer would fit in something like that.'

He nodded again. 'And those were the two things,' he said.

'Those were the two things,' she confirmed.

'That wasn't worth making too much of a fuss about,' Schyman said, with a smile.

She sighed again, and reached for an unopened bar of chocolate.

The editor-in-chief decided to put his cards on the table. 'You know,' he said, 'I think it would be best for everyone if you took some time off while all this is going on.'

Annika stiffened, and put down the chocolate without eating any. 'What do you mean?' she asked.

'You being here means that there's an atmosphere in the newsroom. Your colleagues are worried about getting you into trouble, and they're holding back in their contact with the police to make sure it doesn't look like you've told them anything. To be blunt, it's restricting our activities, and it's spoiling your relationship with your colleagues.'

She looked down at the bar of chocolate, fingering the silver foil. 'You've arranged this very neatly,' she said.

'What?' he said, then bit his tongue, because he knew exactly what she meant.

She let out a laugh, then leaned back in her chair and looked him in the eye. 'I know you're angry,' she said. 'You didn't get the job as head of the Newspaper Publishers' Association, and you think it's my fault.' She laughed again. 'Who am I trying to kid?' she said. 'It *was* my fault. I made you publish that article showing that our proprietors are a bunch of hypocritical hyenas, and I appreciate that they're furious and withdrew your nomination. Are you firing me?'

'Absolutely not,' Schyman said, strangely relieved that she understood him. 'I'm serious about the disclosure ban – your position among your colleagues is unsustainable. I can live with the rest of it, and our proprietors as well. It didn't create that many ripples in other media . . .'

'Of course not,' she said. 'They were just pleased that TV Scandinavia disappeared.'

The editor-in-chief shrugged. 'The general view was that democracy will survive without yet another American commercial cable channel. I want you to take some holiday until things have calmed down on the terrorism front.'

'Not holiday,' she said. 'On leave with full pay. I'll need access to the archives and databases with my own password so I can work from home on my own computer. Ten free taxi-rides each month.'

This had been much easier than Schyman had anticipated. 'Full pay and a password,' he confirmed, 'but no taxis.'

She shrugged and broke off a piece of chocolate. 'Can I go straight away?'

Annika sat like a statue as the editor-in-chief left her office and closed the door behind him.

Shit, she thought. She hadn't thought he'd do it. She'd reckoned he hadn't the stomach to shove her further out into the cold. But he had.

She sat back in her chair with a slow sensation of falling, the usual sign of an imminent panic attack. But nothing happened – she didn't faint.

I'll be quite glad to escape this place for a while, she thought, then immediately felt sad, already missing the reassurance of a context, the vital sense of belonging somewhere.

I can find another home, she thought. She blew her nose into an old napkin, forcing away the self-pity, logged on to the computer and began going through her files and folders. Anything she thought she might need she sent to her personal email account.

'What did Schyman want?' Berit had put her head round the door.

'He's sent me home on indefinite leave,' Annika said. 'He doesn't want me back until the terrorism story is over.'

Berit stepped into the room and closed the door behind her. 'Did he say why?'

'The rest of you think it's a nuisance having to work round me,' Annika said, making a real effort not to sound bitter.

'That's just an excuse,' Berit said, 'and you know it. What terms did you get?'

Annika sighed again. It sounded almost like a sob. 'On leave with full pay and access to the archives. You know what?' She smiled weakly. 'It doesn't feel as bad as you might think. I've nothing against having some time off. We're moving out to Djursholm in the spring, and maybe now I can do some packing, get things organized and do a bit of research without getting stressed. That can't be bad, can it?'

Berit smiled back. 'Definitely not,' she said.

'And you know something else?' Annika said. 'All that money helps. I don't have to work any more if I don't want to. I'd been toying with the idea of handing in my notice and going off to do something completely different anyway. Study law, or maybe Russian, at university.'

Berit was the only person who knew exactly how much money Annika would be getting as her reward. Not even Thomas or Anne Snapphane knew the full amount.

'You'll need something to do,' Berit said, 'or you'll go mad.'

'And it looks like Thomas is going to get a new job,' Annika said, 'so I'll probably be seeing even less of him. He's so full of himself right now that he looks like he's going to burst . . .'

'Why?' Berit said, reaching for Annika's chocolate.

'You know he was looking into how safe politicians are, with the Association of County Councils and the

Justice Department? Now they're talking about him being part of a group drawing up new legislation governing the use of bugging and phone-tapping. I don't know if it'll come off, but he's already entertaining our friends with stories about how vital this new legislation is. You should have heard him at his parents' on Saturday.'

Berit shook her head. 'This legislation has all the signs of being a really nasty business. Do you want lunch before you go home for the last time this year?'

'I just need to check I've got everything . . .' She glanced through the last of her folders, sent off some background notes about an old murder case to her email archive, then switched off the computer. She poked about in her drawers and realized she didn't want to take anything with her. She got up and picked up her bag and coat. 'Okay, my treat this time,' she said.

The door to the government offices at Rosenbad was locked. Thomas gave the cold brass handle, embossed with three crowns, a cautious tug but the door didn't budge. He glanced round to check if anyone was watching him, then pulled hard on the door, which flew open.

'Oops,' he said, hearing how silly it sounded, and stepped inside the building.

His shoes were muddy, leaving brownish grey marks on the white marble floor. He tried in vain to wipe them before going through the swing-doors.

A white marble staircase led up to a white foyer, and his gravelly footsteps crunched under the vaulted ceiling. His heart was in his throat and his hands were damp. He had spent seven years walking past the Cabinet Office on his way to work at the Association of Local Councils on Hornsgatan. Seven years of looking up at the apricot-coloured façade and letting his thoughts run away with him: What would it be like to work in Ferdinand Boberg's art-nouveau palace, to be a small cog in the machine of power?

He had never been in here before. During his previous project, looking into the threats faced by politicians, they had either met at the Association of County Councils, or the Association of Local Councils, or in some bar. Per Cramne, the representative of the Justice Department, had preferred the latter.

Now he looked at the white floor, with its inlaid granite triangles, the four statues along the wall to his left, the marble pillars, the vaulted ceiling.

Two men in overalls were at the security desk, apparently arguing about something, but apart from them the foyer was empty. Thomas stood behind them, forming a short queue, and looked at his watch. Perfect. You had to be careful with your timing: you didn't want to look either too keen or too casual.

'You don't have clearance,' the security guard said, passing back the men's ID cards through a small hatch at the bottom of the glass screen.

The workmen looked at each other in resignation.

'It must be a mistake,' one said. 'We're supposed to be doing a job here.'

The guard was a young woman, with a neat centre parting. She was wearing a tie. 'I can't help you,' she said curtly. 'Your names aren't down here. You don't have clearance.'

'Sorry,' Thomas said, 'but could you just let me in?'

She looked at him closely.

Thomas pulled his driving licence out of his wallet and passed it through the hatch. 'I'm seeing Per Cramne in Justice,' he said, feeling the workmen's stares on his back.

She tapped at her computer and picked up a phone. 'Straight up the stairs,' she said, then turned back to the workmen.

Thomas tried to look relaxed and confident as he went through the doors leading into the government offices. He pressed the button for the lift nearest to him, then glanced up to find himself facing the deputy prime minister.

'Hello,' the deputy prime minister said. 'Do you want right or left?'

'Sorry?' Thomas said, unsure if he had heard correctly.

'Right or left?' the deputy prime minister repeated.

'Er,' Thomas said, 'I was thinking of going up.'

'In that case I recommend you go left. At the moment you're heading for the goods lift. It stops at every half-floor.'

The man was famous for speaking his mind when he thought no one was listening. Now he smiled cheerily at Thomas and held open the door of the lift to the right. 'After you.'

This can't be happening, Thomas thought.

Cramne met him on the sixth floor. 'Come in, come in,' he said, shaking Thomas's hand warmly. 'Welcome! Have you been here before?'

'Not for a long time,' Thomas said.

'Okay, we'll take a quick tour of the corridors of power before I show you where you'll be working. How does that sound?'

Cramne unlocked the doors leading to the offices without waiting for a reply. Thomas was sweating in his thick winter coat and would dearly have loved to take it off.

'There are sixteen sections in Justice, plus the legal secretariat and the metropolitan chancery,' Cramne said. 'The largest section deals with the police, as well as general issues of law and order. That's where you and I belong. Oh, do take your coat off.'

Relieved, Thomas shrugged out of it, hung it over his arm and hurried to catch up with his new colleague.

'This is where the minister, the directors general for legal affairs, the press secretary and the political advisers have their offices,' Cramne went on, gesturing vaguely as they walked quickly down a white-painted corridor.

The carpet was light grey, thick as a mattress. It swallowed every sound and left the air still and clean. From the rooms he sailed past, Thomas thought he could sense focused individuals at their desks, having reasoned discussions in low voices.

'Here, for instance,' Cramne said, stopping outside a half-open door. He lowered his voice, pointing at a woman sitting half concealed behind the door, talking on the phone.

'Director general for legal affairs in L5, criminal jurisdiction. Bloody smart girl, she's spent a lot of time working on sexual violence recently, and compensation for raped children. The permanent under-secretary down there is responsible for legal procedure, courts, police and all the rest of it. He had to deal with the raids on those security transports.'

Thomas straightened his back, feeling power tickle the back of his neck.

'The Blue Room,' Cramne said, pointing to one corner. 'Mondays are departmental days, and that's where we have our briefings. Each section presents its activities to the minister. As one of the pen-pushers, you're bound to end up in there at some point.'

'Where's my office?' Thomas asked, shifting his coat to the other arm.

Cramne laughed. 'Not up here. You'll be with me down on four,' he said, then turned a corner.

Another corridor, with similar white doors and grey carpet, stretched off into the distance. Photographs of justice ministers through the ages hung in three rows along one wall. The voices were louder here, someone laughing, the signature-tune of the lunchtime radio news.

'This is the minister's office,' Cramne said, stopping by a door on the right. He glanced at his watch. 'He's in a cabinet meeting – they meet every day between twelve and one. Usually he doesn't have to go – five ministers are enough to reach quorum – but there was going to be a roll-call today. Difficult to miss something like that . . . His secretary is outside his actual office.'

Thomas put his head in and looked at the justice minister's rooms. It reminded him of a small apartment, with the secretary's space as an entrance hall, then a fairly nondescript office with light, modern furniture, a painting, a desk covered with papers and a computer, then a low bookcase holding files and pictures of children. The room faced the Parliament building and the waters of Norrström, grey as lead.

'At the back there's a small bedroom and bathroom,' Cramne said. 'He's a whiz at Sudoku – we think he sits in there practising. Shall we move on?' He gestured to a door on the left. 'The press secretary. If the minister gets kicked out, she goes too, as well as the under-secretary and the political advisers. Then the caretaker comes along, unscrews all the nameplates and that's the end of them.'

'How many people are we talking about?' Thomas asked.

'What? Political appointees? A handful, six or seven.

164

No more than that. The rest of us faithfully serve whichever master we have. Are you hungry?'

Thomas shook his head.

'Excellent. You've met Karin, head of Planning? She was responsible for your appointment. Shall we say hello to the under-secretary?'

Cramne went on, past several more doors. 'Jimmy? Have you got a moment to meet our new bugging adviser?'

The Under-secretary of State for the Justice Department came out into the corridor in jeans and a checked beige shirt, his hair all over the place. 'Hi,' he said, with a broad smile. 'Welcome aboard. When do you start?'

They shook hands.

'After New Year,' Thomas said, finally starting to relax.

'Bugging's a real minefield,' Jimmy Halenius said. 'You'll have to watch yourself if we're going to steer it through successfully this time. What's the timetable?'

This last question was directed at Cramne. 'Initial inquiry in six months,' the section head said. 'Out to consultation in the Legislative Council this autumn, and a government proposal in February next year.'

'So a new law on the first of July in eighteen months' time,' Halenius said. 'A slightly different tempo from your wife's work. She's on one of the papers, isn't she?'

Thomas was momentarily at a loss for words, and he could feel himself blushing. How the hell did the Under-secretary of State in the Justice Department know who Annika was?

'My best friend bought a car off her once,' Halenius said, looking extremely amused. 'It must be nine, ten years ago. "It's goes like a dream," she said, and it did, until it broke down.'

'Er,' Thomas said. He didn't know what to do with his hands.

'Shall we take a look at your office?' Cramne said.

He doesn't like being outside the conversation, Thomas thought, and shook the under-secretary's hand again.

They walked in silence along the corridors, back out through the glass doors and into the lift.

'Where's your office?' Thomas asked.

'Three rooms from yours. Can you press four?'

They found themselves in the same sort of office set-up as they'd seen on the sixth floor, the same layout but lacking the atmosphere of power. There were more magazine racks, notice-boards on the walls, and a large, colourful tapestry in the hall.

Thomas's room faced out on to Fredsgatan, towards the corner with Drottninggatan. It was a reasonable size, but its position meant it was quite dark. He leaned over and peered out. No view of Tegelbacken. He had never looked up at this window.

'You know what this is all about?' Cramne said, pulling out a chair. 'You're putting together a departmental proposal, which will then be sent out for consultation. Everyone gets to have their say, and we already know how most people are likely to respond. The police and prosecutors are in favour, the chancellor of justice is in favour, and the legal ombudsman against. The Lawyers' Federation is against, they're always against everything, and the authorities that deal with the victims of crime, and the women's support units, will probably be in favour.'

'And then the work starts in the various sections here,' Thomas said.

'Exactly. You listen to God, God's auntie and everyone

166

else, then you pull it all together with the head of section – in other words, me. Then we go to the director general for legal affairs, who says "Think about this and this and this," and when all is okay we get to show up for a Monday meeting in the Blue Room. Which is when it's time to point out the stumbling-blocks for the minister.'

'And what will those be in this case?' Thomas asked.

'There'll probably be a few modifications,' Cramne said. 'The level of suspicion required, what crimes will be covered, synchronization with legislation in other countries, and then possibly the timescale.' He punched Thomas's shoulder playfully. 'It'll be a breeze.'

Thomas smiled and gulped.

12

Annika's head was spinning as she left the office, her feet seeming hardly to touch the ground. The air was milder today, almost warm. For some reason an old memory surfaced, the first day of the summer holidays when she had run over Grandma's meadow down towards Hosjön Lake, grass and leaves scratching her legs as she headed for the first proper swim of the year.

I'm not going to look round, she thought. I might not be coming back, and I want to remember it as it was when I still belonged here, when there was still a place for me . . .

Slowly, a little uncertainly, she walked to the bus-stop. The next bus was due in thirteen minutes. She wondered whether to walk home or sit down and wait. Why hurry?

She sat down on the wooden bench and pulled out her mobile phone. Who to call?

Thomas's mobile was switched off.

Anne Snapphane didn't answer.

She hesitated for a few seconds, then dialled Detective Inspector Q's direct line.

He answered.

'Hello, it's the headline-chasing bitch here,' Annika

said. 'I've been sent on gardening leave. Your disclosure ban has got me out of the office indefinitely on full pay.'

'Congratulations,' Q said. 'Should I get you a cake?'

'No,' Annika said, 'but I thought I might bring one up for you. Are you in this afternoon?'

'In and out. I don't like marzipan.'

The bus pulled up, a couple of minutes early.

'Good,' Annika said. 'I'll bring one with marzipan.'

She got on, showed her season ticket and settled down on the back seat.

Rålambshov Park spread out with a complete absence of colour. Beyond it, the grey waters of Riddarfjärden were scarcely visible through the mist. This is a terrible time of year, Annika thought, and there are months to go before it changes.

She got off by Sankt Erik's Eye Clinic on Fleminggatan and walked down Polhemsgatan towards Police Headquarters. Q must have said something to the receptionist because she was let in at once and headed straight for his office, with its view of Kungsholmsgatan.

'Where's the cake?' the inspector said, gesturing towards a chair on the other side of the desk.

'Damn,' Annika said, pulling off her jacket. 'I forgot. How are things?'

'Our youngest girl's got another ear infection, but otherwise okay,' he said. 'How about you?'

'You haven't got a daughter, have you?' Annika said, sitting down.

He looked at her in surprise. 'No,' he said, 'you're right.'

'You see?' Annika said. 'I know everything but say nothing.'

'And now you've got the sack and it's my fault.'

'Exactly,' Annika said. 'So I thought you could tell me if it was worth the trouble.'

'What? You keeping quiet? God, yes.'

The inspector stood up, and Annika saw that he was wearing a pair of pink gabardine trousers. 'Wow. Are you a member of the Eurovision fan club?'

'I'm on the committee,' he said. 'Milk and sugar?'

She nodded and he disappeared into the corridor to get coffee. His excessive taste for Hawaiian shirts and noisy music hadn't left any noticeable traces on his workplace.

Almost ten years had passed since she had first met Q. Back then he had been leading the investigation into the murder of a stripper, Josefin Liljeberg, a young girl with dreams of becoming a journalist who was found strangled behind a headstone in the Jewish cemetery in Kronoberg Park. Over the years they had exchanged a wealth of information, often, but not always, to their mutual advantage. He had occasionally told her that it was over, but the breaks never lasted long. Annika had no illusions as to why.

Q needed a public mouthpiece in the media. He knew that she almost always placed her articles where she wanted them, which meant that when he needed to he could plant material in the public domain.

'There you go. Don't say we don't work hard,' he said, putting a cup of coffee on the desk in front of her, and managing to spill some on the way.

'Maybe not in this office,' Annika said, 'but I'm sure that's not always the case.'

Detective Inspector Q sighed, threw himself into his chair and put his feet up on the desk. 'Yes,' he said, 'you're quite right. A third of all police officers solve almost all crime, and the rest do virtually nothing. It's a serious problem, the fact that young recruits leaving the academy are so much smarter than their bosses.'

Annika blew on her coffee. It was boiling hot and tasted like tar. 'What do you mean?' she said.

'In the good old days it was so hard to fill the courses that pretty much anyone was accepted. Nowadays only one in every ten applicants is taken on, so only the élite become officers, which means that the standard within the force is extremely uneven. The younger officers are talented and highly motivated, the older ones less so.'

'And the way to solve this is to close down all the police stations in the suburbs and the countryside?' Annika said.

'Do you know?' Q said. 'The problem isn't that we're closing down police stations all over Sweden. It's the ones that are still open.'

'Really?' Annika said.

'They're open every other Tuesday between ten and twelve, and the rest of the time the staff sit there doing crosswords. Obviously the sensible thing would be to close those stations, get rid of the worst officers and replace them with more talented people.'

'And then you'd have been able to solve cases like the killings at the Nobel banquet?' Annika said.

'We're smart enough, and strong enough,' Q said.

'I know,' Annika said. 'Neue Jihad and a family out in Bandhagen.'

'Nothing to do with the Nobel killings,' Q said. 'We know pretty much what happened now.'

'Seriously?' she said.

'We know the killer got in through the main entrance at twenty-two forty-one. By then the dinner was over and the dancing had started. The first guests had already left the party and were on their way out through the courtyard.'

'It was quite chaotic,' Annika said. 'The staff were clearing the tables, people were milling about, going to the loo or heading for the music in the Golden Hall. How did she get in? Did she have an invitation?'

'We think she must have read the *Evening Post*,' Q said. 'You gave a description of how it all works.'

Annika's mind was blank. 'What do you mean?'

'"How I Got into the Nobel Banquet". It was a few years ago now, but it must have been since you started working there. One of your colleagues put on an evening-gown and high heels and slipped past the guards at about ten thirty, saying, "Goodness, isn't it cold!" She didn't have anything remotely like an invitation but still managed to get right up to the royal couple without being stopped. I think you published a picture in the centrefold of her dancing with the prime minister.'

Annika tried to smile but didn't succeed. 'Oh, that Nobel banquet,' she said.

'That's more or less what the killer did. We presume she was carrying a forged invitation just in case, but she wasn't called upon to show it. The officers on the main entrance remember her – she was smoking out on Hantverkargatan, fiddling with a mobile phone, just outside the passageway into the courtyard. A few minutes later she hurried in, with the phone in her hand and her little evening-bag dangling from her shoulder. They could see she was freezing and thought she'd gone out to make a call and have a cigarette, and was on her way back in.'

'And they didn't stop her.'

'One of the guards gave her a hand to stop her slipping on a patch of ice. She thanked him in English without looking at him. He said her hand was very cold.'

172

'How can they be sure it was her?'

'They recognized the Photofit.'

'Do they remember what she was wearing?'

'All the guards have extremely clear memories of her. Unfortunately they don't match. One says she was wearing a red dress, the others that it was grey or beige. Some say she was wearing a shawl, others that her shoulders were bare. We think they're mixing her up with two women in a group who were leaving the courtyard just as she arrived.'

'She had shoulder-straps,' Annika said. 'I'm a hundred per cent sure of that. You said she was smoking, did she drop the butt anywhere?'

'Ground it into a puddle of frozen dog piss. The next sighting is vaguer, from the pillared walkway between the entrance and the Blue Hall. She was on her way up the stairs leading to the council chambers and the Golden Hall. A man who had drunk his own and his neighbour's share of the wine stopped her and asked her to dance. She tried to get past without replying. He persisted and grabbed her arm but she pushed him in the chest and slipped past. The man got angry and tried to catch up with her, but she'd already disappeared into the crowd. He got in touch after seeing the Photofit.'

'There's no chance he's trying to make something out of nothing?'

'It's possible, but the woman should have been thereabouts at that time, so we're presuming he's telling the truth. But we don't know which door she used to get into the Golden Hall, we don't know how quickly she identified her victims, and we don't know why she shot them.'

'Do you know what weapon she used?'

'Probably a Walther 7.65, a fairly common Belgian

gun. No one saw her pull a pistol from her bag, so we can't be sure. More coffee?'

Annika tried to conjure up the picture of the woman with her elbow raised and her hand feeling inside her bag. 'She never took it out?' Annika said. 'She shot through the bag?'

'It looks like it. The ammunition was Israeli, not fully jacketed, with a soft tip.' Q dropped his feet to the floor and stood up. 'Well, I'm going to have another cup.'

'Dumdum bullets?' Annika said. 'I thought they'd been banned?'

'Hardly,' Q said. 'They're even used by the Swedish police – the union seems to prefer them. We used to have Walther 7.65s as our service weapon, but a lot of officers weren't much good with them so nowadays we use nine-millimetre weapons. They're much more powerful and can kill people even if you don't get your shot in properly.'

'But the killer got her shots in properly,' Annika said, to drag the conversation back to the subject.

'Exactly,' Q said. 'She aimed for the heart and blew out the aorta. Why don't you cut the cake while I'm gone?'

He disappeared into the corridor again, leaving Annika with her somewhat bemused thoughts. How did Caroline von Behring fit into all this? And what did the killings have to do with Aaron Wiesel?

Restless, she got up and walked over to the window. A group of children from a nursery, in padded trousers and woollen hats, was going past on the other side of the road, holding hands in a crocodile. Their teachers were walking at the front and back, joking and coaxing them onwards. The colourful procession wobbled slowly up

174

towards Kronoberg Park, the children's swinging arms showing that they were singing.

For some reason groups of nursery-school children walking through the city always made her feel weepy. Her throat tightened. They were so small, their legs so short, but they had grown-ups to shield them from cars and other dangers. Oh, God, she didn't want to move from Kungsholmen. She didn't want to leave the city – this was where she belonged. What on earth was she doing, moving out into an idyllic suburb?

'It doesn't get any better,' Q said. 'I've been standing there as well, trying to summon up the weather gods, but it hasn't worked so far. Bad reception or something.'

Annika closed her eyes and let the children disappear, then turned round and took in the detective's bright-pink trousers again. 'Why von Behring?' she asked. 'Why Wiesel? Did she pick them at random, or did she search them out?'

Q sat down in his chair. 'What do you think, Einstein? Why make her way through the whole building before firing?'

Annika went back to her chair. 'She went through the main entrance at twenty-two forty-one.'

'Exactly.'

'And she made her way in from Hantverkargatan, across the courtyard, through the Blue Hall, up to the Golden Hall, identified the victims and shot them, all within four minutes.'

Q took a sip of coffee, his feet back on the desk.

'So she knew exactly who she was going to shoot and where they were,' Annika said.

'Correct.'

'How could she know that?'

Q looked at her without speaking for a few seconds.

'She got a text message telling her where the victims were,' he said finally, holding her gaze. 'From someone inside the banquet. That's how we're looking at it, anyway.'

Annika felt the hairs on the back of her neck stand up. 'How can you know that?' she asked.

He sat in silence for several more seconds, evaluating her with his eyes. 'A text message,' he said quietly. 'A text message was sent from the relevant mast, from one pay-as-you-go phone to another, containing the words *dancing close to St Erik*. Both phones were on the Telia network, bought at the same time from the Central Station in August this year. The buyer paid cash rather than with a credit or debit card. And because the Central Station is used by about a hundred thousand people every day, he or she can't be traced.'

Annika licked her lips and shuffled on her seat. 'How can you know what text messages were sent from which number and when? And how can you know what this one *said*?'

Q fingered his mug.

'I didn't think that was even technically possible,' Annika said, leaning back. 'Keeping track of every conversation and text message?'

'Of course it is,' Q said. 'How else would the networks get paid?'

Annika reflected for a few seconds, letting this information sink in. 'They get paid,' she said, 'because they know who called whom and for how long, but they don't know what they said or what they wrote in their texts. That's not possible. Those details aren't stored.'

'Right,' Q said. 'And what does that tell you?'

She thought for four seconds. 'You've found a phone.'

Q tilted his head to one side and smiled. 'Bravo! In a

rubbish bin at the bus-stop outside the main entrance, right opposite the Serafen health centre. No finger-prints, just traces of the soap used inside the City Hall. The SIM-card was erased, but we've got guys down in a garage in Nacka who can reconstruct that sort of thing. So, what does the text message mean?'

Annika looked at Q and thought hard. 'An accomplice,' she said. 'She had help, from inside the City Hall.'

Q nodded and drank the rest of his coffee. 'At least one, right, and at least one more outside: the person driving the boat. But we have no idea who these people were. We've got a list of suspects, but no conclusive evidence.'

Annika stared at Q. 'The phones were bought in August, you said. Four months ago?'

'The same time the getaway boat was stolen. Which suggests she knew exactly what she was doing.'

'So she didn't shoot the wrong person? She didn't miss Wiesel and just happen to hit von Behring by mistake?'

Q got up and went to the window, then turned back to her. 'Apparently not.'

The information hit Annika in the chest. 'I knew it,' she said, seeing Caroline's eyes once more. 'I knew she was the target, and she knew it too. Had there been any threats against her? Anyone who wanted to get rid of her?'

'Nothing that's come to light yet.'

'There has to be something,' Annika said. 'You need to dig deeper. Caroline wasn't surprised when she died – I saw it in her eyes.'

Q gazed at her thoughtfully. 'So you say,' he said. 'Was there anything else you were wondering about?'

Annika looked past him and out of the window. So Caroline really was the killer's target. Someone had wanted to get rid of her. 'What happened after the shots were fired?' she asked.

Q sat down again, picked up his coffee-cup, saw it was empty and threw it into the bin. 'We've got more witnesses for that, but not as many as you might think. We know she made her way out using the lift in a service passage leading to the Golden Hall. And from there it's less than a hundred metres to the water.'

He got up, pulled open one of the desk drawers and took out a large rolled-up map. 'Look at this,' he said. 'After Liljeholmen there are no built-up areas along the shore of Lake Mälaren until you get to Södertälje, with the exception of this little road here, Pettersbergsvägen in Mälarhöjden. We've got a witness who saw two people get on to two small motorbikes in Gröndal. They could have driven without being seen all the way from the centre of Stockholm and out into the Baltic, if they'd wanted to. And that's exactly what I think they did.'

'That's impossible,' Annika said. 'Wherever you go, there's always someone.'

'Stockholm's got a hell of a lot of green,' Q said. 'Shore protection and the environment Fascists have made sure of that. Do you have any idea how much coastline we've got in Sweden? Enough to go round the planet nine and a half times, and no one's allowed to build on any of it.'

Annika tried to follow his argument. 'So who did it? Any particular group? What were they trying to achieve?'

The detective inspector sat down again and for once looked quite normal, serious. 'We have one suspect,' he said. 'It was your information that did it.'

Annika blinked. 'You're kidding?'

'The eyes,' Q said. 'Her golden yellow eyes. We got lucky with the CIA. She's American, a professional assassin, expensive and extremely bloody talented.'

Annika was having trouble breathing. 'What's her name?' she said, her voice sounding thin.

'She uses a whole list of identities and nationalities, but the CIA know her by her nickname. It comes from her eyes. She's called the Kitten.'

'The Kitten?' Annika said.

'Yep,' Q said, standing up. 'And I'm only telling you so you understand why it was important that you kept quiet.'

'About her eyes?' Annika said.

'That was the decisive detail for us,' Q said, 'but, as you've doubtless realized, that information mustn't go beyond this room.'

'Why not?' Annika asked. 'Large parts of this aren't exactly controversial. And, however much you try, it'll leak out in the end.'

'Not this,' Q said.

'It will,' Annika said. 'Everything leaks. It's just a matter of time.'

'If this gets out,' Q said, 'it'll be because you've talked. We're keeping this within an extremely restricted team, because this isn't just about us and the Nobel killings.'

Annika let what he had said settle into some sort of order in her head. 'You're waiting for other security services,' she said. 'You're working with foreign police on other crimes, other murders. Where?'

Q looked faintly amused. 'The USA, Colombia and France, among others.'

'You've got something else as well,' Annika said. 'What?'

'We've linked her fingerprints to the investigation, and this is the first time anyone has managed that.'

'How?' Annika asked.

Q couldn't help smiling. 'She dropped one of her shoes on the steps down to the water,' he said. 'Can you believe it?'

'Cinderella of Death,' Annika said.

'You can see the headline,' Q said. He rolled up the map and put it back into his drawer.

'So, when can I use it?'

'All in good time,' Q said, heading towards the door. 'If you've eaten enough of my marzipan cake, maybe you can do the washing-up in the kitchen because I've got to load my great big gun with some dumdum bullets and catch some baddies. I don't want to end up among the two-thirds that never do anything.' He stopped. 'And we're not just letting the CIA lead us on this one,' he said. 'We've still got problems to deal with here at home.'

'Because you don't know who hired her,' Annika said.

'Correct.'

She got up and pulled on her jacket, hoisted her bag on to her shoulder and left the room. She paused. 'A qualified guess?'

He closed the door behind them. 'Well, it certainly wasn't Neue Jihad.'

Part 2
MAY

Saturday, 22 May

13

Johan Isaksson swiped his card through the electronic reader. He waited for the click to alert him that the door was unlocked, then opened it.

Inside the laboratory corridor he glanced quickly to the right to check his pigeonhole. He paused to examine the notice-board above the table where the post was sorted: *ID-cards must be visible at all times in FBF premises* and *Use colour-coded envelopes for external post!* as well as *In case of faults, call* . . . No new notices. Most of them had been there since he had taken up his postgraduate post in the department four years before. The absence of news made him feel a bit safer.

With some trepidation he went over to the individual pigeonholes.

His contained two circulars about new summer opening hours in the café and a reminder that carbon-dioxide cylinders could only be exchanged between eight and nine a.m., Monday to Friday. He glanced through the papers in several of his colleagues' boxes; they had received the same as he had.

He breathed out. No general offers, no odd invitations to make some quick money, nothing that looked as if it could be meant for everyone but was actually just for him.

No *Stewarding at the Nobel Banquet! Want to earn some extra money? Help us with our practical joke and save money! Ring* . . .

He had rung. In fact he had practically thrown himself at the phone. When he had got the job he had been delighted, had assumed a lot of them were fighting for it. Afterwards he had realized that the photocopied note hadn't been generally circulated. The message had been directed specifically at him.

How had they known that he would agree to be a steward?

And how had they known he needed the money?

He rubbed his chin – he was sweating.

Now he was here, on a Saturday evening, instead of at Agnes's party. It felt pretty good. He had neglected his research, but that was at an end now. The decision to explain everything in an anonymous letter to the police had made him feel a whole lot better. He headed towards his cramped office. It was dark and there was a sour smell in the corridor, like old *E. coli* bacteria. I ought to let in some air, he thought.

He passed the equipment room with its DNA-sequencing and measuring machines, the centrifuge room on his right, the bacteria lab to his left, all deserted. He stopped at the storeroom behind the photocopier and pulled out a tray of Petri dishes. He hesitated in front of the shelf holding the ten-millimetre test-tubes, then remembered he'd already got some so went to get a tray of sterilized needles. He tapped in the code to unlock his office and put down his equipment, then waited by the door, listening.

An alarm was ringing somewhere. It sounded like the

186

carbon-dioxide alarm, which went off whenever the percentage of the gas sank too low in the incubator and you had to switch cylinders. The whole lab had had trouble with mould and cell-death throughout the spring, and now some poor sod's cells would suffocate unless someone saved them.

He let the door swing shut behind him and headed towards the sound. The alarm got louder as he reached the corridor at the far end. A slender girl with a ponytail, wearing a lab coat, was standing at the airlock to one of the cell labs, looking bewildered.

'Do you need any help?' he asked, and she jumped.

'Oh, shit,' she yelled, in English, staring at him in horror. 'You scared the hell out of me. Can you turn this thing off?'

She was evidently American.

'It's the carbon-dioxide alarm,' he replied, also in English. 'Have you tried changing the cylinder?'

'Are there more than two of them?' she asked, opening the door to let him into the airlock.

He went over to the equipment to the right of the door and checked the pressure gauge. Both cylinders were empty: someone had forgotten to change the reserve tube. He shook his head. 'You can only call to get the cylinders changed between eight and nine in the morning. It's a nightmare. Sorry.'

The girl looked like she was going to burst into tears. 'But,' she said, 'what's going to happen to my cells? I got a new batch last week, and with the mould and everything I'm running out of chances. The carbon dioxide in the incubator is already down to one point one per cent so they won't last till Monday. What am I going to do?'

She looked so wretched in her big wooden sandals and clumsy glasses that he felt obliged to stay and help.

'Have you checked to see if there's any extra gas in one of the other labs?' he asked.

She looked even more horrified. 'But surely you're not allowed to do that?' she said.

He smiled and suppressed an impulse to put a hand on her shoulder. 'Well,' he said, 'you can borrow the reserve cylinder from my lab. I'm in the next corridor on the right.'

'No kidding?' she said, taking off her glasses, and now he could see that she was actually very pretty. She had a red scar at the top of her right cheek, shaped like a little bird.

'Sure,' he said. 'I'll help you carry it. Can you pass me that?' He gestured to the large wrench that was lying on the radiator behind the cylinders, left there for precisely this eventuality.

She followed close on his heels as they went down the corridor, and watched as he closed the valve and unscrewed one of the cylinders from its place in his own lab and put it on to a small sack-barrow. 'They're really heavy,' he said apologetically, as he set off with the cylinder.

Positioning it in her lab took less than three minutes. Thank God I used to do so much work on my moped, he thought, putting the wrench back on the radiator.

She was practically crying with joy as the carbon-dioxide levels in the incubator rose and the alarm stopped. 'How can I thank you?' she asked. 'Can I offer you dinner?'

Johan Isaksson laughed, rather embarrassed. 'I have to work tonight,' he said. 'Sorry.'

'What about a beer, then?' she said. 'Please – I'm practically done here. Have just one little *cerveza* with me?' She tilted her head and fluttered her eyelashes.

He laughed again, more relaxed now. 'I suppose one won't do any harm,' he said.

She clapped her hands. 'Great! Hang on, I'll go and get them . . .'

She disappeared inside her lab and emerged with two bottles of American Budweiser.

'I hope you like Yankee beer,' she said, pulling off her lab coat. She handed him the bottles as she kicked off her sandals and pulled on a pair of high-heeled leather boots.

'Cilla,' he said, reading the name from the sandals as she put them by the airlock. 'Is that you?'

She took the beers from him and smiled. 'Shit, no,' she said, then held out her hand. 'I'm Janet.'

He took it and smiled back. 'Johan,' he said. 'Where do you want to sit?'

She went over to the table at the end of the corridor, and he noticed that she was limping. She opened both bottles and passed him one. '*Para mi héroe*,' she said, raising hers.

He drank in careful sips. The beer was bitter, slightly sour, and he couldn't help pulling a face.

'What is it?' she said, looking worried. 'Don't you like it?'

He cleared his throat. 'It's good,' he said. 'I'm just not used to it . . . So you speak Spanish?'

She shrugged her shoulders awkwardly and laughed. 'My family is from Mexico,' she said. 'I'm the first person in our family to go to university. It's a big deal for them.'

He nodded sympathetically. She must be a bright girl.

'We swam across the Rio Grande when I was five years old, just west of Ciudad Juárez.'

She'd been through a lot, he thought.

'I got caught on some barbed wire they'd put up to stop people like us reaching the American dream,' she said, pointing to her cheek and her left leg. 'I never really recovered.'

'Does it hurt?' he asked.

She looked rather sad. 'Only in here.' She laid a hand over her heart.

'Do you miss your family?'

She nodded, smiling sadly. 'So I just have to drown my sorrows.' She knocked her bottle of beer against his. 'Bottoms up,' she said, and downed her beer in one.

He took a deep breath and followed her example, gulping hard several times. He didn't really like beer, and this one was horrible.

'Do you want another?' she asked, and he raised his hand to stop her fetching one.

She tilted her head again. 'There's just one little thing I could use some help with,' she said. 'My samples are on the top shelf inside the freeze-room, and I can't reach them even if I stand on a stool. Could you give me a hand?'

He smiled. She really was very sweet. 'You know,' he said, 'you've got beautiful eyes.'

Dimples appeared in her cheeks. 'Thank you,' she said. 'You're pretty cute yourself.'

He downed the last of the beer with a grimace.

'My samples,' she said, gesturing towards the door of the freeze-room.

He went to the control panel to the right of the door, switched on the light inside and checked the thermostat: minus twenty-seven degrees.

'Where are they?' he asked.

'Right at the back, on the top shelf,' she said, opening the door for him.

He walked in and shivered.

The space between the shelves was narrow and cramped. Boxes of slides, crates of samples, long rows of frozen cellular tissue. He looked along the labels, feeling a bit peculiar.

'What did you say it said on the samples?' he asked, and at that moment the door closed.

He stared at the frozen door without really understanding what he was looking at, noting the emergency release switch and freezer apparatus to the left of the door. 'Janet?' he said.

There was a click and the fluorescent lights in the ceiling flickered, then everything turned black.

'Janet!' he shouted into the darkness. 'The door's closed!'

He put his hands out in front of him, fumbling in the air and dislodging a test-tube that crashed to the floor. He felt his way to the door and pressed the emergency release switch.

Nothing happened.

He pressed again, harder. 'Janet!'

He pushed against the door with his whole weight. It didn't budge.

He screamed until he thought his throat would burst.

The Kitten sighed and tugged at the yellow and white striped overall with the elasticated cuffs. The zip was chafing the back of her neck. Cilla's sandals were too big, flapping when she walked. She pushed the dark-framed fake glasses on to her nose, checked the time and sighed again. She'd been acting the part of lab-rat in this get-up for too long now and had had enough.

Another quarter of an hour.

She glanced through the window in the airlock door.

The gloomy corridor outside was empty. The spring evening was getting dark, no longer reaching far into the long corridors of the building.

God, she was sick of this – and she could use a cigarette.

She took a deep breath, shut her eyes and forced herself to focus on the rest of the chain of events. This whole damn job was a matter of timing and waiting, and the latter was without a doubt her weak spot.

She was utterly fed up with this city and this job. Everything about them sucked. At least the last one had been a bit rock'n'roll, but this? Her negative attitude towards the country wasn't only the result of the scar on her cheek and the pain in her leg. There was something about the blandness of the architecture and the landscape, the naïvety of the people, the hopeful expressions on their faces.

A self-satisfied people, she thought, who saw the world through a haze of insipid loveliness. If everyone was like us there'd be peace on earth. Fucking morons.

The cretinous blabbermouth in the freezer was no exception. He couldn't keep his mouth shut, and just look how that had turned out. What a stroke of luck that she'd kept hold of her wingman's mobile phone. For safety's sake she'd kept it switched on and charged, an intuitive precaution that had been entirely justified.

Little Yappy had sent the first text just as she'd finished cleaning up after the pisshead doctor. It had come from his private number, short and possibly the result of panic: *Call me! I want to talk!* Naturally she hadn't replied, but presumed he must have his mobile set to tell him when messages had been delivered because the next said: *I know you're there. I know what you did. Call me!*

192

Waiting for his next move had become a sort of hobby. Of course she never replied, just let him stew.

Then, on Tuesday, it had stopped being fun.

OK. Fine. I'm going to the police.

She had gathered her things, left the flat in her own good time, locking it carefully behind her, then made her way to the airport. That same evening she had searched his student room. There was a draft of the letter in his computer, anonymous, to the police explaining what Yappy had done, how much money he had been paid, what her wingman had done (so pathetically clumsy!) and the phone number he had used.

She left the document as it was. The boy didn't have broadband in his room, and she hadn't found a modem, so he couldn't use the Internet. She had kept him under close observation for the rest of the week. He hadn't posted any letter: she had got to him in time.

With a deep sigh she struggled over to the carbon-dioxide cylinders on the right of the lab door. The pain below her left knee flared every time she put any weight on the leg. The bone had healed crooked because the Communist quack had been so useless.

She wondered if anyone would notice that both normal cylinders were empty. Probably – scientists were so fucking picky about their precious samples. Her walks through the lab building pushing a cleaner's trolley had taught her exactly how fussy they were. They were bound to notice the cylinders and talk about them, but not about the cleaner who had been in there, wiping and disinfecting. No one sees cleaners, no one would be able to describe her afterwards.

She opened the door to the corridor and listened. No one but Yappy had booked a lab that evening or overnight, but you couldn't be too careful. You could still smell the gas in the corridor, which wasn't good, but there was nothing she could do about that. Not that carbon dioxide was particularly dangerous, she'd checked, but she'd emptied out the contents of two full cylinders so it would be a few hours before the air returned to normal.

She looked at the time and sighed again.

He'd managed to get the whole bottle down him in the end. Okay, so the chemicals had made it taste pretty crap, there was no getting away from that, but it wasn't bad enough for a thirsty young man to turn up his nose at it.

Really, though, it was pretty bloody rich that she should have to clear up other people's mistakes like this. She hadn't hired Yappy, she'd been sure to point that out: he had been her wingman's mistake, the fucking amateur.

There was no serious harm done, though, which was something to be grateful for.

She looked at the time again.

One hour and fifty-three minutes.

That would have to do. The combination of the cold and the drug would kill an elephant within two hours. It was time to pick up the mobile phone and clear the contents of a computer in the student residence.

She pulled off her protective clothing and glasses and put them in the bag with the empty beer-bottles. She kept the latex gloves on (she had already wiped any surface she had touched with her bare hands and had no intention of doing it again). She pulled on her boots and denim jacket, then went to Yappy's office, checked through his things and grabbed his mobile phone. Then she left the door ajar, just as she had found it.

Finally she took out the key and went back to the freeze-room. She listened at the door for a few seconds, even though she knew she wasn't going to hear anything.

Then she put the key in the lock and turned it.

Wednesday, 26 May

14

Annika woke up from a particularly traumatic dream not knowing where she was. The sun was shining on to her bed and the sheets were damp with her sweat. A bird was singing outside the window, and she groaned loudly, pulling the pillow over her head.

She was lying in the bedroom of their house in Djursholm.

Of course.

She sighed and got up. Thomas had already left, she knew. He got to work before seven each morning, the official reason being to avoid rush-hour. The real reason was that his love for his amazing job was greater than his love for his thoroughly ordinary family. At least, that was what she thought in her darker moments.

She pulled on her thoroughly ordinary towelling dressing-gown and went downstairs to the kitchen to make breakfast for her thoroughly ordinary children. The sun was streaming in here too, making the parquet floor shine, and the cherry tree outside the window was in blossom. She stood at the window staring at it. This house isn't ordinary, she thought. I ought to be happy. After all, I've finally found a home.

She swallowed the lump in her throat and put two mugs of milk in the microwave to make hot chocolate. She made some toast and spread it with peanut-butter. Then she sliced a banana, peeled two oranges and divided them into segments, then put it all on to two plates. The microwave bleeped four times when the milk was hot, and Annika yanked the door open, annoyed: everything made so much noise out here. If it wasn't the birds outside the bedroom window, it was household gadgets. Her microwave in the city had bleeped three times, and that was what she was used to.

She put the plates and the hot chocolate on the table and went to wake Ellen and Kalle.

Getting the children into their new nursery had been difficult. The council had kicked up a fuss and said they couldn't start until the autumn, but Annika had employed a combination of research and lobbying and had found a private pre-school that had a nursery and a class for six-year-olds. It was keen to attract more pupils, so both children had got in. The groups were much bigger than they had been used to in the city, but on the other hand there was much more space out here. As far as the other children were concerned, they weren't much different from those on Kungsholmen. They guarded their territory and weren't going to let any new kids in just like that. Kalle, in particular, was having problems: none of the other boys wanted to play with him.

She drove them there in her new SUV, a slightly smaller version of the monster Thomas had gone for. As usual, the children argued about who was going to sit in the front, which ended up with them both in the back. Kalle cried quietly all the way, so hard that he was shaking.

'Come on, Kalle-Balle, cheer up,' she said, looking at him in the rear-view mirror.

'Don't call me that, you *stupid cow*!'

Annika braked sharply and pulled over to the side of the road. When the vehicle had stopped she turned to him. 'What did you call me?'

'You started it,' he said sulkily.

'I'm sorry if I upset you, but I've always called you Kalle-Balle. If you want me to stop, then I will.'

He swiped at the air in front of her.

She caught his clenched fist. 'I didn't mean to hurt you, but you called me that awful name because you wanted to make me sad, didn't you?'

Kalle kicked at the seat in front of him.

'Stop kicking and look at me,' Annika said, managing to keep her voice more or less calm. 'We don't call each other names like that in this family. Now, you're going to say sorry to me, and you're never going to call me that ever again. Is that clear?'

He looked up at her guiltily and nodded. He was on the point of tears again. 'Sorry, Mummy,' he said.

'Oh, darling!' Annika said, undoing his seatbelt. 'Come here . . .' She pulled him between the seats and put him on her lap, rocking and comforting him.

'There, there,' she whispered, 'you're the best boy in the world. Do you know how much I love you?'

'Right up to the stars?' he said, curling up in her arms.

'Much further than that. Right up to the angels! Now, you're going to have a lovely time today. Singing and playing football and eating lovely food and being nice to the other children.'

He nodded into her chest. 'Can I sit in the front now?'

'Not a chance. Into the back with you.'

A woman drove past far too close and honked her horn. Annika gave her the finger.

When she had delivered the children to their respective classes she felt drained. She leaned back against the SUV and gazed at the nursery with an indefinable ache in her heart. A low, single-storey building with large windows to let in the light, and big, bright green lawns, colourful climbing-frames, some swings swaying gently in the breeze, a clutter of tricycles near the fence. The sun was shining in the hesitant way it did in spring, there was the smell of soil and grass, and anxiety throbbed inside her.

She had taken on such a huge burden of responsibility when she had given birth to her children. How could she guarantee that they would have decent lives? What could she do if other children were nasty to them? If someone betrayed their innocent faith in the world?

Clearly it was going to happen. It had happened to her and probably to most other people as well. She'd worked through thirty-three years of life and still couldn't see what the point was. Maybe I'm depressed, she suddenly thought, then felt ashamed of herself.

She'd been able to stay at home all spring on full pay, packing and clearing out their old flat in peace and quiet. She'd started jogging again, and had joined a gym. How many people had such a luxurious life?

The reward for finding the money had been paid out a few weeks earlier, on 1 May, just as she had been promised. She hadn't really believed it would happen until she was standing outside the bank with the statement in her hand: twelve point eight million kronor had been paid into her account. It should have been a moment to savour, but she could only think of it with unease. Her conversation with Thomas on the pavement had gone all wrong.

'We ought to invest the money,' Thomas had said. 'I've got some old friends who are investment advisers. They'll make sure we get the best dividends. I'll give them a call this afternoon.'

'What do you mean, "best dividends"?' Annika had replied. 'In what sense? Do you mean from companies that export weapons, or use child labour, or . . .'

'Don't be ridiculous,' Thomas said.

'Unless there's something even more lucrative? Some really shit factory where they keep the workers in chains to die if the place catches fire?'

Thomas picked up his briefcase and headed towards a taxi. Annika had rushed after him, wanting to hold him in her arms the way she did with Kalle. 'Money doesn't come from nowhere,' she called after him. 'There's always someone working to make it. Any money you get from a good tip-off is the result of someone else's hard work. Don't you get it?'

'That's just sentimental bullshit,' Thomas had said, jumping into the taxi, slamming the door and driving off to his job.

He wasn't very happy with the house. It was better than their flat in the city, but he missed *the classical style*.

'Like your 1960s house in Vaxholm?' Annika had retorted.

She put her hand over her eyes as she thought of how they were behaving towards each other. I've got to be happy some time, she thought. I've got to pull myself together. I'll find something to do, even if it doesn't involve me working. I'll get to know the neighbours and stop fantasizing about murdering Sophia Grenborg.

She got into the SUV and drove towards Vinterviks-vägen.

The house sat on its corner plot, shimmering in the morning sun. Her lovely house – her very own house.

She parked on the road so she could look at it from the outside, see it as other people saw it. In an area like this it was nothing special, but it had been built with the best materials and was well designed. The plot had once been a patch of common land, but the council had sold it off when it had needed extra money. There were no mature trees, which was a shame, but the previous owners had planted fruit trees and some small oaks, which would look good in a few years.

To the left of the house there was a small rockery. It lay in shadow most of the day, and Annika had wondered about trying to get hold of some plants that might thrive there. But the plot didn't offer much opportunity to commune with nature. In front of the house a small flowerbed wasn't doing much, but the real problem was the grass. It was rutted with wheel-tracks, from when the neighbours had used it as a shortcut while the house was empty. Annika had no idea how to put it right. Maybe some topsoil? Turf? Cover the whole lot with tarmac?

She switched off the ignition and got out of the SUV. They'd bought their new vehicles when the money had first arrived, and she was very fond of hers already.

'Good morning!'

Annika spun round to see a young woman jogging towards her. She had a dog running alongside her, shadowing her every move without a leash. The woman slowed and stopped beside her. She was wearing a sweatband and a padded jacket, and was sweating profusely.

'So you've moved in, then?' she said, with a smile.

Now Annika recognized her: she was the woman in the house diagonally across from them. The one she had met during the winter. 'Yes, we're in,' she said, smiling back, remembering her decision to get to know the neighbours.

'Welcome to the area. How do you like it so far?'

Annika laughed awkwardly. 'I don't really know yet. We haven't done much except unpack.'

'I know what you mean,' the woman said. 'I moved in five years ago and I'm still finding boxes I haven't opened yet. Why do we hang on to so much unnecessary stuff? If I haven't missed those things for the past five years, why on earth did I buy them in the first place?'

Annika couldn't help laughing. 'That's so true,' she said. What was the woman's name? Eva? Emma?

'Would you like to come over for a cup of tea?' the woman said. 'Or coffee? I only live—'

'I know,' Annika said. 'I remember. Coffee would be great, thanks.'

Ebba, that was it. Ebba Romanova. So there had to be something foreign in her background. And the dog's name was Italian. Annika bent over and patted him. 'Francesco, isn't it?' she said.

Ebba Romanova nodded and scratched the dog behind the ear. 'I just need to grab a shower,' she said. 'Give me fifteen minutes.' She jogged off down Vinterviksvägen and stopped at her gate, opened it, then was swallowed up by greenery.

Annika stood where she was, looking about her. In winter you could see parts of most of the neighbouring houses, but today they were all hidden by hedges and foliage. She could just make out the dark façade of Ebba's, with its veranda and summerhouse.

So, what am I going to do about the grass? she thought, as her eyes reached her own little plot.

'What do you think you're doing?'

She jumped.

A thickset man with a beer-belly and a cap was standing behind her, hands on his hips, staring at her antagonistically.

'What?' Annika said. 'What have I done?'

'You're blocking the traffic! No one can get past if you leave your tank in the middle of the road.'

Annika stared at her car in astonishment, parked by the verge, then looked up and down the empty road. 'But there's no ban on parking here,' she said.

The man took a few steps towards her, his impressive gut forcing him to walk with his legs far apart, feet turned out. His eyes were small and deep-set, his face dark red. '*Move the car!*' he snarled. 'There's no parking here. How much clearer do I have to make myself? *No parking!*'

'I'm sorry,' Annika said, blinking. 'I haven't seen any signs.'

'You're going to move your car because that's the way it's always been out here. It's an old tradition.' He clenched his fists a few times, flexing his fingers.

'Okay, okay.' She got into the car, turned the key and let it roll into her drive. 'Happy now?' she asked, as she got out again.

To her astonishment, the man was walking across her lawn. He was following the wheel-tracks, kicking at the ground, and vanished into the neighbouring plot.

The man in the Merc, Annika thought. Chairman of the villa-owners' association.

15

Ebba Romanova had changed into black jeans and a white blouse. She'd put on some mascara and pink lipstick. 'Come in,' she said, throwing the door open. 'You've met Wilhelm, then.'

'Did you see what he did?' Annika said. 'He walked right over my grass to get to his house.'

'I heard him,' Ebba said. 'He gets very upset if anyone parks on his road. He was born in that house and seems to think he owns the whole neighbourhood. And he's deeply racist against anyone who can't trace their roots back at least seven generations in Djursholm.'

Annika tried to laugh. 'So he can't stand you either?'

'Oh, he tolerates me because he's got it into his head that I must be related to the Russian royal family. I'm not. It was coffee, wasn't it? Sit yourself down while I get it.' She gestured towards a tall pair of double doors, then disappeared into the kitchen. Annika looked around the entrance hall. The house was enormous, the ceilings more than three metres high. The décor, as far as she could make out, wasn't far from the style of the Winter Palace in St Petersburg. All the furnishings were fine old antiques, and paintings in heavy frames adorned the walls.

The double doors led into a large library, and Annika stepped carefully on to a thick rug. The wall to her right was dominated by a vast open fireplace. She had only ever seen anything like it in old British films. The sofas were brown or deep red, with lots of cushions in various patterns and materials. The walls were covered with built-in bookcases, made from some exotic and probably now banned wood, filled with plenty of modern books. Her eyes fell on a copy of *Who Makes the Decisions About Your Life* by Åsa Nilsonne. It was good – she'd read it.

There were thrillers and some non-fiction in English, and one whole bookcase contained Russian novels, in Russian. Many were leather-bound. Annika traced a finger along the Cyrillic lettering on a spine.

'Milk or sugar?' Ebba called from the kitchen.

'A little milk, please,' Annika called back.

The room contained just one painting, a small, dark picture hanging in a glass cabinet on the far wall. Annika went over and peered at it. The paint looked old, with a barely noticeable tracery of fine cracks. The subject was a sombre young woman with a look of intense sadness in her eyes. She was gazing over her shoulder, right into the eyes of the observer. Her lips were slightly parted. She wasn't much more than a child.

'Who is she?' Annika asked, as Ebba came up behind her with a mug of coffee in each hand.

'Beatrice Cenci,' Ebba said, looking up at the picture. 'She was executed in Rome on the eleventh of September 1599. Beheaded.' She passed a mug to Annika. 'A bit of milk, no sugar . . .'

Annika accepted the coffee without taking her eyes off the girl's face. 'Thanks. What had she done?'

Ebba sat down on one of the sofas, pulling her feet

up under her. 'She killed her father. Pope Clement the Eighth condemned her to death. The painting's a real antique, and this is hardly the ideal environment to keep it in, but if you look carefully you'll see the cabinet has sensors and thermostats to maintain the temperature and humidity.'

'You've got a lovely house,' Annika said, sitting on the sofa opposite her. 'Do you live here on your own?'

Ebba blew on her coffee and took a cautious sip. 'Just with Francesco,' she said. 'Do you think the décor's vulgar?'

Annika almost choked on her coffee. 'Not at all, just . . . unusual. I've only ever seen rooms like this in films.'

Ebba smiled. 'A lot of the furniture's inherited,' she said. 'It belonged to my mother. She's dead now. Alzheimer's.'

'I'm sorry,' Annika mumbled. 'Was it recent?'

'Five years ago, just before I bought the house. She would have liked it. I got rich just before she died.'

Annika drank her coffee and didn't know what to say. Okay, you got rich, great. I got rich too. Was that the sort of thing you said over coffee out here in the suburbs?

'I sold my business,' Ebba went on. 'Or, rather, I got chucked out of a business that I helped set up. So I suddenly had a lot of money I wasn't expecting, at least not just then . . . But tell me, what do you spend your days doing? I understand you've got children.'

Annika put her mug on an elaborate marble-topped table. It felt odd to be sitting here like this. What a difference the move had made to the sort of neighbours she had.

'Two,' she said. 'Kalle and Ellen. Six and four. We'd lived in the city for years, but decided it made sense to move now, before the children start school. I'm a journalist, and my husband works in the Justice Department.' She fell silent, worried she was sounding arrogant. It was bad enough that Thomas was going around boasting to everyone he met about his lovely new job. 'What sort of business was it?' she asked quickly, to change the subject.

'A bio-tech company,' Ebba replied. 'I studied medicine, then got into research after graduation. While I was a postgraduate I discovered an entirely new type of adjuvant, a substance that improves the effect of vaccines, and when I combined it with something known as a vaccinia vector I got fantastic results. I already had the patent by the time I finished my doctorate.'

'Wow,' Annika said, unable to think of anything more intelligent to say.

'My fiancé was at the School of Economics at the time, and it was his idea to set up the business, ADVA Bio it was called, if you've ever heard of it.'

Annika shook her head.

'It was just when SARS was starting to spread, and the first people in South East Asia were getting bird flu, so anything to do with vaccines was really hot,' Ebba went on. 'My fiancé and a friend of his gave up their courses and started negotiating with various multinationals about the rights to the patent. The first offer was ten million dollars, and the second was fifty. Round about that time the boys realized they no longer needed me. I wasn't contributing anything substantial to the company, as they put it. By then it was valued at seventy-five million dollars, more than half a billion in Swedish kronor. They bought me out for a hundred and eighty-five million kronor.'

Annika had to lean back in the sofa. And she'd been

thinking she was rich. 'Were you happy to be bought out?' she asked.

Ebba gave a wry smile. 'I didn't really have much choice,' she said. 'But now, in retrospect, I'm not too upset about it. The week after I got my money my former partners flew to the USA to negotiate and agree terms with a multinational pharmaceutical company, Xarna. The first evening they drank so much champagne that my fiancé, or rather my ex-fiancé, fell asleep on a sofa in the company's R and D department. That wasn't the problem. The problem was that his partner didn't fall asleep, but sat chatting to the researchers and management, showing off about the patent and about how my discovery worked, until he'd pretty much explained how to get round it altogether. The next day they were shown the door, without a single penny.'

'Never!' Annika said.

Ebba shrugged lightly. 'The multinational went on to use an alternative method to achieve the same results as I had, which made ADVA Bio and my patent more or less worthless. ADVA Bio went bankrupt owing a quarter of a billion kronor.'

'Bloody hell,' Annika said.

'She who laughs last . . .' Ebba said, with a smile. 'More coffee?'

'Please.'

Ebba got up and took both mugs out to the kitchen.

Annika sat on the large sofa, with a faint buzzing in one ear. Why would you tell someone a story like that the first time you met them? And it wasn't the first time Ebba had told it, that much was obvious, but why so soon?

The whole chain of events must still be at the front of her mind, Annika decided. She must think about it

211

every day, an untreated trauma, rumbling away in her head the moment she relaxed. How important it is to have a context, a place where you belong.

Ebba came in with more coffee and a plate of fruit. There was a smile on her pink lips.

'What do you do these days?' Annika asked, when her hostess had sat on the sofa.

'I'm researching the signal pathways of cells,' Ebba said, taking an apple. 'I've donated fifteen million to Karolinska to fund a research project into the causes of Alzheimer's, with the condition that I lead the research. Our little team has been working for three years now.'

'Wow,' Annika said. 'Have you found anything yet?'

'Only that an imbalance occurs in the patient's brain,' Ebba said, biting into the apple. She chewed for a moment, then swallowed. 'For some reason there are too many hyperphosphorylated proteins in these patients' brains, which means that the proteins start to cluster together inside the cells, forming tangles, and that's one of the first stages of the illness. We're trying to find out what causes the imbalance, and how to slow it down or stop it.'

'It would be amazing if you could do that,' Annika said.

'Yes, it would,' Ebba said. 'Have you ever watched someone fade away with Alzheimer's? It's terrible. Mum spoke seven languages, as well as Russian, her mother tongue. She lost them all, along with her grasp of time, where she was, and everything else that makes a person who they are. I just hope we might be able to find one piece of the jigsaw that will eventually get rid of the disease.'

'That sounds quite a long way from what you were doing before,' Annika said.

'Not as far as you might think,' Ebba said. 'There's one theory that suggests Alzheimer's develops as a result of an inflammation. We know that the interleukins of the immune system are involved, and the signal pathways in the cells are the same . . .' She fell silent and looked away.

'Is Alzheimer's hereditary?' Annika asked.

'Only about five per cent. Most cases depend on something else. Obviously the goal is to find a vaccine to stop it developing at all, giving the body something that can help it prevent these proteins from clumping and so stop the imbalance in the first place.'

'Do you think you'll succeed?'

She shrugged her shoulders. 'Either we will, or someone else will. Whoever gets there first stands to make a fortune. There are two other research projects looking into this at the Karolinska Institute alone.'

'Private funding for specific research projects is becoming more and more common, isn't it?' Annika asked, realizing that Ebba hadn't answered her question about whether or not they'd found anything.

'It's very common,' Ebba said. 'A number of projects in my department alone are external commissions. We got the big one last winter, an American pharmaceutical company trying to develop a vaccine against a future superbug.'

'Your old territory, then?' Annika said.

Ebba dabbed at the corners of her mouth with a pale-blue napkin. Annika saw traces of lipstick on it.

'Yes,' Ebba said, 'in some ways. They're trying to understand the mechanisms governing the mutation of the virus in order to control it.'

'Medi-Tec,' Annika said.

Ebba raised her eyebrows. 'It's a huge company,

conducting research into a whole load of different areas. You know it?'

'I was at the press conference,' Annika said. 'The MD was there, inaugurating the project. He's a Swede.'

'Bernhard Thorell,' Ebba said.

'Quite young,' Annika said. 'Quite cute.'

'Quite unpleasant,' Ebba said. 'I don't know why but I don't trust him. Did you interview him at the press conference?'

Annika laughed rather sadly. 'I haven't interviewed anyone at all for the past six months. I've been frozen out at work, on leave with full pay. I've got a meeting with the editor-in-chief tomorrow. I'm expecting him to try to buy me out.'

Ebba tilted her head and looked at her thoughtfully. 'Do you want to give up your job?' she asked.

'I don't know,' Annika said, looking down at her hands. 'I've come into some money too, so I don't have to work, at least not at the moment, but I don't know.'

'Think carefully,' Ebba said, 'before you let yourself be bought out. It can be hard getting over the feeling that you're not needed.'

Yes, Annika thought. I've already worked that out. 'It would be nice to do something else for a while,' she said. 'Study, maybe, or set up my own business and start freelancing.'

'It's always good to have options,' Ebba said. 'Where do you work?'

I might as well put my cards on the table, Annika thought. Either she likes me or she doesn't. 'The *Evening Post*,' she said. 'I mainly do crime. Sometimes I get a bit of variety – celebrity stuff, political scandals, other types of violence. My most recent job was the Nobel banquet, which was a bit out of the ordinary.'

214

'That's where I recognize you from,' Ebba said. 'I always read the evening papers – I grew up with them. Mum used to love the tabloids because they were so disrespectful. She grew up with the newspaper *Pravda* – she got out of Russia when she was twenty.'

'How?' Annika asked.

'She fled over the border into Finnish Karelia. The guards shot at her, but she thought they were intentionally trying to miss her. That's what Mum was like, always thinking the best of people . . . Are you happy with your work?'

'Sometimes,' Annika replied truthfully.

'You've never thought of writing about the academic world?' Ebba said. 'About the research itself, of course, but there needs to be far more careful coverage of the actual institutions, their funding and their methods.'

'How do you mean?' Annika asked, her interest growing.

'Some people will do practically anything to get ahead,' Ebba said, her eyes darkening. 'They spy on other people, steal their results, publish their discoveries as their own. In some institutions it's got to the point where everyone locks all their material away the moment they leave the room.'

'That's astonishing,' Annika said.

'Not really,' Ebba said. 'There's so much at stake. Take that project we got last winter, for instance – three-quarters of a billion kronor but not a mention of it in the media.'

'I got the impression that it wasn't really such a lot of money in that context.'

'That's true,' Ebba said, 'and that's exactly what I mean. You could find plenty to write about if you took a closer look at the scientific establishment.'

'That's not a bad idea,' Annika said. 'I'll give it some thought.'

'Ask if you need help,' Ebba said, getting up from the sofa. 'I'm going into the lab this afternoon. Maybe you'd like to come and have a look round some time.'

Annika picked up her mug and got up. 'I'd like that,' she said. 'Thanks for the coffee.'

They went out into an enormous old-fashioned kitchen with huge cupboards on the walls and a huge table in the middle. 'Oh, let me,' Ebba said, taking Annika's mug and going to the dishwasher. She stopped halfway and turned back. 'Hang on,' she said, 'if you were at the Nobel banquet, does that mean you saw what happened?'

Annika rubbed her forehead. 'Caroline von Behring was looking at me when she died,' she said. 'I dream about her several times a week. It's starting to get a bit unpleasant.'

Anders Schyman was looking out across the newsroom. He preferred his modest new office to the huge old corner room with its view of the Russian Embassy. And this was the best part of all – access to the working environment, people coming and going, the blue glow of the computers during the dark nights. The only thing he missed was the guard in his hut beside the embassy gates.

The old man can't help but be happy, the editor-in-chief thought, as he watched the chairman, Herman Wennergren, stride across the newsroom.

'Well, it does feel rather a tight fit,' Wennergren said, as Schyman opened the door to his cubbyhole. He couldn't tell if the chairman was referring to the newsroom, Schyman's office or his own blazer.

'It's probably best if we go and sit in the cafeteria,' Schyman said. 'I don't have any extra chairs. But let me hang up your coat while we're here . . .'

'Hmm,' Wennergren said, handing it over. 'I understand that you haven't exactly been letting the grass grow here.' He looked as if he wasn't particularly pleased with the pace of change at the paper.

'We've started up experimental ventures with both television and radio,' Schyman said. 'And the website has been completely redesigned. We felt it was important to get everything working as quickly as possible, to give the board something to base its decisions on.' I'm using the royal 'we', he thought, and decided to carry on with it.

'So the pace of change is in no way an attempt to pre-empt the decision of the board?' Wennergren asked sourly. 'After all, it's much harder to say no to something that's already up and running.'

'I have to say,' Schyman took out a folder of designs and other documents, 'that the reorganization has gone much more smoothly than anyone could have guessed. Because every department was getting less space, including management, neither the union nor the employees' forum had any objections.'

'The Swedish mentality,' Wennergren said. 'As long as everyone goes without, it's fair.'

'Precisely,' Schyman said, stepping out of the room and leading the chairman to the right and down a narrow corridor. 'If I could just show you? The whole of Sport now fits into my old office.'

They stopped outside the open door to the editor-in-chief's former territory and the chairman craned his neck to look in. 'Remarkable,' he said, 'that you can squeeze so many computers into such a small space.'

'And it's working extremely well,' Schyman said, walking on. 'To the left here we've done away with all the private offices and installed the whole of the marketing department in the space. That's had some unexpected advantages, largely because Marketing and Advertising are cooperating much better.'

'What were these rooms used for before?'

'The dayshift reporters,' Schyman said. 'We've given them all laptops and are encouraging them to work from home as much as possible. They're all very happy.'

'Hmm,' Wennergren said. 'I believe in keeping your staff where you can see them.'

Spike came over from the news desk, looking like he wanted something. 'The Parliamentary Ombudsman's report into the security problems at the Nobel banquet is due out tomorrow,' he said. 'Who can we use to try to get hold of it today?'

Schyman was extremely annoyed at the interruption, and even more annoyed when he realized he couldn't hide it. 'Use whoever you like,' he said. 'It doesn't matter that much.'

'I've spoken to some of the lads on the online edition,' Spike said. 'They don't appear to know what or who the Parliamentary Ombudsman is.'

The editor-in-chief avoided Wennergren's gaze and wished Spike would just vanish. 'Sort it,' he said, then turned towards Wennergren. 'Over there,' he said, pointing, 'was where Entertainment used to be. Now we've squeezed in Planning and Advertising. You can't see the wages office from here – we've fitted it into the left-hand corner. We've rebuilt the staffroom as a television studio, and the stationery cupboard is now a control room. Basically, we've managed to fit our entire broadcast operation into space that was wasted before.'

Wennergren turned to him with a slightly strained look in his eyes. 'To be honest,' he said, 'I'm not really interested in questions of space. Why haven't we got an editor who can solve the problem with the ombudsman's report?'

Schyman wanted to clear his throat, but suppressed the urge. 'If I could just . . .' He held out his arm and showed the way to the newly built cafeteria, a small area beside the lift with a coffee-machine and an automatic sandwich dispenser. A few members of staff were sitting in one corner, talking into their mobiles. Schyman fetched coffee for the pair of them, and put the cups down on a rather unsteady table. He opened his folder of documents and contracts and leafed through them.

'At the moment I'm negotiating with several different commercial radio stations with a view to supplying radio news and possibly some talk-shows. The website has been designed so that everything we broadcast anywhere can also be put up on the Internet. There's a lot of potential for the future: television via broadband.'

Wennergren took off his glasses. 'But no editors with the sense to call the Parliamentary Ombudsman?'

'The digital television network will be integrated with the Internet,' Schyman said, pretending he hadn't heard Wennergren's comment. 'It's only a matter of time, and it's going to affect everyone in this business. How is the government going to tackle the complete freedom this gives anyone in this area? What does it mean for the various regulatory bodies? For taxes on advertising? There's a lot to consider. But what's unique about us is our basic approach, exploiting that previously untapped market in the media. In other words, tabloid news on television.'

The chairman of the board put his glasses back on and

reflected for a few seconds. 'In purely concrete terms,' he said, 'what are we talking about here? Live coverage of things like those American car-chases?'

'Car-chases, of course,' Schyman confirmed. 'In-depth personal interviews, hidden-camera footage of important people, scandals and accidents. Natural disasters and fires, children crying in every broadcast, politicians in hiding, love-rat celebrities. Revealing footage from behind the scenes at big events like the Eurovision Song Contest, of course. But I still maintain that the personal approach is the unique factor in our new venture. People speaking out, telling us their personal experiences of events, big and small.'

'I see,' Wennergren said, and sighed. 'I can already hear the objections of our proprietors. More gutter journalism isn't exactly what anyone wants right now.'

'No,' Schyman said. 'What they want is at least a hundred million to cover the financial disaster of our illustrious morning-paper stable-mate.'

'Perhaps,' the chairman said, 'you should choose your words with a little more care. As you can imagine, you're not exactly top of their list of favourite people at the moment.'

'That's been made abundantly clear,' Schyman said curtly, wishing his bitterness wasn't quite so obvious.

Wennergren took off his glasses once more and leaned forward. Schyman could see the pores on his nose. 'I understand,' he said, 'that you're annoyed with the individual who wrote the piece about TV Scandinavia. I've explained to the family that you didn't have much choice. If you'd said no she would just have taken the story somewhere else. At least we had a chance to steer the whole process of publication and claim the moral high ground.'

He leaned back, his blazer creaking as he did so. 'What's happened to her, anyway? I never see her name in the paper now.'

'She's on leave,' Schyman said, choosing not to mention such details as pay and conditions.

'Excellent,' Wennergren said, standing up. 'And is there reason to hope that this might become permanent?'

If Schyman hadn't known better, he could have sworn that Wennergren was smiling, but it must have been a trick of the light. Herman Wennergren never smiled.

'I'm going to deal with that,' Schyman said.

'And find someone who can call the Parliamentary Ombudsman,' Wennergren said.

16

Annika was peeling potatoes when she heard the outside door open and close. 'Hello,' she called, over her shoulder.

No answer.

She put the potato-peeler on the draining-board and listened. 'Thomas?' she said, a bit louder. 'Is that you?'

Still no answer.

She took a few steps towards the door, suddenly anxious. 'Who's there?' she said. 'Hello?'

The door to the cloakroom under the stairs was half open, and she heard coat-hangers rattling. Annika ran over and pulled the door open. Inside, a blonde woman was crouching to look for something on the floor. It took Annika a couple of seconds to realize it was Anne Snapphane. She laughed in relief. 'Bloody hell!' she said. 'You gave me a fright. What on earth are you doing?'

Anne looked up at her. 'Hello, country bumpkin. I thought I'd dig out those shoes you borrowed before I forget. Are they in here or the bedroom?'

'What – the stilettos?' Annika asked, surprised. 'But I gave them back to you when you were going to Crazy Horse.' It must have been more than six months ago, she thought. Back when Anne was still drinking.

Anne stopped. 'So you did,' she said. 'And both heels snapped that evening so I threw them away. Crazy Horse is a such a dump. Never go there!' She stood up and brushed off some invisible dust. 'Can I borrow these instead?' she asked, holding up Annika's new cowboy boots from NK.

Annika's smile faded. 'I haven't had a chance to wear them yet,' she said.

'Okay, forget it,' Anne said, dropping the boots on the floor.

'No, no, take them,' Annika said. 'I don't need them when I'm here all the time.'

Anne looked at her for a few seconds, then bent over and picked up the boots. 'That's really nice of you,' she said, with a smile. 'I have to change my clothes between lectures – I can't do one performance after another looking exactly the same. The media would start making fun of me.' She gazed admiringly at the boots. 'These really are very nice. It's so lucky we're the same size.'

'Do you want to stay for dinner?' Annika asked, going back to the sink. 'I'm doing steak with potato gratin and garlic bread.'

'You really haven't got the hang of the GI index, have you?' Anne said, walking round the open space that made up the ground floor of the house, kitchen, dining room and living room in one.

'Are you staying?' Annika asked again.

'No, thanks,' Anne said. 'I'm trying to eat a bit more healthily. I've got to lose weight. My agent wants to get some pictures done for new posters, and the camera puts five kilos on you.'

'How can it possibly do that?' Annika wondered, bringing out the food-processor to slice the potatoes. 'If that's true, there must be something wrong with the lens

– it's not reproducing the perspective properly or something. Can you pass me the cream?'

'It's so unfair,' Anne said. 'You're skinny even though you eat stuff like this every day. So, where's the man who's going to save us from terrorism?'

'Out on the battlefield, of course,' Annika said. 'I thought you were him just now . . . Where's Miranda? Is she at Mehmet's?'

Anne glanced round quickly, maybe to check the children weren't anywhere near, then moved close to Annika. 'You haven't heard anything from Sophia Grenborg?' she asked, in a low voice.

Annika stuffed the funnel full of potato on to the machine and switched it on. 'Why should I have done?' she yelled, over the noise.

'Maybe he's got someone else,' Anne shouted. 'Once they've started, they usually carry on.'

Strips of potato piled up in the processor. Annika switched it off and tipped the contents into an oven dish. The silence echoed as she seasoned it, scattered some chopped onion and garlic over it, covered it all with grated cheese and poured in the cream.

'I'm just worried you're going to get hurt again,' Anne said quietly. 'How are you getting on, anyway? You ought to get some therapy. Trust me, it works wonders. I've learned to see the world in a completely new way, I understand my old patterns of behaviour much better now. Can't you sit down for a moment? You haven't even told me what you think of my lecture.'

Annika rinsed her hands and dried them on a tea-towel, then went and sat on a sofa. 'I've only skimmed the new version,' she said. 'I know I promised, but this last week has been so crazy, with the kids starting at the new nursery.'

Anne threw up her hands in despair.

'I know,' Annika said, 'I promised and I will help you write it, but I didn't know you were going to be coming out here today.'

'But what do you think of what I *have* written?'

Annika felt distinctly uncomfortable. 'It's good,' she said, 'but it's very similar to the last one.'

'I knew it!' Anne said triumphantly. 'They're just moaning about nothing at that bloody agency!'

'But didn't they want you to do something completely new?' Annika said. 'So that you get more bookings? If that's the case, you might need to start again from scratch. Pick something else to talk about – you've got so many experiences to choose from.'

Anne stared at Annika. 'What do you mean, *more bookings*? You don't think I'm in demand?'

'Of course I do,' Annika said. 'That's not what I meant, but I thought the agency said—'

'Don't you start as well! It would be nice to have just *one* person on *my* side sometimes!'

'I'll come and see you next week and we can do it together,' Annika said. 'When are you free?'

Anne considered. 'I'm really busy next week,' she said. 'But maybe Tuesday afternoon would work.'

'Okay,' Annika said. 'I'll come round to yours. How are things otherwise? Do you like the flat?'

Anne looked up at the ceiling. 'There was a meeting of the residents' association yesterday evening,' she said. 'Wine, canapés, all that shit. We've got a new chairman, von Dummkopf from the third floor, who water-combs his hair and wears a silk cravat. Honestly, the people in that building are so up themselves it drives me mad. It must be almost as bad as out here.'

Annika's neck stiffened. 'I had coffee earlier with a

neighbour over the road,' she said. 'A girl the same age as us, who sold her biotech company for millions and millions and is now doing research into Alzheimer's at Karolinska.'

'Amazing!' Anne said. 'So you can sit there comparing your bank balances. It's terribly nice of you to let us guttersnipes from the city come and breathe some of your lovely fresh air.' She laughed raucously.

'I have to finish cooking,' Annika said, getting up.

'Have you got a bag?' Anne wondered, picking up the boots.

Annika pulled out a plastic one from a kitchen drawer.

'"Nordéns ICA, Djursholm",' Anne read. 'Whatever's happened, Anki? Have you abandoned the Co-op after all these years?'

Annika turned to face her friend, leaning back against the worktop and folding her arms. 'Why are you being so nasty?' she asked quietly, and Anne's laughter died away.

'Nasty?' Anne said, surprised. 'What do you mean? Come on, you've got to be honest in a decent friendship. That's something I say in my talks, about the importance of self-criticism and not always insisting on being the focus of attention.'

Annika could feel her face colouring. 'That's not what I meant,' she said. 'I would have loved to stay in the city, but this is better for the kids before they start school.'

'You should stand up for your decision,' Anne said. 'You weren't exactly forced to move to the place with the highest number of millionaires and the lowest council tax in the country. Did you really do this for someone else, or were you just satisfying your own needs?'

Annika opened her mouth to reply, but couldn't find any words.

At that moment the doorbell rang. 'Move that car!' a male voice shouted angrily outside. 'You're not allowed to park on the street. Is that so hard to understand?'

'Oh, no,' Annika said, horrified. 'Where did you leave it?'

'Outside the house. Why?'

'This road isn't a public car park!' Wilhelm Hopkins yelled. 'Open this door!'

'Please,' Annika said breathlessly, 'would you mind moving your car? That's our neighbour. He gets so angry if anyone blocks the road.'

'But I'm not blocking anything,' Anne said. 'I parked really close to the kerb.'

The bell went on ringing as the man kept his finger on it. Annika ran to the door and opened it.

Wilhelm Hopkins's solid bulk almost filled the doorway. 'If this carries on I shall phone the *police*!' he roared.

'It's my friend,' Annika said. 'She's just leaving.'

'Fucking hell,' Anne said, pushing past Annika and looking derisively at the man. 'How can you bear it out here?'

The bag containing Annika's new cowboy boots had caught on the door-handle and Anne tugged to free it, then marched off towards her car.

The man took two steps inside Annika's porch.

'I'm terribly sorry,' Annika said, backing away. 'That was my friend. She didn't know.'

'It's always people like you,' the man said, sounding hoarse. 'I know exactly what sort of person you are.'

Annika blinked. 'What?'

'You're the sort who moves here to *change* things. You want to *change* things, and we don't like that. We don't like it at all.' He stared at her for several long seconds.

Then he turned and walked across the ruined lawn towards his own house.

Subject: The Greatest Fear
To: Andrietta Ahlsell

How abandoned he is, how vulnerable! A decade before his death Alfred Nobel writes to Sofie Hess: *When one is left alone in the world at the age of fifty-four, and the only person to show one any friendliness is a paid servant, the darkest thoughts arise . . .*

His greatest fear is not death but the lonely walk towards it: lying forgotten on his deathbed.

And he worries about his funeral, and about what will happen after that. Above all, he doesn't want to be buried underground.

To his brother Robert he writes:*Even cremation seems to me to be too slow. I want to be dropped into hot sulphuric acid. Then the whole business would be over and done with in a minute or so . . .*

He has friends, of course, although they are often his employees. He has relatives, but they also work in his companies. Sofie Hess has married a riding-master, Kapy von Kapivar (and now both she and her husband write for more money).

He has two friends in England, Frederic Abel and James Dewar. They work in his British company and Alfred is generous; he pays them well.

But then he is informed of a new patent, someone in England has registered a discovery that is exactly the same as his own *ballistite*.

Someone has stolen his work.

Frederic Abel and James Dewar.

Alfred refuses to believe it's true. He refuses! And he refuses to use the law against them, against his friends, but he has no choice. The lawsuit grinds on for years, and in the end Alfred loses.

By then he has just a year or so to live.

On 7 December 1896 he is sitting at his desk in his villa in San Remo in Italy writing letters, always writing letters. He is commenting upon a shipment of powder samples from Bofors, *they are particularly beautiful*, and that's when it happens. He slumps down, just slumps.

None of his friends is close at hand, none of his relatives, his colleagues. The servants carry him up to the bedroom; an Italian doctor diagnoses a massive stroke.

Alfred tries to talk. He talks to his valet but his memory is damaged. He, the cosmopolitan gentleman who could communicate fluently in Russian, French, English, German, can remember only the Swedish of his childhood.

He lives for another three days.

For three days he lies paralysed in his bed, trying to talk.

The staff understand one word, one single word – *telegram*.

So they send word to his colleagues in distant Sweden, but they don't get there in time.

And so he dies, at two o'clock on the morning of 10 December, exactly as he had feared: entirely alone, without anyone who was able to understand his last words.

Thursday, 27 May

17

The rain was tipping down. Annika was caught under a cycle shed in the nursery playground, staring out at the sheet of water surrounding her. The car was parked on the road, ten metres away, and there was a whole ocean between them.

I can't do it, she thought. I can't go on like this.

Her chest ached non-stop, wearing away at her. She tried to take a deep breath, and raised a hand to massage away the pressure.

The children were safe and dry, sitting in circles for Assembly; there were people to look after them; there were children the same age who wanted to be with them.

I can't stand here like this any longer, she thought. Everyone will be looking at me, wondering what's wrong with me, standing here snivelling: what effect will it have on the children? Look at that funny lady under the cycle shed. Is that Kalle and Ellen's mum? Kalle, why's your mum so weird? Why's she standing there, Ellen? Hasn't she got a job?

Oh, yes, Annika thought. She's got a job but she's not allowed to do it because they don't want her there.

Suddenly it was too much effort even to stand up. She

slumped on to the cycle-rack. The rain was bouncing off the ground, splashing her.

Moving house had kept her going, but now that was done and life had taken over: routine, waiting, patience, basic maintenance. She stared out at the rain.

I've got to find something to do, she thought. I've got to have some sort of meaning in my life.

What about the children?

She started, taken aback by how self-centred she could be.

I have responsibilities, she thought. Everything depends on me. I have to cope.

There was a buzzing sound from her bag: a text message.

She dug out her mobile, pressed *read*: *Hi Annika! Is it raining where you are? Hope the move went well. Coffee next week? 'Wet & Lonely'* x

The warmth spread from her stomach through her whole body, easing the burden on her chest a little.

Bosse.

She couldn't help laughing. He never gave up, never lost touch. No matter how far out in the cold she was, he didn't care. Her colleagues on the paper never got in touch, apart from Berit, and Jansson very occasionally, but one of their rival reporters cared about how she was.

Maybe, she texted back. *Seeing the Big One today, don't know what he wants. Might have all the time in the world . . . 'It's never too late to give up'* x

She dropped the phone back into her bag and she hoisted it on to her shoulder. She stood up, steeled herself and made a dash for the car.

Her mobile rang as she was searching for her keys. It rang and rang as the rain found its way under her collar and down her neck.

'Hello?' she yelled, trying to unlock the car while holding the phone and balancing her bag on her knee.

'Are you standing in the middle of Niagara Falls?' Q asked.

The car's lights flashed as the central locking clicked. Annika managed to get the driver's door open, but dropped her bag on the ground, spilling the contents.

'Fucking shit,' she said, trying to hold back the emotion from her voice.

'Nice to hear your voice as well,' Q said. 'I've got a picture I'd like to show you.'

Annika leaned down to pick up her Filofax, wallet, lip-balm, a pack of painkillers and half a pack of tampons from the puddle they were lying in. 'I didn't know you'd taken up painting,' she said, throwing her soaking bag on to the passenger seat. And to think she had promised herself she would never let the inside of the car get dirty.

'It's a man,' Q said. 'I'd like you to take a look at him, see if you recognize him.'

She settled into the driver's seat, shut the door and took a deep breath. 'God, this rain.'

'It's not raining in this part of Kungsholmen,' Q said. 'In fact, it never rains anywhere on Kungsholmen. How soon can you get here?'

The traffic ought to have eased a bit by now, but the rain was slowing it. There's no point in getting worked up, she thought. You'll only get stressed and die of a heart-attack. She tuned the radio and thought about Bosse.

She didn't have to be at the paper until the afternoon. Anders Schyman had sent her an email saying he wanted to see her at three o'clock. The very thought of the meeting made her stomach churn. Well, if he wants to buy me out, he'd better have his biggest cheque-book handy, she thought. She tried to think rationally, in terms of the numbers: how much was she willing to sell her job for? For what amount would she be prepared to walk away from something she had put so much time and effort into?

Ebba Romanova had got 185 million kronor. And even that didn't seem to have bought her peace of mind. You probably couldn't sell the things that gave your life meaning.

God, she thought, roll on three o'clock so we can get it over with.

Suddenly she remembered something an American multimillionaire had said on television a week or so before: *Those who say you can't buy happiness don't know where to shop.*

The car in front of her rolled forward two metres.

'Bloody hell, you're soaked,' Q said, as she walked into his office. 'So, have you moved out to the suburbs?'

'The closest parking space was on Pipersgatan,' Annika said. 'There must have been some serious climatic change on Kungsholmen after we spoke.'

Q looked out at the rain running down the window-pane. 'Look at that,' he said. 'Go and dry yourself off. You're ruining my Persian rugs.'

'Where's the picture?' Annika said, sinking into an armchair.

Q handed her a photograph of a man of about twenty-five standing in front of a yacht. His dark hair was ruffled by the wind; he had bright blue eyes, a suntan and a smile. She stifled an impulse to smile back at him.

'Cute,' she said. 'What about him?'

'Do you recognize him?'

She studied the photograph carefully. It showed only

his top half, which made it hard to judge his height and bearing. 'Don't know,' she said. 'I don't think so.'

She screwed up her eyes and held the picture closer. Had she seen him somewhere? Was there something familiar about him? Would she remember him if she bumped into him? She put the picture in her lap. 'I suppose it's something to do with the Nobel banquet?' she asked.

Q sighed. 'Great, we've got to *Twenty Questions* already,' he said. 'Can you think of where you might have seen this lad?'

Annika picked it up again. 'No,' she said, after a long minute. 'No, I've never seen him before.' She put the photo on the desk. 'Sorry,' she said. 'He's dead, isn't he?'

'Frozen to death,' Q said, picking the picture up. 'He was found dead in a freeze-room in one of the Karolinska Institute's lab buildings on Monday morning.'

A shiver ran down Annika's spine. Frozen to death? 'How is that possible?' she said.

'We don't know,' Q said, putting the photograph in a desk drawer. 'There's no indication of any crime, so we haven't begun an official preliminary investigation yet. The door was unlocked and the emergency release was in working order.'

'So how could something like that happen?' Annika said. 'How cold was it? How long was he shut in there? Why couldn't he get out?' She paused. 'He's something to do with Nobel, isn't he? How?'

'Time's up,' Q said, standing. 'Well, we'd like to thank you for taking part in *Twenty Questions*. Thanks so much for coming.'

Annika left large puddles of water on the floor and the chair. 'What's his name?' she said.

'Johan Isaksson,' Q said.

Johan Isaksson. His whole life ahead of him.

'Hang on,' Annika said. 'He must have been a student or researcher out at Karolinska, seeing as you don't think it's odd that he was found in that freeze-room. So either he won a ticket in the lottery for students, or he was a steward . . .'

She studied the expression on Q's face. 'A steward,' she said. 'He worked at the banquet. You think he was involved somehow. Could he have been the contact on the inside? The one who sent that text message, *dancing close to St Erik*? What makes you think that? What had he done that makes you think he was involved?'

Q sighed. 'He may not have been involved. It's not certain he knew what the information was going to be used for.'

'So he started behaving strangely after the killings?' Annika said. 'Guilty, irrational? The other students hardly recognized him? And you'll have checked all the texts and calls and God knows what from loads of innocent people for months to see if you can find some sort of link between the inside contact and the Kitten, but presumably you haven't found anything. Which is why you're wondering if I saw them together.'

'The lad was always a straight-A student,' Q said. 'But after the attack he started to neglect his research. The post-mortem indicates that he'd consumed a number of different things before he died, and he must have screamed like a lunatic – his vocal cords were in tatters. No crime suspected, though.'

Annika stared at Q. 'The Kitten?' she said.

'No one knows if she works like this,' Q said.

'How does she normally work?'

Q looked at her, suddenly seeming very tired. 'You've

been off work too long,' he said. 'You're not really tuned into this, are you?'

'Come on,' Annika said.

'All we know is that she shot two men in Jurmala in Latvia four days after the Nobel banquet, a doctor and an American, a former marine.' He looked carefully at her for a few seconds. 'And how do we know that?'

Annika's mind was racing. 'The gun,' she said. 'The bullets and the gun were the same, and the fingerprints from the shoe you found on the steps. You found her fingerprints at the crime scene in Latvia.'

'Almost right,' Q said. 'Our Latvian colleagues found them. They were all over the house. Have you got any theory about why?'

'Why she shot them, or why she was so careless? Something went wrong. You said one of the victims was a doctor? She was wounded somehow.'

'A bucket of hardened plaster-of-paris was found by the bodies,' Q said. 'Well, if you'll excuse me, I think it's time to bring in the next contestant.'

Annika stopped in the doorway. 'How much of this can I write?' she asked.

'I thought you were in quarantine.'

'If I'm lucky, I'll be let back into the fold today,' she said. Or thrown out head first.

'I'll tell you when it's time,' he said. 'We've got to smoke out the Kitten's client.'

'What do you know about him?' Annika said, hoisting her sodden bag on to her shoulder. 'Apart from the fact that he's got access to a great deal of money.'

'If it is a he,' Q said, shutting the door in her face.

She got out of the lift, stepped into the newsroom and a whole new world.

The news desk was gone, as was Sport, and the coffee room contained three television cameras, its walls now covered with blue sheets.

She stopped for a moment to get her bearings, unsure of where to go. Berit had told her about the changes, but Annika hadn't grasped how comprehensive they were. Across the sea of unknown faces she could just make out the news desk where the opinion-piece desk used to be. Entertainment and Culture sat next to each other where IT support had once been. A new world, a new age.

I hope Schyman knows what he's doing, she thought, as she headed for her office on the far side of the news-room.

The curtains were gone, the sagging beige drapes that had always hung in her room. Now the glass walls were covered with the same blue sheets as the walls of the cafeteria. Above the door there was a flashing sign with the words *on air*, and she paused for a few seconds before opening the door and going in.

Where her desk used to be there was now a large mixing desk with hundreds of controls and flashing lights. A girl with a ring in her nose and enormous headphones was perched on top of a bar stool speaking into a large microphone as she adjusted the controls. She gave Annika a completely blank look as she talked about a traffic accident on the Essinge motorway.

Annika was frozen to the spot, as the girl ended her report, then slid one of the controls. A Madonna track started to play.

'What are you doing here?' Annika said to the girl.

'What do you mean?' the girl said, pulling off the headset. 'I'm doing a live programme. What do you want?'

'This used to be my room,' Annika said.

'Back in the dark ages, you mean?' She put the headset back on, turned away and started to type into a computer. Annika took a step forwards and saw a list of hit songs flash past on the screen. She walked out of the room and closed the door carefully behind her.

Berit was sitting by what had been the stationery store working on a laptop. Annika recognized her old bookcase and the filing cabinet containing court reports and other background material. 'So they let you keep your furniture?' she said, and Berit looked up over her reading glasses.

'Annika!' she exclaimed, taking off her glasses. 'How lovely! Are you back for good?'

'Don't know,' Annika said, pulling over a chair. 'I'm seeing Schyman at three o'clock.' She looked round as she sat down. 'God, this place really has changed,' she said. 'There's a girl talking on the radio in my old room.'

Berit sighed. 'Just be grateful you missed the whole circus,' she said. 'It's been so chaotic that I just wanted to go home and hide. But things seem to have settled down, at least in terms of the move.'

'What happened to the crime desk?' Annika asked, craning her neck to look at where Berit's desk used to be.

'The online edition is based there now,' Berit said. 'And Crime is just me and Patrik now, of course. That's his chair you're sitting on. This is where we hang out, but we're allowed to work from home as much as we want.'

'That sounds good,' Annika said, then pointed at Berit's desk. 'Nice new laptop as well.'

'Oh, yes,' Berit said. 'So we don't have to drag ourselves

in to work, and the paper doesn't have to provide space for us all. How are things with you?'

'Not great, to be honest,' Annika said, her shoulders slumping. 'I'm worried about what Schyman's going to say. I don't want to be kicked out. You can't just sell your lifelong ambitions, no matter how much money's on offer. I need something to do with my time.'

Berit looked at her thoughtfully. 'It's normally possible to have a proper conversation with Anders Schyman,' she said. 'Don't back down! And, remember, you don't have to give him an answer to anything he suggests there and then. Go home and think about it, whatever he's offering.'

Annika nodded, suddenly on the verge of crying again. 'Sod it,' she said, forcing the tears away. 'What are you up to? Have you got anything good in the works?'

Berit arched her back and picked up several printouts. 'Oh, yes. Wait till you hear this,' she said. 'Are you okay for time?'

'I'm free until fourteen fifty-nine,' Annika said.

'Bandhagen,' Berit said. 'I've been to see the woman and the girls several times, and this story just keeps getting weirder.'

The block of flats in the darkness, the overexposed film, shadows in the windows, police in riot gear, Annika remembered. 'Is the father still missing?

'Jemal's being held in a prison just outside Amman,' Berit said. 'There was a hypothetical connection between the family and the Nobel killings, but it's absurdly tenuous. Here.' Berit put her glasses on and leafed through her papers. 'Do you remember Neue Jihad?'

'The guys who went missing in Berlin,' Annika said.

'Exactly. The mother of the family in Bandhagen, Fatima Ahmed, is the cousin of the youngest lad. Five

242

years ago, when the boy was fourteen, he was here on holiday for three weeks, staying with the Ahmeds.' Berit waved a sheet of paper. 'This is a copy of the visa application from when the family invited the boy to visit Sweden. Non-Europeans often have to prove they have somewhere to stay. This is the only official paperwork anywhere in Europe that connects them, so it must be behind the raid on the flat.'

She put the document down and picked up another. 'This is a letter saying that Jemal's temporary residence permit to stay in Sweden has expired and won't be renewed.'

'Can they just decide something like that?' Annika asked. 'Without really looking into it? Surely the decision can be appealed against.'

'Good questions. No answers,' Berit said.

'And what about his wife and the girls? Are they being chucked out as well?'

'Fatima and Dilan, the older daughter, have permanent residency so they're safe. The younger girl, Sabrina, is a Swedish citizen because she was born here.'

'So why can't the father have permanent residency?'

'A pure technicality,' Berit said. 'To get a permanent residence permit you mustn't be away from Sweden for more than ten months if you're intending to stay. Jemal has spent time in Jordan helping his elderly parents – they've got a small farm outside somewhere called al-Azraq ash Shamali. On one occasion he was gone for fourteen months, although that was several years ago. He was at the front of the queue to get a permanent residence permit, and would have got it at the beginning of this year if he hadn't been arrested and thrown out.'

'But why is he in prison?' Annika said. 'No one

243

actually believes any of that stuff about Neue Jihad any more, do they?'

'Don't be too sure,' Berit said. 'Over the past six months I haven't heard a whisper about any other theory.'

'But the police didn't believe in Neue Jihad,' Annika said. She moved her chair closer to Berit's desk and leaned forward. 'This is how it is,' she said. 'The woman who shot Wiesel, von Behring and the security guards on the quayside is an American assassin known as the Kitten. She got away on a motorbike on the footpaths along the edge of Lake Mälaren, and to Latvia by boat. Her accomplice in the boat that she escaped from the City Hall in was probably a former American marine.'

Berit's eyes were wide.

'The Kitten's very good, and very expensive,' Annika said. 'Whoever hired her has access to a lot of money.'

'But she must have made mistakes,' Berit said, 'or you wouldn't know any of this.'

'She's made several,' Annika murmured. 'First she dropped one of her shoes on the steps down to the water, with her fingerprints on it. Then something must have gone wrong while she was making her getaway. She must have broken her leg or something, because she was patched up by a doctor in Jurmala outside Riga. After that she shot and killed the doctor and her accomplice.'

'Cinderella of Death,' Berit said.

Annika smiled.

'How the hell have they managed to keep this quiet?' Berit wondered. 'And why has Q told you?'

'National Crime and the Security Police have been collaborating with several different police and security forces abroad on this,' Annika said, 'so the pressure to keep it quiet has been greater than their desire to let any of the details leak out. Telling me was evidently a big deal so I haven't said a word in six months. I wouldn't have done that if he'd left me to dig out the details one by one.'

'But now you're telling me . . .'

'My loyalty has been with the investigation,' Annika said, 'and Q knew that. But now I don't know what the hell's happening. I don't know if I'm still going to have a job in a few hours' time. If I keep it, it's time for me to write something. And if I get the sack, I'll happily hand it all over to you.'

'Thanks a lot,' Berit said, suddenly sounding rather weary. She sat back and pinched the bridge of her nose. 'How confident are the police about this?' she asked. 'Are they sitting there guessing, or is this all based on facts?'

'Witness statements,' Annika said. 'They've got finger-prints, they've got international support from police authorities abroad, and there's the whole business of the mobile phones. They've been checking text messages, numbers used to call other numbers . . .'

'We could spend a long time talking about that,' Berit said, reaching for another folder. 'Telephone surveillance and bugging are particularly interesting aspects of the Justice Department's new legislation.'

'Guess what my husband thinks about that,' Annika said.

'Listen,' Berit said, reading from one file. '*The meaning of the term "involvement" shall be understood in a broader sense than merely referring to those suspected of actions punishable by law. This means that a person need not be a presumed culprit in order for him or her to be regarded as likely to commit a crime. It can thus be deemed sufficient grounds if a person is objectively*

245

thought likely to promote a future criminal act.' She let the paper fall to her lap.

'And that means?' Annika asked.

'In future it will be possible to break terrorism laws without doing anything at all,' Berit said. 'Planning or preparing to commit a crime is already against the law, but from now on it will be possible to convict someone of terrorism simply because they might be suspected of planning a crime at some future date.'

'But that's completely mad,' Annika said. Was this what Thomas did all the time he was at work?

'It's nothing but superstition,' Berit said. 'The Security Police can sit and listen in to see if people are thinking bad thoughts, or if they might possibly – and *entirely* objectively, of course – be capable of thinking bad thoughts in the future.'

'But maybe that's necessary,' Annika said weakly, in an attempt to defend the people making the decisions. 'Maybe that has to be done to protect democracy.'

'Democracy?' Berit said. 'What are the actual threats against democracy?'

'Well,' Annika said, 'terrorism, from al-Qaeda. They want to bring down democracy . . .'

'Really?' Berit said. 'They've said that the attacks were revenge for the American military presence in the Middle East, for the USA's various wars, a million or so dead Iraqis and not least their hard-nosed support for Israel's policy of occupation. They picked targets that represented the USA's supreme global financial and military power: the Pentagon and the World Trade Center.'

'But their real motivation was hatred of Western democracy and the liberated status of Western women,' Annika suggested.

'So, now democracy has to be defended by placing

246

restrictions on it?' Berit said. 'You see how stupid that sounds?'

'Why haven't you written anything about this in the paper?' Annika asked.

Berit sat for a few moments without saying anything. 'I've tried,' she said eventually. 'The article was rejected. It was biased, apparently.' She stood up. 'Okay,' she said, 'let's go and get some lunch. At least the canteen is still there, and the food hasn't changed. They've been warming up the same dishes since you . . .' Berit let the sentence die away, embarrassed.

'Since I left?' Annika said, with a smile. 'You don't have to worry. I've made my decision so I don't have to wait for the axe to fall.'

'I still think you should hold out for as much money as you can,' Berit said.

Annika clutched the strap of her bag tighter.

The Kitten unlocked the front door of her apartment, then stopped and listened for a few seconds to the sounds around her: the roar of the motorway in the distance, the beep from a reversing lorry, some kids laughing and playing in the pool.

Everything normal.

She pulled the door open and stepped on to the marble floor.

This place was one of her favourites.

She sighed with contentment, and let her little cabin bag fall to the floor.

The apartment was completely white. White marble floor, white walls, white south-facing terrace with the Mediterranean as a backdrop. The furniture was white or pale beige. She liked to relax properly when she wasn't working.

The apartment was one of four she owned through various companies along the Spanish coast. When she wasn't away working or planning jobs she moved around between them. Three times a year she let an agency rent them so the neighbours would be confused about who owned them and unwilling to get to know her better. Not that anyone had ever shown any sign of wanting to get to know her.

The Costa del Sol could have been made to fit her requirements.

People from all round the world gathered in the little port of Puerto Banús and along the narrow streets around Orange Square in Marbella, so she never had to worry about fitting in. She could come and go between her apartments without anyone paying her any attention at all. Tens of thousands of apartments along the coast stood empty for months at a time until their wealthy northern European owners deigned to show up for a bit of sun and golf. In newly built complexes like this one, no one kept an eye on who was doing what.

She posed as an insurance broker, which her research had shown to be the most suitable job as far as the neighbours were concerned. Everyone backed away quickly on the few occasions when she mentioned what she did, terrified that she was going to try to sell them insurance they didn't need.

Another advantage of the area was its location, and that it was so well connected. Málaga was a small regional airport with direct flights to all the major cities in the northern hemisphere. She was half an hour by boat from North Africa (on clear days she could see the Atlas Mountains from her bedroom window), two hours by car from Portugal, and three-quarters of an hour from Gibraltar.

She almost never felt homesick. Her mother was always nagging at her to come home for turkey at Thanksgiving, but she avoided the USA as much as she could. Passport controls with fingerprints and photographs were out of the question now, of course, and not just since she had dropped that shoe up at the North Pole. For years she had made her way in and out of her home country by water, usually from Toronto, across Lake Ontario to the forests outside Buffalo. From there it wasn't too far to her mother's family estate outside Boston.

She knew she was a source of constant disappointment to her mother, but that was something the old woman would have to live with. Her brother and sister were very well behaved, after all: her brother was a brain surgeon and her little sister an opera singer. An opera singer! Whose idea of a fucking career was that? The Kitten snorted.

Leaving her cabin bag on the hall floor, she went to open the electric blind in the bedroom. It was such a relief to get away from the North Pole at last. Hardly surprising that so many Scandinavians turn up down here every winter, she thought.

She went out on to the bedroom terrace, happy with the decision she had made on the way back: never again. No more jobs up there among the icebergs. Her client had been a real loser anyway, and she didn't want to work for people like that. It could be dangerous, even though only her agent had any idea of who she was and how to get hold of her.

She admired the view, enjoying the deep blue sky, breathing in the scent of eucalyptus and gardenia. The bright pink bougainvillaea was tumbling over the terrace railings, and the jacaranda had started to shed its lilac blossom across the tennis courts.

She sighed contentedly. It felt good to be able to take a bit of a break.

Humming to herself, she went back to the hall and took her laptop out of the bag, started it up and logged into the Happy Housewives chat-room.

Her whole body froze when she saw that her agent had left a message.

For fuck's sake, don't say something else has gone wrong.

But it hadn't.

The client was happy and had another job for her.

She laughed. Typical. Once someone got a taste for her work, it was easy to get addicted. Which was good for her, of course, but not this time.

Never in hell, she said, and logged out.

She was a pro, and if anything ever went wrong during any of her jobs, then of course she tidied up after her, there was no question about that. Like Yappy in the freezer, for instance. An incredibly dull little job, but very neatly done now that she could look back on it. She'd given the lad time to reflect upon his sins and feel a bit of remorse, while still making it look like an unfortunate accident.

The Kitten pulled off her shoes and stepped out into the sun.

The loser would have to find someone else. Or why not take responsibility and manage without outside help?

18

Annika was clutching her bag so tightly that the strap was sweaty. Even though she'd made her decision, she wasn't looking forward to this meeting.

She couldn't leave her fate in the hands of a powerful editor-in-chief, who was governed by a dictatorial capitalist board. She had to decide for herself what she wanted to spend her time doing, and that would take time. The children came first, of course, and Thomas. She wasn't very good at looking after any of them, but she needed more than the house and the garden. She had to find something to get properly involved in.

And it was stupid to turn money down. There was no reason for her to leave the *Evening Post* without a seriously good redundancy package.

At least two years' pay, she thought. Ideally three. And I want to keep my computer.

That would hardly be a problem: her PC was ancient.

At last the editor-in-chief opened the door to his little room behind the culture desk. 'Come in,' Schyman said. 'It's a bit of a squeeze but you can have my chair. I'll sit on the desk.' He shut the door. 'What do you think?' he said, trying to sound light-hearted. 'A lot of changes, eh?'

'It's hard to believe it's the same place,' Annika muttered, her mouth completely dry.

'Would you like something to drink? Coffee, water?'

'No, thanks. I'm fine.' She sank on to his chair.

The editor-in-chief settled on top of some printouts spread out over his desk, put his hands into his lap and looked at her.

'I've been doing some thinking,' Annika said, taking a deep breath. 'I've been doing an awful lot of thinking. About my job, about my future here at the paper, about what I can imagine doing in the future.'

Schyman made himself more comfortable on the desk and looked curiously at her. 'I see,' he said. 'And what conclusions have you reached?'

'You have to be careful what you do with your ambitions,' Annika said. 'I don't think you can put a price on them. I've got a neighbour who . . .' She fell silent, biting her lip. 'My job is incredibly import- ant to me,' she said. 'Maybe not the fact of being employed, really, but what I do with my time. What I spend my time getting involved with, that's important, and to do it you need money, and if you haven't got a job . . .'

She cleared her throat, as Schyman gazed at her, his brow furrowed.

'What I mean,' she said, 'is that money is really just money, but at the same time we all have to live, and money is extremely important when it comes to how you live. And people are prepared to do pretty much anything for money.'

The editor-in-chief nodded thoughtfully. 'That's true enough,' he said.

'It's not that I've turned into some ridiculous materialist,' she said, 'it's not that at all, but I can't ignore the symbolic significance of money, and what it, in spite of everything, represents.'

He frowned as though he weren't quite following her.

'That's what I wanted to say,' she said quietly.

'Have you had any contact with the team investigating the Nobel killings?' he asked.

Annika blinked, taken aback. 'Er, yes,' she said. 'Why?'

'How come they're just treading water? Nothing's happening! Haven't they learned anything from the Palme case?'

'I get the impression they're still working,' Annika said, 'but for once they've managed to plug all the holes. Nothing's leaking at all.'

'I've been thinking a lot about proper journalism recently,' Schyman said. 'Serious digging, the sort of thing you usually do. Knowing how to get hold of a report from the Parliamentary Ombudsman a day early, for instance. That sort of knowledge is on the verge of dying out on this paper.'

Annika was bewildered. 'What report do you mean? The one looking into security at the Nobel banquet?'

'It's time you came back and started work again,' Schyman said. 'What do you think? Would that be possible, or is your information about the killer still too sensitive?'

Annika's head was blank. Come back? 'How . . . how do you see it, then?' she said.

Schyman got up and went over to his bookcase. 'I suggest that you come back to work from the first of June,' he said, leaning over and searching in the bottom drawer of one of his cupboards. 'That's next Tuesday. How does that suit you?'

She stared at her boss, feeling her own arguments

tumbling around her. Come back and start working as if nothing had happened? As if she hadn't been left out in the cold for six months, excluded from any sense of group identity, stripped of her place in the world?

'Yes, sure,' she heard herself say. 'Tuesday will be fine.'

Schyman straightened up and turned round, his nose red, his hair untidy. 'Here it is,' he said, putting a bag containing a new laptop on the desk. 'You're one of the dayshift reporters from now on. You choose your hours and your workplace, but you have to be at the disposal of the news desk. You can't just head off round the world without us knowing where you are and what you're doing.'

'Okay,' Annika said, reaching for the computer. It was just like Berit's.

'If you want to sit and work up here, there are desks behind the op-ed section, which are available to the day-shift reporters, for the time being at least. We'll have to see how much they get used.' He pointed to the computer. 'It would be a good idea if you could check that the installations have worked. These new machines have had teething problems . . .'

Annika pressed the on button and the laptop whirred into life, pre-programmed with her as its user.

Schyman sat on the desk again. 'Then I'd like an up-date on the Nobel story,' he said. 'You said you were still in touch with the investigators. Have you heard any-thing else? Anything we could publish?'

Annika's fingers slid over the keyboard. 'I'll have to see,' she said, glancing up at her boss with a smile. 'I can take a look and see what I've got hidden away.'

He stood in front of her awkwardly. 'I've been really pushing ahead recently,' he said. 'It's had more of an impact on the actual content of the paper than I imagined. Sometimes . . .' He stopped and turned away.

'What?' Annika said.

He stood still for a few seconds, as if he were wondering whether or not to go on. 'Sometimes I get the feeling that we've managed to lose the paper's soul along the way,' he said. 'That we're developing all these new outlets, but have forgotten why.'

'I'll go and check that the laptop's working,' she said.

She went out to the temporary desks behind the op-ed section and tried to log into the paper's wireless network. After a few seconds the *Evening Post*'s homepage appeared on the screen. It worked.

She settled on a dusty office chair, exhausted by a build-up of tension she had hardly been aware of. Belonging. A place to be. As early as next Tuesday . . . I should have made up my mind to fight, she thought. How could I ever have considered giving up what I've got, selling everything I've achieved?

She stretched her back, then tapped experimentally at the keyboard. She went on to Google, the site flashing up in an instant. What a great computer, especially compared to her old wreck at home. She wondered what to look up. 'Caroline von Behring', *search*. 17,100 hits, far more than when she was alive. As a powerful, living person you weren't very interesting, Annika thought. As a dead murder victim you're fascinating.

Most of the results were reports in various papers, but there were other, more recent, items. Women's groups and various research set-ups had posted pages in memory of Caroline, and the Nobel Committee had a section of its own devoted to her work. There was also a discussion group, but you needed authorization and a password to get into that.

Annika went on, typed 'Nobel Committee', *search*.

10,800 hits, most of them news-related. 'Nobel Committee Stirs Up Hornet's Nest', ran one headline, referring to the decision of the Norwegian Nobel Committee to award the Peace Prize to a UN organization, the International Atomic Energy Agency, a couple of years ago.

Her eyes were drawn to another hit further down the list. It came from a discussion group, written by someone calling themselves 'Peter No-Tail'. 'Today I found out the truth about the decision to appoint Professor Ernst Ericsson as chair of the Karolinska Institute's Nobel Committee after von Behring: there was a huge bust-up!' Annika read. 'One group thought it was obvious that the vice chair, Sören Hammarsten, should take over, while another thought that Ernst should carry on von Behring's work. We know what happened. Ernst won and now we're waiting for the follow-up. Clash of the titans . . .'

Those men at the press conference, Annika thought. So, there's trouble at the top. And who was Peter No-Tail?

Typed 'Peter No-Tail', *search*.

73,600 hits.

'Peter No-Tail' and 'Nobel', *search*.

392 hits, among them a site about children's books. She scrolled down the list but found nothing to tell her who Peter was.

Typed 'Alfred Nobel', *search*.

Almost 1.5 million hits. She picked one of the first, and clicked on a link in the left-hand column to reach an archive of articles about the inventor. There were facts about his early years (impoverished), his education (private tutors), his inventions (numerous, dangerous and ingenious). And there was one article about his love of literature and feeble efforts in that field. Alfred Nobel had written a stage-play, the story of a young girl who was the victim of incest. It was said to be poor and had never been performed. It was called *Nemesis*, and showed the young girl getting her revenge by murdering her father. Her name was Beatrice Cenci, and she was sentenced to death for her crime and beheaded in Rome on 11 September 1599.

Annika stopped reading. Beatrice Cenci? That date *again*? She knew what Beatrice Cenci had looked like. She was the childlike woman with incredibly sad eyes, looking over her shoulder, staring hard at anyone studying her, from the wall of Ebba Romanova's library.

'So, you're sitting over here? Well? Tell me what happened.' Berit was striding towards her.

'Oh,' Annika said. 'Er, yes, it was really good.'

'What happened?' Berit asked again, glancing at Annika's new laptop.

'I'm staying,' Annika said, unable to hold back a smile. 'I start work again officially on the first of June.'

'Brilliant!' Berit said. 'Have you got anything to work on, or shall we talk on Monday afternoon and come up with a plan?'

Annika pulled a face, looked at her watch and turned off the computer. 'I'm not in Crime. I'm working directly for the news desk,' she said. 'Schyman was pretty clear on that, and I can't just drift about doing what I like. I'll have to be one of Spike's slaves and do as I'm told.'

'We'll soon see about that.'

Annika put the laptop away in its bag and zipped it up. 'Berit,' she said, 'did you know that Alfred Nobel wrote a play about incest just before he died?'

About to walk away, Berit stopped. 'A play about incest? You mean a proper theatre play?'

'A tragedy in four acts,' Annika said.

'I had no idea,' Berit said. 'It's weird that we've never heard of it. Do you think that's really true?'

'It was called *Nemesis*,' Annika said, 'about a young woman who murders her father. Apparently she was a real person. Her name was Beatrice Cenci.'

'And I dare say things didn't end happily ever after for her,' Berit said. 'Could it possibly be that Nemesis punished her soon afterwards?'

Annika hung the laptop over her shoulder and picked up her bag. 'Bingo,' she said.

'You have to be careful if you're going to start playing God,' Berit said, with a wave.

Although Annika couldn't see any connection, an image of Sophia Grenborg popped into her head.

Having finished work for the day, Thomas was leaving the office. The door opened, quickly and silently, and he put up his umbrella. The rain was still lashing the pavement with such intensity that the drops bounced, forming a hazy carpet a few inches above the ground. He paused for a few moments, staring at it, feeling oddly content.

It had been a good day, a really good day. At last he felt as if he was finding his feet, starting to belong there. His formal role was approaching its conclusion – he wasn't supposed to be staying on after the briefing on Monday – but this afternoon he had been led to believe that he would be staying on. He'd tried to call Annika, but her mobile had been switched off.

Now she'll see, he thought. She never really believed I could pull this off, but now she'll have to accept that she was wrong.

Annika hadn't been enthusiastic about the project. Sometimes he thought she was jealous, that she couldn't bear his career to have overtaken hers. She wanted to feel important, and when her imposed period of leave had coincided with the job of a lifetime for him, their marriage had suffered. On the few occasions when she had shown any interest at all in his work, she had barked at him a series of angry questions. A lot of commentators had questioned the government's proposed legislation. He'd read them all and had concluded that they were very confused. People were arguing against existing laws, against consultations, investigations and referrals to the Legislative Council, and it was all getting mixed up. He knew Annika was driven by a genuine belief in justice. Maybe her questions were serious, but that didn't mean she was right.

He took a deep breath and set off into the rain. He jogged quickly up Fredsgatan, past the Foreign Ministry and up towards Malmtorgsgatan.

This morning he had had to park in the multi-storey on Brunkebergstorg. Usually he managed to find a cheaper spot in one of the streets nearby, but today the spaces had been filled by the time he arrived.

He was soaked to the knees when he reached the car park. His car was on the lowest level, and the exhaust fumes were so thick that he tried not to breathe more than he absolutely had to.

His meeting with the director general for legal affairs had gone smoothly. She had been attentive and encouraging, had had very few questions and merely pointed out that the minister would probably want very clear notes when it came to the parliamentary debate.

His task had been to draw up the proposal for new legislation about bugging, and above all he had had to look into what would be done with all the surplus information gathered during surveillance operations against criminals. What would happen if Joe Bloggs said: 'Yesterday I sold fifty kilos of gear to Olle, and then I beat my wife'? Or: 'Tomorrow I'm *going* to sell fifty kilos of gear to Olle, and then I'm *going* to beat my wife'?

The question was how the police should handle everything they found out that wasn't directly connected to the drugs trade. And that was what he had been working on. He thought he'd got it just about right. In the first instance, Joe has already sold the drugs and beaten his wife, so he can be prosecuted for the drugs but not for physical abuse. In the second case, where neither drug-dealing nor physical abuse has yet taken place, the police would be allowed to intervene to stop the abuse taking place. Anything else would be immoral and unreasonable, as most people would surely agree.

But not everyone, he was aware of that.

He took criticism very seriously.

The traffic heading out of the city was terrible. It took him three-quarters of an hour to reach the motorway heading out towards Norrtälje, and it was gone half past six before he turned off towards Danderyd Church.

Tomorrow morning he was due to meet Jimmy Halenius, the under-secretary of state, and go through everything with him. If he thought it was okay, there'd be a briefing on Monday.

He was looking forward to it. All the civil servants seemed to think there was something special about the presentations to the minister in the Blue Room. He had only spoken to the minister once. He had walked into Thomas's office on the fourth floor one day, just after lunch, and asked him how it was going. Departmental gossip had it that he liked to do this occasionally, un-like his predecessor. Thomas had been startled and had fumbled nervously with his papers as he explained the situation.

'Remember, there are innocent people in bars and brothels as well,' the minister had said, when Thomas had stopped talking. 'Not everyone who works there is a criminal, and they won't like being kept under surveillance. We'd be breaching their human rights, and that's the strongest argument against this legislation.'

Thomas had replied that he was aware of that.

The minister had got up, and stopped in the doorway on his way out. 'One of my first jobs as a lawyer was a bugging case,' he said, more to himself than to Thomas. 'I was acting for the Kurds who were bugged in the Ebbe Carlsson affair. I don't think I asked a single question throughout the entire trial.' With that, he had left.

Thomas turned into Vinterviksvägen and let the car roll towards his drive. He grabbed his briefcase, not bothering with the umbrella, and dashed for the front door.

The children came rushing over from the television, Kalle first, with the speed of a leopard on the prowl, then Ellen, hopping over with Ludde and Poppy under her arms. 'Hello, darlings,' he said, bending over and catching both of them. They squealed in delight, kissing and hugging him.

'Daddy, we made a car out of boxes, a proper one with a wheel, and, Daddy, I made the salad today.'

'Daddy, Daddy, can you see that Poppy's a bit broken here? Can you mend her?'

He couldn't hold them any longer and sat down on the floor. 'Careful,' he said. 'Let me take off my jacket.' But they threw themselves on him, tickling him, Daddy,

Daddy, and he felt the wet and the dirt from the hall-floor soaking through his suit trousers. 'Okay,' he said. 'Can I get up now, please?'

They let him go. Kalle, so like his mother, and Ellen, who looked just like he did at her age: they pulled him by the fingers until he was on his feet again and could brush off the dirt.

'Have you had a nice day?' he asked. 'Did you do anything good at nursery?'

'*Pre-school*,' Kalle corrected. 'Made a car with boxes, I told you. And I got to join in, because the teacher said everyone could join in.' Suddenly he looked tearful, his bottom lip jutting out.

Thomas ruffled his dark hair. 'Of course you could join in,' he said. 'You're a proper rally-driver. What about you, Princess Ellen of Vinterviksvägen? What did you do today?' He picked her up with her dolls, making her squeal again. 'You're tickling me, Daddy!'

He put her down and she wriggled out of his arms, running off towards the television as the *Tom & Jerry* signature tune started.

Thomas let out a deep sigh, then unlaced his shoes and pulled them off with relief. He took his briefcase upstairs and put it down beside the desk in his office. It was great having his own room to work in again – he'd forgotten how much he had taken that for granted long ago. He could hear Annika clattering with some dishes downstairs, then paused before turning on the computer and logging on to his emails. He'd invited several of his colleagues round on what would have been his last day, Monday, and he wanted to see who had replied.

Cramne, naturally, he never missed a party, and two other supervisors on the same floor, with their partners. And Halenius, the under-secretary of state.

He read it once more. Yes, Halenius had replied that he'd like to come, even though Thomas had only invited him out of politeness. He had been discussing the party with his colleagues when Halenius had appeared, and it would have been rude not to ask him. Thomas had assumed he wouldn't accept the invitation. The politicians tended not to socialize with the civil servants, particularly the under-secretary and the minister.

Okay, so there'd be eight of them. Maybe the children could eat a bit earlier than usual. Perfect.

He took off his suit and hung it up. The back of the jacket and left trouser-leg were smeared with mud. He'd have to remember to ask Annika to take his suit to the dry-cleaner's. He dropped his shirt into the laundry basket and pulled on a pair of jeans and a rugby shirt.

When he went down to the kitchen, Annika was standing by the sink with her back to him. 'Hello,' he whispered, putting his hands on her shoulders and blowing on her neck. 'And how's my darling girl?'

She stiffened under his touch and dropped the washing-up brush into the bowl. 'Fine,' she said. 'We've already eaten. The children were so hungry that we couldn't wait for you.'

He leaned over her and picked up a half-eaten carrot from one of the plates on the draining-board. 'Sorry,' he said. 'The traffic was terrible.'

'I know,' she said. 'I was up at the paper today, went to see Schyman.'

'How did it go?' he asked, chewing the carrot.

'Good,' she said. 'I start work again on Tuesday.'

It was his turn to stiffen. He stopped chewing as the likely consequences raced through his head. 'I see,' he said. 'You don't think we should have talked about this?'

'About what?' she snapped. 'About whether or not I can have permission to leave the house?'

'Don't be ridiculous.'

'Anyway, your job ends soon, doesn't it?' she said. 'It was a six-month appointment, wasn't it?'

'It's being extended,' he said. 'I found out today.'

She threw the dishcloth at the draining-board. It fell into the sink with a splash. 'And we don't need to talk about that? We only have to talk about me and my job?'

He picked up a glass from the worktop, rinsed it and filled it from the tap. 'Okay,' he said. 'We'll start with me. What do you want to talk about?'

She turned round and leaned back against the dishwasher. 'Why is this new terrorism law that you've been working on really necessary?'

He sighed. 'I thought we were going to talk about the practicalities of work,' he said.

'Why should Sweden be at the forefront of this bugging crap?' Annika said. 'Why are we the ones pushing issues like this in the EU?'

'They think I've done a good job,' he said, 'and they want me to stay on in the department. Or shall I go and sign on instead?'

'You're not answering my question,' Annika said.

Thomas ran his fingers through his hair, making it stick up. 'The fact is,' he said, 'that the other Nordic countries already have this legislation. We're fifteen years behind, because the former Social Democratic ministers never wanted to deal with the fuss that kicks off whenever anyone tries to discuss these issues.'

'What about the EU, then?' Annika said. 'They said on the news last week that Sweden is pressing for service providers to be obliged to store any information sent over their networks.'

'That's a different question,' Thomas said. 'All that information is already kept, and we want that to carry on, just as before. We just want its use and the associated costs to be regulated. At the moment there's a load of horse-trading every time the police want to get hold of any information from the networks. Do you think that's a better system?'

'What do you mean, "horse-trading"?'

'The police say, "We can solve this rape if we find out who called this mobile at this time." The network replies, "Okay, twenty-five thousand kronor." The police say, "We can let you have fifteen thousand." Network: "Nope, at least twenty."'

'I don't believe that,' Annika said.

'The fact is that the Swedish police have become a hell of a lot better at negotiating in recent years,' Thomas said. 'The cost of getting information out of the networks has gone down from seventy to fourteen million.'

Annika bit her bottom lip and balanced on one foot. He knew she was thinking hard.

'Terrorists usually commit crimes like murder, kidnapping, sabotage, and destruction constituting a public danger, don't they?' she finally said. 'Unless I've been misinformed, there are already laws covering those crimes.'

Thomas drank some water, not saying anything.

'I don't know how you can live with yourself,' she said. 'How can you justify what you're doing? That we need special laws for terrorists – what sort of rubbish is that?'

'It's about intent,' Thomas said, putting the glass down on the kitchen table. 'The important thing is the *purpose* of the crime, if the act is likely to threaten the entire system. Because that means it has to be treated differently. If the whole point isn't to blow up a building but to scare people senseless, we're talking about terrorism. Or about some other form of organized crime, like motorcycle gangs or international narcotics syndicates, or groups smuggling weapons or people.'

'Motorcycle gangs aren't terrorists, are they?'

'Their criminal activities could still be part of an attempt to destabilize and instil fear in society. This is about gathering evidence! You don't need to bug petty thieves and out-of-control kids – they get caught anyway.' He threw out his hands, aware that he was pleading with her. 'We're talking about drug Mafias and motorcycle gangs here, the sort of people no one dares to stand witness against. Which means we need technical evidence, and we have to bug their hang-outs and listen to their phone calls. For God's sake, this is about national security!'

She looked at him with her arms wrapped tightly round her body, so small and dark and jagged. He suddenly felt utterly worn out. He wanted to take her in his arms, stroke her hair and forget the rest of the world.

'Berit showed me a proposal for a new law today,' she said.

'Did she?' Thomas said, sinking on to a chair. 'What law?'

'The one saying that the Security Police should have the right to listen to whoever they want to,' Annika said. 'That's completely insane!'

'That's not a new law,' he said. 'That's a comment on a piece of legislation, and it's doubtful it will get passed, but what it's all about is trying to prevent—'

'Exactly,' Annika said, her eyes flashing. 'If the Security Police start arresting people before they've decided to do anything criminal, that's certainly taking preventive action.'

'What this is about,' Thomas went on, in a monotone, 'is a minor change to legislation that can be used in two specific types of scenario where the police are acting to prevent—'

'It's like the old witch trials. You threw the suspected woman in a river and if she sank and drowned she was innocent, and if she floated she was pulled out and burned at the stake!'

Silence erupted between them, filling the kitchen and creeping downstairs to the basement.

'Do you want to know what those scenarios are or would you rather I didn't bother?' he asked.

She wrapped her arms even more tightly round herself and looked down at the floor.

'Suppose two men come here seeking asylum,' Thomas said, 'but the police hear that they're really here to carry out an attack. They know that the target is the Muslim community in Malmö, but they don't know where, when, how, who or what the exact target is. The legislative proposal you mentioned would mean that the police, in this instance, would be able to tap their phones. Today that's permitted only if you know who or what the target is. The proposal is that the line be drawn at an earlier stage of events, instead of everyone having to sit and wait for the bang.'

She didn't answer.

'The second scenario,' he said, 'is also about stopping attacks in advance. And we're talking about phone-tapping, not arrest. If the Hell's Angels are due in court and the police find out that someone is going to be killed – the prosecutor, the judge, a police officer – then they would be allowed to tap their phones and intercept their post. If the intention is to stop the trial, that would be regarded as a threat to the system, which would allow the new law to be applied.' He gulped audibly. 'But you and your oh-so-liberal mates will probably see to it that it never gets passed.' He stood up, toppling the chair behind him. 'The result will be that we have to sit twiddling our thumbs until the next terrorist bomb goes off. Then this proposal will sail through Parliament at the speed of light. And you know what? When that happens, you and Berit and all the others will be sitting there screaming, "Why didn't you *do* anything? Why didn't you *act* on the tip-off? Resign, *resign*!"'

He walked out of the kitchen and out of the house to the small rocky outcrop at the corner of the garden. As the rain drummed against his back, he put his head in his hands and bit his cheek until he could taste blood in his mouth.

Friday, 28 May

19

Annika was sitting on her bed looking out through the open window. It had stopped raining but the sky was ash-grey. The wind was tearing at the trees, and the pennant on Ebba's flagpole was whipping in the air.

She had had nightmares again last night. It was a long time since she'd had so many so close together. For the first year after Sven, her former partner, had died they had tormented her almost every night, but since she had met Thomas they'd become much less regular. After that night in the tunnel under the Olympic Stadium all those years ago, they had got worse. In her dreams last night, Caroline von Behring had died again, her eyes crying out to Annika through time and space, but the message was garbled and she didn't understand what Caroline was trying to say.

She stood up and brushed her hair from her face, then made the bed. She tossed the bedspread over it and straightened the sides.

Thomas had hung his filthy suit on the door of her wardrobe, and she felt a little stab of anger. He was assuming that by some miracle it would be hanging in his own wardrobe in a few days' time, neatly pressed and in a plastic bag from the dry-cleaner's. She had never been good enough for him, no matter how hard she tried.

Yesterday he had *promised* to come home in time for dinner. He had *promised* to play with the children and repair the puncture in Kalle's bicycle tyre. Instead he had gone straight up to his office and sat in front of the computer. Then he had drifted down to the kitchen, expecting a plate of hot food on the table an hour later than they had agreed.

He never listened to her; he didn't care about her opinions and ambitions. It didn't help that they had bought the house in Djursholm.

She slapped the wall hard, so hard that her eyes watered with pain.

She went slowly down to the kitchen. She cleared away the breakfast things, wiped the granite worktop, got out the vacuum cleaner and did a quick circuit of the ground floor. Made coffee. Drank it. Looked at the clock: loads of time before she had to start preparing dinner.

She pulled on her jacket and went out into the gale. The grass was begging for her attention, with its brown ruts full of water, but she turned her back on the lawn and walked out into the road. Ebba's red Volvo was parked outside her house, and Annika went up the steps to the door. Perhaps you didn't just go over and ring on your neighbours' doors out here. She pressed the bell, hearing it echo inside the thick walls.

Almost a minute passed before Ebba answered, with Francesco trying to push his nose past her legs, waving his tail happily. 'Oh, hello!' Ebba said, surprised. 'It's you! Come in.'

'Thanks,' Annika said, stepping into the hall. 'I don't want to take up too much of your time, but I was wondering . . .'

Ebba smiled. Today she was wearing a grey jacket and trousers. 'Yes?'

Annika cleared her throat. 'Would you mind if I took another look at your painting, the girl who was beheaded?'

Ebba seemed rather taken aback. 'Of course not,' she said, gesturing towards the library. 'I have to head off to the lab soon but, please . . .'

Annika kicked off her shoes and walked quickly into the room with the enormous fireplace, padding soundlessly over the thick rug towards the painting.

The background was different shades of brown, and the child-woman's face was very pale, her slightly parted lips soft pink. She was wearing a white turban round her hair, and her dark blonde locks curled down her neck. Her body was swathed in something white and shapeless, possibly a sheet, or a gown that was too big for her.

Ebba came and stood next to her, and together they looked into the painted light-brown eyes.

'Beatrice Cenci,' Annika said. 'I was reading about her on the Internet yesterday, that Alfred Nobel wrote a play about her.'

'Poor Beatrice,' Ebba said. 'A young girl couldn't win against men and the Church in those days.'

'So she really did exist?' Annika wondered.

'Oh, yes,' Ebba said. 'Her fate has fascinated people for centuries. Alfred Nobel wasn't the first to write about her. The English poet Shelley wrote a play in blank verse in 1819, and Alexandre Dumas devoted a whole chapter to her in his epic work *Celebrated Crimes*. Why do you ask?'

'Who was she?' Annika asked.

'Beatrice was the daughter of Francesco Cenci, a rich and powerful nobleman.'

'And she murdered him?'

Ebba nodded. 'With the approval of her brothers and step-mother. During the trial it emerged that her father had been a tyrant. He used to lock Beatrice and her step-mother inside his castle near Rieti, and would subject them to pretty much every sort of abuse you can imagine.'

'But that didn't count for anything in the trial?'

'Francesco was rich. The Pope thought he would be able to get his hands on the family's assets if he got rid of Beatrice so she was beheaded on the Ponte Sant'Angelo, the bridge that crosses the Tiber at the edge of the Vatican. There were huge crowds there to watch. She became a sort of symbol for anyone who was the victim of an unfair trial, practically a saint.'

'But not in the eyes of the Church,' Annika said.

Ebba smiled. 'No. How are you getting on with your job?'

'I start again on Tuesday,' Annika said, smiling back at her. 'I have to admit that I'm really pleased. I need something to do besides pairing socks.'

'I understand,' Ebba said, heading back towards the door. 'Have you given any thought to what we talked about, moving away from violence and taking a look at the world of scientific research instead?'

Annika was watching her hair bounce as she walked. 'As far as I can see, the world of research can get pretty violent at times,' she said. 'Did you happen to know Johan Isaksson?'

Ebba stopped mid-step and turned round slowly. 'Isaksson?' she said. 'Do you mean the boy who had that awful accident? Shut inside one of the freeze-rooms?'

Annika nodded.

'I knew who he was. His lab was in my department

and his research area was quite close to mine. He was looking into neuro-degenerative diseases, Parkinson's, I think. At any rate, he was working with signal pathways and proteins, like me. Why do you ask?'

Annika took a breath, about to answer, but for some reason she changed her mind. 'I – I was locked in a room with a temperature of minus twenty not too long ago,' she said. 'Last winter, actually. There were several of us. One man died . . .' She wasn't sure why she hadn't also told her that she'd been called in by the police to talk about Johan Isaksson's death.

'Do you want to come and have a look?' Ebba said. 'Then you'd have an idea of whether it's worth covering.'

'Would that be all right?'

'Of course,' Ebba said, 'but if you haven't got official access you'll have to go incognito. Do you need to get anything from your house or can we set off straight away?'

The Volvo was an estate model, so that Francesco could travel in the boot. He was evidently used to it. He protested loudly when he wasn't allowed to go with them. The car still smelt new, with a hint of damp dog. Ebba drove down the Norrtälje road, then turned on to the highway through Berghamra.

'The research world is a bit odd,' she said. 'I'm very glad I'm slightly detached from it. I don't have to fight with everyone else for grants and status.'

Grey viaducts slid past the car windows.

'What makes it odd?' Annika asked.

'So many are called and so few are chosen,' Ebba said. 'I've got two friends who are on their way to becoming professors but their nominations keep getting challenged, to the point that they'll be lucky to get their

275

appointments before they retire. Is it like that in journalism too?'

'Not quite,' Annika said. 'Most of the Swedish media are privately owned, apart from the papers published by unions and similar organizations, plus Swedish Television and Radio Sweden. The owners decide who gets the top jobs. They usually go for the people who are most commercial and fit in well with the board and management.'

'Naturally,' Ebba said. 'It's like that for us as well. Although your work is much more public than ours, of course. With us, there's a constant stream of gossip, speculation and rumour about what everyone else is doing.'

'Is it very competitive?' Annika wondered.

'You bet!' Ebba said. 'When I started my postgraduate degree, that was the first thing my supervisor told me. "Turn all your papers face down whenever you leave your desk. *Never* let anyone read anything you're working on. *Never* tell anyone what you've achieved or what you're trying to do." The levels of suspicion and secrecy are absurd.'

'What a nuisance,' Annika said. 'But surely you have to be able to confide in someone?'

'Your supervisor,' Ebba said, 'although that can be a disaster as well. I know supervisors who have stolen their doctoral students' research and published it as their own. On the other hand I've seen the opposite too, students stealing their supervisors' results.'

'Bloody hell,' Annika said. 'I thought having a story pinched was unique to our industry.'

They drove on to the campus via Nobels Väg, passing the Nobel Forum on their left, then rolled down narrow roads between large red-brick buildings.

276

'That's where we used to have lectures when I was a student,' Ebba said, pointing at a building on the corner of Von Eulers Väg.

Annika looked up at a three-storey brick building, the windows dating it to the 1950s.

They swung left, then right, and ahead of them loomed a modern white steel-framed building. Ebba had her own parking space outside the main entrance.

'This can't have been built all that long ago?' Annika said, gazing at the sparkling façade.

Ebba locked the car door. 'Sometimes I wonder if the right hand knows what the left is doing,' she said. 'The politicians put up new buildings and pull old ones down all at the same time. You've heard they want to spend five billion tearing down the entire hospital and building a new one? . . . You can go in, it's not locked, then aim for the stairs. We're going down two floors.'

The building was light and airy. The stairwell was open and stretched up through all the floors, making the entrance-hall seem much bigger than it was. They headed down the broad dark-oak steps to a large open space that functioned as the canteen. One floor below the stairs stopped at a series of heavy doors with coded locks.

'First right,' Ebba said.

Annika stood to one side to let the scientist past. She pulled her card through the reader on the door, and there was a faint click as the lock slid open. 'My office is straight ahead, then right. I'm just going to check if I've got any post.' Ebba stopped at the pigeonholes to the right of the main door. A notice-board shouted the sort of messages that notice-boards usually did, telling you to have your ID clearly visible, and which numbers to call in case of problems and faults.

'Are you going to get into trouble because I'm here?' Annika asked.

Ebba was sifting through a pile of envelopes. 'I doubt it,' she said. 'There are so many people coming and going that no one will notice you.' She put all the envelopes except one back in her pigeonhole. 'Just a load of junkmail,' she said, slipping the letter into her handbag.

The corridor felt cramped and dark, even though the walls were white and the floor light grey. Annika could see daylight further ahead, but it didn't reach far into the passageway.

'Shall I tell you a bit about what we do here?' Ebba said, glancing at Annika over her shoulder. Without waiting for a reply she pulled open the first door on the left. 'The centrifuge room,' she said, and Annika followed her in.

Yes, she could recognize centrifuges. They looked like washing-machines, only bigger. 'What do you need them for?' she asked.

'We use centrifugal force to separate substances from the medium they're suspended in,' Ebba said. 'Suppose I want to extract a particular protein from a solution. I'd put it in a centrifuge and the proteins would form a lump at the bottom.'

Annika stared at the machines. 'The heaviest elements end up at the bottom?' she asked.

'Exactly. Very practical when you're trying to get at things held inside cells and membranes, for instance.'

The door opened and a plump little woman came into the room, her hennaed hair all over the place. It was Birgitta Larsén, Anna realized, the professor who had been friends with Caroline von Behring. 'Ebba,' the woman said, handing the scientist a polystyrene box. 'Can you do me a favour and send this out, please?

278

Thanks so much. Remind me that I owe you lunch one day. By the way, we need to get on to the couriers about those missing antibodies. Have you put in a claim yet?' She moved quickly through the narrow space without waiting for a reply, passing close to Annika without appearing to notice her.

'I did it on Monday,' Ebba said, in answer to the professor's question.

They went out again, passing a huge photocopier surrounded by polystyrene boxes. 'For when we need to send things,' Ebba said. 'Most of our stuff needs packing in dry ice to keep it cool. I'll just make sure that this one gets sent out.'

Somewhere behind Annika a door opened and the sound of men laughing drifted towards her. She turned to see three men in suits come round a corner and along the narrow corridor. They were focused entirely on each other, talking loudly in English. Annika recognized the man in the middle but couldn't quite place him.

'Wait here,' Ebba said, disappearing into a small room. Thirty seconds later she was back without the package. 'Our professor hasn't quite worked out that we've got people who do this for us,' she said.

Annika was watching the men disappear. 'Who were those guys?' She pointed at the door through which they had vanished.

'Bernhard Thorell and his fan club,' Ebba said. 'They've been here all week. This is my room.' She tapped a four-figure code into the keypad to unlock the door, then let Annika into the smallest office she had ever seen. Three desks piled high with computers and heaps of paper were crammed into just seven square metres.

'And I thought I'd had some cramped offices!' Annika

said. Bernhard Thorell, she thought, the head of the American pharmaceutical company who was at the press conference in the Nobel Forum last winter.

'I gather this used to be the smoking room,' Ebba said, 'so at least we've got good ventilation. Would you like to see my lab?'

'You have your own?' Annika said, who was starting to get a grip on the perspectives of the research world.

'I share it with seven other people. Left, then the first corridor on the left.'

Annika let Ebba go first and followed her with a sense of claustrophobia. The corridor was pressing in on her from every angle, above, below and on each side. Admittedly, it was a bit lighter here – all the lab doors had round windows in them – but the feeling of being shut in was worse. Maybe it was because of the bookshelves, computers and printers that had been squeezed between the different offices, with rows of test-tubes, Petri dishes and flasks. There were posters and notices taped up all over the place. Some of the doors bore timetables, for people to book themselves in.

'This is an airlock,' Ebba said. 'You have to change your shoes and put on protective clothing before going into the cell lab. Here you go – it fastens at the back of the neck.'

Annika took the yellow and white striped tunic, which reminded her of the surgical outfits she had seen in A&E. It had long sleeves with tight, elasticated wrists. On a shelf to the right of the door there was a row of white wooden sandals, next to a pair of large gas canisters. 'Which ones should I use?' she asked, reading the names above the shoes.

'Doesn't matter,' Ebba said.

They went into the laboratory.

An Asian woman was crouching in a fume cupboard, concentrating hard on dripping something into a test-tube with a large pipette. She was wearing the same yellow and white protective clothing, with gloves that covered her wrists.

'There are loads of Chinese people here,' Ebba said, then said hello to the woman. She didn't answer.

'What's she doing?' Annika asked.

'Don't know,' Ebba said, glancing quickly at her. 'She's so tense, I think she must be preparing cells to try to detect proteins with the help of antibodies. Antibodies are expensive – a big experiment can cost up to sixty thousand kronor. And a whole delivery has just gone missing . . .' She moved a bit closer to Annika and lowered her voice. 'You never ask what other people are doing,' she said. 'And you never tell anyone else what you're doing. It's best not to get your research mixed up with anyone else's.'

Ebba stepped away. 'My cells are in this incubator,' she said. She opened something that looked like a normal fridge, but inside it was warm rather than cold. 'They need thirty-seven degrees to thrive. Add a bit of nutrient and five per cent carbon dioxide, and they almost always do what you want them to. Unless something happens, of course.'

'Like what?' Annika asked.

'It could be something as simple as picking up the wrong bottle when you're working on an experiment,' Ebba said. 'There are any number of ways of messing things up, like confusing different growth cultures. So many of the bottles look the same.' She closed the door of the incubator and went to a large bucket with a lid. 'This is where I keep the cells when I'm not using them,' she said, unscrewing the lid and pulling out the insulation. 'This is liquid nitrogen, minus 196 degrees.'

White vapour drifted out of the container and Annika instinctively took a step back. 'Talking about cold,' she said, 'could I see the freeze-room?'

Ebba replaced the polystyrene bung and screwed the lid back on. 'Sure,' she said. 'It's in the next corridor along. We'll have to go through the airlock again.'

The freeze-room was at the far end of a section of corridor that received no natural light. Shadows from the doors along the corridor cast strange patterns over the walls.

'As you can see, light and temperature are controlled from out here,' Ebba said, pointing to a control panel on the right of the door. A display indicated that the temperature inside was minus 25 degrees.

'What was Isaksson doing in there?' Annika asked.

'I suppose he was fetching something,' Ebba said. 'We store samples in there, as well as quite a bit of useless stuff, like waste blood and so on. We can go in for a moment, but I have to warn you, it really is extremely cold.' She pressed a switch to turn the lights on and pulled the door open. The cold hit them, making Annika gasp.

'I think we'll leave the door open,' Ebba said.

The room was very narrow, lined with shelving on both sides. Bottles, flasks and boxes were piled up to the ceiling – every inch of space had been used.

'How on earth could he have got stuck in here and frozen to death?' Annika said, fighting her claustrophobia.

'The emergency door-opener has been a bit temperamental – I was almost shut in once,' Ebba said. 'And rumour has it that he was under the influence of alcohol and something else, so his wits probably weren't at their sharpest.'

Annika knew she would soon have to get out of that room. 'But there's an alarm over there,' she said, pointing to a button close to the floor at the far end. 'Why didn't he press it? And why didn't he yell until someone came and opened up?'

'He was on his own here on a Saturday evening. His lab was the only one booked.'

Annika stepped quickly into the corridor and breathed out, relieved, as the door closed behind them. A moment later there was a commotion as man in a grey cardigan stormed past them. '*Birgitta!*' he roared, the name echoing along the walls.

'Bloody hell,' Annika said. 'What on earth's happened?'

The man stopped outside one of the labs and stared in through the round window. 'Birgitta,' he yelled, 'you bloody collaborator! I know you're here somewhere!'

Birgitta Larsén backed out of a room further down the corridor, holding another polystyrene box in her arms. 'Goodness, Lars-Henry,' she said, 'what a terrible noise. What do you want?'

He was the professor who had written the confused article in the *Evening Post* last winter, Annika remembered, and who had been dragged out of that rather eventful press conference.

Birgitta Larsén walked past him and came up to Ebba again. 'This one is going to the same place, darling. When do you think you'll hear back about our claim?'

'Don't think you'll get away with this,' the man shouted, waving a printout. 'I want an explanation of this.'

Ebba took the box with a neutral expression on her face.

'My dear professor!' Birgitta Larsén said, looking up

at him – he was at least a foot taller than her. 'Why are you so upset?'

'I've had an email from Pubmed and saw this,' he said. 'We got a citation in the *Journal of Biological Chemistry* and you didn't think to mention me!'

Annika looked from one to the other in surprise.

'Hmm,' Ebba said quietly, 'a case of wounded vanity, and I have a feeling it's my fault . . .'

'But, Lars-Henry,' Birgitta Larsén said, 'things like that aren't my business, as you know. What's this about?'

'My doctoral student is listed as the author of the article, but not me, her supervisor! How could something like that happen?'

Ebba passed the polystyrene box to Annika and walked up to the man. 'It was my decision,' she said. 'I came to the conclusion that you hadn't contributed to the research, so there was no reason for you to be listed in the article.'

'Because I've been pushed out of the assembly!' he shouted, standing right in front of Ebba. 'You all take every opportunity you can to humiliate me!'

'I haven't pushed you out of the Nobel Assembly,' Ebba said calmly. 'I merely concluded that you've hardly been here over the past four months.'

The man's eyes found Annika's. 'Are you responsible for this?'

'She's a reporter for the *Evening Post*,' Birgitta Larsén said, without looking at Annika. 'I have no idea what she's doing here, but I intend to find out just as soon as you finish shouting.'

Lars-Henry jabbed the printout towards Annika and Ebba. 'You should watch out,' he said. 'You're ignoring Nemesis, all of you. Just remember that I've warned you!' He marched off towards the main door and disappeared.

'What was all that about?' Annika said, as the door closed behind him. She was still holding the box.

Ebba took it from her. 'I'll take care of this,' she said, vanishing round the nearest corner.

Birgitta Larsén moved closer to Annika. 'You thought I didn't recognize you. Of course I did. What are you doing here?' Her eyes were bright and serious.

'Caroline wasn't surprised that she'd been shot,' Annika said. 'I was there, on the floor next to her. She was looking at me when she died. I can't escape it. I keep dreaming about her.' She was surprised by how agitated she sounded.

Birgitta Larsén was standing quite still, her eyes fixed on Annika's. 'What do you dream?' she asked very quietly.

'Caroline is trying to tell me something,' Annika said, lowering her voice, 'but I can't understand her. What do you think it could be? *What?*' She felt tears welling and bit her lip. God, she never stopped crying, these days.

'Some food,' Birgitta Larsén said, turning on her heel and heading off down the corridor. 'Bring Ebba, and we'll go over to the Black Fox.'

20

They left the building by the main entrance and stepped out into hazy sunshine. The lawns around them were bright green, and newly unfurled leaves danced on the trees. Ebba and Birgitta carried on talking about the missing consignment of antibodies and what to do next in their claim for compensation. Annika was walking behind them, admiring her surroundings.

It was lovely out there. It reminded her of films she had seen of Ivy League colleges on the east coast of the US. Narrow roads, big buildings, lots of green.

The faculty club, the Black Fox, was on the edge of the campus, at 6A Nobels Väg, not far from the Nobel Forum where Annika had been with Bosse. She realized she hadn't replied to his email with a time when they could have coffee the following week.

They had met several times during the spring, quietly in some café, all completely innocent, not a single inappropriate word spoken.

Did she want to carry on like that? Did she want to see him at all? Did she want more?

She didn't know, and was having trouble separating her emotions: expectation, shame, excitement, happiness, anxiety.

'Dear old Lars-Henry,' Birgitta said. 'He's become quite excitable.' She skipped up the granite steps leading to the heavy copper door of the faculty club and held it open for Ebba and Annika. 'He's always been vain,' she said, 'but he wouldn't have made such a fuss a few years ago about nothing more than an acknowledgement under a minor piece of research. But why, Ebba dear, didn't you include him? You put my name in. What would it have cost you to add his?'

Ebba held her head high. 'It was purely a matter of principle,' she said. 'Cilla, the post-grad who has him as her supervisor, has been trying to get hold of him all spring, and he's never responded. She's pretty desperate. At some point you have to take responsibility for your behaviour, even if you're a miserable old professor.'

Birgitta beckoned a neatly dressed waiter. 'Have you got a table for three? Splendid! By the window? Never mind. We'll take this one in the corner – is that all right with you, girls?' She sat down with a sigh and spread the napkin on her lap. 'Being excluded in the way that Lars-Henry has been shouldn't be possible,' she said, 'but the assembly did it anyway. I can understand that he feels bitter about it. I would, too, in his position.' She rubbed her hands together. 'But I don't have to wonder about that – I was promoted rather than being kicked out. I'll have the trout, that's always good. And a large low-alcohol beer, please.'

'What's this business about Nemesis that he keeps going on about?' Annika asked, choosing the trout as well.

'It's from Greek myth,' Ebba said, 'an endless maze of ideas about crime and punishment, cause and effect, injustice and retribution. Fundamentally, I think Lars-Henry's reaction is based on scepticism about Darwin's theory of evolution. He belongs to the minority who think we should have greater respect for God in science, the so-called creationists.'

'Yes, dear me,' Birgitta said, with a sigh.

Annika stared at Ebba. More God in science?

'Supporters of creationism claim that the universe arose in line with the description at the beginning of the Book of Genesis. They want the story of the creation to be seen as a parallel and an equally valid frame of reference to Darwin's theory of evolution, in both education and science.'

'As you can appreciate, it's hard to take them seriously,' Birgitta said, raising her eyebrows.

'You said you'd been promoted,' Annika said.

'Moved from the assembly to the committee, to fill the gap after Caroline,' Birgitta said. 'You understand what that means?' Annika shook her head. 'The assembly's task each year is to choose the recipient of the Nobel Prize for Medicine. It consists of fifty members, all professors here at the Karolinska Institute. The committee is the executive board of the assembly, five members plus a chair and vice chair. Everyone knows that the real decisions are taken by the committee.'

'Wasn't there some trouble about who was going to succeed Caroline as chair?' Annika asked, remembering Peter No-Tail's post on the Internet.

Their food and drinks arrived, and Birgitta took a deep swig of her beer. 'We wanted someone who would carry on in the spirit of both Caroline and Nobel,' she said, 'not an opportunist who would bend with the wind, depending on whoever was offering most money.'

'Strong words,' Ebba said, taking the bones out of her fish.

'True, though,' Birgitta said. 'Sören Hammarsten

simply isn't made of the right stuff to give moral leadership. It was a great relief that Ernst was able to take over. But tell me, Annika, what was it you were saying about Caroline? That she speaks to you at night?'

Annika put down her knife and fork. 'I know it sounds silly,' she said, 'but I can't stop thinking about the look in her eyes. She was staring at me, right at me, and I was looking into her eyes when she died, and it was as if she *knew*, as if she *understood*, and it was just so awful having to watch and not be able to . . .'

Tears welled yet again, and she noticed that Birgitta was crying too. The professor sniffed loudly and wiped her nose with her napkin. 'I wish I knew,' she said. 'If Caroline was going to confide in anyone, it would have been me. I'm not saying that out of arrogance,' she said. 'I was the one she talked to, but she didn't say anything about this. I've no idea what she could have been thinking as she died.' Birgitta shuffled in her seat and took a sip of her beer. 'She didn't actually say anything? Not a word? Nothing that you might have heard but not understood?' She looked hard at Annika with her bright eyes.

'No,' Annika said. 'Caroline was dead in a matter of seconds. She didn't even have time to gasp.' She picked up her cutlery and looked down at her plate. Birgitta Larsén was a bad liar.

Ebba and Annika sat quietly beside each other in the car on the way home. Birgitta Larsén was still with them somehow, indefinably present in the back seat.

'Where did she recognize you from?' Ebba eventually asked.

Annika pushed her hair back. 'I interviewed her about Caroline the day after she died,' she said. 'She was fairly upset, which was only natural, and it ended with her getting quite aggressive.'

'Birgitta's an odd person,' Ebba said. 'You never really know what she's thinking. She can seem confused and blasé one moment, only to be sharp and focused the next.'

Annika nodded. She had noticed that too. 'Did she really know Caroline von Behring as well as she makes out?'

Ebba indicated right and turned off the motorway at Danderyd Church. 'You'd see them together at JJ fairly often. There aren't many women at that level, so I suppose it was natural for them to stick together.'

'JJ?'

'Jöns Jakob, the staff canteen. And they used to arrange seminars together that were slightly outside the area of medicine, about things like leadership, equality and such, so they probably were quite close.' Ebba glanced at Annika. 'So, what do you think? Is there anything worth writing about in the world of scientific research?'

Frozen researchers, shouting matches in the corridors, grants worth billions of kronor.

Annika nodded. 'Absolutely.'

They were back in Djursholm and the sun was shining, making the colours clearer. Annika gazed at the palatial villas as they drove past them. Imagine, *she* was living out here. 'Do you ever think about how lucky you are?' she asked Ebba.

Ebba indicated and turned, evidently considering her answer. 'Sometimes,' she said. 'Some things have turned out well for me, but others haven't. Mum left me nothing but furniture and books so I've had to work for everything I've got. Nothing ever comes for free, and the price gets higher the further up you get.'

The Volvo swung into Vinterviksvägen. Annika's house was sitting there, white and sparkling in the afternoon sun. 'There's something I've been wondering about a lot,' she said. 'Can you think of any reason why Caroline might have been killed? Who could have had a reason for wanting her dead? Can you think of any explanation, any reason at all?'

Ebba switched off the engine. Silence filled the car. 'Maybe,' she said, 'the price gets so high that it can no longer be paid. Maybe that's what happened to Caroline.' She opened the car door and stepped out on to the gravel.

Francesco started barking from his kennel.

Annika crossed the road towards her own house, feeling a peculiar swaying sensation. Caroline von Behring was with her, Birgitta Larsén was drifting above her, Ebba Romanova was walking silently behind her.

What happened to women in the academic world? The space available to them seemed more limited, the boundaries more sharply drawn, their territory more important than anywhere else.

Only four per cent of women who finish their doctorates become professors, compared to eight per cent of men. Both Birgitta and Caroline had made it, all the way to the top, and Caroline had climbed to the very summit.

That had to have something to do with it.

It had to be important.

Annika dodged the troughs of rainwater in the grass and headed for the door. A movement in the corner of her eye made her look over towards the rocky outcrop. And there stood Wilhelm Hopkins, digging a hole in her lawn. His back was towards her, an iron spike stuck in the ground beside him. He was pressing his whole weight on the spade as the blade sank into the wet ground.

Annika stopped mid-stride, almost unable to believe her eyes.

Her neighbour? Digging a hole *in her garden*?

'What on earth do you think you're doing?' she said, and her feet started moving again, automatically, flying towards the thickset man.

He ignored her, driving the spade into the grass beside him and pulling out the iron spike.

'Are you *mad*?' Annika shouted, grabbing the spike. 'You're standing here digging *on my land*.'

The man yanked the spike from her with such force that he had to take a couple of steps back, his face bright red and his eyes flashing. 'We've always had our midsummer pole here,' he said hoarsely. 'Every year since I was a child we've held our celebrations here, *right here*, and you're saying that the tradition has to be abandoned!'

'But the council sold this land a long time ago,' Annika snapped. 'We live here now. This is our home! You can't come and dig up the grass just because you used to when you were a child. That's insane!'

Her neighbour took a long stride towards her, so quickly and aggressively that Annika came close to stumbling into the hole.

'We celebrate midsummer here,' he said, stressing every word. 'All of us, whether you like it or not. No one asked us if they could sell our communal land.' He picked up his spade and iron spike and turned his back on her.

'So why didn't you buy it, if you want it so much?' Annika said.

The old man spun round. 'It *was* mine!' he shouted.

'Why should I have to pay for it?' He trudged away across her lawn.

Annika stood where she was, staring after him. Only when he had disappeared from view behind the house did she realize that she was trembling. Her heart was thudding so hard that she was having difficulty breathing. Silently she took a couple of steps after him, her mind blank.

How was this possible? How could anyone behave like that?

She carried on to the corner of the house, then stopped and looked along the rutted tyre-tracks to where they disappeared through the gap in the hedge. At that moment a car engine started up and two semi-circular lights shone right into her eyes. Wilhelm Hopkins put his big Mercedes into gear, accelerated and drove out across her lawn. The water in the ruts splashed up from his wheels, cascading away from the tyres.

Without taking any notice of Annika he drove so close to her that mud splashed halfway up her thighs.

I'm going to kill him, Annika thought, as the rear lights disappeared through her gateposts and out into the road.

Subject: Disappointment
To: Andrietta Ahlsell

In the summer of 1889 Alfred Nobel drafted his first will. He told Sophie Hess about his plan:

> *I doubt anyone will miss me. Not even a dog named Bella will shed a tear over me. Although she would probably be the most honest of all, because she would not be able to sniff around*

for any remaining gold. But those beloved
individuals are likely to be disappointed on that
score: I take pleasure in the anticipation of all the
wide eyes and all the swearing that the absence
of money is likely to bring.

Alfred, Alfred – Sofie isn't the right person to confide in! When will you realize this?

Because Sofie complains about the will several times while Alfred is still alive.

Three times he revises his last will and testament, three times, and he writes it himself. He doesn't like lawyers, calling them *niggling parasites*.

Alfred wants to write from the heart, and does so: on 27 November 1895 he signs his last will and testament. The document is less than four pages long, handwritten in Swedish. Three sides deal with which of the *beloved individuals* will get what, and less than one page with the new prizes he wants to set up and which his enormous fortune will finance.

The will is deposited at Stockholm's Enskilda Bank. It is unevenly written in jagged handwriting, with a number of notes in the margins. It is opened on 15 December 1896, five days after Alfred's death, and no one has cause to celebrate its contents.

No one at all.

Quite the opposite, in fact: everyone is disappointed. His relatives are deeply disappointed, feeling themselves practically defrauded. He gives his brother's children a million kronor, *a million kronor* at that time, a dizzying, immense sum, but they want more, much more, and they take their case to law, and in the end they win, they are drowned in money, all the income from the entire estate for one and a half years.

And they leave their uncle's grave, counting the notes clutched in their fists.

The future archbishop Nathan Söderblom is disappointed, he who spoke beside Alfred's coffin in San Remo, yet even so he does not get the hospital he had hoped for.

Even the Swedish king, Oscar II, is distantly disappointed, believing that the intention to establish prizes in order to reward not only Swedes but also *foreigners* is *unpatriotic*.

The future prime minister, Hjalmar Branting, editor-in-chief of the newspaper the *Social Democrat*, calls the donation a *major bungle*.

But Alfred, he has thought and pondered. He wants five prizes to be awarded, five prizes in line with his life's work and passions: physics, chemistry, medicine, literature and – perhaps most remarkable of all – peace.

His women are there, both of the women who have meant most in his life; they are both mentioned in the will, albeit in completely different ways.

Here she is again, the woman he never captured. He does not mention her by name, but he gives her his greatest gift: in future the Norwegian Parliament is to be instructed to reward *the person who shall have done the most or the best work for fraternity between nations, for the abolition or reduction of standing armies and for the holding and promotion of peace congresses.*

Bertha Kinsky, who married von Suttner, the beautiful countess from the Grand Hôtel in Paris, who has become famous for arranging peace congresses, becomes the second woman ever to be awarded a Nobel Prize (the Peace Prize in 1905; the first is Marie Curie, awarded the Physics Prize in 1903).

Sofie Hess (now Mrs Kapy von Kapivar) is mentioned by name, and of all the disappointed parties perhaps she is the most gravely overlooked. The will bequeaths her the equivalent of half a million kronor each year for the rest of her life, but Sofie wants more, she wants much, *much* more, and she is holding a trump card, 218 of them, in fact: Alfred's letters to her over the years. She contacts the executor, Ragnar Sohlman; she fawns, she pleads, she cajoles. She has so many debts, they are such a burden to her, they are pressing her to the ground: could not the estate pay them off?

When this fails she makes threats: 218 letters. Naturally, she doesn't want anyone else to read them, an outsider, it would be *shameful* if that were to happen, she certainly doesn't want that, considering the good name of the late Mr Nobel . . .

One million, that's what she wants, the equivalent of one million kronor. Cash. Otherwise she will sell the letters, the scandalous letters, to the highest bidder.

And Sohlman pays.

The blackmail has worked.

So ends Sofie Hess's long connection with Alfred Nobel.

She manages to exploit him even after his death.

Saturday, 29 May

21

The Kitten stretched in the sun, letting the chlorinated water from the pool run on to her towel. The kids were racing around her, shrieking at each other in their private-school British English (she could imagine them heading off to school in shiny Range Rovers driven by their neat, suntanned mothers).

There were too many permanent residents in this complex now. She'd have to start looking for a new one soon. She pushed her big round sunglasses more firmly on to her nose and picked up a copy of *Cosmopolitan*: how to be hotter, thinner, richer.

The beach-ball hit her head, dislodging her sunglasses. She let out a cry and sat up. The ball was lying next to her, and two pale, chubby British brats were standing in front of her, looking scared. The Kitten smiled. 'Is this your ball?'

They nodded mutely, eyes wide.

'Here,' she said, tossing it back to them. 'But make sure you don't hit anyone else. Who knows? They might get cross.'

The children nodded again, one of them picked the ball up and wandered off, but the second, smaller, one didn't move. 'Where are you from?' he asked.

The Kitten, who had adjusted her glasses and settled back on her sunbed again, sat up once more. 'I'm from America,' she said. 'The best country in the world. Much better than Spain or England.' Then she leaned back and raised her magazine demonstratively.

That usually worked. Arrogant Americans were the worst thing stuck-up Europeans could imagine. If praise of the USA didn't work, she usually moved on to how great President Bush was. That always meant she was left in peace.

But the little brat didn't move. 'Why don't you live there?'

She lowered the magazine. He really was incredibly annoying, pale, freckled, red-haired and evidently as stupid as they came. 'You know what?' she said, standing up, picking up the magazine and her towel. 'That's a really good idea, thanks a lot.' She smiled at the brat and headed for the entrance that was furthest from her own flat. No point letting the whole pool know exactly where she lived.

'What did you do to your leg?' the kid shouted after her, but she pretended she hadn't heard.

Up in the apartment everything was cool and white. She hung the towel (white, of course) to dry in the bathroom, and put the magazine in the wicker basket next to the linen-covered sofa. Her bathing suit was wet and cold, chilling her stomach pleasantly in the heat. She never wore a bikini. The large scar on her chest was too noticeable, the sort of detail people tended to remember. Heart surgery, she had said, on the few occasions when someone had seen it and asked. But she could just as easily have told the truth – no one lived very long after asking: an injury at work. I was shot once a long time ago but that's all

300

forgotten now. Forgotten, and long since buried.

She went into the bedroom, switched on the computer and fetched a new towel, which she folded and laid on the office chair so the seat wouldn't get wet. Logged into Happy Housewives and looked for any sign of her agent.

A new message was waiting for her.

The shit has hit the fan. Erase your hard-drive.
Avoid all usual hangouts. Person who identified
you: Bengtzon, Annika, Stockholm, Sweden.
DO NOT USE THIS CHANNEL AGAIN.

The message had been left at 09.13, central European time, the same zone as her. In other words, twenty minutes ago.

The Kitten read the message three more times. Then she turned off the computer, opened her desk drawer and took out a small screwdriver. She unscrewed the base of the computer and pulled out the hard-drive. It was grey, its size and shape reminiscent of a cigarette packet. The RAM memory could stay: any information on it was erased as soon as the power was switched off. Then she left the bedroom, taking the hard-drive with her, and headed into the bathroom. She took off her swimsuit and pulled on a pair of dark jeans and a blue T-shirt. She pulled her still wet hair up into a ponytail and hung her sunglasses from the neck of the T-shirt.

This was what she had always suspected, that her agent was another clumsy idiot.

Erase your hard-drive. As though that would help! Everything could be reconstructed, and then they'd have emails and websites and chat and IP addresses from here, there and every-fucking-where. *Erase your hard-drive? Kiss my fucking ass.*

301

She put the hard-drive into her handbag and grabbed the car keys from the hall table. She didn't bother about fingerprints: that stage was over now.

She shut the door without looking back: never look back. Instead she focused on the future, and on her future markers.

Bengtzon, Annika, Stockholm, Sweden.

Annika woke up with the sun streaming on to her face. It was making her sweat so much that her hair was stuck to her neck and back. Without opening her eyes she lay there for a minute or so, listening to the sounds of the house. There was a radio on somewhere – she could hear loud chatter on P1, accompanied by a newspaper rustling. Children were shouting, and she presumed they were hers.

She ought to get up. She had to pull herself together.

She would have to go and buy a proper roller-blind from Ikea.

With an effort she heaved herself out of bed and over to the bathroom. Thomas was whistling downstairs, the sound cutting into her head.

The weekend: a whole weekend that they were obliged to spend together, unable to hide behind their jobs.

She pulled on a pair of jeans and a hooded top and went down to the kitchen.

'Good morning,' Thomas said, without looking up from the paper. 'There's coffee in the pot.'

She went over to the worktop and poured herself a large mug. 'I don't know what we're going to do about Wilhelm Hopkins,' she said. 'If he doesn't stop using my garden as his private playground, I'm going to do something silly.'

'So it's *your* garden now? I thought we lived here

together,' Thomas said, leafing through the paper, still without looking up at her. He was wearing a tracksuit and trainers.

Annika sat down opposite her husband and put her hand over the article he was reading. 'He can't carry on using *our* garden as a shortcut every time he takes his car out. That must count in law as arbitrary conduct.'

Thomas pulled the paper away from her and held it up. 'There'll be six people coming to dinner on Monday evening,' he said, from behind it. 'Larsson and Althin and their wives, and Cramne and Halenius.'

'And digging holes in the grass because that's where midsummer always used to be celebrated is insane,' Annika said.

Thomas turned the page. 'We have to show a bit of understanding,' he said. 'These are old traditions, and until recently people living in the area had the right to use this piece of land. It's natural if they're upset that they've lost it. What were you thinking of cooking?'

'Fish soup,' Annika said, to the copy of *Svenska Dagbladet* that shielded Thomas. 'But the council sold the land, we live here now, and the neighbours can't just carry on doing as they like.'

Thomas lowered the paper, folded it and finally looked at her. 'You have to be a bit subtle when you live in a villa,' he said, standing up. At the front door he stopped. 'Mum phoned,' he said. 'She's coming over this afternoon. Wants to see how we've settled in.'

'Okay,' Annika said. So she can reassure herself that this isn't Djursholm *proper*, and point out yet again that there's no sea view except from upstairs, she thought.

Thomas went out, closing the door behind him. She pushed her mug away, darted over to the window and watched him jog out of the gate and down

303

Vinterviksvägen with short, easy strides, his shoulders rolling slightly. She saw him vanish into the greenery down towards the shore and the pressure grew in her chest. Why was he being so distant?

She went back to the worktop, gathered together the breakfast things and put them into the dishwasher, wiped the table, then wiped it again.

She had to pull herself together. Had to do something.

She rinsed her face under the kitchen tap, dried it on a tea-towel and went out to see the children. They were playing with trucks and spades in the hole that Wilhelm Hopkins had dug. 'Look, Mummy,' Kalle cried, when he caught sight of her. 'We've got a volcano! It spits fire, but Spiderman is going to stop it – *vroom*!' He was holding a plastic bucket that was standing in as the flying superhero.

Ellen picked up a dumper truck and followed her brother's example: 'Vroom, vroom . . .'

'Would you like to do some more digging?' Annika asked, making an effort to sound cheerful. 'How about planting some flowers?'

The children dropped their toys and ran over to her, grabbing a leg each.

'I like you lots, Mummy,' Ellen said, hugging her thigh.

Annika crouched and took both children in her arms. 'And you're the best in the world,' she whispered, the pressure growing in her chest again. She hugged them, rocking them, then let go, stood up and cleared her throat. 'Bring your spades and we'll start digging.'

She fetched her own spade from the basement and led the children over to the hole in the hedge where Wilhelm Hopkins drove his car through. The Merc was parked with its front bumper just a metre from the boundary of her garden. 'Here,' she said. 'We're going to plant a really nice flowerbed.'

With the children milling round her legs, she quickly dug a three-metre-long strip of the churned-up grass, laying the turves as a barrier against her neighbour. 'There,' she said. 'Now we can go and buy some flowers.'

The children rushed off towards her car, scrambling up on to the back seat without arguing. She locked the house, putting the key into a boot outside the door so Thomas could get in, jumped into the car and drove off to Hortus out in Mörby.

There were masses of people at the garden centre, and she had to keep telling the children to stay close to her. In return she let them choose some of the plants they were going to put in the new bed. Ellen selected pansies and summer phlox, while Kalle wanted ox-eye daisies and busy lizzies. Annika chose different sorts of marigold – her grandmother had grown trays of them on the windowsills of her flat in Hälleforsnäs before planting them out in front of her cottage at Lyckebo. A young lad helped her carry three big bags of compost out to the SUV, and then they were done.

When they got home the children were tired of their gardening adventure. They ran back to the volcano and carried on digging with the Spiderman tractor.

Annika took the bags of compost out of her car and started dragging them towards the new bed.

'You could have told me you were going out,' Thomas said behind her, making her jump and drop the compost. He was sitting on the terrace at the back of the house reading the evening papers.

'I put the key into one of the boots by the back door,' she said, bending down to pick up the bag.

Thomas got up and walked round the side of the

house. He's going to help me, Annika thought. He'll soon be back with the rest of the compost. She tore open the bag and emptied it on to the flowerbed, glancing at the corner of the house round which Thomas had disappeared. He'll be pleased that I'm making an effort, she thought. We can have the house and garden as a shared project. Together we'll turn it into our own little oasis, a place to relax and recharge our batteries.

But Thomas didn't come back. Instead she saw him walking about inside the kitchen, standing at the sink and talking into his mobile. For some reason the sight of him there made her feel like crying. Disappointment was forming a noose round her neck, making it hard to breathe. Nothing she did was any good. No matter what she did, it was never good enough.

'Hello there!' Ebba called from the road. 'What are you planting?'

Annika spun round and forced a smile, then drove the spade into the soil and walked over to the fence. Francesco started barking and wagging his tail when he spotted her.

'Hello, boy,' Annika said, bending down to pet him and taking the opportunity to wipe her eyes and nose.

'Wilhelm won't be very happy about where you're putting your new bed,' Ebba said, waving at the bare soil.

'Guess that was the intention,' Annika said. 'Would you like a cup of coffee, or some lunch? I was planning to do an omelette . . .'

'Thanks,' Ebba said, taking a few involuntary steps as the dog tugged her towards a squirrel. 'That would have been lovely but I'm on my way to the institute. Francesco! Come here!'

'You work on Saturdays?' Annika asked, trying to sound relaxed.

'The Nobel Assembly has organized a really inter-esting seminar,' Ebba said. '"The Global Challenge of Neuroprotection and Neuroregeneration". There'll be drinks and nibbles afterwards. It's become something of a tradition, open to staff and post-docs – it's usually very popular.'

'A sort of staff party?' Annika said, glancing at the house. She could no longer see Thomas.

'Yes,' Ebba said. 'The Nobel Committee is meeting today to draw up its preliminary list, and that usually means a lot of heightened emotions. By the way, could I ask a favour?'

Annika looked back at her. 'Of course,' she said.

'I'm going up to see my cousin in Dalarna tomorrow for a few days, and I was wondering if you could keep an eye on the house.'

Annika nodded. 'Of course,' she repeated. 'What do I have to do? Water the plants, water the dog, bring in the post?'

Ebba laughed and dug for something in her jacket pocket. 'Francesco's coming with me, but it would be great if you could take the post in once or twice. The plants should be okay. Here's the key to the letterbox. Thanks so much. Just call me if anything happens – my mobile number's on my card.' She handed Annika a small key-ring and a business card, gave a little wave and jogged after her dog, who was on his way into Hopkins's garden. 'No, boy, not there, this way.'

Annika put the card and keys into her pocket, then looked at her car again. The bags of compost were on the ground next to the open boot. No one was going to help her with them.

Monday, 31 May

22

As Anton Abrahamsson entered the room his knees felt like jelly. Early-morning meetings at the top of the central building of the police complex on Kungsholmen were notorious, particularly the ones in the corner rooms with a view of the treetops in Kronoberg Park.

And now it was his turn.

The head of the Security Police and his boss, Bertstrand, were standing by the window with cups of coffee, talking quietly. The early-morning sun reflected off the building opposite, casting uneven shadows on their faces.

'Well,' Abrahamsson said, rubbing his hands together to warm them, 'so this is what it's like up here.'

The men by the window put their cups down on a small, round wooden table and walked towards him. 'Welcome,' the head of the Security Police said, as they shook hands. 'Coffee, or perhaps some water?' He gestured towards a side-table with a range of refreshments.

Abrahamsson shook hands with Bertstrand, then poured himself a glass of sparkling water. His hand felt slightly unsteady and he didn't want to risk spilling anything. I wonder if everyone gets this nervous before meetings to discuss promotion, he thought.

'Sit yourself down, Anton,' said the head of the Security Police.

They settled into a group of low armchairs, comfortable, dark-blue fabric. Abrahamsson stretched out his legs.

'I hope all's well with your family?' his boss said.

Abrahamsson couldn't help laughing – they were actually interested! 'Thanks, yes,' he said. 'Our son's getting big now, nine months old . . . We had a bit of trouble for a while with colic and so on . . .'

Bertstrand leaned forward and clasped his hands together. 'Anton,' he said, 'we'd like to talk to you about the extradition from Bromma back in the winter.'

Abrahamsson nodded and smiled. He remembered that very well indeed. 'A tricky job,' he said. 'I'm just glad it went so well.'

His superiors exchanged a quick glance, which, for some reason, made him feel a little uncomfortable.

'The report you wrote,' the head of the Security Police said, 'I presume it was accurate?'

Abrahamsson took a sip of water. Yes, indeed, it had been entirely accurate.

'There are a few details we've been wondering about,' Bertstrand said. 'We're hoping you can help to clarify the course of events for us.'

Abrahamsson grinned and let his knees fall apart. 'Shoot,' he said.

'At what point did you realize that there were members of the American CIA present at the extradition?'

At what point?

At what point?

'Well,' he said, slightly hesitant, 'it must have been when George said he'd brought some men with him to look after the transportation.'

'George?' the head of the Security Police said.

'The man who presented himself as the head of the American team,' Bertstrand clarified.

'George?' the head of the Security Police repeated, looking blankly at Abrahamsson.

'He was very polite and correct,' Abrahamsson said.

The head of the Security Police shuffled awkwardly, the chair's upholstery creaking slightly.

Bertstrand moved to the very edge of his seat. 'Were you wearing a mask at any point?' he asked Abrahamsson in a rather accusing way.

A mask?

'At any stage in the proceedings?'

'Absolutely not. Why would I have been?'

'You didn't think it odd that all the American personnel were wearing masks?'

'Not George,' Abrahamsson said quickly. 'He wasn't wearing a mask. He was very . . .' Polite and correct, he had been about to say, but he had already said that.

His bosses exchanged another glance.

'One more thing,' Bertstrand said. 'Why did you walk out?'

Walk out? When?

'Why did you and your colleagues leave the room while the CIA were conducting their humiliating treatment of the prisoner?'

'We stayed,' Abrahamsson said. 'We stayed for almost the whole thing.'

'Yes,' Bertstrand said, very gently and very slowly, 'but why did you walk out when you did? I mean, towards the end?'

Sitting in the grand meeting room at the top of the central building on Kungsholmen, Abrahamsson heard the prisoner's screams echoing round the room, the rattle of ankle-chains, the slicing of scissors through thick fabric. He heard the crying and calls for help, saw bloodshot eyes stare at the ceiling as the man's naked body tensed while his anus was invaded. 'I thought it was rather unpleasant,' he said.

The head of the Security Police stood up and walked over to stare out across the treetops in the park.

'Anton,' Bertstrand said, 'there is a legal problem with this extradition, as you can probably understand.'

Abrahamsson blinked. *A legal problem?*

'You were responsible for the extradition, yet the fact of the matter is that you handed over official control to the Americans,' Bertstrand said. 'And that isn't permitted under Swedish law. There will have to be an investigation, and the result will, sooner or later, be made public. Do you understand what this means?'

Abrahamsson was gripped by an extremely unpleasant suspicion. 'It wasn't my fault,' he said. 'There was nothing I could do.'

'I quite understand your position,' Bertstrand said. 'We'll have to help one another to get to the bottom of this.'

'I wasn't the one who authorized the transportation,' Abrahamsson said. 'That was the Foreign Ministry. The foreign minister.'

'Yes,' Bertstrand said, 'but it isn't the transportation *per se* that's the problem.'

'I could hardly help it if something happened once they were in the air. Then it's the captain who—'

'Abrahamsson,' the head of the Security Police said, turning to face him again. '*George* is the problem. Haven't you grasped that?' He walked slowly towards the chair where Abrahamsson was sitting. 'How,' he said slowly, 'are we going to explain that you handed over

314

official control at a Swedish airport to the *American fucking CIA?*' He shouted the last three words.

Abrahamsson pushed back hard in his chair and clutched the armrests.

'Let's deconstruct this,' Bertstrand said. 'The government decided that the terrorist needed to be extradited so we're in the clear on that. Whatever might have happened to him after that is also regulated by legislation that only the government can call upon, so we're fine there as well. We might be able to make the transportation itself the issue here, in which case it would be the Foreign Ministry's problem.'

'*The American fucking CIA?*' the head of the Security Police yelled again, staring red-eyed at Abrahamsson. '*George?*'

'If we can keep the public focus on the flight itself rather than on who was exercising official authority we should be okay,' Bertstrand said. 'Most editors find aeroplanes much sexier than legal paragraphs, don't they?'

The head of the Security Police groaned loudly, then went and sat at his desk.

'We have to handle this in the right way from now on,' Bertstrand said. 'It's important that we say the right things. And it's important that other things are, ideally, not said at all.' He smiled thinly. 'How did you say your son was doing, Anton? Nine months old? Have you ever thought about spending a bit more time with him?'

Abrahamsson merely nodded. He was unable to speak.

The sun was already warm. It was going to be a lovely day, the first real summer's day.

Annika was strolling in the garden while the children

315

put their shoes on. The new flowerbed by the gap in the hedge wasn't, if she was honest, a thing of great beauty. The plants looked tired and untidy, leaning limply against each other, and there weren't enough of them. But with a bit of luck they'd fill out over the summer and look healthier.

Her mother-in-law had wrinkled her nose and wondered if Annika couldn't have helped the children plant the bed. 'I planted it,' Annika had replied. 'Don't you like it?'

And Doris Samuelsson had changed the subject.

Kalle was coming towards her, dragging his heels. He took her hand and burrowed his face into her jeans. 'I want to stay at home today, Mummy,' he said.

'Why's that, then?' she said, squatting beside him. 'Aren't you feeling well, or are you just a bit tired?'

'I want to stay at home,' he repeated.

'But I've got to go to work,' Annika said, stroking his back. 'In a few weeks' time Daddy will be on holiday, and then you can be at home, and go swimming with him for almost the whole summer. That'll be good, won't it?'

He nodded. She took his hand and led him to the SUV.

Ellen had climbed up into the back seat by herself. Annika helped her with her seatbelt, and they set off.

When they arrived at the nursery the little girl ran off with Poppy and Ludde under her arms, chatting to the staff, but Kalle hung back by the car. 'What's the matter, Kalle?' Annika asked. 'Why don't you want to go in?'

'Come over here,' said Lotta, the member of staff who was making sure he settled in. 'You're so early today that you've got time to go on the computer before breakfast, if you'd like to.'

Kalle took her hand and disappeared into the building.

Help him, Annika thought. Help him where I can't. Please, someone, look after my children when I'm not able to.

She got into the car and drove home for the last day of her leave.

She cleared away breakfast. She wrote a shopping list of things she needed for dinner that evening. She made coffee. Drank it. She sat at the kitchen window feeling the pressure in her chest grow.

Then she put her mug into the sink and went back to her computer.

Yesterday she had tried writing on the terrace, but the brand new laptop battery was dead so she was stuck with the cable and plug inside the house. The office was small and Thomas's papers, books and reports were scattered all over the place. She wondered if his office in the department was as much of a mess. She gathered together the documents on the desk into a pile, moved Thomas's computer to one side and put hers in the middle.

She went on to the Internet and checked the *Evening Post*'s homepage, but there were so many flashing headlines that she had to freeze it before she could read it. Sunday had been relatively uneventful. Rumour had it that Princess Madeleine had decided to learn to sail, there'd been some sort of sexually motivated attack on Darin, a big pop star, and the police had shot an eighteen-year-old in Borlänge in the leg. And Zlatan had scored a goal.

Nothing about Caroline von Behring.

Nothing about the Nobel killings.

It was as if nothing had happened. People had already started to say, *Oh, yes, the Nobel banquet, didn't some-one die there? Someone who fell over the railings into the water, or something?*

She almost couldn't remember it properly herself. After just six months her memory was hazy. The music was almost silent, the food had lost its insipid taste. Only Caroline remained, the look in her eyes when she had realized what was happening, her silent plea.

As she had so many times before, Annika logged into her personal email account and pulled up her text about the Nobel banquet. It was fortunate that she'd written everything down straight after the event: her thoughts were there, her reactions unclouded by time. She read about the lights, the glasses, the dancing and Bosse, of course. Then the push, the bruise on her foot, the shoulder-strap, Caroline, the blood, those yellow eyes.

Those yellow eyes . . .

How quickly things fade.

She closed the article and checked her work email account.

She had three new messages.

Party at the nursery – bring cakes, we'll provide coffee and juice!

She stared at it for a long minute. The nursery in question was the one on Kungsholmen, and the email had reached her by mistake, a mass email sent to a mailing list from which her name hadn't been erased. They didn't belong there any more.

She clicked to open the second: *New battery.* She could pick up a replacement battery from Spike in the newsroom any time after eleven. Great.

Her hand stopped, hovering over the keyboard as she read the title of the third: *You're lying, and you're going to be punished!* The sender's name made her lean closer: *Nobel Lives.*

What the hell?

She clicked to open the email.

You're one of the hypocrites. You've set yourself up as a champion of the truth, but all you bring are lies and darkness.

She scrolled down and read on:

I know the truth about the Nobel Assembly. The high-priest of hypocrisy, the Machiavelli of the Nobel Committee, the man who has turned dissembling into an art and despotism into a virtue, he thought he'd silenced me when he banished me, but that would take a far more serious offence. Just ask Nemesis, ask Caroline von Behring! And ask Birgitta Larsén!

Aha, she thought, and went back up to the signature: *Nobel Lives.* She highlighted the name, clicked to bring up *properties*, and found the real address behind the signature.

She let out a deep breath. Lars-Henry. She might have known.

But what did he mean? Who was he referring to? Ernst Ericsson, Caroline's successor as chair of the committee?

Everyone knows but no one's saying anything, they're all joining in this filthy game. The most

319

powerful man has been bought, lock, stock, and barrel, by the pharmaceutical industry, and is resting safely in the monster's maw. He drinks too much and lets through unreliable results – and now his MS treatment is being tested on people, but what happened during the tests on animals? Why were they buried in secret? We must all take responsibility. Whose life is more important? The powerful man's, or the sick man's?

Annika's unease grew the more she read.

Your friend is an opportunist who manoeuvred her partners out of the way. I know what happened, only money counts, only Mammon matters – god of wealth and property. Now she has bought herself a position in the world again, a place at the table of the hungry, in the room where Sæhrimnir the hog is slaughtered day after day without any thought of the consequences . . .

The last section was addressed directly to her:

You have a responsibility to the world, the responsibility you took upon yourself to safeguard the truth, but you are betraying it.

This will not go unpunished.

WILL NOT GO UNPUNISHED!

The email wasn't signed.
She stared at the screen until her eyes burned.
It wasn't unusual for nutters to contact you when your byline appeared above articles in the evening paper. Up

in the newsroom she had a shoebox full of peculiar and threatening letters, faxes and printouts of emails.

But this was something else. The unhinged, ostracized professor really did want something from her. He hadn't signed the email, but had sent it from his usual address at the Karolinska Institute so, clearly, he wasn't bothered about concealing his identity. In that respect he was just like the member of staff at the Social Democrats' headquarters on Sveavägen who had conducted a smear campaign against the leader of the Moderate Party. He could easily have set up a hotmail address and called himself something like *single mum Alice*.

That his signature was *Nobel Lives* was perhaps a bit odd, but she knew someone who popped up as *Sherlock* when his name was Anders, so maybe it wasn't that unusual.

She rubbed her forehead. This was quite straight-forward, really. Either Lars-Henry Svensson was a paranoid obsessive, or there was something in what he was saying.

She looked at the time. It was already a quarter to nine. She reached for the phone on the desk, dialled Reception at the Karolinska Institute and asked to be put through.

Professor Birgitta Larsén picked up after the first ring. Annika said her name, but the professor cut her off abruptly. 'So what's Caroline been telling you this time, then?'

'I've got a different source today,' Annika said. 'I've received an anonymous email from the Karolinska Institute, and I think I know who wrote it.'

Birgitta sighed. 'I see,' she said. 'So Lars-Henry is writing to you as well, is he? What's he threatening you with?'

'I'm betraying the truth,' Annika said, 'and this won't go unpunished. And I'm supposed to ask you about crimes that silence people.'

There was the sound of a chair scraping the floor, as if Birgitta were sitting down. 'There's something mentally wrong with Lars-Henry,' she said. 'One of the girls in our network is a university lecturer in medical psychiatry. She'd probably have a fancy name for it. I just think he's mad. Don't worry about him.'

'Does he always carry on like this?'

'He has his moments, but this time he's gone way over the limit. Do you feel threatened?'

Annika thought about it. 'Not exactly,' she said, 'but it has made me think. Why is he sending this now, and why to me? Has anything happened?'

For once Birgitta was silent. 'You've spoken to Ebba since the seminar?' she said finally.

The seminar? 'Ebba's in Dalarna,' Annika said. 'I haven't spoken to her for a couple of days.' The seminar? On Saturday? After the Nobel Assembly held its first meeting about this year's prize, with drinks and nibbles afterwards?

'What happened after the seminar?' she asked. 'And why am I being dragged into it?'

'There was a bit of a fuss,' Birgitta said. 'What else does he say in the email?'

Annika hesitated. 'He makes accusations against various people,' she said.

Birgitta groaned. 'And now you're wondering if there's any fire behind all the smoke,' she said. 'Well, I think you should bring a printout of that email up here so we can take a look at these accusations. I've got a meeting at ten, so you'll have to be quick.'

'I'll set off at once,' Annika said.

'It really is time for us to sort this madman out once and for all,' Birgitta said, and hung up.

Annika sat with the phone in her hand for a few seconds. She had evidently struck a nerve in Birgitta Larsén: she wanted to see what Lars-Henry Svensson was saying, and to know what he knew.

Annika printed off a hard copy of the email.

23

Birgitta Larsén's department was much brighter and airier than Ebba's. There were rows of double windows, all the doors were glass, and the ceiling was noticeably higher. The walls were yellow, white, blue, and the floor a warm red.

'These were Astra's old premises, before they merged to form AstraZeneca,' Birgitta said, striding down the corridor. 'Say what you like about the private sector, but they know how to build a decent workplace. I send up a little prayer of thanks to Håkan Mogren every morning that they decided to move the whole business down to Södertälje. This is my office.'

She unlocked the door as Annika peered in through the glass wall. Desk, computer, a small microscope, test-tubes and pictures of children of various ages.

'You have children?' Annika asked, hearing the surprise in her own voice.

'And grandchildren,' Birgitta said, stopping in front of the photograph collection. She sighed happily. 'I can't believe they're all mine!' With a swift gesture she pulled out two office chairs and waved Annika into one.

'Don't worry about the radiation warnings,' the professor said, pointing at the yellow tape with red symbols that ran round the edge of the floor. 'They've assured me that it's all been sorted out now. If they're lying, there'll soon come a time when I won't have to switch the lights on in a dark room. Have you brought the email?'

Annika handed over the printout. Birgitta held it out in front of her and scanned it, her eyebrows rising. 'Hmm,' she said. 'Okay, I see . . .'

Then she let out a deep sigh, and Annika could have sworn it was prompted by relief.

'This is just his usual nonsense,' she said. 'Nothing you need to worry about.' She handed it back to Annika.

'I presume Machiavelli is Ernst Ericsson,' Annika said. 'And *my friend* is obviously Ebba – he saw the two of us together. Ebba's told me what happened to her business, and obviously there are different ways of looking at that, but what does he mean about the dead animals? Could Ernst have cheated with some research results?'

Birgitta stood up, irritated. 'In this business you keep your work to yourself,' she said. 'It's not like journalism where you stand up and pour things out in public every single day, no disrespect intended. Here you work in secret for several years before you reveal your conclusions, so Lars-Henry obviously has no idea how Ernst's research is going. This is nothing but a classic case of jealousy. Ernst's animals are fine, and he happens to be very fond of them. I'm on my way over there now. I've got a meeting with Bernhard Thorell to discuss renovation of the premises.'

'Can I come with you?'

Birgitta looked at her in surprise. 'We don't usually let people in just like that,' she said. 'After all the attacks by animal-rights campaigners the buildings are kept anonymous. There's no indication of what they're used for from the outside. Why do you want to see them?'

Annika looked steadily at her. 'I'm interested,' she said.
'Interested in what?'

In what you're hiding, Annika thought. In what you're not telling me. In everything you don't want me to know about Caroline, and in what happened on Saturday. 'In science,' she said. 'In development and progress. You're the ones who do the work. I'm just a megaphone.'

Her answer seemed to work on Professor Larsén. She pulled a bunch of keys from a drawer and headed to the door. 'It's quite a walk,' she said. 'And I need to get a decent cup of coffee on the way.'

They went out of the building into the sunshine, heading across a lawn towards the Jöns Jakob restaurant. Steel-edged glass doors slid open automatically as they approached. Inside it smelt of school dinners: boiled vegetables and gravy. Their steps echoed on the dark-red stone floor. Metre-thick wooden beams crossed the ceiling. Long rows of rectangular birchwood tables only added to the school-canteen atmosphere.

'It hasn't got any Michelin stars,' Birgitta said, 'but they do a decent latte.'

They ordered one each, and Annika paid for both. 'Do you use test animals yourself?' she asked, as they came out into the sunlight again.

'About fifty at the moment,' the professor said, turning off on to a footpath. 'Mostly mice, but a few rabbits as well. They're awfully sweet.'

'Isn't it hard, having to make them suffer?' Annika asked, hurrying to keep up with the solid little woman.

The professor glanced at her. 'My dear,' she said, 'my research primarily requires behavioural studies. I teach the mice to take hold of sweets with either the right paw or the left, to swim across a little pool or

326

pick up breakfast cereal in the middle of an open area.'

'What exactly are you researching?'

'The ageing process,' Birgitta said. 'The biological effects of ageing, mainly on the nervous system but also on the organs governed by the nervous system. Why do you ask?'

'You need to do tests on animals to look into that?'

'The truth is that there are a lot of similarities between the ageing process in yeast, worms, mice and human beings. So I wish I could say no. But unfortunately we aren't quite at the stage where we don't need to conduct tests on animals. Difficult questions that affect an entire organism, plant and animal alike, can't be answered simply by studying cell samples.'

They turned on to a path lined with a low hedge.

'Have you reached any conclusions?' Annika asked.

'That I can reveal to you? Well, the fact that glial cell-line-derived neurotrophic factors are actually produced in greater quantities when we age. This is where we go in.'

'So you know how old I might get?'

'That depends mainly on your genes, darling, and obviously how well you look after yourself, but as far as we understand it today, the biological age limit for a human is somewhere between a hundred and twenty and a hundred and thirty.' She patted Annika's cheek. 'You've got a bit of time left. Would you mind switching off your mobile? We conduct electrophysiological studies in Faraday cages in here, and we don't want any more radiation than necessary. We'll have to finish these before we go in.'

They sat down on a low bench outside the entrance with their coffee. Annika switched off her mobile, shut her eyes and enjoyed the sunshine.

'What was Lars-Henry arguing with Ernst about on Saturday?' she said. 'What exactly did he say?'

Birgitta let out a noise that was halfway between a laugh and a snort. 'Lars-Henry was picking fights with everyone, me included. I saw him attack several people, individually and in groups. Ebba Romanova was one, and Bernhard Thorell, Sören Hammarsten and his little gang, and he had a go at the head of department for a while, but he only really exploded when he got to Ernst.'

'What about?'

She took a sip of her latte. 'More or less what he wrote in your email. That Ernst was fiddling his results, that he had been told to rerun the experiment but had failed and published the results anyway.'

'Meaning that he'd falsified his conclusions? About what?'

Birgitta finished her coffee. 'It's all just nonsense. Nothing worth worrying about.'

Annika looked out across the lawns surrounding them. 'In that case it doesn't matter, does it?' she said. 'You may as well tell me.'

Birgitta Larsén sighed. 'You don't give up, do you? It was to do with multiple sclerosis. You know about MS? An inflammatory disease of the central nervous system?'

'President Bartlet in *The West Wing* had it,' Annika said.

'I don't know about that,' Birgitta said. 'The treatment is fairly new, about ten years old, and Ernst was one of the main people involved. His team confirmed that the new interferon beta treatment, the disease modifier, in other words, was sometimes neutralized by the body's own antibodies. And it was his attempts to stop this neutralization that Lars-Henry accused him of falsifying.'

'How?'

'Ernst succeeded with his trials, and wrote an article about them, which was accepted by *Science*. You've heard of *Science*, one of the most prestigious scientific journals?'

'I know the editor-in-chief,' Annika said, remembering her dinner partner at the Nobel banquet.

'Oh, well, then! The article was accepted on one condition, that Ernst repeated his trials and got the same results again. That much is true. What Lars-Henry claims is that Ernst cheated, that he faked the experiments the second time round and submitted false results.'

'And did he?'

Birgitta snorted. 'Ernst had already done everything twice and was absolutely convinced by the results. But despite this he did everything a third time. It took another four months, but he succeeded again. MS sufferers the world over will reap the benefits from now on. Have you finished your coffee?'

Annika crumpled the empty paper cup.

'Good,' Birgitta said. 'You're about to find out that these buildings aren't quite as nice as the others.'

She opened the main door, using a plastic card and a code. They walked into a hallway with grubby walls and a dark-grey linoleum floor. They went down a flight of steps, then took a lift down several more floors before stepping out into an underground hallway. A single strip-light in the ceiling cast a bluish-white beam and sharp shadows over their faces. Four light-grey doors with coded locks led in different directions.

'These days, the animals are kept completely isolated, both from each other and from external influences,' Birgitta said, 'so we'll have to change our clothes. I hope you haven't got anything too valuable in that bag of yours?'

'Only money, credit cards and car keys,' Annika said.

'Oh, well, then . . .'

They stepped into an airlock, with changing rooms on either side, women to the right and men to the left. The women's was cramped and messy.

'For your hair,' the professor said, passing Annika a blue paper cap. 'You'll find a coat, gloves and wooden sandals on those shelves over there. And wash your hands too, especially under your nails and round your cuticles. That's where they're dirtiest.'

Annika pulled her hair up and tied it into a loose knot, then put the cap on and pulled on an enormous green lab coat and a pair of pale-beige sandals. She scrubbed her hands and put on a pair of milk-coloured latex gloves.

Another coded lock, and then they were inside the laboratory with the test animals.

'Hello, Eva. Have you seen Bernhard Thorell?' Birgitta asked, walking up to a woman in similar clothing who was leaning over a bench.

She didn't look up, just carried on focusing intently on something. 'Should I have?' she asked.

Annika saw that she was holding a small mouse. With a swift movement she cut off its little black head, tossed the body on to a heap of other corpses and examined the head.

Birgitta looked at her watch. 'We were supposed to meet here, but I might be a bit early. This is Annika Bengtzon. I'm showing her round.'

The woman glanced up at Annika. 'Hello,' she said, then went back to her mouse's head.

'What are you doing?' Annika asked, staring at the woman's nimble fingers.

'I need to take a slice of the mouse's brain to check its dopamine levels,' she said. 'Looking at the signal substances, in other words. From the marks on the ear here I can see if it's been genetically modified or not.' She held the animal's severed head towards Annika, who nodded mutely. Then she pulled out the mouse's brain with a practised movement and laid it on a small glass tray. It was the same colour as raw sausage.

'I'll just have to wait,' Birgitta said. 'Shall we take a look at my animals?' She headed off down the corridor and Annika supposed she should follow her.

'You know Bernhard Thorell?' Annika asked.

Birgitta laughed. 'Not really,' she said. 'He got his doctorate here a hundred years ago, then did an economics degree in Britain. But now he lives in the States, where he's MD of Medi-Tec, the pharmaceutical company. They've got a very talented group of scientists over there. A year or so ago they published something of real significance.' She rounded a corner, with a slightly embarrassed shrug. 'Well,' she said, 'the significance of what they discovered is open to debate, of course, but I suppose I'm interested because their area of research is related to mine: ageing. They discovered a way to inhibit dystrophy in axons. And that affects pretty much everyone – you start to see the first signs at the age of nine or ten.'

'They've found a way to stop the ageing process?' Annika said.

'So they say,' the professor said.

'The wellspring of life,' Annika said. 'Wow.'

'Well,' Birgitta said, 'there are various other teams round the world that have reached similar results, so it isn't quite the case that the Medi-Tec team were either the first or the best, but they've certainly demonstrated

331

that they're skilful and serious. This is where we go in.' She opened a door, revealing row after row of animals in Plexiglass boxes. 'This is where the mice live,' she said. 'As you can see, they've got sawdust in their cages, and that white stuff is their toys. All the ones on this row are mine.'

'Their toys?' Annika said.

'We've done experiments to let the mice choose what they think is most fun to play with – little plastic houses, egg boxes or Kleenex tissues. It turned out that they love tissues. They chew them, tear them to pieces, build nests with them. Next best were egg boxes, but they were completely uninterested in the plastic houses. What they liked best of all was dragging the tissues into the egg-boxes and rearranging them.'

'That's amazing,' Annika said, and sure enough, the mouse she was watching really was playing with the tissues. 'What would have happened if Lars-Henry was right?'

Birgitta gave her a quick look, then pulled down a file and leafed through it. 'You mean if Ernst had cheated and sent in false results? If someone could actually prove that was what happened?'

'Yes. What consequences would that have had for Ernst's career?'

The professor carried on leafing through the notes, pausing before she answered. 'If he'd been exposed as a liar? Well, what do you think would have happened?'

'He certainly wouldn't have been appointed chair of the Nobel Committee,' Annika said.

Birgitta stopped and looked down the corridor. 'His career would have been left in ruins, of course. Maybe he could have got a job as a lab assistant somewhere.' She closed the file with a snap and put it back on the shelf.

'Mice aren't social creatures,' she said. 'The females can put up with each other, but the males kill each other as soon as they're given the opportunity. Rats, on the other hand, are pack animals – they're further down the corridor. The rabbits are on the other side. In total, we've got about two thousand cages here at the institute.'

'No cats or dogs or monkeys?' Annika wondered.

'That was a long time ago,' Birgitta said. 'In the late 1980s new regulations were introduced and the whole animal-testing industry was tightened up. But before then there were all sorts of animals all over the place.'

She closed the door and swept on. They passed a room marked *Termination* and emerged into what looked like an operating theatre. 'Have you seen Bernhard Thorell?' she asked a young man, who was busy taking blood samples from a box of rodents.

'What's that?' Annika asked, looking at a steel contraption on one of the tables.

'A stereotactic instrument,' Birgitta told her. 'You use it to hold animals in place when you're operating on them. Over there, on the wall, is the equipment for anaesthetizing them first. As you can see, this one's got screws and drills so it can cut through the skull with millimetre precision. This is a fairly small version. We've got larger ones too.'

Annika looked at the contraption, with all its spokes and arms, and shivered. She'd seen pictures of animals strapped into instruments like this.

'Ah, there you are!' the professor exclaimed happily, bouncing off down the corridor. 'You see what awful conditions we have to work in?'

A man replied, but Annika couldn't tear her eyes from the operation instruments at the end of the table. 'What are those?' she asked the young man beside her. He had just finished taking the samples from the mice.

'Various tools,' he said, pointing. 'Scalpels, clamps, needle-holders, pincers, forceps . . .'

'And it doesn't hurt the animals?' Annika asked.

He smiled shyly. 'Well, they're unconscious, and any that need to be put down are just given a bit of extra anaesthetic.'

'Do you always use drugs when you put them down?' Annika asked, glancing at the door to the termination room.

'The easiest way to put mice down is a quick tug of the head. You break the spinal cord, basically. Larger animals are put in a cage and given a mixture of oxygen and carbon dioxide.'

A gas-chamber, Annika thought, nodding.

Birgitta came over to her with Bernhard Thorell at her side. He, too, was wearing a blue cap and green coat. 'This is Annika Bengtzon,' the professor said.

Annika's latex glove shook Thorell's latex glove.

'It's doctoral students like you who are the future of science,' he said, with a smile so wide it gleamed.

Birgitta giggled. 'Annika's a reporter,' she said. 'She's here to write about the world of scientific research. Annika, perhaps you'd like to write something about Bernhard. He's promised to help finance the renovation of our facilities.'

'I'd rather see it as the subject of negotiation,' Thorell said, smiling.

'Imagine,' the professor said, throwing out her arms, 'bright yellow walls, a soft colour scheme, better lighting, smarter floors.' She turned to Annika. 'Bernhard is a huge asset to the institute,' she said, taking the MD's arm. 'We're so happy to have you here!' She patted his latex glove. 'Niklas, can you show Ms Bengtzon out?'

A young man who looked after the animals appeared behind them in a green coat and blue cap.

She seems extremely fond of him, Annika thought, as Birgitta disappeared into the room containing the rats with Thorell glued to her side.

24

Thomas glanced nervously at the time. Ten minutes to go. He rubbed his shoulder and tried to relax. This was all rather ridiculous. It's not like I'm getting married, he thought, it's just an ordinary work briefing. They take place every Monday, so what am I getting so worked up about?

He stood up, unable to sit still, and wandered down the corridor to Per Cramne's room. 'Shall we go?' he said.

Cramne was trying frantically to squeeze a large bundle of papers into a plastic folder that was far too small. 'You're going in as item number five,' the section boss said. 'First, Crime will be running through something about the courts, employment practices, if I remember rightly. Then there are several different matters regarding the police, so it'll be fine if you come up at eleven or so. I'm dealing with the new document of appropriation so I'm heading up now.'

Thomas nodded, feeling a little flushed. He knew that the document governing the work of the police authorities over the coming year usually took time to go through. It was all about the nuances in formulation, the order in which things should be listed, and deciding which priorities should be emphasized on the first page.

'Were you thinking of moving in, or what?' Cramne said, from the door.

Thomas hurried out of his colleague's office and back to his own room. He couldn't think of anything more he could do. On Friday he had thrashed his way through all the material one more time with Cramne, the director general for legal affairs, and the under-secretary of state. After that his work had gone off to be copied, so that the minister could read everything over the weekend. Thomas had happened to see the heap of papers being carried in to him later that afternoon. Even if he read round the clock, there was no way he could possibly have got through everything.

With an irritated sigh, he sat down at his computer again. He double-clicked on Free Cell. The statistics showed he had 87 per cent wins, and had won his last eleven games. He clicked on *New Game* and got a really tricky layout, with three kings at the bottom and two aces right up at the top. Nothing can really go wrong now, he thought. The results wouldn't have been passed if they'd been too thin or inconclusive.

He put two nines and a three in the free cells to the left and uncovered an ace.

The thought of what would happen after today's briefing made him feel slightly dizzy. The government and parliamentary group would be informed of the proposal; it was possible that the matter would reach the Management Committee. And if everyone was happy with it, a legislative proposal would be drawn up. Then the Supreme Court and the Supreme Administrative Court in the Legislative Council would check it to make sure that it didn't contravene the constitution.

His work. *His work.*

His mobile started to ring somewhere at the bottom of his briefcase and he let go of the mouse to dig it out. He didn't recognize the number – and didn't have time for any nonsense right now.

'Is that Thomas Samuelsson, Kalle's father?'

Shit, the nursery.

'I'm afraid there's been an accident,' the nursery teacher said, sounding pretty upset. 'Kalle's fallen off the climbing-frame. He has quite a deep cut on his forehead, and we're worried he may have concussion as well. The cut needs stitching. How soon can you get here?'

Thomas felt his stomach clench into a rock-hard ball, and looked at the time. Ten to eleven. 'I'm ridiculously busy at the moment,' he said. 'Have you tried ringing Annika? I know she's not working today.'

'We can't get any answer at home and her mobile is switched off.' The teacher's voice was harder now.

Fuck. He tugged at his hair and stood up. 'I can't come right now,' he said. 'I'm in the middle of a meeting until about a quarter past eleven. I can't leave before then.'

'Your son has got concussion because the other children pushed him off a two-metre-high climbing-frame,' the woman at the other end said, sounding angry now. 'How soon can you get here?'

'How long does it take to drive from Rosenbad?' he said, trying to sound icy and important.

She didn't notice that he had given the address of the seat of government. 'We'll be waiting for you,' she said, 'but if he loses consciousness we'll call an ambulance.' She hung up.

He was left holding the phone and staring at the screen. Then he finished the move he had been contemplating before the phone rang, a six on a seven. The whole screen shuddered. He had just one more move left to make and he would have lost the game.

What was he supposed to do? Should he hand over the briefing in the Blue Room to someone else? Let someone else row his boat home?

He put a nine on the ten.

Sorry, you lost!

Thomas turned off the screen, gathered his papers, pushed his chair under the desk and adjusted his collar. He didn't usually wear a tie to work, but this morning he had considered it. He had decided against it, hadn't wanted to look conspicuously well dressed: it would seem amateurish somehow.

He took the lift up to the sixth floor, opening the security door with his passcard.

This was his work, his proposal, his influence.

After the Legislative Council the proposal would be passed at a cabinet meeting. Then the whole package of legislation would be presented to Parliament in the form of a government proposition.

Good God, what was he doing? He ought to leave – he should be with Kalle.

A few civil servants were waiting in the foyer out-side the Blue Room, tapping their feet, hands in pockets. Thomas sat at a table at the end of the corridor. They'll probably get hold of Annika, he thought. What was he supposed to do? Leave everything to Cramne?

A moment later the double doors of the briefing room opened and a dozen or so people streamed out. Last of all came Cramne, who stopped when he saw Thomas and gestured him in.

'Rock'n'roll,' he said.

Thomas walked past the civil servants, feeling their

eyes on him. He stepped into the Blue Room and Cramne closed the doors.

It was bigger than he had expected. The walls really were light blue, with white panelling, giving the room a fresh, almost chilly atmosphere. The windows were large, letting in light from both south and west. Behind thin white curtains he could see the spire of Storkyrkan in Gamla Stan, as well as the tower of the City Hall, topped with its three golden crowns.

'Bugging,' Jimmy Halenius said. 'Welcome! There's bottled water in the fridge if you'd like some.' He pointed to a fridge just to the left of the door.

Thomas shook his head, then followed Cramne to the far end of the room and sat down with his back to the waters of Riddarfjärden. Around him were the seven or eight civil servants who had taken part in the previous discussion and were evidently going to be part of this one as well.

He cleared his throat quietly. Should I say something about Kalle? he thought. The minister has children. I'm sure he'd understand.

Jimmy Halenius leaned over to talk quietly to the minister, who listened and made notes.

Thomas tried not to look anxious. The other children had pushed Kalle off the climing-frame. His friends had hurt him so badly that he needed to go to hospital and be *stitched up*?

The room was dominated by a circular birchwood table, and there was an octagonal blue-grey rug on the floor. The minister and his assistants sat beside each other with their backs to a large painting.

I'll give them a thrashing, Thomas thought. No one hurts my son and gets away with it.

On one wall there was a large fireplace, the mantelpiece holding the flags of Sweden and the EU. There were chairs round the table and along the walls, also birchwood, pale leather seats. He looked at the ceiling. Up there, beyond the white porcelain lamps, was the prime minister's office.

'Can you give us a summary of the content?' Halenius said.

Thomas straightened his back. He stumbled slightly as he explained the main points of the project he had spent the past six months working on.

Kalle, dear God, I'm on my way! I'll make it better!

The minister sat and read and leafed through the papers and made notes. 'It's good that the legal safeguards are highlighted,' he said. 'Anyone who is bugged must have the right to legal representation. All instances must be approved by a court and reauthorized every month. That's good.' He read in silence for a few seconds. 'But there's one section of the proposal I'd like to remove,' he said. 'Bugging for the purposes of prevention, on page forty-three. That's going too far.'

Birger Jarlsgatan, Thomas thought. That ought to be quicker than Sveavägen and Valhallavägen at this time of day.

'Forty-three,' Cramne said quietly, next to him, and Thomas felt the heat rise to his face as he turned to the right page.

'We'll limit the preventive measures to phone-tapping and intercepting post,' the minister said. 'We'll restrict bugging to crimes that have already been committed. Good!'

He put the folder to one side and picked up the next and, as if at a given signal, Cramne and most of the other civil servants stood up.

Was it over?

Could he go now?

'It's the Security Police now,' Cramne whispered, 'which means that anyone without clearance has to leave.'

Thomas gathered his papers and stumbled out after the others. 'I have to go,' he said breathlessly to Cramne. 'My son's had an accident and I've got to get him to hospital.'

'Oh dear,' Cramne said. 'Are we still having dinner this evening?'

'Of course,' Thomas said, and managed a smile. He could feel sweat breaking out on his brow.

'Is it true that Halenius is coming?' Cramne asked.

'Yes – he emailed to say he'd be there.'

'Well,' Cramne said, moving to stand closer to Thomas and lowering his voice, 'one doesn't usually invite politicians, just so you know . . .'

Thomas felt his cheeks burning as the section head moved away again.

'Eight o'clock or so, then? Vinterviksvägen, Djursholm?' Cramne asked.

The lock whirred and Thomas pushed the door open. 'Vinterviksvägen,' he said, and fled through the foyer.

Annika walked into the newsroom, which, once again, felt oddly surreal. Everything was familiar yet different. Her eyes lingered on the glass room with the bright-blue curtains: her old office, now the radio studio. I wonder where all my files and papers and pens ended up, she thought.

Berit was sitting at her computer with her reading glasses on, writing.

'Anything exciting?' Annika asked, settling on Patrik's chair.

'I'm going through all the legislative proposals that restrict the integrity of the individual,' Berit said, staring at the screen. 'Exciting probably isn't the right word.' She peered over her glasses and smiled. 'But it's really good to see you here again.'

'Do you know where all my files went when they emptied my office?' Annika asked.

'I saved anything I thought you'd want and put it in that cabinet over there.' She pointed to a grey metal one next to the water-cooler.

Annika went to it and opened the top drawer. Inside lay all her bundles of papers, for the first time ever in some sort of order. District-court judgements, appeal-court judgements, government propositions, reports, summons applications, old newspaper articles and pages of notes. Berit had filed everything by case and date. 'This is amazing!' she said. 'Thank you!'

'It was actually quite fun going through it,' Berit said, taking off her glasses. 'It was a bit of a walk down Memory Lane. They were all things I didn't write about, so it was quite useful to get a reminder of them.'

Annika looked through a few files as Berit carried on writing. She found the judgement in the Josefin Liljeberg case, and the verdict against her boyfriend Joachim, five and a half years in prison, not for her murder but for dishonesty to creditors, false accounting, tax fraud, tax evasion and obstructing tax control. I wonder what he's doing now, she thought.

There was a telegram from the Associated Press dated 7 April seven years ago. It was about Ratko, the man who had killed a young woman and had run the cigarette-smuggling industry in Scandinavia after the war in Bosnia. She put it back and pulled out a cutting from the *Evening Post*, an interview with Anders Schyman when he had been appointed editor-in-chief in place of that old stiff Torstensson. It was written by Sjölander. The fact that the economic unit of Stockholm Police was looking into the suspected insider dealing of the former editor was dealt with in a box alongside the interview. Behind the cutting was a report dated 27 June the previous year. Annika had found evidence that proved Torstensson had exploited his inside knowledge when he had sold his shares in the company Global Future.

I made Schyman captain of this ship, she thought. Maybe I ought to remind him of that.

A year later Torstensson had been found guilty of insider dealing and sentenced to one hundred days' community service. Annika scanned the report of the verdict. The fact that he had been slammed by the press and had lost his job was regarded as an extenuating circumstance. 'Imagine,' she said. 'The fact that we write about crooks is seen as so awful that they don't have to go to prison.'

'The state wants to have a monopoly on imposing punishment,' Berit said. 'And now they want the right to raid our homes without any evidence, and to bug our phones because they feel like it.'

Annika put the files back into the cabinet and returned to Patrik's chair. 'If I've got this right, all our neighbouring countries have this sort of law,' she said. 'Norway, Denmark, Finland . . .'

'Yes,' Berit said, 'but they don't have the same baggage as us. They haven't had what amounts to single-party government by the Social Democrats for the best part of a century, listening and registering and pursuing people for no other reason than that they parked in the wrong place at the wrong time, like outside a building where a "suspect" meeting was taking place.'

'Undeniably an aggravating circumstance,' Annika said.

'Now the Social Democrats are claiming that they're all being nice and kind and that these tools would *never*, *ever* be used for anything other than the very best of reasons. They're saying that they won't carry on doing what they did when it was illegal, as long as they can make it legal. Do they think we were born yesterday?'

'Annika!' Spike called from the news desk. 'What are you doing over there? You're not in Crime now. Come here!'

Annika pulled a face and stood up. 'Lunch?'

'Definitely,' Berit said.

Annika went over to Spike and put her bag demonstratively on top of his paperwork. He pulled out a sheet of paper and held it up to her without looking at her. 'Robbery in a shop out in Fittja,' he said. 'Can you take a look?'

She picked up her bag again and hoisted it on to her shoulder. 'Nice to see you too,' she said. 'I don't start until tomorrow. I'm here to pick up a new battery for my laptop. Apparently you have one.'

Spike put the sheet of paper back on the pile, pulled out his bottom drawer and passed Annika a battery.

'How are we going to do this from now on?' Annika said. 'I won't be coming in every day, after all. Will you call me, or shall I call you?'

At that moment Spike's phone rang and he grabbed it.

This could turn out to be rather trying, she thought, as she headed towards the canteen.

After lunch Annika drove slowly towards Fridhemsplan, heading for the indoor market at Östermalmshallen. Fresh mussels, she thought, prawns from Smögen, sole,

345

Norwegian salmon, tuna, some really creamy aïoli, lots of saffron and some medium dry white wine. Strips of lemon peel and some thyme, onions and tomatoes. Lobster stock, of course, masses of dill, and freshly baked garlic bread with flakes of sea-salt and plenty of basil.

Thomas had already bought the wine. He didn't trust her to do that, which was fairly justifiable.

She crossed Barnhusbron and headed along Tegnérgatan. The traffic-lights changed to red and she stopped.

Did she have any bay leaves? Any white peppercorns? She had thrown away a lot of old herbs and spices when they'd moved. Probably best to buy some more.

A car pulled up alongside her and she glanced at it.

A red Volvo estate, with a woman behind the wheel.

She looked up at the traffic-lights again, still red.

She looked back at the car alongside her . . . Wasn't that Ebba? Had she come back early? Wasn't she supposed to be away until tomorrow?

Annika waved, but the woman didn't see her.

Still red.

She fished her mobile out of her bag on the seat beside her so that she could call her neighbour. It was still switched off after her visit to the lab.

A large lorry beeped behind her. She dropped the phone and drove off across the junction. The red Volvo turned left and disappeared from view.

She hit another red light up on Västmannagatan and took the chance to tap in her pin-code to unlock the phone. Seconds later it bleeped to tell her a text had arrived. Then another, and another.

What the . . . ?

The text at the top of the list was from her message

service: *You have . . . eight . . . new messages. To listen to your messages, press one.*

She pulled up at a pedestrian crossing outside the Enskilda secondary school.

'Hello, Annika, this is Lotta. Kalle's had a fall and is bleeding quite badly. Can you call as soon as you get this?'

Beep.

'Annika, Kalle seems to be getting worse. We think he may have concussion, and the cut looks like it needs stitches. Can you call us, please?'

Beep.

'Kalle's not at all well. Can you call us? We're about to ring for an ambulance.'

Her hands started to shake. She put the car in gear and drove off.

Beep.

'Annika, where the hell are you? I've left the briefing and I'm in A&E at Danderyd Hospital with Kalle. Call me!'

She started to cry as she drove, listening to the messages.

Beep.

'You'd better be doing something really fucking important. Call me.'

Beep.

'I've been to see the doctor now, Mummy, and I've got a white plaster on my head. It's really big. When are you coming, Mummy?'

Beep.

'We're home now. I'm getting us some lunch. I have to go back to work, so it would be nice if you could call as soon as you hear this.'

That was from Thomas, his voice ice-cold.

347

This isn't fair, she thought, wiping her tears. I have to be able to go about as I like. I have to be able to switch my phone off for four hours without the world coming to an end.

She drove far too fast all the way home, skidding to a halt in the driveway, throwing the door open and running into the house. 'Kalle!' she called, rushing upstairs to his room. 'Kalle, where are you? How are you feeling?'

He was sitting on the floor of the office, painting, with Thomas at the computer.

'Hello, Mummy. Look at my huge plaster!' He got up and came over to her.

She knelt down and took him in her arms, rocking him gently. 'Sorry,' she whispered. 'I was out and I didn't have my phone on, so I didn't know you'd hurt yourself. What happened? Did you fall?' She loosened her grip on him and stroked his hair, looking intently at his forehead. His lip started to tremble and his eyes filled with tears. 'Is it hurting? Are you feeling sick?'

He shook his head.

'What's the matter?' she said. 'Tell Mummy what happened.'

'They were being mean,' he said. 'The other boys are mean to me. They pushed me and made me fall off.'

Annika looked at Thomas, who was getting up from his chair. 'Is that true?' she said. 'Did those little bastards at the nursery do this?'

'Think about your choice of words,' Thomas said. 'But, yes, it looks like it. I've spoken to the staff, and they're going to talk to the children about it this afternoon.'

She let go of her son and stood up. 'Right,' she said, 'that does it. I'm going to—'

Thomas took a long stride towards her and grabbed her upper arms. 'Annika,' he said sharply. 'Calm down. The staff are going to talk to the parents of the boys involved. We don't want to make things any worse.'

Tears spilled down her cheeks. 'I can't bear it,' she whispered. 'I can't stand not being able to do anything.'

Thomas let go of her and sighed. 'The doctors did a scan and couldn't find any swelling or bleeding in the brain,' he said. 'But you'll have to keep an eye on him this afternoon. The symptoms of concussion can take a few hours to develop. He's allowed to sleep, but you'll have to wake him up at regular intervals to make sure he isn't unconscious.'

'Do I have to give him any medicine?'

Thomas looked at his watch. 'They gave him some painkillers at the hospital, but he can have another paracetamol in an hour's time. I'm going back to work.' He walked out of the room and down the stairs.

25

Kalle slept for a while once Thomas had left, and when he woke up he was lucid and bright-eyed. He didn't want to rush about, and clung close to Annika, helping her lay the table out on the terrace. They used the dark-blue cloth, the best glasses and the plain white china. He said his head didn't hurt, and he wasn't feeling sick.

Afterwards Annika read him a story, letting the child's heavy warmth fill her own body as she rocked him in her arms.

Thank you, Someone, that it wasn't worse, thank you for letting him be here with me, thank you for the fact that he's here at all.

They drove out to Arninge and bought some ready-made fish soup that just needed warming up, some baguettes and a large bunch of lilies. Then they went to pick up Ellen, ten minutes before the nursery shut. The other children had already left. Just like in the city, everyone out here seemed to play *whoever picks up first is the winner*, and Annika always lost.

'Which boys pushed Kalle?' Annika asked Lotta quietly, as Ellen clambered into the back seat.

Lotta, who had been working a double shift, sighed

deeply. 'Benjamin and Alexander,' she said. 'You know who they are, don't you? They didn't mean any harm, not really.'

'Of course not,' Annika said calmly. 'Have you spoken to them?'

'Yes, and to their parents . . .' She let the sentence fade away.

'And?' Annika said.

Lotta looked at the ground. 'They said it was an accident.' She kicked a plastic ball towards the store-cupboard. 'They thought I was making too much of it. Boys will be boys, and all that rubbish. I told them exactly what had happened, that their boys had pushed Kalle off the climbing-frame. There's no doubt in my mind that they did it on purpose.'

'You saw it happen?' Annika asked.

'No, but Malin did. She teaches the younger children. She's absolutely sure.'

'Okay,' Annika said. 'Thanks for trying.'

They drove home and put the soup on to heat. Annika had forgotten to put the wine in the fridge, so she stuck a few bottles into the freezer and hoped she wouldn't forget them, like she usually did. Both children were hungry and she gave them fish-fingers and instant mash on the best china. Then they were more than happy to curl up in front of the television and watch a DVD.

Annika tidied away the crayons, drawing pads and comics from the dining area and set out a tablecloth and flowers in there too. She vacuumed the floor and wiped the kitchen worktops. She did a quick tour of the house, putting clothes, dirty washing and toys in their respective places, gave the toilets and hand-basins a quick scrub, and put out some fresh towels.

Candles? Should you have candles at the end of May? She decided against it.

There. That would have to do.

She went up to the bedroom to find something to wear. A dress, perhaps, or would that be too much?

It was still warm outside, above twenty degrees, even though it was half past seven.

Surely Thomas ought to be home soon.

She brushed her hair and put on a cotton dress, then some lipstick and a pair of gold earrings. She examined herself in the mirror and decided she looked like a cheerleader from Hälleforsnäs dressed up as a Djursholm housewife.

She took off the dress, wiped away the lipstick, then put on a pair of jeans and a neatly pressed white blouse. She kept the earrings – her grandmother had given them to her.

The doorbell rang. Shit. Thomas still wasn't home. What on earth was she going to do?

She ran downstairs barefoot and opened the door.

Startled, the man outside took a quick step back, then said, with a laugh, 'Oh, hello! Are we in the right place? The Samuelsson household?'

He was tall, dark and a bit gangly, his wife small, neat and beautiful.

'Absolutely,' Annika said, her mouth dry. 'Come in, please.' She opened the door wide and took several steps back. 'Thomas isn't home yet, but please, come in.'

The couple shook her hand and introduced themselves as the Larssons. Annika had heard of him: he was another who was working on restricting people's private space with surveillance and more legislation. They had brought flowers and a bottle of red wine.

'Would you like a drink?' Annika asked, suddenly

feeling that her hands were too large for the rest of her body.

'A dry martini would go down well,' Mr Larsson said.

'Yes, why not?' his wife said, with a smile.

Annika felt her own smile turn brittle. How on earth did you make a dry martini? Were there really people who actually drank that sort of thing? She realized she had to make a quick decision. Either she tried to live up to something she wasn't capable of, which would get more and more embarrassing as the evening wore on, or she gave up at the start and got the embarrassment over and done with. 'I don't know how to make them,' she said. 'Thomas might, but we don't have much in the way of spirits. I put some bottles of white wine in the freezer. I don't know if they've had long enough to chill, but if you can help me get one open we can give it a try?'

The Larssons raised their eyebrows but decided to put a brave face on it. He managed to get the cork out, even though it had almost frozen solid, and declared the wine to be at the perfect temperature.

'Great,' Annika said. 'Maybe we should put the others in the fridge now. It's such a nuisance when they freeze.'

They had just settled into the wicker sofa on the terrace with their glasses when Thomas appeared. 'God, sorry, I really didn't mean . . .' he said, rushing up and greeting his guests breathlessly.

'It's quite okay,' Mr Larsson said. 'I'm not God.'

Everyone laughed, except Annika, who went inside to check on the children. 'How are you doing, Kalle?' she asked, looking at him closely. 'Does your head hurt at all?'

'You're standing in the way of the television, Mummy,' he said, leaning to one side so he could see.

'Ellen,' she said, 'it's time to put your pyjamas on. Do you want me to help you?'

'Is there any popcorn?' the little girl asked hopefully.

'Not today. It's only Monday. We'll have popcorn on Friday.'

'But Daddy's got wine,' Ellen said.

'Five more minutes,' Annika said. 'Then it's time for bed.'

She went over to the kitchen to stir the soup. It was simmering on the lowest heat with the lid half off. By the time she served it, it would probably have boiled away to a lumpy fish sauce, but she couldn't have cared less.

Kalle didn't seem too badly shaken after his accident. But he'd have to get used to the scar on his forehead.

The Althins had arrived and were drinking wine on the terrace with the others when she went out again. Thomas handed Annika her glass. 'Hans tells me you don't know how to make a dry martini,' he said, with a slightly strained laugh.

'Have you ever, over the past seven years, seen me mix one single cocktail?' Annika asked quietly, taking the wine.

The doorbell rang again and the last guests arrived simultaneously, Per Cramne and the under-secretary, Jimmy Halenius. They were each given a glass of wine and presented to Annika.

'Nice to meet you,' Halenius said, smiling. 'I've heard a lot about you.'

'Well, cheers,' Thomas said, 'and welcome!'

'I thought only small-time gangsters had names ending in y,' Annika said to Halenius. 'How come there are never any escaped prisoners called Stig-Björn, for instance?'

'My grandfather was actually called Stig-Björn,' he replied. 'He was convicted of the laundry-room murder in Angered in the sixties. You may have heard of it . . . But I don't think he ever escaped so you're right there.'

Annika stared at him. He was fairly short, nowhere near as tall as Thomas, his light-brown hair was uncombed, and he was wearing a checked shirt. He looked terribly serious. 'You're teasing me,' she said.

His face cracked into a wide smile, making his eyes narrow. 'Whatever makes you think that?'

He thought he was so charming. He went round imposing limits on people's freedom just to help his career, and no doubt he thought he was a really great guy.

'How come you've heard about me?' she asked.

'You used to have an old Volvo, didn't you?' he said. 'A 144, dark-blue, lots of rust?'

Annika felt the blood rising through her body and settling in her face. 'My then boyfriend had one like that,' she said. 'I sold it for him.'

'That was pretty nice of you,' the under-secretary of state said. 'You must be one hell of a car saleswoman. No one knew how you managed to get five thousand for that old wreck.'

'Sven couldn't sell it himself,' Annika said. 'He . . . he died.'

She put her glass on the table and went into the kitchen, her hands trembling. Why on earth had she said that? I'm an idiot, she thought, her cheeks burning.

Thomas was showing his guests the garden while Annika put the children to bed and read them a quick story. Then she went down to the kitchen and squeezed the aïoli she had bought from the supermarket out of its

355

tube into a glass dish, adding a couple of extra cloves of crushed garlic for good measure. She followed the group's progress round the garden from the window as she put the baguette, smeared with garlic butter, into the oven. She saw her husband gesturing with his wine glass as he explained something.

He's proud of us, she thought. He wants to show his colleagues what he's got. All of this means something important to him. We're going to be fine.

Wilhelm Hopkins was moving about on the other side of the hedge. He was busy doing something Annika couldn't see, but it looked like he was trying to move something heavy. He's probably being nosy, she thought. I bet he wants to know who our guests are.

The two men's wives had scarcely spoken to Annika. They were both over forty, wearing fashionable mid-length skirts and smart jewellery. They were slim, with the sort of very fine hair that demanded expensive cuts and loads of product. Now they were walking behind the men, chatting to each other and sipping their wine. They both had teenage children who were probably out in the city somewhere, or hanging out with their friends.

Am I going to be like them? Annika wondered. Will I end up sipping chilled white wine in different suburban gardens for the rest of my life? The thought sent an uncomfortable shiver down her spine.

She served the soup on the terrace – she hadn't managed to boil the life out of it. It was salty and full of dill, and the aïoli was quite palatable. The bread was a bit singed round the edges, but it wasn't a disaster.

'Well, your good health again, everyone,' Thomas said. '*Bon appétit!*'

They all seemed hungry, and ate in silence for a while.

The breeze was mild, and smelt of lilac blossom.

'There's plenty more,' Annika said, and they all had a second helping.

The men started to talk more animatedly about people at work, about various proposals that had flopped, and about how recalcitrant the Legislative Council was. Now that they were bit drunk, they were very entertaining.

'You're a journalist, aren't you?' Larsson said, re-filling everyone's glasses.

'Thanks, not for me,' Annika said, stopping him as he got to hers. 'Yes, I'm on the *Evening Post*.'

'What sort of thing do you write about?' his wife asked.

'Violence and politics, mainly,' Annika said, swirling the last of the wine in her glass.

'Really?' Larsson said. 'Maybe you should come and work for us.'

Annika put her glass down. 'We both invade people's privacy, but in different ways,' she said. 'Was that what you meant?'

'What – you hang them out to dry on the front page and we make sure they go to prison?' Jimmy Halenius said.

To her surprise, Annika couldn't help laughing.

'Let's drink to that!' Thomas said.

They raised their glasses again, and over the rim of hers, Annika could see that Thomas was relieved: he hadn't been sure if she would handle the situation or the conversation particularly well.

A moment later Wilhelm Hopkins started up his lawnmower. Not the modern little electric one that he usually used but a petrol-driven monster. The vibration made the windows rattle.

'I don't believe it,' Annika said.

'What?' Jimmy Halenius shouted to her.

Incredibly slowly, their neighbour steered his ancient lawnmower along the other side of the hedge, just ten metres from the terrace where they were sitting and eating.

'Does he usually behave like this?' the under-secretary of state yelled.

'Not quite,' Annika replied, 'but I'm not exactly surprised.'

Halenius looked in astonishment at the man's heavy frame through the foliage. 'He's really not joking,' he shouted in Annika's ear.

A few moments later the exhaust fumes hit them. Annika started coughing and put her hand over her nose.

Thomas got up and came over to her. 'This isn't on,' he said in her ear. 'We'll have to go inside.'

Annika nodded, picked up her glass, plate and napkin and stood up. She gestured to their guests to do the same. They went into the dining room, carefully balancing the fine china and the crystal glasses that had belonged to Thomas's grandfather.

Annika closed the terrace door behind them, but the sound of the machine still found its way in through the panes of glass.

'He's a little eccentric, our next-door neighbour,' Thomas said apologetically.

'Our house is built on what used to be a piece of common land,' Annika said, 'and he can't accept that Danderyd Council sold it with planning permission. He claims that he still has the right to use it.'

She glanced at Thomas and saw that he wanted her to shut up. 'It's a fact,' she went on, 'that disputes between neighbours lead to murders practically every year in Sweden. People fall out about stairwells, laundry rooms, playground swings, you name it.' She raised her glass. 'But of course you know all that. You're the professionals,' she said, taking a sip. God, it was vile. She really couldn't stand white wine.

'Not so long ago we had a neighbourhood dispute in the Supreme Court,' Halenius said.

'Did someone die?' Annika said.

'Only a cherry tree. It was all about a ditch that had been filled in, if I remember rightly, somewhere outside Gothenburg. The neighbours pushed the case through the legal system for ten years without coming to any agreement. Even the Supreme Court couldn't reach a unanimous verdict in the end.'

'Things like that are tricky,' Larsson said. 'I read about a case in Torslanda recently, one neighbour intimidating the other, something about a boathouse.'

A moment later Annika saw Wilhelm Hopkins through the gap in the hedge that he usually drove through. He was pushing the vast lawnmower ahead of him, straining so hard that he was dripping with sweat. Without pausing, he turned out of his own garden and drove into Annika and Thomas's. He flexed his muscles, then set off across Annika's newly planted flowerbed.

She stood up, utterly speechless.

At that moment Hopkins stopped, looked up at the house, then turned the lawnmower through ninety degrees and continued along the length of the flowerbed. Summer phlox, marigolds and busy lizzies flew through the air as the whirling blades cut them to shreds.

Something snapped inside her head. All those flowers, the children's flowers, which she had planted and watered and nurtured. 'Right, you bastard,' she said, throwing her napkin on to the floor. She flew to the terrace door and tore it open, dashed down the steps and across the grass. She shoved Hopkins with both hands, forcing him to let go of the mower, which spluttered and died.

'Help!' Hopkins cried theatrically. 'She's attacking me! Help!'

'Are you completely fucking mad?' Annika yelled, her voice echoing in the sudden silence. 'How can you just drive your mower over my flowerbed?'

She was about to give him another shove, but he took a step backwards, pulling the mower with him. 'You little worm,' he sneered. He stared down at his chest to see if she had left any mark, then took another stumbling step backwards. 'You'll pay for this,' he shouted. 'I'm going to call the police. You hear me? The police!'

'Be my guest,' Annika shouted back. 'By all means. Half the Justice Department just witnessed what you've done.'

Suddenly Thomas's arms were wrapped round her, picking her up and swinging her round to face the other way. 'I really must apologize for my wife's behaviour,' Thomas said to the man.

'Like hell!' Annika yelled, trying to wriggle free.

Thomas was red in the face with embarrassment and anger. Their guests had gathered round the terrace door and were staring at Annika, who was still seething, with expressions of shock on their faces. All apart from Halenius, who had walked on to the grass and was laughing so hard that tears were pouring down his cheeks.

'And someone's parked in the road!' the man was shouting. 'You've gone too far this time!'

'Sorry,' Thomas said to his colleagues 'I really am terribly sorry about this. Annika, I don't understand what's got into you . . .'

'I can't go on like this,' she said quietly to him, pulling free. 'You have to back me up, or we'll have to move. Why do you think the last people who lived here moved? After all, you worked out that they must have lost at least two and a half million on the sale. Now do you understand?'

He grabbed her again, but she pulled away and walked quickly towards the front door.

At the corner of the house, Halenius was still unable to stop laughing.

'What's so funny?' she said, as she passed him.

'Sorry,' he said, wiping his eyes. 'Sorry, really, but it looked so . . .'

'I'm glad I was able to entertain you,' she said, going back inside the house.

She was halfway up the stairs when the phone rang.

I'll let Thomas get it, she thought. All of a sudden she felt completely drained. Her whole body was shaking and she could hardly get up the stairs. Is life supposed to be like this? she wondered. Why isn't anything easy?

The whole idea had been that they would move somewhere peaceful and secure. That was why they were here. This was supposed to be their safe place, and Thomas would finally be proud of her, but she simply didn't fit in. No matter how hard she tried, it just kept going wrong.

Oh, God, she thought. Why don't I ever make anything easy for myself?

'Annika,' Thomas said, behind her. 'Annika, it's the paper.'

She swallowed hard and closed her eyes, pressing a hand to her forehead. 'I don't start work again until tomorrow.'

'That's in two hours' time, and they say it's important.'

I can't do this, she thought. I can't go on like this.
'What?'

'Someone's died. Drowned in his bath, and apparently he lives close to us.'

'Who?'

'They said you knew him, something to do with that whole Nobel thing. His name's Ernst Ericsson.'

Subject: Nobel's Will
To: Andrietta Ahlsell

The person who occupied Alfred Nobel's thoughts most during the last years of his life had been dead almost three hundred years: Beatrice Cenci.

The *Nemesis* project closes the circle of Alfred Nobel's life.

He was born a poet. If he is certain of anything, it is this.

You say I am a riddle, he writes as a teenager, a 425-line poem about Paris and love. He writes other poems, a lot of poems, *Thoughts of the Night*; he starts a novel, *The Sisters*.

He is seventeen years old when his father Immanuel realizes that Alfred's ambition to become a writer – dear Lord! – is completely genuine. They live in Tsarist Russia, in St Petersburg close to the banks of the Neva. Anyone who can't pay his debts is thrown into prison. His father's business has gone badly: does Alfred want to see his father in the fortress? Can Alfred shoulder this burden? Is he prepared to take responsibility?

Alfred, Alfred, they shouldn't demand this of you! It isn't fair!

But he burns his poems. He burns them all, every

362

last one. Only two remain, as copies in other hands. *The Sisters* is finished, but is never published.

And the decades pass. Alfred reads, he writes letters, he collects an enormous library. Of all the loves that remain unrequited in Alfred Nobel's life, literature is the greatest. Eventually he decides that he must finally – *finally!* – be true to himself.

In a prose drama written for the stage Alfred *the poet* will tell the truth about life and death. As a framing device he chooses the classic tale of the Cenci family's tragic fate.

And the poet creates a remorseless settling of scores with Church and society. In the very first scene he writes: *There is no justice, neither here nor beyond the grave.*

Disguised as the young Beatrice he cries: *I am the avenger of wronged innocence and downtrodden justice.*

The settling of scores is extremely violent. Beatrice the rape victim tortures her father, the rapist, to death. She pours molten lead into his ears and knocks his teeth out, all the while enjoying it: *Ah, your cries cannot touch me. No music has ever sounded so sweet to my ears.*

Alfred is very happy with his play. He writes to Bertha von Suttner that he has written a play in *poetic prose*, and that its scenic effect is *very good*. He tries to have it translated into German, into Norwegian, but fails. Instead he decides to have the work printed as it is, in Swedish, and he employs a young parson's wife, Anna Söderblom, married to Nathan and living in Paris, to read the proofs.

The printer has his premises at 19 rue des Saint-Pères.

The proof-copy, to be delivered to the young woman, is stamped: *Expédiée le 10 DÉCEMBRE 1896*.

The play is finished, Alfred! It is ready now, on the day that you die!

The newly printed books, the spiritual testament of Alfred Nobel the poet, lie in piles in Pastor Nathan Söderblom's office at 6 rue de Tour des Dames.

And the pastor read, his relations read, his colleagues read, and they are agreed.

It is the industrial magnate who must be remembered, not the person.

His money is praised, not his creativity.

No one wants a critical settling of scores with the Church, or a violent drama about incest, or harsh words about society from the grave.

No one wants to recognize Alfred *the poet*.

So the pastor burns the books. He burns the entire print-run, apart from three copies, which remain hidden for a hundred years.

And so you are silenced, Alfred, once and for all.

So you are fooled, one final time.

But that's all over now.

Part 3
JUNE

PART 3

JUNE

Tuesday, 1 June

26

At midnight it started to rain. Out of nowhere, the skies opened and a crystal-clear bolt of lightning lit up the entire area for a split second.

Annika rushed back to her car, which she had left on the other side of the fence. At the same time forensics officers poured out of the house, covering the ground around the house and driveway with large tarpaulins.

They don't want any evidence out here to be washed away, Annika thought. They've still got a lot to do inside the house, but they know they're going to have to examine the garden as well.

The men moved quickly and efficiently under the heavy rain, then disappeared back into the house.

Annika bit her lip. This was starting to feel really odd. What could be taking them so long in there? She pulled out her mobile and called the duty desk of the police crime unit again, listening to the ringing tone as she stared at the house through the rain-streaked windows.

Ernst Ericsson's home was just a kilometre or so from Vinterviksvägen, down towards Djursholms Torg. The house was a classic 1920s villa, yellow, two floors. The garden was flat and anonymous, not dissimilar to her own, but it had a large pool at the back.

The house was a hive of activity, lit up like a Christmas tree. The forensics team's arc-lights matched the flashes of lightning outside, showing that they were carefully searching the entire house. She had caught a glimpse of a garish Hawaiian shirt through one of the upstairs windows, so she knew that Q was there. Both the regular police and the crime unit had been there when she arrived, and the forensics team had turned up fifteen minutes later.

She stared up at the house, at the shadows moving inside. It was obvious that the police thought Ernst Ericsson had been murdered, but why? Drowned in his bath, according to the tip-off to the paper, from one of the guys who spent all day listening to the police radio.

It could be right, or it could be completely wrong.

The officer who was guarding the cordon at the end of the drive wasn't the talkative sort. She'd got no more than five words out of him, *Can you move back, please*, so he hadn't exactly helped with any of the question marks.

There were no other media here, just her and the paper's photographer, the idiotic Ulf Olsson. He was sitting in his car, and she was quite happy for him to stay there.

Thank goodness I didn't drink any more wine, she thought. Then the duty desk answered her call.

'I just wanted to check if a lead investigator had been appointed to the preliminary investigation into the murder of Ernst Ericsson,' she said, and held her breath as she waited for the reply.

She heard the officer shuffle some papers. 'We're still working on that,' he said.

Confirmation of murder, Annika thought, making a

mental note. 'Will it be Brolin?' she asked, then held her breath again.

This time the officer was saying nothing. 'Don't know,' he said.

Linda Brolin, senior public prosecutor, was leading the investigation into the murders of Caroline von Behring and the two security guards at the Nobel banquet. 'Anyone else would be a bit impractical,' Annika suggested lightly, but the officer knew he had said too much.

'You'll have to get back to us later,' he said, and hung up.

She took out her ear-piece and looked at the house again. No visible movement. No flickering shadows. They're sitting inside talking, Annika thought, working out what to do next. Maybe they're almost done.

At that moment a dark vehicle swung into the road ahead of her, and she instinctively raised her arm to shield her eyes from the headlights. The vehicle rolled slowly down the road through the rain and pulled up at the end of Ernst Ericsson's drive. The lights were switched off and the engine died.

She peered through the windscreen. What was it doing there?

She gasped when she saw what sort of vehicle it was.

A police van, not an ambulance.

The police had called for Transport to remove the corpse. Which meant that the body really was indisputably dead, but it also meant something else.

According to the regulations, it meant that the head must have been separated from the body. Over the years she had seen similar vehicles arrive at other crime scenes, which had all had one thing in common: the victim had suffered a brutal and violent death.

Ernst, she thought, what have they done to you?

Another vehicle turned into the road, behind her this time. She followed the progress of the headlights in the rear-view mirror until they passed her and the vehicle pulled up just ahead of her. An unmarked car, a Saab 95. Annika craned her neck to see who was inside. The coroner? More forensics officers?

Two men got out, one holding a large camera case.

The competition had arrived. It would have been nice to be alone here when they brought out the body.

The photographer put up his hood to keep the rain off, then took a camera out of the case and started checking the available angles. The other man stared at the house for a moment, then turned and looked at her SUV. He leaned forward, squinting, then took several hesitant steps before opening the passenger door. 'May I?'

It was Bosse.

Annika felt her throat tighten, and she merely nodded.

He sat beside her and closed the door.

'Terrible weather,' she said, staring ahead through the windscreen.

'Christ, yes,' Bosse said. She could tell he was smiling at her and turned to him. God, he was handsome. 'How have you been?' he asked, and she drew a very audible breath.

'It's all a bit much . . .'

He brushed a wet strand of hair from her cheek, his fingers leaving burning tracks on her skin. 'You haven't been answering my texts,' he said quietly.

She looked at her lap. 'I . . . I can't,' she said.

A heavy silence filled the vehicle, and the drumming of the rain on the roof seemed to get louder.

'Would you rather not see me?' Bosse said, his voice oddly muffled.

Annika glanced at him again, but his face was in darkness. He seemed to fill the whole car – she could feel his presence as physically as if he had been holding her tight.

She looked away. 'I can't,' she said.

'Okay,' he said, after a short pause. 'Okay.' He opened the car door and got out into the rain and she opened her mouth and reached out her hand to stop him, leaning towards him, but he closed the passenger door behind him. At the house the front door opened and the trolley carrying the body was pushed out into the rain.

Thomas was asleep when she got home. She closed the bedroom door, went into the office, switched on the desk lamp and called Jansson.

'Is it murder?' the night editor asked.

'Without a shadow of a doubt,' Annika said. 'I imagine they'll appoint a lead investigator within the next few hours, and I'd put money on it being Brolin.'

'How much is publishable?'

'So far, not much. Just observations of the crime scene, and the fact that a prosecutor is being appointed. But Q was there, so I'm hoping to get hold of him later on.'

'How did he die?'

'Don't know, but it was probably violent.'

'How come?'

'Police van, not an ambulance.'

'That doesn't necessarily mean anything,' Jansson said. 'There've been a lot of accidents tonight. Maybe the ambulances were busy elsewhere. Anything else?'

She bit her lip. 'No.'

'So, correct me if I'm wrong,' Jansson said, 'we've got a death that *might* be murder, but which hasn't been confirmed officially, and which *might* have been violent, but we can only speculate about that. Is this really much of a story?'

'Well, it's the second time in six months that the chair of the Nobel Committee has been murdered,' Annika said. 'It's huge. What's the competition for the front-page?'

The night editor sighed. 'We've got great pictures of Princess Madeleine on a yacht out in Sandhamn.'

Annika took a deep breath. 'Listen,' she said. 'Get someone to put together an obituary of Ernst Ericsson, his life in words and pictures. There's a lot to choose from. Our illustrious colleagues on the morning paper did a big thing about him last winter when he got hold of a research grant worth three-quarters of a billion from an American pharmaceutical company.'

'It all feels pretty limp,' Jansson said.

'Wait till you get my piece,' Annika said, and hung up. She tried to get Q on his direct line. No answer. She called the duty desk again. They'd put a lid on the whole story.

She called the emergency calls control centre and asked if they'd had any calls about a death in Djursholm the previous evening.

Two, plus another in Mörby.

Anything that looked suspicious?

The one in Mörby was a suspected stabbing, and one of the cases in Djursholm was still undetermined; the police had been called to the scene. The third was a heart-attack.

So who had made the emergency call about the unclear case in Djursholm?

The report didn't say.

Oh, well.

She called Q again. Still no answer.

Who else could she contact?

Who had known Ernst Ericsson and might have something worth saying? She went into the online telephone directory and typed in the simplest of searches. There were twenty-nine Birgitta Larséns, four of them in the Stockholm area: one in Haninge, one in Bandhagen, one on Kungsholmen and one in Resersberg. The last one was the only one spelled with an accent on the *e*.

Annika took a couple of deep breaths before dialling the number.

'Good evening,' she said, when a sleepy male voice answered. 'My name is Annika Bengtzon and I'm calling from the *Evening Post*. I wonder if I've got the right number? I'm trying to reach Professor Birgitta Larsén of the Karolinska Institute.'

The man breathed loudly down the phone. He sounded as if he'd got a cold. 'What?'

'I'm trying to contact Professor Birgitta—'

'Birgitta,' the man said, evidently to someone next to him. 'It's some professor who wants to talk to you.'

'What?' Annika heard a sleepy woman's voice say.

There was a lot of crackling and rustling at the other end of the line.

'Hello?' the woman said.

The voice wasn't the professor's. 'Sorry to bother you so late,' Annika said. 'My name's Annika Bengtzon, I'm calling from the *Evening Post* and I'm trying to get hold of Professor Birgitta Larsén of the Karolinska Institute. But you're not her, are you?'

'Who?' the woman said. 'Has something happened to Mum?'

'No, not at all,' Annika said. 'I've just got the wrong number. I was trying to get hold of a different Birgitta Larsén. I'm sorry to have disturbed you.'

The woman breathed out. 'Okay,' she said, and hung up.

Damn.

She logged on to the the national population register and searched for Birgitta Larsén.

318 hits.

This wasn't going to work. She had to think of a way to limit the search. How old was she? Where did she live? What was her husband's name, assuming she was actually married?

Annika groaned.

She went on to Google instead.

Professor Birgitta Larsén, *search*.

8,700 hits. Articles about her research, more research, still more research, cultivation of roses . . .

Cultivation of roses?

She clicked the link.

Professor with rose hobby was the heading. Some text from *Gardening News*: *Professor of biophysics, Birgitta Larsén, has many strings to her bow. In her beautiful garden in Mälarhöjden south of Stockholm . . .*

Annika checked the postcodes for south Stockholm. Mälarhöjden came under Hägersten, where they began with 129. The article in *Gardening News* was three years old, but Annika didn't imagine she had moved. Not if she devoted all her spare time to her garden.

She went back into the Infotorg site and limited the search to *birgitta larsén 129*, and bingo!

One result. Number 7, Bisittargatan. Her husband's name was Tage Friberg. And he was listed in the phone directory.

Birgitta answered on the first ring.

'This is Annika Bengtzon,' Annika said.

'Fancy that,' Birgitta said. 'I had a feeling you were going to get in touch.'

'So you're awake, then,' Annika said. 'I presume you know why I'm calling.'

Birgitta blew her nose loudly. 'This is all too much right now,' she said, with a sniff. 'I don't know if I can do this any more – it's all gone too far. Now Ernst! When they phoned to tell me I thought, No, not Ernst as well . . .'

She started to cry, sniffing loudly. Annika listened quietly.

'Do you know what happened?' the professor asked. 'Do you know how he died?'

'Ernst Ericsson lived quite close to me,' Annika said. 'I spent tonight sitting outside his house. The police have cordoned off the garden, and they've been searching the whole house. It looks like they think it's suspicious.'

Birgitta was still crying. 'It's just like I said!' she cried. 'Now they've taken Ernst too – I said they would, didn't I, Tage? Was he murdered? Do you know anything about it? Has anyone said if he was murdered?'

'No,' Annika said. 'But it looks very likely.'

The woman fell silent, and blew her nose once more. 'That's what I thought,' she whispered. 'As soon as Sören called, that's what I thought. Now they've got rid of him as well . . .'

'Who are *they*?' Annika asked carefully.

'Oh, but, my dear,' Birgitta said, completely lucid now. 'If I knew that we wouldn't have any problems, would we? We could just go and pick them up and lock them away, couldn't we?'

'I suppose so,' Annika said. 'What did Sören say when he called?' She presumed they were talking about Sören Hammarsten, the vice chair.

'Only that Ernst's son had found him drowned in the bath, and that the police had taken Lars-Henry in for questioning, as if he could have had anything to do with it . . .'

Annika stiffened. So they had already apprehended someone?

'But he might just have fallen asleep in the bath,' Birgitta said. 'I'd rather you didn't mention it on the front page but sometimes Ernst drank a bit too much. And in my opinion he was a little too fond of Cipramil, and when he'd had too much whisky on top of that he could be a bit of a handful.'

'Like last Saturday?' Annika asked. 'After the seminar?'

Birgitta snorted. 'It was all completely uncalled for, what Lars-Henry did. I know I ought to take more care of him now that Caroline is gone, but it's very tiring, it really is.'

'Why should you have any responsibility for Lars-Henry? Did Caroline?'

The professor sniffed and blew her nose again. 'This is absolutely dreadful,' she said. 'Do you really think he was murdered? Couldn't that be a mistake? Maybe he just fell asleep.'

'Maybe,' Annika said. 'I'm about to talk to the police, and things will be clearer tomorrow.'

'Thanks for calling,' Birgitta said.

I'm the one who should be thanking you, Annika thought. 'Call me whenever you want to,' she said, and gave the professor her mobile number.

Q still wasn't answering. Annika was absolutely certain he was at work, but he wasn't necessarily in his office and she didn't have his mobile number. She hadn't managed to wrangle it out of him yet.

378

But she did have his email address. She took a chance and sent a provocative message: *How long is Brolin going to hold Lars-Henry Svensson? Call me. Annika.*

Thirty seconds later her mobile rang.

'We aren't going public about Brolin yet, and definitely not about Svensson,' the detective inspector said, in a loud, angry voice.

'So what are you going public with?'

'Whose side are you really on?'

Annika looked at the time. 'I started work again three and a half hours ago, and I've got thirty minutes to my deadline. Either I write what I think is true, or I write what I know.'

Q groaned loudly. 'Okay. We can talk about Brolin, but not Svensson.'

'How about someone taken in for questioning during the night?'

'Oh, what the hell? Okay.'

'Murder?' Annika asked.

'Absolutely.'

There were a few moments' silence.

'You're ruling out accidental death?' Annika asked. 'Sudden illness? Suicide?'

'Of all the suicides I've seen, this would be one of the hardest ones to explain,' Q said, hanging up.

She wrote thirty lines about how yet another chair of the Karolinska Institute's Nobel Committee had been murdered within six months. How unconfirmed reports suggested that a relative had found him dead and that the police were convinced it was murder. A short description of the crime scene and the police work out there, the fact that the lead investigator of the Nobel murders, Linda Brolin, had been allocated this case as well, ending with the fact that the police had already taken someone in for questioning.

She called Jansson as soon as she had emailed him the text, and waited in silence as he read it.

The night editor was no longer sighing. 'You're right,' he said. 'This is hot. Madeleine's off the front and into the box at the top of the page.'

'Have you done "Memories of Ernst Ericsson"?'

'I took you at your word, so that's sorted.'

When they had hung up Annika sat staring out of the office window. It had stopped raining, and the sun was coming up. She could hear the birds singing in Wilhelm Hopkins's hedge. If she listened carefully she could hear her family sleeping, Thomas's rhythmic breathing on the other side of the wall, Ellen whimpering in her sleep, unless she was imagining things. Was it just her own pulse she could hear?

Tiredness overwhelmed her. Her thoughts grew fuzzy, words faded away, her body ached and her head felt full of lead. God, she thought, I have to go to bed. She went into the bathroom, undressed, brushed her teeth and crept into bed beside Thomas. He didn't wake up.

27

The water in the bath was cloudy and grey. There were long threads swimming about in it, like algae, sticking to the sides and stirring up small waves on the surface.

Annika was standing in the doorway staring at the bath. She didn't want to be there at all: she wasn't supposed to see this. She had a feeling she had already gone too far.

'It's your deadline now,' Anders Schyman said behind her. 'If you're going to keep your job on this paper you'd better hurry up.'

She knew he was right and took a long stride into the bathroom.

There was a woman floating at the bottom of the bath. The algae was her hair, drifting through the water like snakes.

'We need a police van,' Annika said, but at that moment the woman opened her eyes.

They had no irises, were just blank and white.

She tried to scream but no sound came. She turned to run, but where the door had been there was just a plain tiled wall.

The woman sat up in the bath, her blind eyes staring at Annika. She was naked, her skin covered with slime.

She was trying to say something, but only a hissing sound came out, and Annika realized that the woman was Caroline von Behring.

Annika pressed back against the wall, trying to catch her breath. 'I don't understand,' she managed to say. 'I don't know what you want.'

Then something in her chest gave way and she could breathe again. 'Leave me alone!' she shouted. 'Let me be! It wasn't my fault!'

Her shouting echoed around the little room, and she turned to run again, but another woman was standing right behind her. It was Sophia Grenborg, and she was pale blue, ice-cold and wet. When she opened her mouth there was nothing but a black hole, her throat gurgling like a drain.

'I'm the one he loves now,' the gurgling said.

'Annika, what is it?' Thomas was leaning over her, shaking her shoulder. 'Can you hear me, Anki? Are you ill?'

Annika turned away from the terrible pale-blue Sophia Grenborg and stared in the other direction, into the tiled wall. 'What?' she said.

'Annika, you have to wake up. I'm going to work now.'

'What about Kalle?' Annika said, screwing her eyes shut.

Thomas sat on the bed beside her and sighed. 'He'll have to stay at home and rest today.'

She lay still for a few seconds, feeling sleep and the bad dream tugging at her. 'Today's my first day back,' she said thickly. 'I can't stay at home.'

'What do you mean?' Thomas said. 'You were working all night. When did you actually get to bed?'

Annika threw the covers aside. 'This is my first day back after six months away,' she said. 'I can't be at home, not today.'

'But you're supposed to be able to work from home!' Thomas said, standing up. 'You've got the laptop and everything.'

Tiredness was sending flashes of lightning through her head. *Fuck*, she couldn't deal with this sort of debate the moment she tried to use her brain for something other than *housework*. 'I can't do this!' she shouted. 'I can't deal with this sort of crap the moment I have a good reason to leave the house.'

She grabbed a dressing-gown and marched out to the bathroom, feeling giddy and sick. As she stepped through the door she realized that this was where she had been until a few minutes ago. Caroline von Behring had been lying dead in her bath. She turned in the doorway and went back into the bedroom.

'You said you were going to be working until you presented the briefing,' she said, 'and that was yesterday, and now you're saying you're going to carry on with that fucking job. Well, what about me? Who gives a damn about me? When's it going to be my turn?'

Thomas walked past her and into the office, his jacket flapping. 'Your turn?' he said. 'You've taken over the whole desk, look at this, all your fucking notes all over my memos.'

'For God's sake!' Annika ran in and grabbed her notepad. 'I'm so sorry! Sorry that I dared to take up the tiniest bit of space, sorry for existing!'

'I'm going now,' Thomas said, heading towards the stairs.

Annika moved to stand in his way. Her dressing-gown slid off her shoulders. 'Like hell you are!'

383

His eyes flashed with anger. 'I'm going, even if I have to move you out of the way by force,' he said.

'I can't look after this entire household on my own,' Annika said, in a muffled voice. 'Cleaning and cooking and washing *and* all the responsibility for the children *and* working full time without leaving some kind of sign of it in the office. Surely even you can see that.'

He was breathing heavily, looking down into her face. His jaw was clenched so tightly his skin was turning white. Then he seemed to relax and took several deep breaths that sounded like sobs. 'Oh, God,' he said, going back into the bedroom with one hand over his eyes.

She watched him, the jacket stretched across his broad shoulders, his dark jeans and shiny shoes. 'Thomas,' she said, going after him and wrapping her arms round his waist. 'I'm sorry. Forgive me. I didn't mean to shout.'

He pulled her to him, kissing her hair and rocking her gently. 'It's my fault,' he said. 'Sorry. Of course I realize that you can't be at home today of all days.' He held her away from him and looked at her seriously. She evaded his gaze. 'But you can hardly have slept at all. You mustn't burn out the moment you go back to work.'

She slipped her fingers under the waist of his trousers, pulled out his shirt, finding a strip of hot skin, and kissed his neck. 'I love you, you know,' she whispered, unless she merely thought it, because he didn't answer.

He slid his fingers through her hair, and for the first time in ages she experienced that sensation, the one she had felt with Bosse.

'Why are you shouting?' Ellen was standing in the doorway, clutching Poppy and Ludde.

No, Annika thought. Not now.

'Are you cross?'

Thomas let go of Annika and went to pick up the

little girl. 'Not any more,' he said. 'Do you want to go to nursery today, or would you rather stay at home with me and Kalle?'

'Home with you, Daddy!' Ellen cried, wrapping her arms round his neck.

Annika shut her eyes and leaned against the door-frame. The whole house spun. 'I'm going to grab another hour's sleep,' she said, but no one heard her.

The children were sitting at the dining-table, drawing. The sun was shining, and the window frames were casting patterned shadows over the oak parquet floor. The terrace door was ajar, letting in the hum of insects and the smell of grass.

Thomas sank down at the breakfast bar in the kitchen with the morning paper and a cup of coffee and sighed happily. Cramne had been understanding when he had called and explained that his son wasn't well, and had even managed to sound sympathetic. 'Poor sod,' he had said, although it was unclear whether he was referring to Thomas or his son. As if staying at home with your child was some sort of punishment, Thomas thought. Which it wasn't. In fact, it was rather nice. A whole day with the paper and some magazines and a bit of Eurosport in the afternoon. Really not bad.

'Daddy,' Kalle shouted crossly. 'She's taken my pen.'

Thomas looked up from the editorial and glanced at the dining-table. 'What's all the fuss about?'

'She's got the brown pen and it's *mine*.'

'But I'm doing trees,' Ellen said, concentrating hard on her drawing.

Kalle leaned over the table and hit his sister's head with his fist. The little girl dropped the pen and put her hands to her head as she let out a whimper that soon

385

turned into a howl. Kalle snatched up the pen with a triumphant grin.

'Daddy! He hit me!'

Thomas put down his paper and went to the dining area. 'Listen,' he said, sitting next to Ellen. 'We aren't going to spend the day fighting. We're going to have a nice day together, aren't we?'

'She started it,' Kalle said smugly, drawing long brown lines with the pen.

Ellen was crying, and Thomas stroked her back. 'Okay, little one,' he said, picking his daughter up. 'Does it still hurt?'

'He hit me, Daddy! He hit me *hard*!'

'I know,' Thomas said, blowing on her hair.

Annika came downstairs, dressed and made up, with her oversized bag on her shoulder. 'What's going on?' she asked.

'Nothing,' Thomas said.

Ellen wriggled out of his arms and ran over to Annika. 'Kalle hit me really hard, here.' She pointed to just above her forehead, and Annika bent down to take a closer look.

'Oh, you've already got a bump, darling,' she said. 'We can't have that.'

She kissed her, then went over to Kalle. Taking hold of his chair, she spun him round, forcing him to look at her. 'You mustn't hit your little sister,' she said, looking him right in the eyes.

'But she was the one who—'

'Quiet!' she said, in a loud voice. 'You are absolutely *not allowed* to hit your little sister. You're not going to turn into the sort of boy who hits girls, do you hear me? *Do you hear me?*'

'Yes,' Kalle said.

'Calm down,' Thomas said, but she ignored him.

'Look at me,' she said to Kalle, and he peeped up at her under his fringe. 'Kalle, you've got to stop telling lies and saying everything is someone else's fault, and you've got to stop fighting. You don't like it when other children are mean to you, do you? How do you think Ellen feels when you're mean to her?'

He looked down again. 'Sad,' he said.

She pulled him to her and hugged him. 'I'm going to work now,' she said, and he wrapped his arms tightly round her neck.

'No!' he cried. 'Stay at home, Mummy! Stay at home with me today!'

'But Daddy's at home,' Annika said, and Kalle glanced at Thomas, quickly and shyly, before burrowing his face into Annika's long hair.

'I want you to stay at home, Mummy,' he said.

She freed herself from his grasp and looked at Thomas. 'It's a good idea to wipe the table before they start drawing,' she said. 'They put their pictures all over the house, and we end up with stains everywhere.'

A feeling of exhaustion hit him. 'Get off to work now,' he said, standing up and turning away.

She left without another word. He waited until the door had closed behind her before sitting down with his coffee. She just couldn't help it, pointing out that the table hadn't been wiped. If it was that damn filthy she could have done something about it. Larsson and Althin's wives had cleared the dishes from the dining-table and put them into the sink last night. He noted with irritation that they were still there.

What contribution had she made yesterday? She'd picked up some ready-made food that she had heated in the microwave. She had made a fool of herself in front of his colleagues and behaved appallingly towards their neighbour. And she'd left him with their guests and the dishes and everything.

He started to feel heated as he thought about it, the way she had shouted at their neighbour, and the way the other wives had looked at him, and how the men had started talking about something else. To his surprise, they had all stayed until past one in the morning. Cramne had downed his cognac and asked for another, before Althin had pulled on the brakes and reminded everyone that they all had to work the next day.

Maybe it was because the under-secretary of state had been there. Thomas understood that he had slipped up by inviting Halenius, but he was an easy-going sort and his presence had probably had something to do with the fact that the party had gone on so late. Things had been a bit different simply because he was there.

Unless they had all been waiting for Annika to get home and cause another scandal.

He poured himself some more coffee, now cold and unpleasant.

And she never wanted to have sex. He had never been so utterly starved of sex before, not even when things had been at their worst with Eleonor. At least his ex-wife used to go through the motions now and then for the sake of it, but ever since that business when Annika got too involved with a news story about a terrorist who called himself Red Wolf, she had hardly touched him. It was as if she hated him, as if he was no longer good enough for her.

And now she was starting work again, as if things weren't tough enough for him already. First she'd wanted to move, and now, when he really needed to focus on his career, there was a whole load of painting and decorating to do. Is this what it's going to be like from now on? he wondered. Am I going to spend the rest of my life sitting here? Isn't there more to it than this?

He felt his pulse throb in his neck and pushed the questions aside, too tired and hung-over. He picked up the paper again and turned to the editorial. Maybe this evening she would come home and make dinner and want to have sex and everything would be the same as it used to be.

The editorial was about the responses to the consultation on his bugging proposal. The Association of Lawyers was against, as was the Parliamentary Ombuds-man. They were making a big deal of it, suggesting that these were objective reasons for abandoning the whole proposal. We knew this would happen all along, Thomas thought. The papers have no idea what they're writing about.

'Daddy,' Ellen said.

Thomas sighed. 'What?'

'I'm thirsty.'

He swallowed, put the paper down, fetched a glass and filled it with water. He put it in front of his daughter and went back to his paper. 'I want squash.'

'You're not having squash,' Thomas said. 'You can drink water if you're thirsty.'

The editorial went on to criticize the measures, saying they were an attack on individual integrity, and claiming that the proposed methods were unnecessary because they were ineffective. They said the entire EU directive on the storage of data was ill-considered, and—

'Daddy!' Ellen said.

'What is it now?!' Thomas shouted, throwing the newspaper down.

She stared at him, open-mouthed. She didn't say

anything, just grabbed Poppy and Ludde and went upstairs to her room.

'What are we having for lunch?' Kalle asked.

Thomas put his hands over his eyes and groaned.

Spike was sitting with both feet on his desk. 'What's the deal with the dead guy, then?' he said without looking up at her.

'The second chair of the Nobel Committee to be murdered in six months,' Annika said.

He sighed rather theatrically. 'Yes,' he said, 'I can see that from the paper. Anything else?'

'I've only just got here,' Annika said. 'About fifteen seconds ago.'

He threw her a glance and dropped his feet to the floor, grabbed the desk and pulled himself towards it on his wheeled office chair. 'Personally, I think it's a pretty dead story,' he said. 'Keep an eye on it today, but don't expect to write a novel about it for tomorrow.'

'I thought I wasn't supposed to cover crime,' Annika said, picking up a pear that was lying beside Spike's phone.

The head of News leaned over with surprising speed and snatched the fruit from her hand. 'Leave that alone,' he said.

Annika stared at him for a few seconds, and realized he was slightly slimmer than he had been. 'Spike,' she said, 'you're on a diet!'

'Berit's busy on another story,' he said, biting into the pear. 'A really good lead. Maybe you could have a word with her, pick up a few tips . . .'

Annika picked up her bag and went over to see Berit. 'Hi,' she said, flopping down on Patrik's chair. 'What's going on?'

Berit looked up over her glasses. 'Great job last night. We left the competition at the starting gate. Bosse didn't manage to get anything. Was he even there?'

Annika felt herself start to blush. 'Yes,' she said, 'but they got there too late.'

'Who've they taken in for questioning?' Berit asked.

'Another professor at Karolinska,' Annika said. 'He's a bit of a nutter. He's got it into his head that it's his duty to make threats against people and tell them what they're doing wrong. And he's a creationist as well.'

'What?' Berit said.

'Thinks there ought to be more God in science. So, what's this story you've got on the go?'

'Jemal,' Berit said. 'The father from Bandhagen.'

Annika nodded – yes, she remembered.

'It's completely crazy,' Berit said. 'The Swedish government decided that Jemal should be deported from Sweden, and they didn't waste any time. The CIA picked him up from Bromma airport the same night.'

Annika gave her a sceptical look. 'Not the CIA?' she said. 'That sounds like a bad film.'

Berit took off her glasses and moved her chair closer to Annika's. When she spoke, her voice was low and intense. 'American agents with hoods over their heads picked him up from a room inside Bromma airport. They cut off his clothes, dug around in his mouth and backside, drugged him with suppositories and put a nappy on him. Then they put a hood over his head and dragged him out to their private chartered plane. They chained him to the fuselage and left him like that all the way to Amman.'

Annika's mouth was hanging open. 'Who on earth sanctioned that?' she whispered, hearing the shock in her voice.

391

'The government took the decision to deport him, and the foreign minister was informed about the means of transport, but the ministry claim that she wasn't aware of the involvement of the CIA or of any abuse. It was just a run-of-the-mill deportation for a run-of-the-mill terrorist and the nice Americans offered to give him a lift.'

'So the American secret service can just go round picking up people from our airports and no one's allowed any say in the matter?' Annika said, far too loudly.

'The government isn't allowed to dictate how the police should conduct their business, and the Security Police are blaming one unfortunate officer who was sent out there to oversee the deportation,' she said quietly. 'It's all his fault, apparently. The problem is that he handed over control of the deportation to the Americans, but do you know what else he did after that?'

'What?' Annika asked.

Berit sighed, as if she were collecting her thoughts before answering. 'When the abuse got too painful to watch he went out and threw up. So the plane took off without him having any idea of what had happened.'

'Christ . . .' Annika said. She sat quietly for a minute, thinking hard. 'Mind you, we're hardly alone in this,' she said eventually. 'The CIA have evidently been hiring private planes and picking people up from all over Europe in the past few years.'

'They've given him a life sentence in Jordan,' Berit said. 'They tortured him with beatings and electric shocks until he confessed. Then a military tribunal declared he was guilty of planning and carrying out acts of terrorism. His lawyer wasn't allowed to call any witnesses, and the verdict can't be appealed against. He'll end up dying in that prison, and his daughters will never see their father again.' She moved her chair back to her desk.

Annika stared at her. 'How the hell did you find out about this?' she asked.

'Fatima has visited him in prison, and he told her he'd been tortured.'

'And the CIA?'

'I got hold of the details of the plane. A Raytheon Hawker 800, registration number N168BF. It's owned by a small American company.'

'And?' Annika said.

Berit looked up at her. 'I called and said I'd like to hire it.'

'And?'

'They said they have just one client: the American state.'

'Christ,' Annika said again.

'Patrik's checked out the plane. It's been flying around picking up people all over the world. It often takes them to Cuba, for instance, to Guantánamo.'

'But someone has to be responsible for this,' Annika said. 'Someone has to be made to answer for it. Sweden's a constitutional state. We don't send people to be tortured and killed.'

'The government claims that they were given guarantees by the authorities in Jordan that Jemal was going to receive a fair trial and obviously not be tortured. Well, we can see now how much that promise was worth.'

'When are we running this?'

'Tomorrow, I hope,' Berit said, standing up. 'I've got to go. I've got a meeting with the foreign minister.'

'You won't get anything out of her,' Annika said.

'Of course not,' Berit said, as she picked up her handbag and headed out.

28

Annika sat down at Berit's desk and started making calls.

No answer from Birgitta Larsén, either at work or at home.

Q's number redirected her to Reception.

The duty desk of the crime unit was still refusing to comment on Ernst Ericsson's death.

The press office merely referred to a press conference planned for later that afternoon.

She tried to find Ernst Ericsson's children on the national database, hoping to discover a son of the right age, but the surname threw up far too many results. And it turned out his ex-wife had moved to Provence.

She called the Nobel Forum and spoke to a very polite but apologetic secretary who was unable to tell her anything about anything.

This was hopeless.

Perhaps Ebba knew something.

She pulled out her mobile and checked the number she had saved in its memory.

'Hello?'

'Ebba!' Annika said. 'God, am I glad to hear your voice!'

'Annika?' She sounded surprised and slightly worried.

'Yes! Have you heard what's happened?'

There was a lot of noise at the other end of the line. 'What? Has there been a break-in? A fire?'

Annika blinked several times. Her eyes felt gritty. 'A break-in? No, no, nothing to do with the house. It's Ernst. Ernst Ericsson. You haven't heard the news?'

'I'm in the car, on my way to the Co-op in Vansbro, in Dalarna, to pick up some food and a paper.'

All of a sudden the call wasn't so straightforward any more. 'Ernst Ericsson is dead,' Annika said. 'He died last night.'

There were a few moments of silence on the line.

'Ebba?'

'Yes, I'm here. Are you sure?'

'The police think he was murdered.'

'You're kidding?'

'I'm afraid not,' Annika said.

'Murdered how?'

'Don't know yet. They haven't released the cause of death.'

The background noise got quieter, as if Ebba had pulled over to the side of the road and stopped.

'That's awful,' she said. 'I only saw him on Saturday.'

'I know,' Annika said. 'You said you were going to go to that seminar. How was it? Was it good?'

'Really good, but there was a bit of a fuss afterwards. Lars-Henry Svensson came to the buffet and he was completely out of control. It ended with the police coming out to pick him up. I feel so sorry for him.'

'And he spoke to Ernst?'

'I don't know, I think so. He probably spoke to everyone. Why do you ask?'

'The police have pulled him in for questioning,' Annika said.

Ebba snorted audibly. 'That's ridiculous,' she said. 'Lars-Henry would never hurt a fly.'

Cliché of the month, Annika thought. 'Did he say anything to you?'

Ebba sighed. 'He was angry because he thinks I bought my way into the scientific community, and he can't seem to forgive me for that. He doesn't mean anything by it, he's completely harmless. The police are bound to let him go soon.'

Annika heard Ebba put the car in gear again, then the crunch of gravel as she pulled away. Suddenly she had a flashback to her own car, standing at the traffic-lights at the end of Barnhusbron the day before, a red Volvo estate in the next lane, a woman behind the wheel. 'Where are you?' she asked.

'I've just passed Hulån, and I'm on my way to Skamhed.'

'You weren't in Stockholm just after lunch yesterday?'

'I should be back tomorrow afternoon, unless I have to set off earlier because of this business with Ernst. Well, I suppose I'd better . . .'

Annika closed her eyes and tried to imagine Ebba driving her car, listening hard to see if she could pick up any sounds in the background. What did it look like outside the vehicle? Dark pine forest? A built-up area? Surely she ought to be able to tell the difference. 'Okay,' she said. 'Call me if there's anything you want to know.' She hung up.

She held the handset for a couple of seconds, then dialled the reception desk of the Karolinska Institute. Asked for Sören Hammarsten.

Not available.

Asked for Ernst Ericsson's personal secretary.

Was told he wasn't there.

She hung up and stared at the screen of Berit's computer. Who else could she call? Who might know something about what happened on Saturday? The people who were there, obviously, but who would want to talk to her?

She picked up the phone and dialled the Karolinska Institute again. 'I was wondering if you had a Bernhard Thorell there?'

There was the sound of tapping on a keyboard.

'Thorell, with an *h*?'

'I think so.'

More tapping.

'Yes, I've got him here. It's a mobile number. Wait a moment and I'll connect you.'

The phone rang again, three, four, five times . . .

'Thorell.'

Annika took a deep breath and cleared her throat. 'Yes,' she said, 'good afternoon, my name's Annika Bengtzon and I'm calling from the *Evening Post*. We met very briefly yesterday, in the animal-testing lab. I was there with Birgitta Larsén . . .'

'Ah, yes,' he said. 'The doctoral student.'

Annika smiled. 'Am I phoning at a bad time?'

'That depends on what you're phoning about,' the pharmaceutical-company boss said, as if he was smiling back at her.

'The death last night,' she said. 'I'm interested in how it might affect your work.'

'As far as I'm aware, the matter is being investigated by the police,' Thorell said. 'Obviously it's very tragic, but it won't have any noticeable impact on our research project.'

His accent was upper-class Swedish, not American English.

'One professor is dead,' Annika said, 'and a second is being questioned about the incident. Surely that would affect relations and the working atmosphere within the institute. I know they had an argument after the seminar on Saturday, and I know you were there . . .'

He breathed in so quickly and deeply that Annika paused. 'I've no idea what that was about,' he said, rather abruptly, 'so naturally I can't say anything about it.'

'I completely understand,' Annika said. 'I just wanted to get an impression of what happened that evening, and I know that Lars-Henry Svensson confronted several other people, yourself included.'

Thorell was quiet for several seconds. Then he said, 'That is correct.'

'I realize that you don't want to speak out of turn,' she said, 'but I was wondering if you might be able to tell me what he said to you personally?'

There was crackling on the line. 'I have a lunch appointment at the faculty club,' Thorell said. 'Meet me outside there in half an hour.' He clicked to end the call without waiting for an answer.

The faculty club? Was that the same as the Black Fox?

Annika parked her car outside an old wooden building at number 2 Nobels Väg. It was a red-painted cottage with yellow shutters outside the windows and white curtains. She got out, locked the car and peered curiously through one of the windows. Some sort of conference seemed to be going on in there.

With its mature trees and extensive lawns, the whole area exuded peace and quiet, with the noise of the motor-

398

way only a distant rumble. Ponytails and shirts fluttered in the wind, footsteps and laughter echoing between the buildings. The spokes of bicycle wheels twinkled from the footbridge over to the Karolinska Hospital.

Annika walked slowly down the dead-end road, passing the Medical Society and a Friskis & Svettis gym, heading for the restaurant where she had had lunch with Ebba and Birgitta last week. Yes, the faculty club was the Black Fox. She checked her watch: she was on time. Just to be sure she walked past the windows, looking in, but she couldn't see any sign of Bernhard Thorell – or of Birgitta Larsén, for that matter.

She sat down on the steps leading up to the copper door. The sun was beating down on her head. She turned her face to the warmth and closed her eyes. Still with her eyes shut, she let her head fall forward, on the brink of dozing off. She jerked and shook herself, pushing her hair off her face.

Bernhard Thorell was heading towards her from further inside the campus, his hands in his trouser pockets. His suit, grey and slightly shiny, fitted him like a second skin. The wind ruffled his hair, and his eyes crinkled as he squinted against the brightness.

I can see why Birgitta is so taken with him, Annika thought, as she stood up and went to meet him.

He took his hands out of his pockets and reached for Annika's. 'Sometimes Sweden really is lovely,' he said, his eyes looking her over.

To her surprise, she felt flattered, a little shiver of heat running through her. She pulled her hand away. 'So have you moved here for good?' she asked.

Thorell laughed, flashing even white teeth. 'Not at all,' he said. 'I kept the family farm in Roslagen after my parents' accident, and I try to spend at least a week or two there every year, to keep in touch with my roots.'

Annika's smile stiffened. Should she have known about the accident? 'Your parents?' she asked, feeling very stupid.

He looked down at the gravel briefly, then met her gaze with a hint of melancholy in his eyes. 'They died when I was a teenager,' he said.

Hadn't Berit said something about them, about his father being a venture capitalist and a car-crash in the Alps? 'Oh,' she said. 'I'm sorry.'

He laughed. 'Don't worry,' he said. 'I've got over it – it was years ago. Right now I'm only here to see how work on our research project is going.'

Annika sneaked a glance at him. He was taller up close. 'Is it going to lead to a Nobel Prize?'

He laughed again. 'You never know. There are so many worthy candidates, and often you don't know until later which discoveries are going to stand the test of time. Nobel wanted the prize to benefit humanity in the long term, so it's a good thing that the committee takes its time in making its choice. You wanted to know what Professor Svensson said to me?'

'If you don't mind telling me.'

Thorell looked out across the grass, deep in thought for a few moments. 'The professor was very critical about our work,' he finally said, 'because we've found a way to slow down the ageing process, even to stop it. He accused us of wanting to discover the secret of eternal life, but that isn't what our research is about at all.'

'He thinks you're playing God,' Annika said, with a smile.

Thorell smiled back at her. 'Sadly it isn't possible to conduct any sort of reasonable discussion with the dear

400

fellow. I would have to describe him as a fairly extreme creationist.'

'So the pharmaceutical industry is the jaws of the monster?'

'Exactly. And we have to watch out because otherwise *retribution awaits*.' He said the last words hoarsely with his eyes wide.

Annika laughed. 'So Nemesis is going to punish you?' she said, and Thorell's smile broadened. Two dimples appeared in his cheeks, and the colour of his eyes seemed deeper. Annika looked into them and thought, *Oh, no, not again, not another Bosse*, but she still couldn't help smiling back.

'So you know about Nemesis?' Thorell said, taking a step closer to her.

'The goddess of retribution,' Annika said, 'and the title of a play by Alfred Nobel.'

He tilted his head, smiling so that his teeth sparkled. 'Not many people know that,' he said. 'That Alfred Nobel was so interested in Beatrice Cenci.'

He was standing so close to her that Annika's head was spinning. 'She was a fascinating woman, who met a very nasty end,' she said. Her voice sounded strange – too high, too soft, she thought.

He bowed his head while keeping his eyes on hers, then stuck his hands into his trouser pockets, making the shoulders of his jacket ride up slightly.

God, Annika thought, he's so handsome.

'So young,' he said quietly, 'and so beautiful . . .' He might almost have been caressing her.

'I know,' Annika said breathlessly. 'She was incredibly beautiful. Ebba, my neighbour, has a painting of her in her living room.'

All of a sudden there was total silence between them.

Thorell was staring at her, the glint in his eye dissolving and fading away. 'Not the one by Guido Reni?'

Annika searched her memory. 'I don't know, but I can ask,' she said, with a confused little smile, taking a step back.

'Ebba?' Thorell said. 'Not the one working here at the lab? Ebba Romanova?'

Annika nodded.

His smile was back, just as warm as before. 'What a small world.' He turned without another word and went inside the Black Fox.

The Kitten pushed the bag that contained her tennis racket higher on her shoulder and took hold of the bicycle's handlebars with both hands. She let her ponytail fall down her back as she adjusted the visor over her eyes, her tennis shoes scraping the tarmac under her feet. Okay, off we go, and the bike rolled along beautifully beside her. If there was one thing she was good at, it was melting into affluent suburban settings.

This was the first time she had found anything re-motely good about this country. She had found a shred of reason for these people to live up here at the North Pole.

Naturally, she knew why – she didn't need a shrink to explain it: the area reminded her of where her dad lived just outside Boston. He had moved there after the divorce. Big, comfortable detached houses in muted colours. Small-paned windows that shimmered unevenly in the sun. Well-clipped lawns and blossoming fruit trees in spacious gardens, behind neatly painted fences and trimmed hedges.

She had to admit she was surprised. There was civil-ization up here, after all.

The exception was the reporter's modern monstrosity.

On a flat patch of ground cut up by tyre-tracks she had flung up a showy white house with dead architecture and no sense of tradition or proportion. It had been easy to find the plan of the house in an old advert on the Internet. All open-plan and so-called modern on the ground floor, and four bedrooms upstairs. You didn't have to be Einstein to work out how the Bengtzon family used the rooms.

The two bedrooms at the front of the house were where the little darlings slept, blue curtains with pictures of toys on them for the boy, pastel with flowers for the girl. Christ, it made her want to throw up. At the back lay the master bedroom and a small office, where Mrs Bengtzon had nice, tidy sex with her dull bureaucrat husband and wrote her nasty little articles.

Her skin crawled. She was having trouble breathing and felt strangely uneasy. She had to focus: this was all about planning and marking out her posts. She bit her lip to make herself concentrate, swinging her ponytail. She adopted what she felt was an affluent expression and looked back at the more appealing villas. Immediately behind the crappy house there was a really nice property, where a tall, older man was polishing a Mercedes.

On the other side of the road lay the best house in the neighbourhood. A villa in the national romantic style, three floors plus a basement, with hints of Gothic mystery. The façade was heavy and dark, the effect lightened by the large windows and irregular woodwork of the veranda. The garden was mature and well looked after, with a summerhouse and a well. The far end was given over to a dog-pen.

That, too, the Kitten thought, stopping for a moment. Even a dog-pen.

She could almost guess what the house looked like inside. She knew how it smelt, how it felt, the lofty ceilings, the light through the leaded windows, the draught under the doors in winter. She saw her childhood: this was exactly the sort of house Grant had lived in; a summerhouse, with dog-pen and all. She smiled at the memory of her childhood friend. He had grown up in the house next to her father's, and visits to her father had been restricted. She was allowed to be there when her mother was in the nuthouse. Fortunately this happened every so often, like the time she'd slit her wrists and written drunken letters about *the horrible whore* (Dad's new woman, whom she never heard called anything else).

Those had been magical moments, the times she was allowed to go round to Grant's. She thought back to the Gothic building. The summerhouse, where they had smoked their first joint. The attic room under the roof, where they had their stash of porn magazines.The cellar, where they had trapped mice and practised cutting off their heads with an old kitchen knife. She chuckled quietly.

Grant had been a sweetie. It was a shame he'd got so fucking boring when he grew up. Director of a fucking symphony orchestra: how boring could you get?

She sighed and pushed the bike on again, one, two, one, two, the crunch of gravel under her shoes. She was leaning heavily on the handlebars to relieve the pain in her left leg. You would hardly know she had a limp. Soon her research out here would be done. She just had to get hold of a few things and check her timings.

She glanced back at the trashy white house, the reporter's hideous home.

She'd be doing the area a big favour by wiping it off the face of the earth.

29

Annika returned to the newsroom, feeling suddenly lost and exhausted. What was she doing here? She had no desk of her own; she had her laptop in her bag; she didn't know who she should talk to about her work.

Spike? He couldn't even be bothered to look at her.

Berit? She had more than enough of her own to worry about.

It reminded her of her sixth form, when the experts had decided that group work without a teacher, outside the classroom, was a good idea. Pointless and cheap.

She went over to the desks allocated to the day-shift reporters. They were covered with shrivelled apple-cores, notes and empty cups. So, now she was expected to be a cleaner at work as well. She gritted her teeth, found a large waste bin and swept everything into it without bothering to pick out anything that ought to go into the recycling, then went and got a damp cloth from the cloakroom. She wiped the coffee stains and bits of banana off one of the desks and unpacked her laptop.

It was time to get organized.

What was she going to write about all this?

The murder of Ernst Ericsson was linked to the Nobel killings. She was absolutely convinced of that. There was a pattern here that she couldn't quite put her finger on, threads that ran together in a way that couldn't just be coincidental.

But what would there be room for in tomorrow's paper? How interesting was it really that a few drunken scientists had had a row after a seminar? She sighed. Not very, if she was brutally honest.

If she had managed to find out exactly what had been said between Lars-Henry Svensson and Ernst Ericsson there might have been a story there, but that she knew they had had a row was nowhere near enough on its own.

In the absence of any other leads, she looked up Lars-Henry Svensson in the national register and got an address on Ringvägen on the island of Södermalm in Stockholm. There were two landlines listed in his name, one for Ringvägen and a second to a property on Tavastbodavägen out on Värmdö. No mobile number was listed.

She called both landlines. No answer, and no answer-machine.

She got herself a mug of coffee and went for a stroll around the newsroom to gather her thoughts. During the six months she had been away she had written down all the information she had about the Nobel murders. It was all hidden in her personal email on the Net. She went back to her temporary desk and logged on to her account. Maybe it was time to look at the big picture. To let go of the details and see the whole thing. To look at the vast sums of money in scientific research and the pharmaceutical industry. To chart the path from design to patent, then to drug and finally to consumer.

She looked through all her notes. The texts were unstructured and contained facts, details and reflections all jumbled together. She found the information from Q about the assassin, the Kitten, and about what the killer had done and how the police had pieced it all together. Then details about Nemesis and Alfred Nobel. She found her own research about the money involved in the scientific community, the stuff she had put together after the press conference where Medi-Tec's investment in the Karolinska Institute had been made public. She also found her notes after her meeting with Q to check out photographs in his office the other day.

I've had enough of this, she thought. I've kept quiet long enough.

She reached for the phone and dialled Q's direct line for the tenth time that day. He still wasn't answering.

Damn.

She slammed the receiver down. She couldn't just sit there, entirely dependent on just one source.

In her frustration she decided to do what she had done the previous evening and email him, hoping he'd get in touch. *I'm thinking of going public with the Kitten*, she wrote. *Need to check to make sure I don't blow anything vital.*

The answer came just a minute or so later. *Sorry, honey, I'm on my way out. Don't call me, I'll call you.*

She replied at once: *Okay, honey. I gave you a chance to have your say. You didn't take it. Silly.*

Ten seconds later her mobile rang.

'Meet me at the café on Norr Mälarstrand in ten minutes,' Q said.

'The Mälar Pavilion?' Annika asked.

'How the fuck should I know what it's called?' Q said, and hung up.

Annika smiled and put her laptop away again.

*

The weather really was lovely. There was a warm breeze that smelt of soil and tarmac, the irresistible scent of city and summer.

This is where I want to live, Annika thought. This is where I belong.

She locked the car and put the keys into her bag. It was ridiculously heavy: one of the disadvantages of carrying your workplace around with you.

The Mälar Pavilion was one of her favourite places on Kungsholmen, a little open-air café with rickety tables on neatly raked gravel, big sandwiches and hot chocolate, and blankets you could borrow if you wanted to, which was all too likely in the evening. The waters of Lake Mälaren rippled just a couple of metres from the tables, and on the other side of the water, Långholmen and the towers of Högalid Church rose.

Q was already there, sitting and staring at the Western Bridge through his sunglasses, with an oatmeal biscuit in front of him.

'Do you ever wear anything but Hawaiian shirts?' Annika asked, as she dropped her bag on to the gravel, relieved to let go of it.

'They aren't from Hawaii. They're from Tuki's Pareau in Avarua on Rarotonga. And when I go to weddings and high-class funerals I wear a hand-painted silk shirt I bought from Nelson Mandela's tailor in Cape Town. Have I never told you that before?'

She pulled out the chair facing him and put her pen and notepad on the table. 'Have you found a link between the Kitten and the boy in the freezer?'

'We've managed to tie Johan Isaksson to the Nobel murders,' Q said. 'What are you going to write about the Kitten?'

Annika checked her pen was working by scribbling on

her notepad. 'That she was the one who did it. That she shot the Latvian doctor and her accomplice in Jurmala. That she's suspected of killing Johan Isaksson.'

Q sighed. 'We can't prove that the freeze-room was murder, let alone that she was responsible.'

Annika pulled her pad closer. 'Okay,' she said. 'Instant adjustment. Nothing about Johan Isaksson, except where and how he died, and the fact that you've linked him to the killings. How?'

'His mobile phone.'

'So you've found it?'

'No, it's still missing, but his supervisor gave us the details of his pay-as-you-go number, and we know from his service provider that he sent five texts during the spring to another pay-as-you-go number that had already featured in the investigation.'

'The same number he sent *dancing close to St Erik* to?' Annika said.

Q smiled wearily. 'No, you're wrong there,' he said. 'We're piecing the puzzle together and have found several numbers and several different texts. We're assuming that the Kitten was the recipient of *dancing close to St Erik*, and then a text was sent from her number to another. Obviously, we've been looking at that one as well.'

'So whose phone was that?' Annika asked.

'Whose do you think?' he asked.

Annika stared hard at the biscuit. 'Her accomplice, of course,' she said.

'Right again. And who inherited it once the accomplice was dead?'

'The killer, of course,' Annika said, making notes on her pad. 'So Johan Isaksson sent five texts to the accomplice's phone this spring, and they were received by the Kitten instead. Do you know what he wrote?'

'No. What do you think?'

Annika shrugged. 'He must have been in touch with the accomplice,' she said. 'Maybe it was the accomplice who got him involved. Maybe he had questions after the murders or just felt guilty. Could he have been threatening them?'

'Maybe,' Q said. 'And now he's dead. Have you got it clear now?'

'I think so,' Annika said, scratching her head with her pen.

Q tossed his biscuit to some ducks that were paddling at the water's edge.

'Hang on,' Annika said. 'Why is it okay for me to go public with the Kitten now?'

'It isn't okay,' Q said, 'but I know I can't stop you.'

Annika turned back a few pages in her pad and checked her notes. 'Off the record, again,' she said. 'Could the Kitten have killed Johan Isaksson?'

Q sighed and watched the ducks squabbling over the biscuit. 'It's highly likely,' he said. 'The method fits her profile. Effective, calculated, well planned, and without excessive violence. Controlled, professional.'

Annika nodded slowly. 'She didn't kill Wiesel,' she said.

'He got in the way,' Q said. 'She shot him in the leg to get to her target, von Behring, and she took her out with a single shot. She shot the guards outside to neutralize them, not to kill. One shot each.'

'Ernst Ericsson,' Annika said. 'Did she kill him too?'

'Nope,' Q said.

'No?' Annika asked. 'Why not?' She tapped her pen on the table and looked out across Norr Mälarstrand. Then she put it down on the notepad. 'Ernst's murder was much messier,' she said quietly. 'There was something very personal about his case. Someone did something really terrible to him, didn't they?'

Q looked at her without moving a muscle.

'Yuck,' Annika said, with a shiver. 'Have you released Lars-Henry Svensson yet?'

'This morning. He had nothing to do with the death of Ernst Ericsson.'

'And you're absolutely certain of that?'

'Not a shadow of a doubt.' Q stood up. 'You can have the exclusive on the Kitten until midnight. Then we'll announce a press conference for eight o'clock tomorrow morning, so it's bound to start leaking in the early hours.'

'Wow, that's really good of you,' she said, holding out her arms. 'Here I am, keeping quiet for six months, and I get a couple of minutes to write up the whole story.'

'If I know you at all, you've already got eight different versions of it in that hideous bag of yours,' Q said. He helped himself to a toothpick and walked away.

We know each other a little too well, Annika thought.

She went up to the newsroom and unpacked her laptop for the second time that day. Then she went into her online archive and extracted the various draft articles she had written, three of them, not eight. The first went straight to the point and was an account of what Q had told her the day she had gone on leave from the paper. The other versions were longer and more detailed, and parts of them could be used later as follow-up articles.

She copied the text from her email and put it into a document in Scoop, the word-processing program. She read it carefully, finding a few typos, and amended the information about the accomplice's mobile phone. She saved it to her own folder, and decided to finish the rest of the articles before sending everything to the shared filestore in one big bundle.

Then she pulled out the draft of her article about Johan Isaksson. His death had been reported as a short news item, described as a tragic accident. She updated her text, adding that the police were now linking the death of the doctoral student with the Nobel murders, which meant she had to go back through the article and cover Isaksson's identity. Whenever someone's involvement in the investigation of a crime was made public, their identity was usually concealed. Obviously anyone who knew Johan Isaksson, and everyone who worked at the lab, would know who the article was about, but for the vast majority of readers his identity would be hidden, at least for a while.

Libelling the dead was a serious matter.

Finally she pulled out the fragments of her article about Ernst Ericsson's death. It may have been gruesome, but until she knew exactly *how* gruesome, there was no place for it in the next day's paper.

She sent the whole lot over to the shared filestore. She checked that they had made it to the starting block for tomorrow's edition.

She scanned the headlines she had given the articles: *Nobel Killings Solved* (about the Kitten), *More Murders in Nobel's Wake* (about the killings in Jurmala), *Death at Karolinska Institute Linked to Nobel Killings* (about Johan Isaksson). There they sat, competing for space with Berit and Patrik's mega-scoop about the CIA and the extradition from Bromma.

I have to tell Schyman what I've written, she thought. I have to explain why I've kept quiet so long.

At that moment her mobile rang. She looked at the display: *Anne S calling*. What did she want this time?

412

'Where are you?' Anne asked crossly.

Annika brushed the hair from her forehead with her right hand. 'What?' she said.

'My lecture! You *promised* to help me today – don't tell me you'd forgotten!'

Annika screwed her eyes shut and bit the inside of her cheek. 'Of course I hadn't,' she lied. 'I've just been really busy.'

'What do you mean, *busy*? Folding napkins for your coffee mornings?'

'I started back at work today. I'm in the office.'

'So you can just forget about all the poor losers who haven't found a hundred million in a rubbish bin?'

Annika looked at the time. It was still only a quarter past four. 'I have to talk to Schyman, then I'll come round to yours – in about an hour, if that's okay?'

Anne Snapphane muttered something and hung up.

Shit, shit, shit. Should she phone Thomas to say she was going to be late? She reached for the phone, then stopped herself. *Late?* She would still be home by seven, and did that really count as late? Had Thomas been home before seven once in the past month? Had he ever called to tell her? No and no.

Like hell was she going to call.

She put her laptop away again, threw her cup into the bin and went over to Anders Schyman's little cubbyhole.

He wasn't there.

She sighed deeply and dropped her bag on to the floor. Now she'd have to talk to Spike.

The head of News was eating an apple as he stared intently at his screen. Annika stopped next to him. 'Some idiot's put a load of articles in the filestore saying the Nobel killings have been solved,' Spike said. 'Is this some kind of joke?'

413

'I started working again today,' Annika said. 'I thought the whole point of me being here was to write articles.'

He looked away from the screen and stared at her. 'Why didn't you do any of this before now?'

'I was under orders to stay at home and file my nails for six months,' Annika said, hoisting the dead-weight of her bag on to her shoulder. 'I'll be on my mobile if you need me.'

The traffic was terrible. She crawled along Fleming-gatan, and called Schyman from outside the children's old nursery. As his phone rang she saw Lennart, Kalle's favourite teacher, go past towards the Underground. She waved but he didn't see her. The editor-in-chief's voice-mail message clicked in and she left a slightly confused message, saying that she'd written the story of the Kitten and that the rest of the media would be finding out the details at eight o'clock the next morning. She tried making two more calls, without getting any answer, as she sat in a solid traffic jam at the junction of Birger Jarlsgatan and Runebergsgatan. She sat there for what seemed like at least one and a half eternities, forcing herself not to sound the horn.

When she finally got through the junction she accelerated hard down Karlavägen and swung right into the mess of one-way streets around Jungfrugatan and Sibyllegatan, until she found a space to park, albeit illegally, outside Holy Trinity Church.

Sod it, she thought, as she pulled on the handbrake.

Anne Snapphane's flat was a bit of a walk, and she hesitated for a moment about whether or not to take her bag. She ought to, really, or the damn thing would probably be stolen. She hoisted it on to her shoulder with a groan.

Östermalm really is a weird part of town, she thought, as she trudged slowly past the heavy turn-of-the-century façades. The atmosphere was completely different from that of Kungsholmen, Södermalm or Vasastan. Everything was a bit more sober, a bit better off, a bit duller. It doesn't really suit Anne very well at all, she thought guiltily.

She had been the one who had spotted the flat. She had been the one who had told Anne to buy it. She consoled herself with the fact that she had also been the one who had paid for it, so she shouldn't feel too sorry for Anne.

She turned on to Kommendörsgatan, and groaned at the thought of how far she still had to walk with the weight hanging from her shoulder. Maybe she ought to give in and buy a rucksack, as Thomas had suggested when she had complained about how heavy her bag was.

Over my dead body, she thought, and shifted the bag on to her other shoulder.

At that moment she noticed a woman some ten steps ahead of her on the pavement, a slender woman with a blonde bob who wiggled as she walked. She was wearing a dress that made her shoulders look round and soft, and her knee-length skirt revealed a pair of surprisingly powerful calves. A small handbag swung from one shoulder, and in the other hand she was carrying a light-brown leather briefcase. She was balancing expertly on a pair of high heels and seemed to be enjoying the afternoon sun.

Annika slowed and stared at the woman's back, unsure why she seemed to recognize it.

Then the woman stopped to look in a shop-window and Annika saw her face in profile.

It was another couple of seconds before Annika realized who she was.

She heard herself gasp and felt the ground sway beneath her.

It was Sophia Grenborg.

Annika stopped, unable to move. All sound vanished. *This isn't happening, this isn't happening.*

She was exactly as Annika remembered her, as she appeared in her dreams, as she had been that winter's evening when she had kissed Thomas outside the NK department store, as she looked on the passport photograph that Annika had ordered, then torn into shreds and flushed down the toilet.

And now she was standing there, looking at the window of an antiques shop, curious, interested, on tiptoe to peer at something further inside the shop.

Annika found herself heading straight towards the woman. She was gliding over the pavement, getting closer and closer until she was right next to her, staring at the blonde woman's face.

Sophia Grenborg straightened, with a look of surprise.

'Sophia Grenborg?' Annika asked, in a voice that came from far away.

'Yes?' the woman said, with a bemused smile.

'I'm Annika Bengtzon,' Annika said. 'I'm married to Thomas Samuelsson. I was just wondering what you thought my husband was like in bed.'

The woman continued to smile for another second or so, before gasping and turning pale. Her face twitched as if she had been slapped, and she took a step back, her foot hitting the wall. Her eyelids fluttered. She seemed about to faint.

Annika stood there, staring at her, until she felt she was going to suffocate in her own anger. 'Fucking hell,' Annika said. 'Fucking hell! How could he?' Suddenly she couldn't stay there a moment longer, not a single moment. She didn't want to take another breath in the presence of this person, this *whore*.

She turned and hurried away, walking towards the blinding sunlight. She walked and walked, feeling the woman staring at her back. She saw the buildings sway and felt as if she was going to be sick, and when she reached the end of the street and looked back, she could have sworn that the woman was still standing there, smiling.

30

Anne Snapphane opened the front door with a mascara brush in one hand and a pair of eyelash-curlers in the other. She was more or less concealed by a dressing-gown, and was wearing nylon stockings and suspenders. 'Christ, what's happened to you?' she said. 'You look like you've seen a ghost.'

Annika was clinging to the doorframe and swaying. Her heartbeat was still pounding in her head, her mouth dry. 'Can I have something to drink?' she said, trying to moisten her lips.

Anne stepped back and let her into the flat. The hall was a complete mess, newspapers and clothes piled up everywhere, and in one corner there was a bicycle.

Annika went into the kitchen and poured herself a glass of water, drank it thirstily and refilled it. 'That was horrible,' she said. 'I just bumped into Sophia Grenborg.'

'The scarlet woman?' Anne said. 'Where?'

'Just a couple of blocks away,' Annika said. 'She lives around here, a bit further down Grev Turegatan.' She gestured vaguely towards the south with her glass.

'Why was it so awful?' Anne said, letting her dressing-gown slide to the hall floor and walking into

418

the bathroom. Underneath she was wearing a thong and a transparent white bra.

Annika stayed in the kitchen for a moment, eyes closed, holding the glass to her forehead to cool herself. 'I have nightmares about her,' she said quietly. 'I dream of killing her, and that she's a corpse. I'm scared of her, and I hate her. That's why it was so awful.'

Anne came to the door in her underwear, this time with eye-shadow on one eyelid. 'I hope you didn't do anything silly,' she said, looking at Annika sympathetically.

Annika took a deep breath and sighed. 'No,' she said. 'I didn't. I just told her what I thought of her.'

Anne had been walking away again, but stopped and came back. 'Christ, Annika. What did you say?'

Annika jerked her head back. 'I told her who I was, and who I'm married to. Then I asked how good she thought my husband was in bed.'

Anne stared at her open-mouthed for a few seconds. Then she closed her eyes and banged her forehead against the doorframe three times. 'You're mad,' she said. 'How stupid can you be? I mean, really! You said that? You asked her how good she thought your husband was in bed?'

Annika poured herself another glass of water and resisted the urge to tip it over her own head.

'Talk about making a fool of yourself!' Anne said, throwing her hands out. '*Talk about making a fool of yourself!* Do you know what you've just gone and done? You showed Sophia fucking Grenborg how important she is. You've confirmed that she meant something. You chucked fuel on a flame that was pretty much dead. Fucking hell, Annika, sometimes you're so damn stupid.' She turned and went back into the bathroom.

'I didn't do anything of the sort,' Annika said, aware of the uncertainty in her voice.

'Oh yes you did,' Anne said, 'and you know it. She probably meant very little to Thomas, seeing as he seems to have let go of her so easily. She was just there, and he took his chance. But now you've elevated her to something completely different, to VIP status, someone who affects your family every second of every day. And that's a really stupid thing to do.'

'But she does,' Annika said.

'Wrong,' Anne said, from the bathroom. 'She affects *you*, no one else, and it's all in your head. You should have gone to see a therapist instead of flying at her in the street.'

Annika emptied the glass into the sink, her cheeks burning. 'Do you want to go through your lecture?' she asked.

Anne came out of the bathroom, in full war-paint now. 'I'm so sorry,' she said, 'but Robin called. We're off to the salsa club.'

'Who?' Annika said, feeling lost.

Anne was pulling on a loose, blood-red salsa dress that she had fished out of the mess on the floor and turned her back to Annika. 'Can you help me with the zip? Thanks. Haven't I told you about Robin?'

Annika zipped her up and Anne spun round, making her skirt billow. 'He's so lovely,' she said, trying a few dance-steps on the hall floor. 'So sweet, and only twenty-four. He dances salsa like a *real* man.'

'But what about your lecture?' Annika said, feeling foolish.

'Can we do it later in the week? This feels like a really big opportunity for me.'

Annika stood in the hall, staring at the mess all

around her, thoughts and images flashing through her head like a speeded-up film: Sophia Grenborg's pale face, her illegally parked car, her children, whom she'd be lucky to see at all today, Anne's lecture. She felt her heart sink lower and lower until it landed in the darkest, dankest cellar. 'Okay,' she said. 'We'll do it another day.' She turned and headed for the door, feeling so small that she could hardly reach the handle.

She'd got a parking ticket. Seven hundred kronor for parking in a space marked for deliveries only. Once upon a time she would have appealed against the fine, even though she was in the wrong and the fine entirely justified. She would have written and lied and argued and corresponded and made the council really work for their seven hundred before she gave in and paid up. Now she couldn't be bothered. She tossed it into her bag and forgot about it.

Then she sat in her car, staring out through the windscreen.

Had it been stupid to confront Sophia Grenborg?

She shut her eyes, feeling her cheeks burn again. Yes, Anne was right. It had been a huge mistake. 'I didn't mean it,' she whispered, as tears welled. 'I really didn't.' I just want him to be mine, she thought.

She dried her eyes, then dug out some kitchen-roll from the glove compartment and blew her nose. Really she should go home. Really she should take over from Thomas and put the children to bed, then watch a film with him on the sofa. Or do some gardening, or discuss what to do about the lawn. 'I can't,' she said aloud. 'Not right now. Maybe soon, but not yet.'

She pushed her hair behind her ears and took several

deep breaths, then started the engine and let the car idle in neutral.

She pulled her mobile from her bag and called Schyman.

No answer. Damn.

She took out her notebook and looked through it to find Lars-Henry Svensson's phone numbers. She called his flat on Södermalm. No answer. Then she called the address on Värmdö. No answer.

Where would you go if you'd just been released from questioning by the police? For coffee somewhere in town? Hardly: you'd go home and hide. At your flat on Södermalm? Would you sit there all day, not answering the phone?

Not very likely.

Or would you go to your summer cottage on Värmdö? Maybe sit yourself down in the middle of a patch of lily-of-the-valley and leave the phone to ring as much as it liked indoors.

Much better.

Tavastbodavägen. It sounded nice. So where was it?

She put the address into her sat-nav and got a location way out in the archipelago, in Fågelbrolandet. Past Nacka and Gustavsberg, out towards Stavsnäs.

What if she were to pay him a visit? Ask for a comment as he sat in his garden?

She looked at the time once more. It was time to go home. It was time to call Schyman again. It was time to talk to Jansson, who would just have started his shift.

He answered at once, his voice rough, newly woken.

'You sound shattered,' Annika said, holding on to the steering-wheel, glad that someone else seemed shaky.

'I've got the kids this week,' the night editor said.

'All of them?' Annika asked.

'Are you mad? Just the two eldest. That's bad enough. Can't we hold the Kitten until later in the week? We've got to run Berit's extradition tomorrow.'

'The Kitten will start to leak after midnight,' Annika said. 'If we're lucky, we'll be the only ones running the story if we can do it tonight.'

Jansson groaned. 'It's going to be a pretty full issue,' he said. 'Schyman has forbidden us to add any extra pages. Do you know where he is?'

'I never know anything,' Annika said. 'Ask him to call me when he gets in.'

She sat there with her ear-piece in after she had hung up. She didn't want to go home. Didn't want to remember Sophia Grenborg.

Instead she put the car in gear and headed east, towards the sea, towards Fågelbrolandet.

The landscape grew craggier the closer she got to Stavsnäs. She opened her window and thought she could smell salt and seaweed, though it was probably just her imagination. Clear blue water stretched away to either side of the car, sometimes small lakes, sometimes ice-blue sea. Light grey rocks stuck out from beaches and inlets; gnarled pines and slender birches edged the road. Yellow wooden houses with white gables and silver-grey jetties nestled securely on rock foundations and in meadows.

She had never been out here before.

As she passed the Strömma Channel she found herself in a picture-book version of Swedish archipelago life. How beautiful it was.

Her sat-nav was looking after the directions – she would never have stood a chance of finding her way without it. About five kilometres beyond the channel she turned off to the right and found herself on a twisting gravel road. She drove past Lars-Henry Svensson's cottage and had to do a three-point turn, then drive back. She stopped above the plot, parking behind an old Ford, and looked down at the little house.

The setting was idyllic, on a slope that gave out across the sea, no neighbours, surrounded by nature. The wooden façade was painted rust-red, with white eaves and original old windows, the sunset reflecting off them. It must once have been a fisherman's cottage.

At the back she saw an outside toilet and a large bonfire, and further down towards the water there was another little wooden house, presumably a wood-fired sauna.

Annika turned off the engine and opened the car door. The worst he could do was throw her out. It was cooler here than in the city, crisper and fresher. She took several deep breaths, letting the wind whip at her hair. Maybe this was the way to live. Maybe she could feel at home on Tavastbodavägen.

She walked down into the garden, which was overgrown with clumps of wild flowers; lily-of-the-valley, buttercups, wood-anemones and a large patch of cranesbill beside a little stream. Paths strewn with pine needles ran in various directions, neatly edged with perfectly smooth stones. I wonder if he did all this himself. Does he spend his holidays looking for stones, levelling the ground, laying paths?

Lars-Henry Svensson was listed as single in the national register, but that was no reason to suppose he didn't have lady-friends.

She walked up to the veranda and knocked on the door.

No answer.

She knocked again, harder.

No response.

'Lars-Henry Svensson?' she called, loudly and clearly.

The wind rustled through the pine trees.

She stepped down and went to the back of the cottage, to the outside toilet and the bonfire. The burned wood was flaky and white: there couldn't have been a fire for several days. The toilet was small, painted red in the traditional way, and even had a green heart on the door. It made her think of Grandma and Lyckebo, as a streak of gold flashed past at the edge of her field of vision. 'Beautiful . . .' she whispered.

She went back to the house and knocked again. She tried the door. It wasn't locked. Carefully she pushed it open and peered into a small, pale-blue hallway. 'Hello?'

No answer.

She went in. There was a small kitchen to the left, then a little bedroom. On the right was a larger room, which functioned as both dining and living room. A television was on, with the sound turned down. A plate of herring and potatoes lay on the dining-table, along with a small glass of schnapps. One of the lamps was on.

Lars-Henry Svensson couldn't be far away.

Maybe he's down by the shore, Annika thought. Or perhaps he's gone to get some beer to drink with his meal.

But his car was parked outside, the old Ford. That had to be his, didn't it?

She walked out of the house again, feeling guilty at her intrusion, relieved to be back outside.

The sun was going down in the water below the cottage, and she walked slowly towards the jetty, where a rowing-boat rocked gently back and forth.

Maybe he's out in another boat, Annika thought, checking his pots and nets.

But with a glass of schnapps already poured?

She stopped and stared at the sunset, with a growing feeling that something wasn't right. She went back up to her car, dug out her mobile phone from her ridiculously heavy bag, and called the national vehicle register.

The Ford in front of her belonged to a Lars-Henry Svensson, registered as living on Ringvägen in Stockholm.

She put the mobile into her pocket.

He had to be here somewhere.

How long could he have been gone? Were the potatoes warm? The schnapps cold?

She hurried back to the cottage and went straight into the main room to check the food. The potatoes were cold. There was no condensation on the schnapps glass.

Something was wrong.

She went to the window and looked out at the trees, the sea, the lengthening shadows. The Ford by the road, her SUV behind it. The drifts of wild flowers, a ramshackle garden bench halfway down the path to the little wooden sauna.

The sauna door was ajar.

She leaned closer to the window, screwing up her eyes to see better.

There was no smoke coming from the chimney, and the little window was dark, but the door was definitely open.

She went outside again, then down the needle-strewn, stone-edged path and up to the door of the sauna. From there she could hear the sound of waves lapping against the jetty.

As she opened the door wider, the dusk light fell on a small changing room. There was a pile of wood and a bundle of neatly folded towels, all blue. Apart from that, the room was empty.

On the opposite wall was the door into the sauna.

She took three paces towards it and pulled it open.

He was hanging on the wall.

Somehow she knew at once that he was hanging on the wall, not leaning against it – he wasn't resting. He was hanging.

A large metal nail was sticking out of his right eye.

His left eye was staring at her, bloodshot and bulging.

There was another nail in his neck, through his throat.

She stared at him, closed her eyes, looked again.

She shut the door and went outside, where she threw up over an anthill.

Then she called Q.

31

The first police vehicle was a normal patrol car. It arrived after just fifteen minutes and parked down the hill, not far from the sauna. Two walking clichés got out and looked around.

Annika had locked herself inside her car with the engine running and the heater on. She felt so cold that she was shaking, and couldn't stop looking in the rear-view mirror to make sure no one was creeping up on her from behind. She felt better now that the patrol had arrived.

One of the officers came up the hill to her. When she showed no sign of getting out, he knocked on her window. She opened it a few centimetres. 'Are you the person who called?'

She nodded.

'And the owner of the house is in the sauna, you say. Dead.'

She nodded again.

The policeman sighed. 'Someone from the crime unit will be here to ask you some questions in due course,' he said, then went back to the patrol car.

She closed the window again and went on staring ahead of her.

A nail through his eye, sticking out maybe two or three centimetres.

Which meant that someone had knocked it in, using a hammer to drive it through the professor's head until there was about an inch left.

How long could the nail be? How deep was a skull? Seven inches? Nine?'

And what had Q said about Lars-Henry Svensson earlier that day?

He had nothing to do with the death of Ernst Ericsson.

She heard her own reply echo in her memory: *And you're absolutely certain of that?*

His response: *Not a shadow of a doubt.*

She gasped.

Now she knew why they were so certain Ernst Ericsson hadn't committed suicide.

It might just be possible to drive a nail through your own neck, but not if you've already hammered one through your brain.

She pulled out her mobile, thinking she should call Thomas. She couldn't bring herself to do it. She could feel his anger without needing to hear it in his voice. I'll deal with it when I get home, she thought. Otherwise I'll be punished twice.

Three unmarked cars appeared about ten minutes later.

In the second vehicle she glimpsed a Hawaiian shirt.

She switched off the ignition, pulled on a cardigan she found on the back seat, and went out to meet the detective inspector. She waited patiently beside his car as he went down to the sauna and confirmed that she hadn't been hallucinating.

'Not a shadow of a doubt,' Annika said. 'Great.'

He pointed at the pile of vomit on the anthill just outside the door of the sauna.

'That was me,' Annika said. 'Sorry.'

Q sighed. 'What are you doing here?'

'Is this a formal interrogation?'

He threw out his hands. 'Do I look like a microphone?'

'I was hoping to get a comment on the death of Ernst Ericsson,' Annika said, holding on to the car to stop herself falling. 'There were lights on in the cottage and the sauna door was ajar, so I looked inside.'

'You're sure about that? The door was ajar?'

'I noticed it from the house,' Annika said, pointing at the illuminated window up the hill.

'You were inside the house? What were you doing in there?'

'There was a plate of herring and potatoes on the table. I was checking to see if the food was warm.'

Q groaned. 'So you've been scampering about touching things all over the scene of a crime?'

Annika bit her lip. 'Not the body,' she said. 'I didn't touch him. And I didn't touch anything inside the sauna, except the door-handle.'

Q walked over to his car and dug about inside the glove compartment.

Annika stayed close to him. 'This has to have some sort of personal motive, doesn't it?' she asked. 'It isn't remotely clean or professional, so it wasn't the Kitten, was it? And yesterday Ernst Ericsson wasn't her either, was he?'

He emerged from the car with a small tape-recorder in his hand, and slammed the door. 'Interview with witness Annika Bengtzon,' he said. 'Personal details to be added later, Tuesday, the first of June, time nineteen fifty-five, at the crime scene on Tavastbodavägen in Fågelbrolandet, regarding the suspected murder of Lars-Henry Svensson.'

Annika started walking towards her car.

'Where are you going?'

'The paper,' Annika said. 'Don't even think of imposing a ban on disclosure this time. I'm not going to keep quiet.'

'You'd never put an investigation at risk,' Q said.

She stopped. She was on the verge of tears. 'Please,' she said. 'This is my first day back at work. I can't get myself thrown out again.'

He looked at her, his head tilted to one side, without the slightest trace of sympathy.

'Well, of course I'm going to issue you with a ban on disclosure,' he said, 'according to chapter twenty-three, paragraph ten of the Judicial Procedure Act. I want you to stay here until we're done, so that I can interview you properly.'

'I drove here and got out of my car,' Annika said. 'I looked round for twenty-three minutes before I found the body. Then I threw up and phoned you. I haven't seen anyone else here since I arrived. No cars have gone past, no boats. I've been in all the buildings, including the outside toilet, and I've touched pretty much everything. Okay, I'm going now.'

'I forbid you to leave,' Q said.

'So shoot me,' Annika said, walking to her car.

She pulled out her mobile and called the paper.

Anders Schyman tossed his briefcase on to the desk in his little office. He'd had a terrible day. The family who owned the paper had been given early warning of the morning paper's disastrous results for the first half of the year and had pulled the emergency cord as hard as they possibly could.

There had been a meeting out at their villa on

Djurgården, practically an inquisition. All costs were to be reviewed. All new initiatives were to be put on hold. Every single part of the company was to freeze all new recruitment. They were no longer allowed to use freelancers.

Fortunately there were several wise men and women among the editorial managers of the business. Together they had bullied the owners and the board into understanding that putting the brakes on was not the way to get out of a crisis. Acknowledgement of a state of crisis was all very well, but you had to find ways for people to vent their frustration, an inevitable side-effect. You had to be able to push ahead as well.

He wasn't sure if his message had really sunk in, but he knew he was going to have to spend the next month trying to rescue the new initiatives that he had thought were safe.

He rubbed his chin with the palm of his hand. Why on earth was he doing all this? These cuts were enough to trigger his already somewhat battered parachute, which would carry him safely and securely to the ground as the media world collapsed. But he already knew the answer to his question. It had been formulated by an old hack at Swedish Television who had covered every global conflict from Vietnam to Iraq: *It's never hard to step up to the mark in wartime. You only feel like curling up and dying in times of peace.*

And right now war was raging all round him, with a new front opening up against the idiotic priorities of the paper's owners, alongside the ongoing battle against the other evening paper and future battles about ill-considered technological investments and negotiating positions.

His wife would be waiting for him. He ought to go home.

He sighed deeply.

She would rather he go home late with the battle behind him than show up early with it still raging. Which was why he answered when the phone rang, even though he should have been on his way home.

'I've done it again.'

It was Bengtzon, the walking disaster. He slumped into his chair and put his feet up on the desk. 'I know,' he said. 'I saw it. *The Kitten*, what sort of alias is that? How long have you been sitting on that story?'

'I'm not talking about the Kitten. I've just stumbled across a body, but this time I'm not going to keep quiet.'

He blinked several times against the light from the ceiling lamp. 'What?' he said.

'The professor who was questioned about the murder of Ernst Ericsson is dead,' she said.

'Who?' Schyman said.

'Another professor from the Karolinska Institute. I found him. He'd been nailed up in his own sauna, a nine-inch nail through one eye and another through the throat.'

He stared at the lamp until he was forced to close his eyes. Flecks of light danced in front of his eyes. Nausea bubbled in his throat, bringing with it the taste of vomit. 'Nailed up?'

'He was dead when it happened, strangled. Ernst Ericsson's corpse was mutilated in the same way.' She sounded too wound up to be doing anything. 'I'm not allowed to write anything myself,' she said, 'except maybe an overview. Someone else will have to deal with the news angle.'

'Are you allowed to talk about it? They haven't imposed another ban on disclosure?'

'They're trying to, but I'm not going to let them. I've kept quiet for long enough. Someone who understands the meaning of the disclosure ban will have to interview me. Then it'll be up to you to decide if we publish it. Is Berit there, or Patrik?'

'They're working flat out on the extradition from Bromma. We've got to run that tomorrow.'

'Is anyone else there who knows what rules we're trying to get round?'

He sat down again and propped his head on his hand. 'Jansson, but he's putting the paper together.'

'I see,' she said. 'So I just go home and give up on the whole thing?'

'Me,' he said. 'I can do it. Come up to the newsroom and I'll interview you.'

She said nothing for a few moments. 'What – *Interview by Anders Schyman*?' she said sceptically.

'Do you suppose I've never had to knock something together in the past?' he said.

Wednesday, 2 June

32

Annika thought she was going to die when the alarm clock rang. Her whole body ached with tiredness. She felt as if she hadn't slept in years. She rolled over on to her back, glancing cautiously at the other side of the bed. Someone was there, a warm body, only it wasn't Thomas's but Ellen's. Her tousled hair was spread across the white pillow. Annika leaned over and pulled the covers away from her face. The child's eyelashes were flickering, a sure sign that she was dreaming.

My darling, she thought, stroking her daughter's hair gently.

Then she lay back and listened hard for sounds from the kitchen. No running taps. No rustling newspaper. No chink of crockery.

I hope he's gone, she thought. Which would mean she had managed to postpone the confrontation for a while longer.

She hadn't called the previous evening, and neither had Thomas. When she had got home he was already asleep, and she had managed to creep into bed beside him and Ellen without waking him.

And now he had gone without waking her, and she breathed a sigh of relief.

Ellen shifted uneasily, then stretched out in a slow, leisurely gesture that reminded Annika of Whiskers, her old cat. I have to get up now, she thought. I have to make breakfast and drive the children to nursery.

Kalle would have to go back to pre-school today. Her stomach knotted when she thought about how vulnerable he was. If only she could do something. If only she had some sort of power.

But I have, she thought.

She stared up at the ceiling, letting her thoughts settle. There were ways and means of getting power, if you didn't already have it. It was easy, in fact: she had spent her whole life working with it. Power didn't come for free, it always had a price, but in this case she was prepared to pay.

I have a choice, she thought. I can do it, if I want.

She rolled over to Thomas's side of the bed and cuddled up to her daughter. 'Ellen,' she whispered. 'It's time to get up now.' She stroked the little girl's hair until she opened her eyes, looking round blindly for a moment until she caught sight of Annika.

Then the smile, oh, that smile, radiating complete confidence and unconditional love, and the sleepy voice. 'Mummy!' Sleep-moistened arms around her neck, the sweet smell of a child's skin and cotton pyjamas. Annika rocked the little bundle in her arms and wanted never to get up. 'Are we going to nursery today, Mummy?'

'Yes,' Annika whispered. 'Today's a nursery day.'

Ellen wriggled out of her arms and jumped up, bouncing happily on the absurdly expensive mattress. 'I'm going to finish my bag today,' she said, her hair flying about. 'I'm making a bag, Mummy, with red pockets and lots of buttons.'

'That sounds lovely,' Annika said.

She pulled up outside the nursery. It was just before nine o'clock and the playground was full of children. She stopped and stared intently at the crowd for two solidly built little boys with expensive haircuts and trainers.

There they were. They were standing by the fence, kicking a tricycle.

'Come on,' Annika said, switching the engine off. 'It'll soon be time for Assembly.'

Ellen undid her seatbelt and jumped out, but Kalle hung back. His fingers went to the large plaster on his forehead. 'Can I take this off, Mummy?'

'Absolutely not,' Annika said. 'You might get dirt in the cut. You have to promise me that you'll leave it on, okay?'

He nodded. 'But what if they're mean again?' he said.

Annika bent down to him. 'Kalle,' she said, looking him in the eye. 'I promise you this. Alexander and Benjamin will never be nasty to you again. I'm going to make sure of that.'

He sighed and nodded, then climbed out of the car.

'Hi, Kalle,' Lotta called from the entrance. 'Can you come and help me with Assembly today? You can hand out the books.'

A smile slipped out. He let go of Annika's hand and ran off.

Soon they would all be going indoors – she had only a minute or so.

Annika felt her pulse race until it filled her head. She made her way through the crowd of children as her field of vision shrank. It got narrower and narrower until it became a tunnel, with just two small figures at the end, two six-year-olds who were kicking a tricycle at the far end of the fence.

Finally they were standing in front of her but they still hadn't noticed her. They were yelling and shouting as they kicked the tricycle, and she leaned down towards them.

'Benjamin,' she said quietly, grasping the boy's arm.

The child looked up at her in surprise, stopping mid-yell. She put her face just a couple of centimetres from his and saw the surprise in his eyes turn into vague unease.

'Benjamin,' she said. 'Have you been mean to Kalle?'

His mouth opened and his tongue stuck out a little way.

'I want you to know something,' Annika whispered, her heart thudding so hard that she could hardly hear her own words. 'If you are ever mean to Kalle again, and I mean *ever*, I'll kill you. Got it?'

His eyes grew as big as saucers and gradually filled with terror.

She let him go and grabbed the other child. 'Alexander,' she whispered, her breath enveloping his face. 'If you're ever mean to Kalle again I'll come and find you in the night and kill you. Understand?'

He started to tremble and stared at her in horror. She let him go and looked at them both. 'And you know what?' she said quietly. 'That doesn't just go for Kalle, but all the other children as well.'

Then she straightened, turned her back on them and walked through the sea of children towards her car.

She drove into the city with the peculiar sensation of piloting a plane, not driving a car: the wheels didn't seem to be touching the ground – she was steering through clouds and sky.

Was it stupid?

440

Who cares? she thought. I'd do it all over again if I had to.

The sky was the colour of smoke, and rain was hanging in the air as she parked.

She made her way up to the newsroom, and was struck once again by the cramped but oddly deserted space.

Berit was already there, writing at her desk with her reading glasses on.

'Follow-up?' Annika asked.

'Who knew what?' Berit asked rhetorically. 'Who gave permission for what? Who sanctioned the abuse? Who negotiated with the Jordanian government? I'm not going to leave any stone unturned in this horrible mess. How are you getting on?'

Annika sank on to Patrik's chair. 'Something must have happened on Saturday,' she said. 'Some sort of Nobel group had a meeting. Then there was a seminar, then a bit of a drinks party, and some time during that afternoon something must have happened that triggered the murders of Ernst Ericsson and Lars-Henry Svensson.'

'Can you all listen, please?' Spike yelled from the news desk. Annika and Berit turned.

Schyman clambered on to the news desk, just like he would have done in the old days, standing there barefoot, legs apart in the middle of the desk as people used to when the evening papers appeared in the afternoon and everyone had spent all their time writing, editing and taking pictures for a print newspaper whose earliest edition went to press at 04.45 somewhere in the basement. He was behaving as editors used to.

It didn't have quite the same effect now. Schyman was standing on a much smaller desk, and there were far fewer, and far less enthusiastic, staff standing round to see him do it.

441

The editor-in-chief held a copy of that day's paper above his head, turning to show it in every direction. 'This,' he said, 'is the best edition in the history of this newspaper. Never before has every single news page been full of global scoops. We're being cited by AP, AFP, Reuters and CNN.'

The staff glanced at each other, slightly embarrassed. Most of them didn't work on the dusty old print edition but on the online version, local television, commercial radio or some shiny supplement. Many of them didn't even read the actual newspaper.

'Berit's revelation that a foreign power has been permitted to operate on Swedish soil is being followed up here today,' Schyman said triumphantly, from his lofty position. 'You can already see how everyone else is jumping on the story. We're going further with Annika's detailed story of the Nobel murders. Today we've got the revelation of who carried out the murders, and the fact that they're still going on. This is a great day for all of us. Now let's get back to work!'

In the past a speech like that would have been greeted by shouting and applause. Now people were glancing awkwardly at each other and scuttling away.

Annika and Berit were sitting, arms crossed, looking worried.

'He hasn't really moved with the times,' Berit said. 'Sometimes I wonder if he knows what he's doing at all.'

'I think he's starting to get it,' Annika said. 'He has to make it work again, which he just tried to do. He has to get everyone working here to pull in the same direction. He has to shift the focus back to real journalism.'

'You mean the important thing is what we say, not what sort of broadband we use?' Berit wondered.

'More or less,' Annika said. 'By the way, do you know

what I did this morning? I scared the shit out of some kids who've been bullying Kalle.'

'Uh-oh,' Berit said. 'That'll come back to haunt you.'

Annika sighed. 'I really don't care if it does, as long as Kalle doesn't suffer. So, who do you think knew what about the Bandhagen extradition?'

Berit put her glasses back on and reached for a sheaf of papers. 'Okay, this is how it looks: the government authorized the extradition. They used one of the paragraphs dealing with terrorism, the law about the control of foreign nationals, the one they always fall back on when they don't want anyone to see what they're doing. You know, safety of the realm and all that, with the government as the highest authority.'

'And that's recent legislation?'

'No, it's been around for more than thirty years, and has been used roughly thirty times, so they're not exactly wearing it out. But every time they use it, it makes you just a little bit suspicious because they very rarely reveal what was behind the decision. If the cases aren't deemed to be *particularly urgent*, the government is supposed to ask for a report from the Migration Office, and then the process is supposed to be authorized by a district court. But for some reason these cases are almost always *particularly urgent . . .*'

'But surely they can't just kick people out when they know they're going to be tortured?' Annika said.

'No, they can't,' Berit said. 'According to the same legislation the government must stop or block the extradition if there's any risk of capital punishment or torture, and instead impose compulsory registration of the suspected terrorist. He has to report to a police station a certain number of times each week to prove that he hasn't got his hands dirty. This can go on for three years, and then the case has to be referred to court.'

'Much easier just to throw someone out, then,' Annika said.

'Especially if the Americans happen to be passing,' Berit said.

'Who are we pinning this on?'

Berit tossed the bundle of papers down and took off her glasses. 'In purely formal terms, the Security Police officer out at the airport buggered it up. His name's Anton Abrahamsson. He relinquished official control to a foreign police authority. That's the technical error here, but it isn't the real scandal. How can we allow a locksmith from Bandhagen to be labelled a terrorist and chucked out without any evidence at all?'

'What's the Security Police officer saying?'

'I haven't been able to get hold of him,' Berit said. 'He's on paternity leave.'

'How convenient,' Annika said.

'Isn't it just?'

'And what are they saying in the Justice Department?' Annika asked, thinking of Thomas.

'That the minister was only informed about the extradition on the seventh of January. Several weeks later, in other words.'

'Do you believe that?'

Berit sighed. 'It doesn't really make any difference to Jemal,' she said. 'The Foreign Ministry claim they obtained guarantees that he would be treated fairly. Our ambassador is visiting him once a month and says he's absolutely fine, whereas Fatima says he's been deeply scarred by the torture he had to endure.'

'Well, you'll just have to go and see him,' Annika said.

'I'm going to find out from the embassy this afternoon if I can go with them next time,' Berit said.

444

Annika grabbed her bag and headed off to the day-shift reporters' desks, to let Berit get on and to make a few calls herself. Something had happened last Saturday, she was absolutely certain of it. Something had triggered these new Nobel killings – maybe she should think of them as Karolinska Institute killings. Perhaps they had nothing to do with Nobel.

She dialled Reception at the Karolinska Institute and asked to speak to Birgitta Larsén.

The phone rang four, five, six times . . .

Birgitta usually answered on the first ring, so Annika was about to hang up when the phone was picked up and a voice said hesitantly, 'Hello?'

'Birgitta? Hello, this is Annika Bengtzon from—'

A drawn-out sob interrupted her.

'Birgitta?' Annika said. 'How are you? You know about Lars-Henry?'

'It's the animals,' she said, sounding as though she'd been crying for hours.

'The animals?' Annika echoed.

The professor blew her nose loudly and took several panting breaths over the phone. 'All my test animals are dead,' she said shakily. 'Someone killed them last night.'

Annika saw the rows of Plexiglass boxes in front of her eyes, little black and white mice making nests with tissues and rearranging their egg boxes. 'Killed them? How?'

'The mice had their necks wrung. The rabbits and rats were beaten to death.'

'God,' Annika said. 'Who would do something like that?'

'The police suspect one of the animal-rights organizations, but I don't believe that. No one knows where the lab is. There were no signs of a break-in and only my

445

animals were killed, no one else's. And Lars-Henry – have you heard? It's so awful!'

'I found him,' Annika said.

Birgitta blew her nose again. 'Oh, of course you did. They did tell me. Is it true that he was beheaded?'

Annika gulped hard. 'Not really,' she said. 'Well, almost.'

'You must tell me all about it,' Birgitta said.

'Maybe I could come out and see you,' Annika suggested tentatively.

Birgitta sighed. 'Well, all right. Yes, why don't you?'

Annika hung up and went over to see Spike, dragging her bag with her. 'I'm heading out to the Karolinska Institute,' she said. 'I'll write it up at home.'

The news editor grunted.

'And I was wondering if I was going to get any petrol money, seeing as I'm driving around in my own car on work business?' Annika asked.

Spike looked up at her in surprise. 'I haven't a clue,' he said.

'So who do I ask?' she said.

He shrugged and reached for a ringing phone. 'You can use a bicycle for all I care,' he said. 'Or swim. Hello, Spike here . . . Fucking hell, *hello*!'

Annika headed into the murky grey outside.

Rain was hanging in the air as Annika parked outside the Black Fox, but it didn't seem to want to fall properly. The wind was tugging at the trees, with an odd smell of autumn. Has summer already been and gone? she wondered.

She headed over to Birgitta Larsén's department, Astra's smart former premises, and was let in by a group of students.

'So, tell me all about it,' Birgitta said, pulling out a chair for her the moment Annika stepped into the bright office with its radioactivity warning tape.

The professor of biophysics had evidently been crying for a while. She was putting on a brave face but it wasn't very convincing.

'Have the police been here?' Annika asked, settling into the chair. 'What did they have to say about the dead animals?'

'I've already been questioned,' the professor said. 'They're down in the lab now. What happened last night?'

'I drove out to Lars-Henry's summer cottage in Fågelbrolandet to ask him some questions,' Annika said.

'Ah, I see.' Birgitta put a packet of biscuits on the desk between them. 'Why did you do that?'

'I thought something had happened here on Saturday and I wanted to talk to him about it,' Annika said, turning down the offer of a biscuit. 'Something happened, either at the meeting, during the seminar or at the buffet afterwards, something that triggered Ernst's murder, and then Lars-Henry's. I'm even more convinced now that that was the case.'

'Yes, well,' Birgitta said, wiping her fingers on her white lab coat, 'I was there the whole time and I didn't notice anything unusual. What could it have been?' Her tone seemed too animated. Her words sounded forced, and her eyes were too anxious.

'That was what I was hoping to ask you,' Annika said.

'Oh, I don't know anything,' she said, staring at her chocolate biscuit.

Annika followed her instincts and leaned closer to her. 'Birgitta,' she said, looking the woman in the eye like she did with Kalle when he was playing up. 'There's something you're not telling me, something about Caroline, and I think you're starting to get very scared about the fact that you know it. Ernst is dead, Lars-Henry is dead, and do you know how they died? Someone murdered them, then mutilated their bodies. The killer drove a nine-inch nail through one eye, right into their brains, and then another through their throats and into the spinal cord. Same thing with both of them. What does that tell you?'

Annika didn't look away from the woman, and as she spoke, the terror in Birgitta's eyes grew until they were overflowing with tears.

'Oh, my God . . .' she said.

'Now your animals are dead, and what does that say to you, Birgitta? It's a warning, wouldn't you say? What is it you know, Birgitta? What's so important?'

The professor blinked a few times. Then her face crumpled and she hid it in her hands and wept.

Annika waited without saying anything.

'It's got nothing to do with this,' Birgitta said, once she had calmed down. 'It was so long ago and only Carrie and I knew. It only concerns us, we're the only ones who . . .'

'What?' Annika said.

Birgitta sighed heavily and her shoulders slumped. 'I don't want you to make this public,' she said. 'It could destroy Caroline's reputation and sabotage my own career.'

Her voice sounded different. Deeper, calmer.

'You're my source,' Annika said. 'Your identity is protected by law. I can't write anything without your express permission.'

Birgitta nodded, twisting a handkerchief between her fingers. 'This isn't easy for me,' she said. 'I've kept quiet about it for twenty years.'

Annika said nothing.

The professor sighed deeply and closed her eyes, collecting herself. 'Carrie's big, international breakthrough came when she developed Hood and Tonegawa's discovery of the identification of immunoglobulin genes,' she said eventually. 'Her research was published in *Science* in October 1986, and that was the article that led to her appointment as professor, and to her joining the Nobel Assembly.'

Annika nodded. She had heard this before.

'The problem was that *Science* didn't accept her first version of the article,' Birgitta said, her voice suddenly thin and dull. 'They wanted her to replicate the results, a common routine control, but Carrie knew they were strong enough.'

'As happened with the results of Ernst's research into MS,' Annika said.

'Exactly,' Birgitta said. 'So why should she spend three months doing something when she was absolutely confident of her results?'

All of a sudden Annika realized what she was being told as she met Birgitta's eyes. 'Caroline cheated,' Annika said. 'She didn't replicate her findings, and submitted false results instead.'

Birgitta nodded. 'It wasn't that the research was incomplete or inaccurate. Everything held up. She just skipped the routine control. And she wasn't the one who fabricated it. I was. During the week in question Carrie was at a conference in Helsinki, so I filled in her test results and sent them off.'

Annika stared at the woman, unable to believe what she was hearing. If you'd spent years working on something, why take risks right at the end? 'Why?' she asked.

Birgitta blew her nose. 'There was nothing wrong

with the research,' she said. 'Carrie knew it was absolutely watertight. The people at *Science* were just being overzealous, and she really wanted to attend that Finnish conference.'

'But someone found out,' Annika said.

Birgitta hesitated, then nodded. 'I don't know who, Carrie never told me. But she did something that she was extremely ashamed of to make sure that that person never said anything. I don't know what it was.'

'Someone was blackmailing Caroline,' Annika said. 'Someone demanded something in exchange for not speaking out about her fabricating those results.'

Birgitta sighed and nodded again. 'I don't know when it happened, but the person in question must have got in touch again, not long before Carrie died.'

'What makes you think that?' Annika said.

'Last autumn she once said that she wasn't going to give in to threats any more. Not again. That was what she said. She had allowed herself to be frightened into doing it once, but she wasn't going to do it again.'

'When was this?'

'Right after the names of last year's prize-winners, Wiesel and Watson, were announced.'

'Are they gay, by the way?' Annika asked. 'And a couple?'

The professor looked up at her in surprise. 'Of course they are,' she said. 'Didn't you know?'

'Sorry,' Annika said. 'I'm getting sidetracked. Then what happened?'

Birgitta rubbed her forehead with her fingertips. 'This is where it gets complicated,' she said. 'Carrie said something very cryptic just a few weeks before she died. *Just so you know*, she said, *if anything ever happens to me, it's all in my archive. I've written it all down.*'

'And what did it say?' Annika asked.

'That's the problem,' Birgitta said. 'I told the police that Carrie felt threatened and that she'd written about it in her archive, but we haven't found the archive. I've looked, the police have looked, her husband Knut has looked, but we haven't found anything that reveals what she was so afraid of.'

'Have you told the police that Caroline cheated with her big scientific breakthrough?'

The professor's neck jerked. 'I don't think there's any need to use that sort of language,' she said.

'But you haven't told them?'

'No. I didn't think it was necessary.'

Annika looked at the little round woman, at her energetic movements. There was something else she didn't want to reveal. 'Out of all the people who were there on Saturday afternoon, how many of them knew Caroline in the mid-1980s?' Annika asked.

Birgitta raised her eyebrows a touch and thought for a moment. 'About half, maybe. Why?'

Annika looked at her watch. 'I have to write an article about Lars-Henry Svensson,' she said. 'Can I quote you about his death? Is there anything that you'd like to say, as one of his colleagues?'

'He was a real troublemaker,' Birgitta said. 'If he hadn't gone and died we'd have had to find a way to get rid of him somehow.'

Annika nodded thoughtfully. 'I might not put that in the opening paragraph,' she said. 'By the way, why did you say that you should have taken more care of him after Caroline's death?'

Birgitta stood up. 'Caroline wanted to look after everyone and everything,' she said. 'If it wasn't Alfred Nobel and his memory, it was Lars-Henry Svensson and his career. It could be quite frustrating at times, as I'm sure you can appreciate.'

So where were you yesterday evening? Annika wondered suddenly. And how did you know that Ernst Ericsson was dead? Did Sören Hammarsten really phone you?

'Well, I must go and sort out my poor animals,' Birgitta said.

Annika followed her out of the door. 'Who knew exactly which animals were yours?'

But Birgitta Larsén didn't hear: she disappeared down the corridor.

Annika drove straight home and hauled her laptop up to the study. It was starting to be a real nuisance, having to sort out cables and wireless connections every time she wanted to check her email or make notes. It was much better with my own office at work and a separate computer at home, she thought.

Once she had unpacked and connected everything she called Q. There was no answer, so she emailed a plea to talk to him some time during the day. Because she was planning to ignore his ban on disclosure, she knew that she wasn't one of his favourite people at the moment.

Schyman had interviewed her the previous evening about what she had seen in Fågelbrolandet, then written an article that she had amended. She hadn't got home until two o'clock in the morning, and she was starting to feel the effects. What if she were to lie down for a little while before she got going? She just needed something to think about while she rested.

Lars-Henry Svensson wasn't important enough to warrant a full-page obituary: he was just a grumpy, bitter old professor who had had a nail hammered through his eyeball.

The mutilation of corpses was always interesting, but if she remembered correctly the *Evening Post* had run an article about it after another recent murder case. Maybe she could dust it off, make a few calls to check the facts, and pretend it was a new piece. She went into the *Evening Post*'s online archive of articles and found the text, written by Patrik just three weeks before. It felt a bit cheeky to recycle it so soon. Perhaps something about the two most recent murders having nothing to do with the Kitten because they were so different from the Nobel killings. She had already written the outline of an article along those lines.

She went back to the Internet and checked her personal email account, but just as she was typing in her password her fingers stiffened.

Just so you know, if anything ever happens to me, it's all in my archive. I've written it all down.

Annika stared at the screen.

My archive. Written it all down.

She picked up the phone and called the Karolinska Institute.

Birgitta Larsén was in the lab with her test animals.

'Did Caroline have another email address apart from her official work address at KI?' Annika asked rather breathlessly.

'No,' Birgitta said blankly. 'I don't think so. Why?'

'Did you used to email each other?' She heard something fall to the floor.

'All the time. There were always a million and one things going on, work and meetings and seminars, and our network, of course. She had so many irons in the fire—'

'And she always used the institute's email server?' Annika interrupted. 'And her work address?'

Birgitta took a deep breath and was quiet for a moment. 'Yes,' she said, 'except for the women's group.'

'The women's group?'

'Our network. Alfred's Amazons.'

Alfred's Amazons?

Birgitta cleared her throat. 'It wasn't my idea,' she said. 'I'm not the Nobel fanatic. It was Caroline who set up the network's addresses. They all had something to do with Alfred Nobel. I was Sofie Hess, which I always thought was an insult. As if I was somehow supposed to embody the leech of the group, spendthrift and stupid, always begging for more money. I mean, what was she thinking?'

Annika tried to grasp what the woman was saying behind the torrent of words. 'So Caroline allocated email addresses to everyone in the women's group, to Alfred's Amazons?'

'She said Alfred was very fond of Sofie and that I shouldn't take it badly because Sofie Hess was also very persuasive and charming. Otherwise Alfred wouldn't have—'

'Birgitta,' Annika interrupted, 'did Caroline have an email address on the Internet that was different from the one she used at work?'

'Well, yes,' Birgitta said, sounding indignant. 'That's what I'm trying to tell you.'

'She had an email address with a name that had some sort of connection to Alfred Nobel? Which one? Bertha von Suttner?'

'No,' Birgitta said. 'She was Andrietta Ahlsell.'

Who?

'Who?'

'Alfred Nobel's mother. I think that's how Carrie saw herself, as if she had a responsibility to Alfred and his memory. She seemed to think it was her role in life to carry on his vision, and I have to say that sometimes she took it a bit too personally.'

'What was the domain name?' Annika asked.

'The what?'

'The domain. Was it hotmail or yahoo or nameplanet or what?'

'How am I supposed to know that?'

Annika stifled a groan. 'Who knew what address you were sending emails to?'

'Do you know? I always thought it was a bit ridiculous. And as I didn't like being Sofie Hess I didn't pay much attention. Why do you want to know?'

'You can keep an electronic archive in your email address,' she said. 'I'll try to follow it up.'

'Well, if you must.' Birgitta sighed and hung up.

Andrietta Ahlsell? Annika stared at the screen. How many combinations could you come up with using that name, without looking at the domain name? You could run the first name and surname together, add a hyphen, or use initials or underscoring. What were the most common domains where you could most easily register an email account?

Hotmail and yahoo, but Google had gmail, and nameplanet was still going.

She went into her own work email and tried putting the most common name combinations together with the biggest domain names.

Sixteen emails in total.

She sent them all off at once. Those that went to non-existent addresses would bounce back to her inbox with a Delivery Error Report from the Mail Delivery System. Any emails that got through would have gone to a registered address.

She watched the emails, all headed *test*, vanish into cyberspace. She could only wait and see.

Andrietta Ahlsell, Alfred Nobel's mother. What did Nobel have to do with all this? Annika rubbed her eyes. What could have happened on Saturday to trigger these latest murders? Something to do with the Nobel Prize for Medicine?

She went on to the homepage of the Karolinska Institute, and found her way to the process for choosing a recipient of the prize. It took almost a year. In September questionnaires were sent to approximately three thousand people around the world, to people and institutions that had the right to nominate candidates. They were members of the Nobel Assembly at the Karolinska Institute, the Royal Swedish Academy of Sciences, previous recipients of the Nobel Prize for Medicine, and selected scientists at universities in Sweden and other countries.

She yawned, and thought about going downstairs to make a cup of coffee, but couldn't be bothered.

These individuals, she read, had until February to write back with suggestions of candidates. Between March and May the proposed names were sent to specially selected experts, who then evaluated the work of the nominees. By the end of May the experts reported their findings to the Nobel Committee.

And that's where we are now, Annika thought.

During the summer, until August, the Nobel Committee put together a recommendation to present to the assembly. In September the committee provided a report containing the names of potential recipients to the assembly. The report had to be signed by the whole committee. It was then debated twice by the entire assembly.

At the beginning of October there was a vote, and the recipient was picked by a majority decision. After that the name of the winner was announced to the public. The decision was final and could not be appealed against.

So, the most important work of thinning out the list was done fairly early, Annika thought. Round about now, in fact.

She read that the prize was presented on 10 December, the anniversary of Nobel's death. It consisted of a medal, a diploma and a document confirming the financial size of the award, currently ten million Swedish kronor.

A lot of money, she thought, for one individual. But nothing compared to the amounts that people in the pharmaceutical industry were used to dealing with. The value is in the prize itself, she thought, in the recognition of being awarded a Nobel Prize. How much could that be worth? Being acknowledged as the recipient of the greatest award in the world, being told that you *have conferred the greatest benefit on mankind*?

Bloody hell, she thought, blinking. I'm exhausted.

She got up from the desk, went into the bedroom and lay down on the unmade bed.

And fell asleep instantly.

33

When she woke up again she had no idea how much time had passed. It could have been anywhere between fifteen minutes and eight hours.

It was still light outside, the same grey light as when she had fallen asleep.

Feeling confused, she got up, noticing that she had drooled on the pillow. She went into the bathroom and looked at the time. She had been asleep for two hours. She sat on the toilet for a couple of minutes, wondering if she would ever have the energy to stand up again.

Then she remembered the emails she had sent and got a new burst of energy.

She had fifteen emails in her inbox. Fifteen messages saying Delivery Error Report from Mail Delivery System. She went through the replies, checking which addresses didn't exist.

They had all bounced back, except the one sent to andrietta_ahlsell@yahoo.se.

So, that address had been registered.

She went into yahoo.se, clicked on *mail* and filled in andrietta_ahlsell as the user ID. Password? What on earth should she try first? Alfred?

Invalid password.

Where to start?
caroline.
Invalid password.
What was her husband called? Knut?
knut.
Invalid password.
She scrolled down the page and read on.

Try the following:

- *Is 'Caps Lock' activated on your keyboard?*

If so, press 'Caps Lock' before trying again.

- *Have you forgotten your ID or password, or spelled them wrong?*

You can reactivate your ID and/or password by confirming your confidential information.

- *Still not working?*

Try Log-in help.

Annika pressed *Get a new password.*
A window appeared on the screen. She rubbed the sleep from her eyes and leaned forward to read.

To get a new password you must answer your secret security question correctly:

What was the name of the first school you attended?

What was Caroline von Behring's first school called?
She picked up the phone and called Birgitta Larsén again. The professor was back to her old routine and answered at once.

'Carrie's first school? There was only ever one. The French School. Caroline was an incurable Francophile, a real snob if you ask me. What are you up to now?'

'I'll tell you later,' Annika said, and hung up.

Filled in *French*.

A new window opened.

Create new password.

Confirm password.

Annika chose *alfred*.

The screen flickered. *Welcome Caroline!*

She gasped. Caroline had an online email account, and she had broken into it.

She glanced quickly over the page. It looked like the opening page of most other online mailboxes.

You have one (1) unread message.

On the left was a list of the usual folders: Inbox, Drafts, Sent mail, Spam, Bin. In the inbox she could see her own email, *test*.

Below the list was a heading marked *My folders*.

It contained one entitled *Archive*.

Annika clicked on it, her pulse racing.

There were six messages, all sent to Andrietta Ahlsell from Caroline von Behring. Their headings were: *In the Shadow of Death*, *The Price of Love*, *The Greatest Fear*, *Disappointment*, *Nobel's Will* and *Alfred Bernhard*.

Annika opened them in order. Her frustration grew with each one she read. These weren't secrets. They were short musings about Caroline von Behring's hero, tragic little commentaries on Alfred Nobel's life and death.

She moved the mouse to hover over the sixth and

last document, taking a couple of deep breaths before clicking on it.

It had been written in September last year, three months before Caroline's death.

Annika read it increasingly slowly.

Subject: Alfred Bernhard
To: Andrietta Ahlsell

That's his name, Alfred Bernhard, just like his name-sake, just like Nobel, but his surname is Thorell.

He used to light up the whole room when he walked in.

Lectures with Bernhard Thorell in the audience were always a bit *magical*, oddly golden, somehow, never dull.

I felt so alive when Bernhard was nearby, so interesting and spiritual, my analyses and conclusions so radiant and clear.

Other people became tongue-tied in his presence, others strangely anxious. I used to despise them.

It wasn't that I was in love (that's not how I would describe it), more like *flattered*, or possibly *fascinated*. He had a quality that really affected people, and if only he had studied a bit harder he would have made an excellent doctor.

But he still chose to be a scientist.

I got it into my head that he was doing it for my sake.

For my sake.

That was the effect he had on people: we all felt specially chosen, all of us grey souls.

He got in touch with me, asked if there were any doctoral positions in my research group, and I was so flattered that I hardly knew what to think: he wanted to work with *me* on *my* project. His wish was confirmation of my own brilliance, my skill as an instructor and scientific superiority. The fact that his career choices were a consequence of his own poor exam results was something I never considered.

Caroline, Caroline, how naïve could you be?

When the first doctoral students came in and started to talk I dismissed them. I shouted at one, a young woman from Czechoslovakia who had staked everything on coming here. I drove her out and my cheeks still burn with shame when I think about it. Her name was Katerina; she was short, with dark hair. She had left her husband and her young daughter as hostages in her home country for the chance to conduct research at the Karolinska Institute (this was before the Iron Curtain was raised), and she would sometimes weep over her test-tubes because she was missing her family so much. She came to see me, reluctantly, and accused Bernhard of the most peculiar things.

He had made an unwelcome approach to her. She had pulled away and gently declined, and then odd things started to happen to her research.

Katerina was adamant that Bernhard Thorell had changed the labels on her samples so that her experiment failed. She was absolutely convinced of it, and I can still remember how upset I got.

How *dare* she come to me with such absurd gossip? How *could* she? Had she no sense of honour? A week later I saw to it that she was expelled from the institute and sent back to the concrete bunker outside Prague where she belonged.

I never found out what happened to her. I still don't know what happened when she got home. Her young daughter must be grown up by now, an adult.

I've thought about you so often, Katerina.

Oh, God, if only I had listened!

The next woman who came to me with stammering accusations was Tuula, a brilliant Finnish girl with her roots in the Swedish settlements of Ostrobothnia. She was on her way to making a remarkable discovery, and had finished the first draft of her article, which had been preliminarily accepted by the *Journal of Biological Chemistry*. She was already renowned within the institute.

She had spent three years on her research, three years of red eyes from being overworked, three years of neglected social life, but it was worth it, she said. It was worth it.

And she smiled as she said it, the only time in three years that I saw her smile.

And she smiled until Bernhard went to see her and reminded her of something she had forgotten: that a few months earlier he had helped with some mundane matter, the sort of thing we occasionally do for each other.

He asked Tuula to list him as the co-author of her article, and naturally Tuula refused. Naturally! There was no reason whatsoever to name him. Bernhard asked her to think about it until Friday, saying it would be for her own good.

But Tuula held firm. She challenged him, and it cost her dear.

When she arrived at the lab the following Monday the plug of her freezer had been pulled out

463

at the wall. The lid was open and three years of research had melted into an evil-smelling sludge at the bottom of her test-tubes.

Tuula left KI that day. She moved to England and repeated all of her experiments at Cambridge. She published her findings in *Science* two and a half years later.

Only after publication did she tell me all of this, in a long letter that I burned at once.

As time went on Bernhard no longer asked for permission. He simply stole other people's research and published it under his own name. He had his unpaid assistants take care of his own doctoral thesis, and he was lucky. One of the young women, I forget her name, was a prodigious talent who secured his doctorate for him.

My own awakening was especially painful.

I have always had a soft spot for the animals. In those days there were all sorts of different ones, and they were all over the place, not only in isolated premises but in all sorts of locations.

I arrived at the lab late one evening to check on a small puppy that was unwell. The lights were off and all the doors were locked in the corridor leading to the lab, but over by the operating table some bright lights were on.

I went over to see if someone had forgotten to turn them off, but halfway there I stopped. An animal's scream cut through the lab, anguish echoing round the bare walls, and I saw shadows moving among the rows of shelves.

Someone was hurting one of the animals. The screaming rolled round the walls, muffling my footsteps through the shadows, and I got myself into a position where I could see what was happening.

It was Bernhard. He had secured a female cat in the stereotactic apparatus and was busy cutting out its womb. The cat hadn't been sedated, and was screaming with a raw anguish I had never heard the like of before. He had secured the animal with a screw through the base of the skull and into its brain. And I could see Bernhard's face in profile, the look of complete ecstasy on it.

He was beside himself with joy.

I felt I was about to faint, but stood my ground.

I stood in the shadows as the cat bled to death, screwed into that contraption, as its screams grew weaker and Bernhard sat there enchanted with its genitals in his hands, a womb containing embryonic kittens, with a pair of small ovaries stuck to the side.

Afterwards he washed the table carefully. He burned the body of the cat in the furnace, the way we did in those days, then filled in a report about his experiment.

Tests on the optical nerve, he wrote.

Then he left the lab, turning off the lights behind him, and whistling as he went.

I spent the following week at home, with a terrible fever and horrible stomach cramps.

When I got back to the institute I summoned Bernhard, the institute's magical charmer. I told him I was terminating his doctoral position with immediate effect. He had thirty minutes to leave the premises.

But Bernhard just smiled. *Why?* he asked simply.

The cat, I said.

465

Oh, he said, tilting his head.

Thirty minutes, I said.

I don't think so, Bernhard said.

Then he told me about the group photograph from the conference in Helsinki. He had it in a safe place, with documentation confirming the date the picture had been taken.

He had also dug out the dates of when the supplementary research for my article in *Science* had been carried out, and – *would you believe it?* – they were the same dates.

The same dates.

Bernhard Thorell laughed. He laughed and laughed.

So, my dear Caroline, he said, standing right next to me, you're going to pass my dissertation, and you're going to do it this spring.

Never, I said, still hearing the cat's screaming through my whole body.

But I did. I did it. I passed his dissertation.

I fell into line, and I am still ashamed.

I have never told anyone, not even you, Birgitta.

But now I have to, because he's come back.

He's here again, and this time he wants more.

The Nobel Prize, Birgitta. He wants the Nobel Prize for Medicine for Medi-Tec's research into the ageing process, or he's going to expose me. Not this time, I've told him, never again. I'd sooner fall.

He doesn't believe me. I can see that he doesn't believe me. For him the choice is so straightforward, and he presumes that it is for me too.

But he's wrong.

He's wrong, and now he's given me an ultimatum.

We make our announcement in three weeks' time, and if Medi-Tec's researchers aren't honoured, I'm going to die.

Spectacularly, he says. Like the cat.

But this is about Alfred now, *Alfred Bernhard Nobel's last will and testament*, and, thank goodness, there are things that are bigger than all of us.

When she had finished reading, Annika stared at the screen, feeling dizzy and sick. She didn't know how much time had passed since she'd started reading.

Bernhard Thorell.

Had he been at the seminar on Saturday? He must have been.

How much would the Nobel Prize for Medicine be worth to Medi-Tec?

She reached for the phone again and called Birgitta Larsén. 'I've found Caroline's archive,' she said, before the professor had time to speak. 'She's written all about her deception, and about the person who was threatening her. Please, Birgitta, tell me what happened on Saturday.'

'Who was it?' Birgitta said. 'Who was threatening her?'

'Tell me what happened on Saturday and I'll forward Caroline's email to you.'

'No! It's not up to you to make the decisions here!'

Annika didn't answer, just stared at the last line of Caroline's text: *But now this is about Alfred, Alfred Bernhard Nobel's last will and testament, and, thank goodness, there are things that are bigger than all of us.*

'Okay,' Annika said. 'You decide. Either we hang up or you tell me exactly what happened on Saturday afternoon.'

'It's confidential,' Birgitta said.

'Oh, well,' Annika said, and hung up.

She sat quietly on her chair, listening to the sounds in her head, and wondering how long it would be before Birgitta dug out her phone number and called back.

One minute and twenty seconds.

'I was the one Carrie told about her archive,' the professor said, sounding hurt and angry. 'How can you do this?'

'Everything,' Annika said. 'From the meeting of the Nobel Committee to the seminar and the buffet. All the background information I need to work out what happened. When you've finished, I'll forward the email to you.'

Birgitta groaned loudly. 'I can't just tell you who said what on Saturday,' she said. 'It's considerably more complicated than that.'

'I'm all ears,' Annika said.

Another groan.

'Okay, then,' Birgitta said. 'This is what happened.' She thought for several long seconds. 'Anything to do with the nominations for the Nobel Prize is only made public after fifty years,' she said. 'The names of the people nominated, which experts were consulted and what they said.'

'Okay,' Annika said.

'The Nobel Committee consists of six people: the chair, the vice chair, three members and the secretary of the Nobel Assembly.'

'I presume this is relevant,' Annika said.

'You'll have to be patient,' Birgitta said, 'because what I'm about to tell you ought to be kept confidential for another forty-nine years. What happened last year was that Caroline refused to sign the nomination papers identifying Medi-Tec's researchers as potential recipients of the prize. None of the other five could understand why, but she refused point blank.'

Annika felt her pulse begin to race. 'What had Medi-Tec done to deserve nomination?'

'I told you – they found a way to inhibit dystrophy in axons.'

'Ah, yes,' Annika said. 'The wellspring of life. How much would it have been worth to them if they had been awarded the Nobel Prize for that particular discovery?'

'A Nobel Prize? In monetary terms? To Medi-Tec?' She pondered. 'It's funny you should ask that because Ernst had actually worked it out. He was the one at the institute who knew about things like that. The recognition and marketing that the prize would have given to what you call *the wellspring of life* would have been worth at least fifty billion dollars, maybe double that.'

Fifty *billion* dollars.

Three hundred and fifty *billion* kronor, Annika thought. Did that much money even exist?

'From a purely objective point of view, Medi-Tec should have been listed in the preliminary report,' Birgitta said. 'But Caroline was adamant. She said she'd resign if Sören carried on pressing their claim.'

'Did you see this for yourself?'

'Of course I didn't. I wasn't elected to the committee until this year. Carrie told me.'

'And last Saturday?'

'A similar situation, oddly enough, seeing as Medi-Tec have been proposed again this year, and by the same person, Sören Hammarsten. Ernst dug his heels in from the outset and refused to put them on the list. Sören was furious, said it was corrupt and underhand. Ernst blew up and said Sören was the one who was corrupt. Well, you can imagine what it was like. The other members had candidates they wanted to promote, or get rid of, so it all got a bit rowdy.'

'And then?'

'After the meeting the committee went down to listen to the seminar. Most of us went on to the buffet. Lars-Henry, who was there last year but had been excluded now, turned up at the seminar. We couldn't stop him, seeing as it was open to all members of staff.'

'And he started shouting during the seminar?'

'He kept quiet during the lecture, then went out and started helping himself to the wine. We provide a buffet and a glass of red for each participant, but after that they have to pay. Nobel's money is supposed to fund the prize, not drinks parties on the institute's lawns.'

'And?' Annika said.

'Oh, he ended up having several heated discussions during the course of the evening – they got quite noisy.'

'Did Lars-Henry say anything to Bernhard Thorell?'

'Yes, he had a go at him and shouted a whole lot of—'

'Anything personal, anything specific?'

'He said he knew what sort of person Bernhard was, that he'd do anything to get his hands on a Nobel Prize. Then he said Bernhard should watch out, that he wouldn't get away with it because Lars-Henry knew what he had done with the test animals. Caroline had told him about the cat, she had seen him, and had said he was evil incarnate.'

'He said that?' Annika said. 'That Caroline told him about the cat?'

'Lars-Henry was very close to Caroline,' Birgitta said, with a degree of irritation. 'He wasn't like that before she died. She probably told him loads of things that—'

'Could Thorell have found out that Ernst stopped Medi-Tec being included in the report?' Annika asked.

'No,' Birgitta said. 'You're straying a long way from the facts there.'

'Birgitta,' Annika said, 'could Thorell have got any inside information about what was said in the meeting? Is there any way at all? Could someone have talked?'

Birgitta was quiet for several seconds. 'He spent a long time talking to Sören,' she said, 'but Sören would never—'

'Have you got access to your email? You'll be getting a message from Caroline in a few seconds.'

'I've got my inbox open on the screen in front of me.'

Annika sent off the text marked *Alfred Bernhard* to the professor's address at the Karolinska Institute.

'Ah, there it is,' Birgitta said. 'Do you want me to read it?'

'I'll wait on the line,' Annika said.

'Literary ambitions,' the woman muttered.

'Carry on reading,' Annika said.

The professor's breathing got heavier. When she had finished she didn't speak.

'Have you said anything to Thorell that might have made him feel angry and insecure?'

'What do you mean?' the professor asked hoarsely.

'He knew which animals were yours,' Annika said, 'didn't he? You showed them to him, and he killed them. What did you say to him?'

'Nothing. We just had a fairly general chat.'

'About ageing, about Medi-Tec's research?'

'Among other things,' Birgitta said.

'If you read the email carefully,' Annika said quietly, 'Caroline admits her deception. But she doesn't mention your involvement. You're in the clear. Do you want me to forward the text to the police?'

Birgitta wept quietly down the line. 'Yes,' she finally whispered. 'Do it.'

And Annika clicked to open the email again, then forwarded it to Q.

34

Annika was nervous when she picked up the children from nursery. She had a price to pay for throwing her weight around, and now might well be the time for her to get her wallet out.

The playground was empty, as a swing swayed in the breeze.

Lotta was playing with Kalle and Ellen when she walked in. None of the other children were there.

'Hello, darlings,' Annika said, hugging them as they ran to meet her. 'Are you the last ones here?'

'I think Linda's in the dolls' corner with some of the younger girls,' Lotta said, with a smile. 'A long day?'

Annika raised her eyebrows. 'You wouldn't believe me if I told you,' she said.

'Ellen's finished her bag,' Lotta said, getting up. 'Do you want to take it home today, Ellen?'

The child nodded.

'I'll go and get it,' Lotta said, and headed off towards the sewing room.

Annika bent down towards Kalle and stroked the plaster on his forehead. It was a bit grubby. 'Did you have a nice time today?' she asked quietly.

'Yes. But Ben and Alex had to go home, and Alex wet himself.'

Annika's cheeks burned. 'Goodness,' she said.

'We teased him about it,' Kalle said gleefully. 'We called him Pissypants!'

Annika's took hold of him, slightly harder than she had intended. 'Kalle,' she said, 'you mustn't call Alexander that. Or anyone else. You wouldn't like to be called Pissypants, would you?'

'But he was mean to me.'

'I know, but you mustn't be mean back,' she said, aware of her own hypocrisy.

'I'm hungry, Mummy,' Ellen said.

'Okay, let's go home,' Annika said.

The children's favourite television programme had just started and Annika let them cuddle up on the sofa while she started the meal. She chopped some vegetables and a couple of turkey fillets, put a small pan of jasmine rice on to boil, and got out a tin of coconut milk, a chilli, the fish sauce and some chopped coriander. She laid the table with napkins and candles as the oil heated in the wok. She usually managed to be at home in time to prepare a meal.

She scampered round the kitchen nervously, trying to get everything done before Thomas got home, wiping the worktops and pressing the rubbish down in the bin.

He walked through the front door as she was taking the wok off the heat.

'Hello,' she said. 'Perfect timing. The food's just this minute ready.'

Thomas put his briefcase down by the door and came into the kitchen with his shoes on. He didn't look at her, just went to the freezer and took out two ice-creams.

'What are you doing?' Annika said. 'I'm about to dish up.'

He turned his back on her without a word and went to the children. 'Kalle, Ellen,' he said quietly, but she could still hear him perfectly clearly, 'I want you to go up to your rooms for a little while. You can each have an ice-cream while I have a little talk with Mummy.'

'But we're not supposed to eat ice-cream before tea,' Ellen said.

'Today it's allowed,' Thomas said, and Annika watched as her daughter took the ice-cream and laboriously tore off its paper.

'Thanks, Daddy,' Kalle said, giving Thomas a quick hug before he ran off upstairs.

He stood facing away from Annika until the children had disappeared. She was standing frozen to the spot, holding the wok and the trivet, staring at his shoulders as he slowly turned round.

His eyes, oh, God, *his* eyes. They're bloodshot and narrow – he looks like a different person. Instinctively she took a step back, her heel hitting the breakfast bar. 'What is it?' she said. 'What's happened?'

He took a few steps towards her and now she could see sadness in his eyes. Good God, what on earth had happened? 'What have you done?' he said.

'What?' Was it something to do with the children – what she had said to Benjamin and Alexander?

He stopped in front of her, took the wok and trivet from her hands and put them on the granite worktop, spilling the coconut sauce. 'How long have you known?'

Oh, no, not *that*.

'What?' she said.

'Sophia,' he said very quietly.

She gulped so loudly that the sound echoed.

475

'Why haven't you said anything?' he asked, much louder now. He was clenching and unclenching his fists, as though he were trying to get his blood flowing.

She turned away. 'I don't know what you're talking about,' she said.

'*Stop lying to me!*' he shouted, grabbing her shoulder and spinning her round so fast she almost fell.

'Ow,' she said, looking up at his face, all red and distorted.

'How long have you been *pretending*?' he yelled. 'How the hell could you *do* this to me?'

She felt anger explode in her gut with such force that she could hardly breathe. '*Me?*' she said. 'How could *I* do this to *you*? Are you mad, you fucking disgusting unfaithful *bastard*?'

She screamed the last word. Saliva flew from her mouth and hit his face.

He stopped in the middle of taking a step towards her and let his arms fall to his sides 'Aha,' he said. 'And there it is.'

'What?' she said, dizzy from a lack of oxygen.

'What you really think of me. Why you never touch me. Why our marriage has become a fucking charade of home decorating and garden design and raising children.' He turned away and threw his arms out, walking round the room shouting. 'I've been living a fucking lie! I've been walking round like the biggest mug in the whole damn world, believing that what I could see was the truth, and I've been trying and trying to be supportive and appreciative and interested in your idiotic picture-book idyll!'

She ran to him and slapped his face, not hard, just to shut him up. 'You spoilt, egocentric pile of shit,' she said, and noticed to her own surprise that her voice sounded fairly calm. 'I love you, and the children love you, and you've got a job where you're appreciated, and I've just spent six million on a house for you. You get food on the table, and you're *whining*! You just sulk and moan and make excuses, and now you've come up with a way of shifting the blame to me.'

'You think you know the answer to everything,' he said, and Annika saw that his hands were shaking. 'You think you know everything, you and your mates at the paper.'

Annika looked at her husband, at his ill-concealed anger, and was suddenly filled with utter contempt. 'Oh, well done,' she said. 'As if the newspaper could have anything at all to do with the fact that you've been having an affair.'

He was so angry he could hardly speak. 'You're so fucking smug,' he managed to splutter. 'Berit, for instance – today she wrote a whole load of crap that she knows nothing about. You're just the same.'

'That's bollocks,' Annika said.

'Does she really believe all those lies about that Jordanian terrorist? Does she seriously believe everything she writes?'

He genuinely imagines that he's the injured party here, Annika thought, feeling her anger dissolve into astonishment. He's standing here in front of me, thinking that he's the victim in this whole story. 'You're incredible,' she said. 'You're the one who's been screwing around, but somehow you're the one we should all feel sorry for.'

Thomas turned his back on her, dug his fingers into his hair, then spun round again. 'You never do anything wrong!' he yelled. 'You've been lying and pretending and fooling me for months, and it's the same with everything you do. You decide what the world looks like, and anyone who doesn't agree with you is an idiot.'

Annika folded her arms on her chest, capping the gesture with a dismissive snort. 'You really have turned into an arrogant shit,' she said, leaning back against the breakfast bar.

Thomas took a long stride towards her and raised his hand.

She made a real effort not to blink. 'Great,' she said. 'Go on, hit me. That's all that's missing.'

'The Danish royal family,' he said. 'The Crown Prince, the Princess and their baby. He was going to blow them and himself up during a visit by the American Navy in February.'

'Just you dare hit me,' she said.

He lowered his arm. 'He's killed children, Annika. He was trained in Pakistan and Afghanistan. The official version is that he was helping his parents on a farm in Jordan when really he was learning about different sorts of explosives close to the Khyber Pass. We've got evidence, Annika. There are things you don't know. There are so many things you haven't got a clue about.'

'Oh, aren't you important?' she said. 'Am I supposed to be impressed?'

He looked as if he was about to cry. 'You never gave me a chance,' he said. 'Why didn't you say anything?'

Annika rubbed her forehead. The room was spinning. 'How did you find out?' she said, suddenly drained. 'Did she call you?'

'Of course she did. She wanted us to meet again.'

Annika laughed, with a vehemence that cut into her brain. 'God, that's pathetic,' she said.

'I'm on my way there now,' Thomas said.

Annika fell quiet so abruptly that all sound died away. She stared at him, at the shirt-collar she had ironed, at the stubble she could almost feel, at his broad shoulders and messy hair. 'If you go,' she managed to say, 'if you go now, you can never come back.'

He stared at her with unfamiliar narrowed eyes, his terrible dead eyes.

'Okay,' he said, and walked away.

And she watched him walk across the parquet floor and pick up his briefcase and open the front door and look out at the grey drizzle. He stepped over the threshold and the door closed behind him and he didn't look back once.

She put the food on the table. She told the children to sit down and eat. She poured milk and served the rice and even managed to eat a few mouthfuls herself.

'Why were you shouting?' Kalle asked.

'We're just tired,' she said.

'Where's Daddy?' Ellen asked.

'He had to go back to work,' Annika said.

The children ate almost nothing, their appetites spoiled by ice-cream. She didn't make them finish their platefuls, and let them watch a film as she cleared the table and started the dishwasher. All her movements were jerky, as in a speeded-up film.

'Mummy,' Kalle said. 'I'm tired.'

She sat down on the sofa and took him in her arms. 'That might be because of the bump on your head,' she said. 'Shall we have an early night?'

'I want to sleep with you, Mummy,' Ellen said, cuddling up beside her on the sofa.

'Me too,' Kalle said, curling up on the other side.

She held her children with both arms and struggled to hold back the tears. 'You can both sleep with me,' she said. 'How does that sound?'

479

'What about Daddy?' Ellen asked.

'There's room for him too,' Annika said, taking their hands and pulling them up from the sofa. 'Off we go!'

They settled down in the big double bed, and she sat with them for a long time, reading stories, whispering and hugging them. I have the children, she thought. He can't take them away from me.

When she had drawn the curtains, she left the room, carefully shutting the door behind her, and went to look in their bedrooms. Ellen was a creative little soul, fussing and making things all day long, always full of energy. Kalle was more reserved; he liked sorting things into alphabetical order, lining his cars up in neat rows.

She tidied a few things away in their rooms, clothes, drawings and pens, but as she was bending down to pick up an apple-core and an ice-cream stick, despair crept up on her. *Thomas*, she thought. *I really do love you. I'm sorry. I'm so sorry.*

The telephone rang. She dropped Ellen's drawing book and ran downstairs. How silly we've been! How thoughtless and destructive! Of course we can sort it out . . . We've got so much to lose. She grabbed the receiver and heard how happy she sounded as she said, 'Hello!'

'What did you say?' a woman's voice said.

Who?

'Hello?' she said again.

'This is Benjamin's mother. Did you threaten to kill *my child*?'

Oh, here we go. She screwed her eyes shut and pressed one hand to her forehead. 'Yes. Yes, I did.'

'Are you completely mad? You go round threatening to kill *little children*?'

'Yes,' Annika said. 'And do you know why?'

480

'You should be *locked up*! How can you be walking around *free*?'

'Your son threw my son off a two-metre-high climbing-frame. He had to have ten stitches in his forehead and he has concussion. The doctors had to do a scan to make sure there wasn't bleeding in his brain. Your son could have killed him, and you and your husband didn't give a damn.'

'That's not the same,' the woman said. 'Not as bad as you threatening to kill little children.'

'No,' Annika murmured, sinking on to a chair. 'It's not. Do you know what's really bad?'

There was silence at the other end of the line.

'What?' the woman said.

'What's really bad,' Annika said, 'is that I mean it. And if my son ever did anything like that to another child, I hope their parents would scare the shit out of him.'

'You can't mean that,' the woman said, now sounding more surprised than angry.

'Yes, I can,' Annika said. 'And I hope you can explain to Benjamin that what he did was wrong. It was wrong of me to threaten him, I can see that perfectly well, but I'm serious. If he attacks Kalle again I won't be responsible for what I do.'

'You're an adult – you should be setting a good example,' the woman said, less aggressive now.

'Tell me,' Annika said, 'what would you have done if Kalle had hurt your son so badly he had to have a brain scan?'

The woman was silent for a minute. 'Probably the same as you,' she said.

'Good,' Annika said. 'Thank you.' She hung up, and suddenly felt that the world was toppling over.

The screaming cat, the nail sticking out of Lars-Henry Svensson's eye, *Did you threaten to kill my child?*, Thomas's raised hand, ready to strike, *If you go now, you can never come back*, the plaster on Kalle's forehead, Bosse's mute plea in the car.

She got up on unsteady legs, staggered to the cloakroom beside the front door and threw up.

You decide what the world looks like, and anyone who doesn't agree with you is an idiot.

He's killed children, Annika.

Panting, she clung to the toilet seat, her head throbbing. I've got to talk to someone, she thought. I can't just sit here.

Slowly she made her way up to the children, opening the bedroom door as quietly as she could. She went into the room, listening to their soft breathing. They were both fast asleep. He'll come back, she thought. Daddy will come back.

She looked out through the bedroom curtains. There was a light on in Ebba's house. She was back from visiting her cousin in Dalarna.

The walls were closing in on her. What if he didn't come back? Was she just going to sit here and wait?

She went back out on to the landing, shutting the bedroom door behind her, walked into Ellen's room, out of Ellen's room, into Kalle's room, out of Kalle's room.

Would they be all right for a little while if she went over to see Ebba?

But what if Thomas called?

She could redirect the calls.

She went downstairs and looked out of the picture window next to the front door.

Was someone moving outside?

Maybe Thomas had come home.

I can't just sit here, she thought. She tapped in the command to redirect her calls, then typed in her mobile number. She checked there was still enough power left in the battery, then put her phone in her pocket and headed for the front door.

35

It was dark outside, even though it was an early summer's evening. The clouds lay like wet concrete across the sky. The suburbs are miserable in bad weather, she thought. All the colour disappears, leaving nothing but shades of grey. In the city there was room for everyone; the streets and squares were public spaces. Out here everything felt cramped, even though there was much more space.

Why am I thinking this now? she wondered. How can I be worrying about peace and harmony between neighbours at a time like this?

As if he had heard her thoughts, Wilhelm Hopkins emerged on to the road in front of her. He pointed at a red sports car parked outside her house.

'I've had enough now!' he said loudly. 'This is the last time. I'm calling the police!'

Annika didn't even glance at him.

Ebba's red Volvo was parked on the gravel drive in front of her house. The fountain was switched off and the dog-pen was empty. Annika went up the steps and rang the bell, hearing it echo inside. Francesco was quiet, and she couldn't hear any footsteps. The echo faded, and she went back down to the garden and looked around.

The car was making little clicking sounds, as if it had just driven a long way and was still cooling. There were lights on in the ground and first-floor windows. She went back to the front door and rang again.

No response.

She looked out at the road.

No sign of Wilhelm Hopkins.

Hesitantly she leaned against the door and tapped on the leaded glass.

'Ebba?' she said. 'Ebba, are you there?'

Maybe she wants to be left in peace. Maybe she's had a long drive and is lying in the bath . . .

There was a sound inside the house, as if something had been dropped on the floor.

Annika stopped on the steps. 'Ebba!' she called, pressing the doorbell hard. 'Ebba! Are you all right?'

The door flew open and Annika took a step back in surprise. 'Goodness,' she said, looking inside the hallway.

It was empty.

'Ebba?' she said, stepping inside the house. 'Ebba? Hello?'

She took a few more steps and looked up the stairs.

The door slammed behind her, making her jump. She spun round.

Bernhard Thorell was standing there, pressed against the wall, holding a long-barrelled pistol in his hand and smiling at her. 'Well, look who it is. The doctoral student,' he said. 'How lovely. Do come in!'

Annika's heart stopped. She stared at him without returning his smile. 'What the hell are you doing here?' she said.

'Oh,' he said, tilting his head slightly. 'Now I remember. You're a reporter, aren't you? One of those people who ask questions and stick their noses where they don't belong.'

'Where's Ebba?'

'Oh, she's very much at home,' Thorell said. 'Do go into the sitting room!'

He gestured with the gun towards the library and Annika took a few hesitant steps towards the double doors, not wanting to turn her back on the pistol. Thorell gave her a hard shove, and her head hit the doorframe.

She clenched her teeth against the pain, unwilling to give him the satisfaction of hearing her cry out. The next shove propelled her into the library. She stumbled into the room and tripped over something, falling headlong on to the floor and landing in front of the fireplace.

She pushed herself up on one elbow to see what she had stumbled over.

It was Francesco. The dog had been shot through the head, probably fairly recently. Blood and brains were still spilling from his body, soaking into the Persian rug.

Annika said nothing and got to her feet.

Ebba was curled up on the sofa, in floods of tears. Her knees were pulled up under her chin and her arms were clasped round her ankles. She didn't look at Annika, just stared at the dog's body.

Annika had no idea what she should do. Thorell was a full-blown sadist, and would enjoy every hint of pain and grief.

The screaming cat, the nail through the eye.

Her knees started to shake. Dear God, was that what he had in store for them? Were they going to be murdered and mutilated?

Don't be frightened, she thought.

She turned to him once more. 'I was serious when I asked,' she said. 'What the hell are you doing here?'

Thorell, who was now standing at the far wall, nodded appreciatively. 'Can you go and sit next to her? Thank you. I'm here to pick something up,' he said, gesturing with his gun towards the painting of Beatrice Cenci.

Annika walked slowly and carefully across the room, not taking her eyes off him.

'I've been looking for this for a long time,' he said. 'I missed it at auction in St Petersburg three years ago, and ever since I'd been trying to find out where it had gone. You managed to keep it well hidden!' He nodded to Ebba and smiled.

Annika sank down beside Ebba and took her hands, which were ice cold. The woman didn't respond. She still wasn't looking at Annika, just at the dead dog.

'Why do you care about an old painting?' Annika said.

'It's not the painting I want,' he said. 'It's Beatrice.'

'She was just a murderer,' Annika said. 'Why are you so interested in her?'

A flicker of annoyance crossed his handsome features. 'You don't know anything about Beatrice,' Thorell said, raising the gun towards them. 'You know she killed her father, Francesco Cenci, but do you know what she used as the murder weapon?'

Annika didn't reply.

Thorell lowered the gun. 'Two nails,' he said. 'She drove one through her father's eye, into his brain, and the other through his throat into his spine.'

Annika felt suddenly sick. 'I thought she poured molten lead into his ear and knocked his teeth out,' she said.

Now Thorell laughed, his beautiful eyes flashing. 'You've been looking too deeply into Nobel's testament,' he said. '*Nemesis* isn't a factual description of the events surrounding Beatrice Cenci's life and death. The play is much more than that. It's a moral reflection on human retribution and guilt, on the power of the Church and the sins of the father.'

Annika stared at him. *Nobel's testament, the power of the Church and the sins of the father.* Why had he started to kill people in the same way as Beatrice Cenci? Why did he identify so strongly with her?

'Do you know how they got her to confess?' Thorell asked. 'Do you know what the Vatican's torturers did to break her?'

Annika looked at the rug.

'They cut off her hair,' he said. 'They stripped her naked and tied her hands behind her back. Then they hoisted her into the air by her arms, which were tied behind her back. Can you picture it? Can you see her before you? Can you see her hanging there, naked, so thin, such small breasts? Higher and higher, until she was two metres up, and when they let her fall, almost to the floor, her arms were dislocated by the jolt. That was when she lost consciousness.'

He laughed.

'But even that didn't make her confess. Only when her brothers came into the torture chamber and gave the game away, only then did she give up. There was no point in fighting any more.'

A thought was circling on the edge of Annika's mind, something Thorell had said, unless it had been Berit.

Sun, heat, grass.

I kept the family farm in Roslagen after my parents' accident . . .

'Perhaps you're wondering how I know all this,' he said. 'Perhaps you think I'm making it up. I'm not.'

Annika's eyes were closed. The newsroom, Berit with

a cup of coffee, crumbs at the corners of her mouth. *Simon Thorell, a venture capitalist, pretty much the first to make a killing from it. He and his wife died in a car-crash in the Alps, if I remember rightly. A tragic story . . .*

'Alexandre Dumas,' Bernhard Thorell said. 'He went through the records and proceedings from Beatrice's trial. It's all described in great detail in *Celebrated Crimes*, volume one, part two. The chapter is called "The Cenci".'

The power of the Church. The sins of the father. All described in Nobel's spiritual testament.

Annika opened her eyes and looked right at the man. 'You see a connection between you and Beatrice,' she said. 'You're fascinated by her because you did the same thing. You killed your father, just as she killed hers.'

Thorell raised his eyebrows and smiled.

'You did something to their car so that they died in a crash,' Annika said. 'How did you do it?'

'It was *such* a tragic accident,' he said.

'How did you know what to do?' Annika asked. 'You were only a child.'

Thorell got up and walked over to the painting, removed the protective glass case and stared at the child-woman's face. 'Sixteen,' he said, his eyes caressing the picture. 'I was sixteen, about the same age as Beatrice.'

Good God, Annika thought. He's a monster. 'What did you do to the brakes?' she asked, forcing her voice to sound calm.

He turned towards her and gestured with the gun towards the road. 'Did you see the Jaguar outside? The red one? A 1963 model, I've restored every last nut and bolt. I got it from my uncle when I was fourteen. Cutting the brake-line on Dad's car took a matter of seconds.'

Annika felt her heart pounding, and dug her nails into her palms to make herself breathe calmly. 'Why? Why did you do it?'

Thorell looked at her and suddenly she knew. Of course, it was so simple.

'You think Alfred Nobel was writing about you, don't you?' Annika said. 'You think that Nobel's literary testament is really the story of your life.'

He tilted his head, listening intently.

'You genuinely think you're Beatrice,' Annika said. 'Your father was rich and powerful, just like Francesco, and he did things to you, didn't he? He raped you, like Beatrice's father did to her.'

Thorell raised the pistol towards her, and she could see it was shaking now.

'But you're wrong,' Annika said. 'You're not Beatrice Cenci, and there's no way you can be like her. No one will ever write a play about you. You're never going to be some great saviour.'

'Ah,' he said, lowering the gun again, 'but you're wrong there.'

'No,' Annika said. 'There is justice, both here and beyond the grave.'

He laughed, but Annika thought she detected a note of uncertainty.

'And you're never going to get the Nobel Prize either,' she said. 'You know that, don't you?'

The smile faded, and he took several steps towards her.

'Caroline made sure you missed out last year,' Annika said, 'and Ernst made sure you won't be getting it this year, and from now on your prison sentence will stop you getting it in the future.'

He laughed again, scornfully this time. 'And who's going to catch me?' he asked. 'You?'

A second later the double doors crashed open, as voices and noise invaded the room from the kitchen. Thorell looked away from Annika and Ebba on the sofa and aimed his weapon alternately towards the doors and the kitchen. Police officers in helmets and riot gear were visible in both doorways, all aiming their automatic weapons at him.

'Drop the revolver!' one shouted.

Ebba started to cry louder.

Thorell looked at the police in horror.

'Put the weapon down and take two steps back,' the police officer said again.

'But I haven't done anything,' he said. 'What are you doing?'

The police started to move forward, one step at a time, and Thorell raised his hands. 'Okay, okay,' he said. 'I'm putting it on the table. Is that okay?' He tilted his head again and smiled at the police.

Bloody hell, Annika thought. He thinks he can charm his way out of this as well.

'It's all just a misunderstanding,' Thorell said. 'I'm only here to pick up a painting.'

They handcuffed him and led him out of the room.

In the doorway he stopped and looked sadly at Ebba. 'You should have taught your dog to behave better,' he said. 'It's shat itself.'

Annika stayed on the sofa after the police had taken Thorell away, unable to get up. Ebba, on the other hand, staggered over to Francesco, where she slumped down and wrapped her arms round him.

Several plainclothes police officers came into the room, then walked out again. They were talking to each other on radios that crackled and bleeped, but Annika couldn't make out what they were saying.

Detective Inspector Q came into the room, stopping in the doorway. 'Are you okay, tough girl?' he asked Annika.

She nodded mutely.

The officer went over to the fireplace and bent over Ebba, saying something to her that Annika couldn't hear. Then he led her back to the sofa, where she slumped next to Annika again.

'How did all this come about?' Annika asked.

'There's an ambulance on its way,' Q said, to Ebba. 'Have you been physically hurt?'

Ebba shook her head.

'You're in shock. I want you to take a quick trip to Danderyd Hospital so that they can give you the once-over,' he said, holding her hand. 'Do you understand what I'm saying?'

Ebba nodded.

'How could you have known?' Annika asked, but Q gestured to her to hold off for a while.

'Can you tell me what happened?' he asked Ebba.

The woman cleared her throat and took a deep breath.

'He . . . he rang the doorbell,' she said in a shaky voice, looking quickly from Annika to Q. 'I let him in. He said he wanted the picture, my Guido Reni, the portrait of Beatrice Cenci.' She shook her head. 'How could he have known I had it?'

'I told him,' Annika said. 'I'm sorry.'

Ebba looked at her for a few seconds. 'I said he couldn't have it, of course, I had no intention of giving him the painting, and that's when he shot Francesco. He said he was going to shoot me too if I didn't do as he said. Then the doorbell rang again.'

'That was me,' Annika said, to Q.

'Your name is Ebba?' Q asked, laying his hand on the woman's arm. 'I'll make sure you get off to hospital, and we'll look after your dog while you're gone. Then I'd like to talk to you some more about what happened this evening, if that would be all right?' He turned to Annika. 'How about you? Did he hurt you at all?'

She shook her head. 'My children are asleep across the road,' she said. 'I've got to get back to them.'

'Wait here,' Q said.

'Just one thing,' Annika said, turning to Ebba. 'Were you driving a car on Barnhusbron on Monday?'

Ebba was clearly bewildered. 'What?'

'I thought I saw you in your car on Barnhusbron on Monday.'

'On Monday?' Ebba said. 'But I was at Johan and Tina's then. I told you.'

'I just thought I saw you,' Annika said, 'but I must have been mistaken.' How many red Volvos could there be in Stockholm?

Ebba tried to smile. 'Don't be sorry,' she said. 'This really wasn't your fault. I'm very glad you came over this evening.' She paused. 'And don't worry about the other neighbours. They'll settle down.'

Q led her from the room and out to the waiting ambulance.

Annika stayed on the sofa as two police officers came and collected Francesco. They handled the dead dog so gently that she felt like crying.

'Do you want to go to hospital as well?' Q said, as he came back into the room.

Annika brushed her hair from her face. 'No, thank you. Now, tell me what you're doing here,' she said.

'Your neighbour called,' he said.

Annika blinked.

'Wilhelm Hopkins?' she said, astonished. 'How did he know that Bernhard Thorell was here?'

'Your neighbour called the emergency services to report a car parked illegally, according to him. He had the registration number written down and rattled it off to the operator.'

Annika leaned her head back against the sofa and shut her eyes. 'How did you get into the house?'

'The door wasn't locked,' Q said. 'I got your email or, rather, Caroline's email. We knew Bernhard Thorell had been in Djursholm at the time of Ernst's murder, and in Fågelbrolandet when Lars-Henry was killed, so he was already in our sights even before we received Caroline's account of what had happened.'

Annika's head was spinning. Again, she felt as if she was going to be sick. 'How could you know that?' she said. 'How could you know where Thorell's been?'

Q didn't answer, and she looked up to see him staring at her.

'His mobile phone, of course,' he said. 'Criminals are often very stupid. He called from his own phone on both occasions. Speaking of stupid criminals, the FBI picked up a purveyor of violent services in San Diego yesterday evening. He'd erased his hard-drive and thought he was home free, but three and a half hours later the lads there had restored it, and Bernhard's name popped up there as well. He used his company's money to hire the services of the Kitten on two separate occasions.'

She shut her eyes again. 'So you're telling me you were actually looking for Bernhard Thorell?'

'And his car, which the duty officer in the emergency calls control centre had just received a national alert about. He could hardly believe it when our officious old friend on Vinterviksvägen called and read out the same number.'

She laughed, utterly joylessly. So Wilhelm Hopkins had helped to save her life. How absurd. 'But how did you know we were here?'

'I have to say, you really do keep an eye out for each other over here. Mr Hopkins knew exactly where you were. But what was Bernhard Thorell doing here?'

'He really was after that painting,' Annika said. 'All because he thought he was like Beatrice Cenci, the avenger of wronged innocents.'

She looked at Q and felt like crying. 'He was raped by his father,' she said. 'And he killed him for it.'

'I didn't know that,' Q said.

Annika stared up at the ceiling. 'The other murders were just about money,' she said. 'A Nobel Prize in Medicine would have been worth fifty billion dollars for Medi-Tec. It would have become one of the biggest pharmaceutical companies in the world. I did tell you that my children are asleep over there.' She pointed towards her house. 'Can we do the questions tomorrow?'

Q nodded. 'Have you got anyone to look after you? Is Thomas at home?'

She smiled through her tears. 'Of course,' she said. 'He'll take care of me. I'll write something for the paper and email you a copy. No disclosure ban?'

'Yes,' he said, 'but I dare say you'll do as you like anyway.'

She walked out of the house and across the grass, then into her own house and up the stairs, where she found the children fast asleep in the double bed. She closed the door on them and collapsed on the landing.

Thursday, 3 June

36

She must have fallen asleep because suddenly it was night and everything was silent around her. She sat up guiltily, giddy and disoriented, got to her feet, and looked in on the children.

Ellen's thumb was in her mouth. Annika went over to her, gently pulled it out and stroked the child's hair. Kalle was fast asleep with his mouth open, making little snoring sounds.

He's coming back, she thought. Daddy's coming home to us.

She couldn't bear the thought of any alternative. She pushed her pain aside in the only way she knew how: she went into the office and turned on the computer.

And she wrote, she wrote about it all, about Caroline's blackmail, her secret and her shortcomings, about what Thorell had said, Ebba, her own conclusions, the arrival of the police. Then she mailed the text to two recipients: Q and Jansson. As a heading to the email she typed *Please note: disclosure ban!* They could do whatever they liked with it.

She switched off the computer, then sat and stared out of the window. The summer night was blue, breezy but warm. There were still lights on in Hopkins's house, in the kitchen and the basement. Ebba's house was dark – perhaps she wasn't back from the hospital yet.

I'm not going to be able to sleep, she thought, her eyes stinging. She headed to the bathroom, then paused in the doorway, staring at the bath. It was empty and clean: she'd polished the enamel with chamois leather. She wasn't going to have any more dead women from her dreams in there.

She took a deep breath, a gasp that turned into a long sigh, then finally a sob.

He'll come back, she thought. He has to come home to us. Dear God, please, *let him come home to me!*

She slumped on the toilet seat and put her head into her hands, listening to her own heavy breathing. Her pulse was throbbing in her ears, her arms shaking.

I need you, she thought. I love you. Forgive me. 'I didn't mean it,' she whispered.

And she cried until she couldn't cry any more, until the house was completely silent and she was completely empty inside.

She stayed there for another minute or so, then stood up, giddy and drained.

It'll sort itself out, she thought. Somehow this will all sort itself out.

She reached for her toothbrush, only to discover that the toothpaste tube was empty. So she brushed her teeth with water, then washed her face with her expensive soap and brushed her hair. She looked into her own eyes in the mirror, puffy and distant. She leaned forward over the basin until the light above her threw dark shadows over her features.

Who am I? she wondered. Where am I going? Am I driving my life and my family straight over the edge? Is there something destructive within me that I can't control? Do I somehow attract death and disaster?

She pulled away from the shadows and looked round the bathroom.

Scrubbed and shining, with an antiseptic smell of bleach.

She switched off the light and went on to the landing. Darkness enveloped her, and she relaxed.

It's up to me, she thought. I can do this, if I try. It's no worse than that.

She'd got halfway along the landing when the crash came. The sound reached her as if in a dream, unreal and far away. It didn't scare her, just came as a surprise, a huge crash followed by a crystal rain of shattered glass.

What the hell . . . ?

She walked towards the stairs and was met by a gust of wind. The picture window next to the front door gaped jaggedly against the night. Fear struck. Someone had broken her window in the middle of the night. Someone had walked up to her house and smashed it . . .

Her heart was in her mouth as she ran down the stairs, three steps at a time, and landed in the middle of all the glass splinters just as a second crash shook the house. She stopped mid-stride. It was above her this time.

Ellen's window.

She turned and raced up the stairs again, yanking open the door to the child's bedroom. At that moment something flew through the smashed window, something dark and heavy and rectangular, with a little sparkling tail.

The instant before it hit the floor she knew what it was: a large glass bottle, full of liquid, sealed with a burning rag. A Molotov cocktail.

She slammed the door as the bottle shattered on the floor and the room exploded in fire. Annika could feel

501

the heat against the door, hitting her like a shockwave. She staggered back, arms flailing, hearing the flames roar on the other side of the thin sheet of wood. Oh, God, this can't be happening. The next moment the window of Kalle's room crashed in, and through the half-open door Annika saw a brick land on his bed. She saw it lying there and knew she should be heading towards it but her body wouldn't move, it wouldn't obey her, and she felt her own distorted face stare at the shattered window, watching another heavy bottle fly through the room, the same rectangular darkness with its burning tail.

The plume of flames in Kalle's room hit the ceiling the moment the glass bottle shattered against the wall above the bed. The petrol turned to gas in an instant, the fire riding on its back, throwing itself at the blue curtains printed with cars, the picture books on the Ikea shelves.

Annika stared at the flames, frozen to the spot. She felt the heat hit her hair and skin and stumbled backwards instinctively, against the closed bedroom door.

The children. *Oh, God, the children!*

She staggered into her room, closing the door behind her. She saw the hazy shapes under the covers. Out – now!

It was the smoke that was most dangerous, smoke that killed, not the flames, at least not at first. She glanced at the closed door and saw the deadly gases already rolling in under it, then threw herself at the bed and dragged the covers off Ellen.

'*Ellen! Kalle!*' she screamed, throwing the covers on to the floor by the door, stamping on them to block the crack at the bottom, then ran back to the bed.

'Ellen!' she shouted, pulling the child upright. 'Ellen, we've got to get out.'

The little girl stared at her in horror, still groggy with sleep. Annika picked her up and ran to the window, Ellen's body slippery and hot under her pyjamas.

'Ellen,' Annika whispered, scarcely able to breathe. 'There's a fire, I'm going to help you get out, and when you get down I want you to run to the hedge and sit there. Wait for me and Kalle. Got it?'

She started to cry, loud and scared. 'Mummy,' she howled, 'Mummy, no, Mummy . . .'

Annika peeled her arms away from her neck and put her on the floor by the window. She ran back to the bed. 'Kalle!' she shouted, shaking him. 'Kalle, go and stand over there with Ellen. The house is on fire!'

He sat up, blinking, his hair on end. The white plaster on his forehead shone in the darkness. Annika could hear the fire roaring on the other side of the door. 'Kalle, over here!'

She rushed back to her daughter, winding a sheet into a thick rope that she tied round the child as she shrieked for Daddy, then ran for the door. Annika caught her and swept her up into her arms. 'Ellen! Ellen, listen to me. Ellen, we're going to die if you don't do what I tell you.'

Kalle had started to howl by the window, his little frame shaking. From the corner of her eye Annika saw a dark stain spread over his pyjama trousers as he wet himself. 'Mummy!' he cried. 'I don't want to die!'

I can't do this, Annika thought fleetingly. We're going to die here. This is impossible.

And somewhere she knew that was the wrong thought. It was entirely up to her. She just had to take control. As always.

She made her way to the window and put the little girl down next to her brother, then crouched beside them and hugged them both. 'Okay, this is what we're going to do,' she said, as calmly as she could. 'We'll start with you, Kalle, because you're a big boy and I know you can do this. It'll be easy. I'm going to tie this sheet round your tummy, like a big rope, and then I'm going to lower you down to the terrace. I want you to wait there and help Ellen when she comes down, okay?'

'I don't want to die,' he sobbed.

'Kalle,' Annika said, lifting his chin and looking him in the eye. 'Listen to me, Kalle, you have to help me now. You're a big boy and you have to help Ellen when I lower her down. She's still very little.'

'I'm not little,' Ellen said.

Annika stroked her daughter's cheek and tried to smile. 'You're just right,' she said. 'Can you help me lower Kalle down, do you think?'

She nodded eagerly, her tears forgotten.

Kalle looked doubtful as Annika knotted the blue sheet round his waist. Can I really do this? Annika thought. What if I drop him?

Smoke was starting to pour into the room, and it looked as if the bedding by the door was smouldering.

'Okay,' Annika said, opening the window. 'Are you ready?'

She forced herself to smile at her son, as his lower lip started to tremble again and he took a step towards the door. Annika quickly lifted him on to the windowsill, turned him round to face the garden, then pushed his legs over the edge so they were hanging down the side of the house. She looped the sheet round the central bar of the window, then nudged Kalle over the edge. There was a sharp jolt and he screamed in terror and slid half a metre.

What if he slips through the loop? she thought, letting

out a bit more of the sheet, then a bit more, and a bit more, until finally there was no more sheet wound round the window-frame.

'Are you down, Kalle?' she called. She couldn't let go to lean out and see.

He didn't answer.

'Have you got far to go?'

No answer.

She had to risk it.

She steeled herself, then let the sheet come free of the window-frame. She heard him land on the terrace, then let go of the sheet and leaned out.

'Kalle? Are you all right?'

He was sitting huddled on the terrace, staring back into the house. 'Mummy!' he shouted. 'The kitchen's on fire!'

Inside the bedroom the smoke was grey and thick. The bedding by the door was alight now.

'Kalle,' Annika said, 'I'm going to lower Ellen down now, and I need you to help her when she gets close to you, okay?'

Without waiting for a reply she crouched beside Ellen. 'Now it's your turn,' she said, trying to smile. 'Kalle's already down, and he's going to help you. That's good, isn't it?'

Ellen nodded and waited as Annika knotted the other sheet around her chest with trembling fingers. Then she sat her in the window, as she had with Kalle, and nudged her out.

The jolt wasn't so violent this time: Ellen was much lighter than Kalle.

The door behind Annika caught fire with a muffled oomph.

She lowered the child down the last metre or so.

The heat hit her from behind, wiping out all concentration. Unable to think rationally, she clambered on to the windowsill and threw herself out. She tumbled through the air, straight out and straight down, falling from the upper floor to the terrace just as the room behind her exploded into a firestorm.

She landed on the terrace table, which shuddered under her weight. Pain shot through her and she almost tumbled head first off the edge, but stopped herself by grabbing one of the chairs in front of her.

The world paused. She shut her eyes and took a deep breath.

The pain subsided. She sat up, straightening her legs. She hurt all over, but nothing was broken.

The children?

She clambered off the table and stood up carefully. Kalle and Ellen were standing close together just below the terrace: she could see their faces peeping above the edge.

'Are you okay?' she asked, going down to them carefully, still not sure that her bones really were intact. 'Did you hurt yourselves when you landed?'

The children shook their heads, their hair blowing in the night wind.

A window behind her exploded, sending a shower of glass through the air, and she ducked instinctively, putting her arms out to shield them.

'Come on,' she said, heading across the grass, 'let's get further away.'

The children went with her in their pyjamas, over the dew-damp grass towards Ebba's house. In the distance she heard sirens, a choir of emergency vehicles, and in the neighbouring houses lights were coming on in the summer night.

That was when she saw him.

Her entire body knotted, making her arms shake.

He was standing behind his hedge, looking into her garden. He hadn't seen her because he was craning his neck to look at the upper floor, dodging and hopping between the branches to get a better view.

'Look!' Kalle said, pointing at Wilhelm Hopkins. 'There's our stupid neighbour.'

Annika hushed him and huddled down in the darkness. I mustn't let him know we're alive, she thought. He didn't see us get out and now he thinks he's succeeded.

On bare feet, Annika and the children crept across the road and into Ebba's garden.

'Why is our house on fire, Mummy?' Ellen said.

Annika tried to find her voice, tried to moisten her lips. 'I don't know, darling. Houses catch fire sometimes.'

Ellen's bottom lip started to tremble. 'But where's Daddy?'

'Daddy's at work,' Annika said. 'He's working late.'

'You had an argument,' Kalle said.

'Where's Poppy?' Ellen said. 'Mummy, are Poppy and Ludde in the fire?' She started to cry helplessly and tried to run back to the house, making Annika grab her again.

I can't stay here, she thought. I can't stay here with the children, letting them watch as their home burns down. I can't let them see that our neighbours have set fire to our home and are now creeping about in the bushes watching us get burned alive.

'Poppy,' Ellen sobbed, 'I want my Poppy.'

Annika still had her mobile phone in her pocket.

She pulled it out and checked the display. No one had called. Thomas hadn't called. No one had sent her a text. She rang Thomas, but his phone was switched off and the messaging service clicked in. What could she say? How should she start?

She clicked to end the call and phoned for a taxi instead.

But she didn't have any money – and where could she go?

She looked at the house.

The last windows shattered. The fire was blazing in every room. The sirens were closer now, but the fire brigade wouldn't be able to do anything. Soon the roof would collapse.

She wanted to cry, but felt paralysed. She wanted to scream, but felt mute.

The children pressed tightly against her and she knew she shouldn't be standing there.

The children had been the target. Their rooms had been firebombed. There must have been three Molotov cocktails: one at the bottom of the stairs, one in Ellen's room and one in Kalle's.

Nothing in the master bedroom.

They knew I'd go to the children. They knew I'd try to save them. We wouldn't have been able to get out. We were supposed to die.

This was personal.

Revenge, for the simple fact that they lived there.

Wilhelm Hopkins emerged from behind the hedge and headed towards his porch. He stopped and wiped his shoes carefully before going inside the house.

You're going to pay for this, Annika thought. If it's the last thing I do, you're going to pay for what you've done.

There was a taxi in the area and it swung into Ebba's driveway just a few minutes later.

Annika slumped into the back seat with the children and gave the driver Anne Snapphane's address. 'Bloody hell,' the taxi-driver said, staring wide-eyed at the burning house on the other side of the road. 'Has anyone called the fire brigade?'

At that moment the first fire engine turned into Vinterviksvägen and pulled up in Annika's drive.

'I'll need to go up to one of the flats,' Annika said hoarsely. 'I haven't got any money. Can you wait when we get there while I go up and get some?'

The taxi-driver looked at her in the rear-view mirror. 'Not really,' he said.

She closed her eyes and leaned her head back. 'That's my house on fire,' she said. 'Please.'

He put the car in gear and drove slowly past all the emergency vehicles that were on their way to the fire on Vinterviksvägen. Past the fire engines and trucks, the blue night shredded by the lamps on their roofs.

Tonight will soon be over, Annika thought.

The taxi drove along the shoreline towards the city. To the west the sky was still dark, but behind her it was lit up by something other than the fire. The sun was on its way over the horizon, or soon would be.

'How did the fire start?' the taxi-driver asked.

'I really don't want to talk,' Annika said.

She sat with the children huddled close to her, one on each side, stroking their hair. The swaying of the car soon rocked them to sleep.

When she was sure they were asleep she took out her phone.

Q answered on his direct line after the first ring. 'I didn't think I'd be hearing from you for a few more hours,' he said.

'My house is burning down,' Annika said quietly.

'Someone set fire to it on purpose. Molotov cocktails in the kids' rooms.'

The detective inspector fell silent. Annika could hear the rustling of paper.

'Are you all all right?' he eventually asked.

'I got the children out through my bedroom window, lowered them down using sheets.'

'Can the house be saved?'

'Not a chance,' Annika said. 'It's gone.'

He sighed. 'You really know how to do it . . .' he said.

'I know who did it,' she said. 'Wilhelm Hopkins, the old man next door, the one who phoned about Bernhard Thorell's car. He was standing in the bushes watching after we got out. He was the one who started it.'

'Why do you think that?'

Annika pushed the hair from her face, and realized she was covered with soot. 'He's been trying to get rid of us since we arrived. He uses my lawn as a shortcut and drives his lawnmower over my flowerbeds.'

'That doesn't necessarily mean he's prepared to murder you and your family.'

'He's been trying to get rid of us since day one. He dug up—'

She fell silent, suddenly unable to go on.

Then she said, 'This was personal. It was done by someone who wanted to hurt me as badly as he could. First he smashed the window next to the front door and set fire to the staircase so we wouldn't be able to get downstairs. Then he smashed the windows of the children's rooms. I saw the brick he threw into Kalle's room, and then he threw petrol bombs through the broken windows. Into the children's rooms. *The children's rooms!*'

She started to cry quietly.

510

'I've still got my hands full with Thorell,' Q said. 'Come up here when you've had some sleep. We'll talk more then.'

'Okay,' Annika said.

She tried calling Thomas again.

Still just the messaging service.

Please leave a message after the tone . . .

She breathed soundlessly into the silence of the phone, watching the lights of the suburbs drift past the car windows. Then she cleared her throat. She had to let him know what had happened, had to tell him his children were safe.

Because he hadn't been there. *He hadn't been there.*

She had had to deal with it alone. He had left her and she had had to get herself and the children out all on her own.

The taxi passed the old city boundary at Roslagstull and headed into the centre of Stockholm.

She clicked to end the call.

The Kitten walked towards Passport Control, breathing shallowly, her palms sweating. She *hated* this fucking country. Even the airport exuded smugness: empty, tasteful, neatly effective. Arlanda: what sort of fucking name was that for an airport, some sort of misspelled attempt at Air Landing?

She had tried to be rational. She'd realized that it probably wasn't the geographic location that was the problem. Naturally, it was to do with her, as always. She had messed up her markers, not by much but enough for it all to fall apart.

It was the fault of the people here.

The police in this country weren't normal. They sat in their nasty little rooms carrying out their nasty

511

little tasks as if they were the only thing that mattered. They didn't shy away from using complicated and controversial technology. How fucking irritating was that?

And then there were the law-abiding, ever-observant citizens. They were everywhere, making notes, carefully and conscientiously, phoning the nice, friendly police as soon as they saw something *suspicious*. What fucking losers! Even out in the middle of fucking nowhere they'd stop walking their dogs and phone to report something. How could they put up with themselves?

But worst of all was the oh-so-wonderful reporter. So conscientious! So good with details! So amazingly careful and thorough!

So they'd identified her. Fine! A lot of her protective barriers had been swept away, but not all of them. The damage was serious, but not irreparable.

The queue for Passport Control moved ahead of her, slowly. She sighed, put her hand luggage down and checked the little box in her pocket. (When she had to deal with any official authority, she always made sure she had the box close to hand.)

The reporter. Well, she wouldn't be doing any more reporting now.

The Kitten tried to locate the sense of calm satisfaction in a job well done, but for some reason it wasn't there.

Death by arson was about as far beneath her dignity as she could get. As a tool it was clumsy and unreliable.

But this time it had worked, perfect Molotov cocktails landing right in the kids' beds. She had watched the house until it was burning properly and the fire brigade had shown up. The front door hadn't opened once and no one had jumped from the burning kids' rooms

512

upstairs. No ambulances had turned up to take any smoke-damaged kiddies away.

That'll teach you, bitch, she thought.

Even so, she still couldn't relax.

There wasn't really any cause for concern. Her Russian documentation was as good as a false passport could be, only used once before. There was no reason to think they could link her Russian identity to her real one.

Don't get jumpy, she thought.

Her apartments on the Costa del Sol had been confiscated, along with the villa in Tuscany. (That one didn't matter: she'd never liked it. The Italians were almost as far up their own backsides as the Swedes.) There was no question of ever going home to the family farm outside Boston. But her Swiss bank accounts were still there, along with the room in the boarding house in the Bekaa Valley. Lebanon was a beautiful little country. In fact, she was almost happiest there, really. She had nothing to feel sorry about, nothing at all.

Then it was her turn. She adjusted the glasses on her nose and handed her passport through the hatch of the glass booth, smiling and trying to look bored.

Come on, let's get it over with.

The police bitch behind the glass inspected her passport, looked a bit closer and touched the photograph, then typed something into her computer. The Kitten felt her pulse-rate increase. She licked her lips and swallowed.

Come on, for fuck's sake!

The woman looked up at her, carefully, intently, then folded the passport back to open it better. *Watch out!* The Kitten wanted to say. *It's new!*

'A problem?' the Kitten said, in broken English.

The police officer ignored her, the arrogant witch. Instead she picked up a phone, dialled a short number and waited. Then she looked up, and the Kitten felt her gaze pass right through her body, like an X-ray. The woman said something into the phone in that Viking gibberish, waited a few moments, then hung up. She got up, tucked her chair under the desk, and emerged through the door in the side of the cubicle. The Kitten followed her intently with her eyes. The woman was coming straight towards her, and she couldn't move, felt not the slightest impulse to run.

'Miss Houseman?' the police officer said, stopping in front of her and taking hold of her elbow. 'Miss Frances Houseman, would you mind coming with me, please?'

They knew her true identity. They had found her core – Frances, after the first woman in the US cabinet. The Kitten put her hand into her pocket and opened the little box. 'I should have listened to Dad,' she said. She found the pill and popped it into her mouth.

I should have married Grant, she thought, then bit down hard on the cyanide capsule.

Author's Acknowledgements

This is a novel, a work of complete fiction. But I do make use of a large number of facts when I am building the foundations of my story.

The Karolinska Institute, for instance, certainly exists, and is in gratifyingly good health. It is consistently ranked in the top 10 medical universities in Europe.

However, neither the Department of Medical Epidemiology and Molecular Biology, nor the Department of Physiology and Bio-Physics, exist within the Karolinska Institute. These departments are entirely the product of the author's imagination, but the way they work is roughly the same as the way similar workplaces function around the world in real life.

Even if the Karolinska Institute's Nobel Assembly and Nobel Committee in purely technical terms function in the way described in this novel, I would like to make it clear that I haven't followed their working practices and make no claims to have depicted their work in a factually correct way.

Nor is there any modern white building at the end of Berzelius väg in Solna. I have simply relocated a building from the Huddinge campus of the Karolinska Institute to its main site in Solna.

The newsroom of the *Evening Post* does not exist either, although it shares some characteristics with many media organizations I have worked for over the years.

Alfred Nobel, on the other hand, most definitely did exist, along with his brother Emil, Beatrice Cenci, Bertha von Suttner and Sofie Hess. Everything I have written about these characters in this novel, about their lives and deaths, is based entirely upon historical fact.

The portrait of Beatrice Cenci painted by Guido Reni, or possibly by his daughter Elisabetta Sirani, also exists, but it belongs not to a private collection in Djursholm in Stockholm, but to the *Galleria Nazionale d'Arte Antica* in Rome.

The whole sad story of the theatrical drama *Nemesis*, a tragedy in four acts written by Alfred Nobel, is accurately depicted. Today just one original copy of the work exists in the National Archives in Stockholm. The whereabouts of the other two copies that Nathan Söderblom spared from the flames remains unknown.

But today Nobel's spiritual testament can be purchased and read by anyone.

On the anniversary of Nobel's death in 2005 the play finally received its world premiere when it was performed at Strindberg's Intima Teater in Stockholm. Both the play and the actors received outstanding reviews. The poet Alfred Nobel finally received public recognition, albeit 109 years too late.

I could not have written this novel without the help of a number of very patient people. Many thanks to you all!

Cecilia Björkdahl, project manager at the Karolinska Institute, for research visits, checking facts and an introduction into laboratory routines (and for letting Ebba

Romanova borrow your research!). I couldn't have done this without you, Cilla!

Åsa Nilsonne, professor in medicinal psychology and author, for help with contacts, discussions of motives for murder and the world of scientific research.

Thomas Bodström, lawyer and former Minister of Justice, for the opportunity to follow the internal work of the Justice Department, as well as checking facts and discussions about the genesis and implementation of legislation.

Brun Ulfhake, Professor of Anatomy at the Karolinska Institute, who showed me KI's animal research facility, its laboratories and halls.

Alexandra Carlberg, official guide at Stockholm City Hall, who showed me large parts of the building, including lifts and goods entrances.

The staff at the *Expressen* newspaper's main premises in Stockholm who allowed me to get in their way, among them Kerstin Thornström and Anders Fallenius, Carolina Ekeus, press secretary for the National Swedish Police Board, for help regarding disclosure bans and legislation covering freedom of speech, according to paragraph ten of chapter twenty-three of the Judicial Procedure Act.

Jan Guillou, author, for help about different sorts of weapons and their areas of use.

Jonas Gummesson, head of TV4 News, for information about the political decision-making process.

Dan Boija, Detective Inspector with Stockholm Police's violent crime unit, for a description of the work involved in putting together photofit pictures.

Anders Sigurdson, Police Superintendent with Stockholm Police Authority and head of security for the 2005 Nobel banquet, for describing the nature of regular security procedures and the division of responsibilities surrounding the Nobel festivities in Stockholm on 10 December each year.

Margareta Östman, chemist with the National Chemicals Inspectorate, for clarifying the characteristics of various flammable liquids and for discussions about how best to burn down a house.

Erik Marklund, motoring expert and my brother, for information about how to sabotage car brakes.

Niclas Salomonsson, my literary agent, and his staff at Salomonsson Agency in Stockholm, for all their great work.

And finally, Tove Alsterdal, dramatist and editor, who always reads whatever I write first of everyone. If you hadn't set up your cabaret in Nobel's old laboratory in Vinterviken, this novel would never have been written.

I have also had a great deal of help from the books *Alfred Bernhard Nobel* by Kenne Fant (Norstedts), *Vem älskar Alfred Nobel?* (*Who Loves Alfred Nobel?*) by Vilgot Sjöman (Natur och Kultur), as well as from hundreds of internet sites. The most important: www.nobelprize.org, www.wikipedia.org, www.mediaarkivet.se, www.ki.se, and www.tv4.se.

Any mistakes or errors which have crept in are, as always, entirely my own.

You can find out what happens to Annika next in Liza Marklund's upcoming novel.

The most famous police officer in Sweden is found murdered in his bed. His four-year-old son has vanished without a trace. His wife, Julia, is under suspicion and no one believes her when she says she is innocent. No one except for her best friend Nina, also a police officer.

And possibly news reporter Annika Bengtzon. Thomas has left her and is demanding custody of their children. The newsroom at the *Evening Post* is in chaos as cutbacks mean many of the journalists are losing their jobs.

So Annika turns all her energies to her work, investigating the life of the murdered man. But if Julia is telling the truth, where is their son?

Turn the page for a sneak preview . . .

Part 1

Thursday 3 June

The call went out at 03.21. It was sent from the regional communication centre to all patrol-cars in the centre of Stockholm, short and to the point:

'Control to all units, report of shots fired on Bondegatan.'

No more details. No house number, no information about casualties or who made the call.

Even so, Nina felt her stomach clench.

Bondegatan's a long street, there must be a thousand people living there.

As Andersson, in the passenger seat, reached for the radio she quickly grabbed it from him, pressing the transmit button on its left-hand side, whilst with her other hand steering on to Renstiernas gata.

'1617 here,' she answered. 'We're one block away. Have you got a house number?'

Andersson let out a theatrical sigh and looked demonstratively out of the window. Nina glanced at him as the car rolled towards Bondegatan. *Okay, sulk if you want to.*

'Control to 1617,' the operator said over the radio. 'You're the closest unit. Is that you, Hoffman, over?'

The number of the patrol-car was linked to the number on her police badge. One of the routines before each shift started was to feed the car's registration number and your badge number into the Central Operations Planning System, handily abbreviated to COP, so that the operator in the communication centre could always see who was in which vehicle.

'Affirmative,' she said. 'Turning in to Bondegatan now . . .'

'How does it look, over?'

She stopped the car and looked up at the heavy stone buildings on either side of the street. The dawn light hadn't reached between the buildings yet, and she squinted as she tried to make out shapes in the gloom. There were lights on in one top-floor flat on the right-hand side, but otherwise everything was dark. It was evidently a street-cleaning night, no parking allowed, which made the street look particularly empty and abandoned. One rusty Peugeot stood alone, a parking ticket on its windscreen.

'No visible activity, as far as I can tell. What number was it, over?'

The operator gave her the address and she went completely cold: *that's Julia's place, that's where Julia and David live.*

'And he's got a flat on Söder, Nina! God, it'll be nice to get away from this corridor!'

'Don't just take him because of his flat, Julia . . .'

'Take a look, 1617, approach with caution . . .'

She wound down all the car's windows to make it easier to hear any sounds from the street, put the car in gear, turned off the headlights and drove slowly down the familiar street, no flashing lights, no siren. Andersson had perked up and was leaning forward intently.

'Do you reckon it's anything, then?' he asked.

I hope to God it isn't anything!

She stopped outside the door and switched off the engine, then leaned forward to peer up at the grey cement façade. There was a light in a second floor window.

'We'll have to assume the situation is dangerous,' she said tersely and grabbed the radio again. '1617 here, we're in position, and it looks like there are people awake in the building. Should we wait for 9070, over?'

'9070 is still in Djursholm,' the operator said, referring to the operational command vehicle.

'The Nobel murderer?' Andersson wondered, and Nina gestured to him to be quiet.

'Are there any other cars in the area? Or the armed response unit, over?' she asked over the radio.

'We're switching frequency,' the operator said. 'All concerned, switching to zero-six.'

'That whole Nobel business was quite a story,' Andersson said. 'Did you hear they've caught the bastard?'

Silence spread through the car, and Nina could feel her bulletproof vest rubbing at the base of her spine. Andersson shuffled restlessly in his seat and peered up at the building.

'This could very easily be a false alarm,' he said, to quell his enthusiasm.

Oh, dear God, let it be a false alarm!

The radio crackled, now on the designated frequency.

'Okay, has everyone switched? 1617, come in?'

She pressed the transmit button again, her mouth dry.

'Zero-six, we're here, over.'

The others responded as well, two patrols from the city centre and one from the county force.

523

'The armed response unit isn't available,' the operator said. '9070 is on its way. Hoffman, you have operational command until the command unit gets there. We need a considered response, hold some units back. We'll form a ring around the location, get cars in place. All units to approach in silence.'

At that moment a patrol-car swung into Bondegatan from the other direction. It stopped one block away, the headlights going out as the engine was switched off.

Nina opened the car door and stepped out, her heavy boots echoing in the street. She pressed her ear-piece tightly into her left ear as she opened the boot of the car.

'Shield and baton,' she whispered to Andersson, as she tuned in to frequency zero-six on the handheld radio.

Over at the next block she saw two policemen get out of the patrol-car.

'1980, is that you over there?' she said quietly into the speaker microphone on her right shoulder.

'Affirmative,' one of the officers replied, raising his hand.

'You're coming in with us,' she said.

She ordered the other patrols to take up positions at opposite corners of a square, to ensure they had all lines of sight covered, one at the corner of Skånegatan and Södermannagatan, the other over on Östgötagatan.

Andersson was rummaging around among the bandages, fire extinguishers, shovels, flares, lamp, antiseptic gel, cordon tape, warning triangles, paperwork and all the other clutter that was stuffed into the boot of the car.

'1617 to Control,' she said over the radio. 'Do you have a name for the person who called in, over?'

A short silence.

'Erlandsson, Gunnar, second floor.'

'He's still up. We're going in.'

The other officers came over, introducing themselves as Sundström and Landén. She nodded curtly and tapped in the entry-code on the keypad beside the door. None of the others reacted to the fact that she knew what it was. She stepped through the door, turning the volume on the radio down to barely audible. Her colleagues filed in silently behind her. Andersson, the last to enter, wedged the door open wide so that they could retreat to the street quickly if need be.

The stairwell was dark, deserted. The only source of light came from the lift, seeping through the oblong glass window in the metal door.

'Is there a courtyard?' Landén asked quietly.

'Behind the lift,' Nina whispered. 'The door on the right leads to the cellar.'

Landén and Sundström each checked a door, both were locked.

'Open the lift door,' she said to Andersson.

The officer wedged the door open so no one would be able to use the lift, then stopped by the stairs and awaited her order.

She could feel panic thudding at the back of her head, and took refuge in the rulebook to conquer it.

Make an initial evaluation of the position. Secure the stairwell. Speak to the man who made the call and find out where the suspected shooting occurred.

'Okay, let's take a look!' she said, heading quickly and carefully up the stairs, floor by floor. Andersson followed her, keeping one flight of stairs below her the whole time.

The stairwell was gloomy. Her movements were making her clothes rustle in the silence. There was a smell of cleaning fluid. Behind the closed doors she could sense the presence of other people without actually hearing them, a bed creaking, a tap running.

There's nothing here, no danger, everything's fine.

Finally, slightly out of breath, she reached the flats on the top floor. It was different to the others, with a marble floor and specially designed security doors. She knew that the housing association had renovated the attic space as luxury apartments in the late 1980s, just in time for the crash in property prices. The flats had stood empty for several years, almost bankrupting the housing association. Today, of course, they were ridiculously expensive, but David was still angry at the poor judgement shown by the previous committee.

Andersson came up behind her, panting heavily. Nina could sense her colleague's irritated disappointment as he wiped his forehead.

'Looks like a false alarm,' he declared.

'Let's see what the man who called in has to say,' Nina replied, going back downstairs.

Sundström and Landén were waiting on the second floor, beside a door marked ERLANDSSON, G & A.

Nina stepped up to the door and knocked quietly.

No response.

Andersson shifted his feet impatiently behind her.

She knocked again, considerably louder.

A man in a blue and white striped towelling dressing-gown appeared through the crack behind a heavy safety chain.

'Gunnar Erlandsson? Police,' Nina said, holding up her badge. 'You called about some suspicious noises? Can we come in?'

The man closed the door, fumbled with the chain for a couple of seconds, then the door swung open.

'Come in,' he whispered. 'Would you like some coffee?

And there's some of my wife's Swiss roll, with homemade rhubarb marmalade. She's dozing at the moment, she has trouble getting to sleep and took a pill . . .'

Nina stepped into the hall. The layout of the flat was exactly like David and Julia's, but this one was considerably tidier.

'Please, don't go to any trouble for us,' Nina said.

She noted that Gunnar Erlandsson had been addressing Landén, the largest of the men. Now he was looking anxiously from one to the other, uncertain of where to look.

'Gunnar,' Nina said, gently taking hold of his upper arm, 'can we sit down and go through what you heard?'

The man stiffened.

'Of course,' he said. 'Yes, of course.'

He led them into a pedantically neat living room with brown leather sofas and a thick rug on the floor. Out of habit he settled into an armchair facing the television, and Nina sat down on the coffee-table in front of him.

'Tell me what happened, Gunnar.'

The man swallowed and his eyes were still flitting between the officers.

'I woke up,' he said. 'A noise woke me up, a bang. It sounded like a shot.'

'What made you think it was a shot?' Nina asked.

'I was lying in bed, and at first I wasn't sure if I was dreaming, but then I heard it again.'

The man pulled out a pair of glasses and started polishing them nervously.

'Do you hunt?' Nina asked.

Gunnar Erlandsson stared at her in horror.

'Good grief, no,' he said. 'Murdering innocent animals, no, that seems utterly medieval to me.'

'If you're not familiar with firearms,' Nina said, 'what

made you think that you heard a shot, precisely? Could it have been a car backfiring, or some other sudden noise out in the street?'

He blinked several times and looked beseechingly up at Landén.

'It didn't come from outside,' he said, pointing at the ceiling. 'It came from the Lindholms'. I'd swear that's where it came from.'

Nina felt the room lurch and stood up quickly, clenching her teeth to stop herself screaming.

'Thank you,' she said. 'We'll be back later to take a formal statement.'

The man said something else about coffee, but she went out into the stairwell and up the stairs to the floor above, two steps at a time, up to David and Julia's door.

David and Julia Lindholm.

I don't know if I can go on, Nina.

You haven't gone and done anything silly, have you, Julia?

She turned and gestured to Sundström and Landén that they should cover the stairs in both directions, and that Andersson should approach the door with her. They took up position on either side of the door, leaving any line of fire clear.

Nina felt the door gently. Locked. She knew it closed automatically if it wasn't held open. She fumbled for the ASP baton in her belt, then opened it with a light flick of the wrist. She pushed it gently through the letterbox and peered in cautiously.

There was a light on in the hall. The air from the flat smelt of newspaper print and cooking. She could see the morning paper on the mat. She quickly moved her baton, laying it horizontally so that it held the letterbox open. Then she pulled out her pistol and made sure there was a bullet in the chamber, then gestured to the others to be on the alert. She nodded towards the doorbell so that Andersson realized she was about to make their presence known.

Pointing her weapon at the floor, she pressed the doorbell and heard it ring inside the flat.

'Police!' she called. 'Open up!'

She listened intently to any sound from the letterbox. No response.

'Julia!' she called in a slightly quieter voice. 'Julia, it's me, Nina. Open up. David?'

Her vest was tight across her chest, making it hard to breathe. She could feel the sweat breaking out on her forehead.

'Is that . . . Lindholm?' Andersson said. 'David Lindholm? You know his wife?'

Nina holstered her gun and pulled out her personal mobile from the inside pocket of her jacket, and dialled the familiar number to the flat.

Andersson took a step closer to her.

'Listen,' he said, standing far too close to her. She resisted the impulse to back away. 'If you have a personal connection to anyone in there, then you shouldn't . . . '

Nina stared blankly at Andersson as the phone started to ring on the other side of the door, long, lonely rings that seeped out through the letterbox.

Andersson took a step back. The ringing stopped abruptly and the answer-machine clicked in. Nina ended the call and dialled another number. A cheerful tune started to play on the floor just inside the door. Julia's mobile must be on the hall floor, probably in her handbag.

She's home, Nina thought. She never goes out without her bag.

'Julia,' she said once more as the mobile's voicemail clicked in. 'Julia, are you there?'

The silence was echoing. Nina took several steps back, pressed the transmitter on her radio and spoke quietly into it.

'1617 here. We've spoken to the informant and according to him he heard what he thought were shots, probably from the flat above. We've made our presence known but there's been no response from inside the flat. What do you advise, over?'

There was a short pause before the answer reached her earpiece.

'The armed response unit is still unavailable. Your call. Over and out.'

She let go of the radio.

'Okay,' she said quietly, looking at Andersson and the other two officers on the stairs. 'We'll force the door. Have we got a crowbar in 1617?'

'We've got one in our car,' Landén said. Nina nodded towards the stairs and the officer hurried off.

'Do you think it's appropriate for you to be leading the operation if . . .' Andersson began.

'What's the alternative?' Nina cut him off, more harshly than she intended. 'Handing over command to you?'

Andersson gulped.

'Wasn't there something funny about Julia Lindholm?' he said. 'Wasn't she involved in some sort of scandal?'

Nina took out her mobile and called Julia's number once more, still no response.

Landén returned to the landing with the necessary equipment in his arms, a length of metal almost a metre long that was basically an outsized and reinforced crowbar.

'Can we really do this?' Landén said breathlessly as he passed her the tool.

'Any delay could just make things worse,' Nina said.

Paragraph twenty-one of police legislation. *The police have the right to gain entry to a property, room or other location if there is reason to believe that someone inside may have died, be unconscious or otherwise incapable of summoning assistance . . .*

She passed the crowbar to Andersson and clicked off the safety catch of her pistol, nodding to the others to take up their positions.

As Andersson inserted the end of the crowbar beside the door-frame, she put her foot down close to the door so that it wouldn't fly open and injure her colleague, in the event that there was actually someone inside who might try to force their way out.

After three carefully judged attempts, the door gave way and the lock broke. The air that streamed out into the stairwell carried with it the last smells of cooking.

Nina listened intently for any sound within the flat. She shut her eyes and concentrated. Then she jerked her head quickly to her left, taking a first glance at the hall, empty. Another glance, this time towards the kitchen, empty. A third, towards the bedroom.

Empty.

'I'm going in,' she said, pressing her back against the frame of the door, and turning towards Andersson, 'Cover me.'

'Police!' she called again.

No response.

Her body tense, she slid round the door-frame, kicking the newspaper aside and stepping silently into the hall. The lamp hanging from the ceiling was swaying slightly, presumably from the draught. Julia's bag was

531

indeed lying on the floor to the left of the front door. Alexander's jacket was next to it. David and Julia's coats were hanging from hooks on the rack to the right.

She stared straight ahead, towards the kitchen, hearing Andersson's breathing behind her.

'Check the nursery,' she said, gesturing with her gun towards the first open door on the left, without taking her eyes from the entrance to the kitchen.

Her colleague slid in, Nina could hear the fabric of his trousers rustling.

'Nursery clear,' he said a few seconds later.

'Check the wardrobes,' Nina said. 'Close the door behind you when you're done.'

She took a few steps forward and took a quick look inside the kitchen. The table was bare, but there were plates with the remains of spaghetti bolognese on the worktop.

Julia, Julia, can't you be a bit tidier? I'm so damn tired of clearing up after you.

Sorry, I didn't think.

The draught was coming from the bedroom, one of the windows must be open. The curtains were drawn, making the room completely dark. She stared into the shadows for a few moments, detecting no movement. But there was a smell, something sharp and unfamiliar.

She reached out a hand and switched on the light.

David was lying on his back across the bed, naked. Where his genitals should have been was a bloody mass of entrails and skin.

'Police,' she said, forcing herself to act as if he were still alive. 'You have a weapon aimed at you. Show your hands.'

Thundering silence in response, and she noticed that she had tunnel vision. She looked round the room, the

532

curtains were moving slightly, there was a half-full glass of water on the bedside table on Julia's side of the bed. The duvet was in a heap on the floor at the end of the bed. On top of it lay a weapon identical to hers, a Sig Sauer 225.

Nina felt mechanically for her radio.

'1617 to Control. We have one casualty at the scene, unclear if he's still alive. Looks like gunshot wounds to the head and groin, over.'

As she waited for a reply she went over to the bed, looked down at the body and realized the man was dead. His right eye was closed, as if he were still asleep. In place of the left eye was a gaping entry-hole into his skull. The flow of blood had stopped, his heart had stopped beating. His bowels had opened, leaving a brown sludge of acrid-smelling excrement on the mattress.

'Where's the ambulance?' she asked over the radio. 'Didn't they get the same alarm as us, over?'

'I'm sending an ambulance and forensics,' Control said in her ear. 'Is there anyone else in the flat, over?'

Andersson appeared in the doorway, glancing at the body.

'You're needed out here,' he said, pointing towards the bathroom door.

Nina put her gun in its holster and hurried out into the hall, opened the bathroom door and held her breath.

Julia was lying on the floor next to the bath. Her hair was like a pale halo round her head, partially smeared in a mess of vomited spaghetti and sauce. She was wearing underwear and a large t-shirt, her knees were pulled up to her chin, in a foetal position. She was lying on one hand, and the other was cramped in a fist.

'Julia,' Nina said gently, leaning over the woman. She brushed her hair away from her face and saw that her eyes were wide open. Her face was covered with pale-red splatters of blood. A string of saliva was hanging from the corner of her mouth down to the floor.

Oh God, she's dead, she's dead and I didn't save her. I'm sorry!

A rattling breath made the woman jerk, as she gasped before her stomach retched once more.

'Julia,' Nina said, loudly and clearly now. 'Julia, are you hurt?'

The woman retched in vain several times before subsiding back on the floor.

'Julia,' Nina said, putting her hand on her friend's shoulder. 'Julia, it's me. What happened? Are you hurt?'

She pulled the woman up into a sitting position, leaning her against the bath.

'1617,' Control repeated in her ear. 'I say again, are there other casualties in the flat, over?'

Julia closed her eyes and let her head fall back against the enamel. Nina caught it with her left hand as she checked the woman's pulse in her neck. It was racing.

'Affirmative, two casualties, one presumed dead, over.'

She let go of the radio.

'Andersson!' she called over her shoulder. 'Search the flat, every inch. There should be a four-year-old here somewhere.'

Julia moved her lips, and Nina wiped the vomit from her chin.

'What did you say?' she whispered. 'Julia, are you trying to say something?'

Nina looked around and made sure that there was no sign of a weapon in the bathroom.

'How much do we want to cordon off?' Andersson asked from the hall.

'The stairwell,' Nina said. 'Forensics are on their

534

way, and people from the crime unit. Start questioning the neighbours. Take Erlandsson first, then the others on this floor. And check to see if whoever delivers the papers saw anything, he must have only just been. Have you searched all the rooms?'

'Yes. Even checked the oven.'

'No sign of the boy anywhere?'

Andersson hesitated in the doorway.

'Is there something you don't understand?' Nina asked.

Her colleague shifted his weight from one foot to the other.

'I think it's bloody inappropriate, you being part of this investigation,' he said, 'considering that . . .'

'Well, I'm here and I've got it,' she said curtly in a sharp tone of voice. 'Get the cordon sorted.'

'Okay, okay,' Andersson said, and lumbered off.

Julia's lips were moving nonstop, but she wasn't making any sound. Nina was still supporting her head with her left hand.

'The ambulance is on its way,' Nina said, as she examined the woman with her free hand, following the outline of her body under the t-shirt, tracing her skin.

No wounds, not even a scratch. No weapon.

In the distance she could hear the sound of sirens and was gripped by panic.

'Julia,' she said loudly, slapping the woman on the cheek with the palm of her hand. 'Julia, what happened? Tell me!'

The woman's eyes flickered and cleared for a moment.

'Alexander,' she whispered.

Nina leaned down close to Julia's face.

'What about Alexander?' she asked.

'She took him,' Julia gasped. 'The other woman, she took Alexander.'

Then she fainted.

As Julia Lindholm was being carried out on a stretcher from the flat she shared with her husband on Södermalm, Annika Bengtzon was sitting in a taxi on her way into the centre of Stockholm. The sun was rising over the horizon as the car passed the city limits at Roslagstull, colouring the rooftops a blazing red. The contrast with the black, empty streets hurt Annika's eyes.

The taxi-driver kept glancing at her in the rear-view mirror, but she pretended not to notice.

'Do you know how the fire started?' he asked.

'I told you, I don't want to talk,' she said, staring at the buildings flashing past.

Her house had just burned down. Someone had thrown three incendiary grenades through the windows, first one at the foot of the stairs, then one into each of the children's rooms. She'd managed to get her son and daughter out through the window of her own bedroom at the back of the house, and now she was clutching them tight as they sat on either side of her in the back seat of the car. Both she and the children smelt of smoke, and her cornflower-blue top had soot stains on it.

I bring death and misery with me. Everyone I love dies.

Stop it, she thought sternly, biting the inside of her cheek. I made it, after all. It's all a matter of focusing and then acting.

'I never usually drive anyone on credit,' the taxi-driver said sullenly, pulling up at a red light.

Annika closed her eyes.

Six months ago she had discovered that Thomas,

her husband, had been having an affair with a female colleague, an icy little blonde called Sophia Grenborg. Annika had put a stop to the relationship, but she had never confronted Thomas and told him that she knew.

Yesterday he had found out that she had known all along.

You've been lying and pretending and fooling me for months, he had yelled, *and it's the same with everything you do. You decide what the world looks like, and anyone who doesn't agree with you is an idiot.*

'That's not true,' she whispered, aware that she was about to burst into tears in the back seat of the taxi.

She wanted us to meet again. I'm on my way there now.

Her eyes were stinging and she opened them wide to stop the tears from overflowing. The stone façades of the buildings flickered and shone.

If you go now, you can never come back.

He had stared at her with his new, strange, narrow gaze, his red, terrible, dead eyes.

Okay.

And she had watched him cross the parquet floor and pick up his briefcase and open the front door and go out into the grey mist. He walked out and the door closed behind him and he didn't look back once.

He had left her and someone had thrown three firebombs into the house. Someone had tried to kill her and the children and he hadn't been there to save her, she'd had to cope alone, and she knew perfectly well who'd thrown the bombs. The neighbour on the other side of the rear hedge, the one who'd ruined her lawn by driving across it, dug up her garden and destroyed her flowerbeds, the one who'd done all he could to get rid of her: Wilhelm Hopkins, chairman of the villa-owners' association.

She held the children more tightly.

I'm going to get you back for this, you bastard.

She'd tried calling Thomas, but his mobile was switched off.

He didn't want to be reached, he didn't want to be disturbed, because she knew what he was doing.

So she hadn't left a message, she'd just breathed into his new, free life and then clicked to end the call. It served him right.

The betrayer. The deceiver.

'What number did you say it was?'

The taxi-driver turned into Artillerigatan.

Annika stroked the children's hair to wake them up.

'We're here,' she whispered as the taxi pulled up. 'We're at Anne's. Come on, darlings . . .'

She opened the door and the night chill swept into the car and made Ellen curl up into a little ball. Kalle whimpered in his sleep.

'I want your mobile as security,' the taxi-driver said.

Annika shepherded the children out of the car, turned round and dropped her phone on the back seat.

'I've turned it off, so you can forget about making any calls,' she said, slamming the door.

Anne Snapphane turned her head to take a cautious look at the man lying on the pillow beside her, at the dark, gelled hair sticking out over his forehead, his quivering nostrils. He was falling asleep.

It was a long time since she'd slept next to anyone, actually not since Mehmet got engaged to Little Miss Monogamous and abandoned their open, functional relationship.

How pretty he is, and how young. Scarcely more than a boy.

I wonder if he thinks I'm too fat, she thought, checking to see if her mascara had run. It had, but not much.

Too fat, she thought. Or too old.

What had been most exciting for her had been the taste of strong lager in his mouth.

She felt rather ashamed at the realization.

It was six months since she last drank any alcohol.

How come it wasn't longer than that? It felt like an eternity.

She rolled onto her side and studied the profile of the young man beside her.

This could be the start of something new, something fresh and fun and good.

It would look great in the little boxes of basic information when the papers interviewed her:

Family: daughter, 5, and boyfriend, 23.

She reached out a hand to touch his hair, the hard clumps almost like dreadlocks.

'Robin,' she whispered in a soundless exhalation, moving her fingers just above his face. 'Tell me you care about me.'

The angry buzz of the doorbell out in the hall woke him with a start, and he looked round in confusion. Anne pulled her hand back as if she'd burned herself.

'What the fuck?' he said, staring at Anne as if he'd never seen her before.

She pulled the sheet under her chin and tried to smile.

'It's just the doorbell,' she said. 'I won't bother to answer it.'

He sat up in bed, and she noticed that all his hair-care products had left a big stain on the pillowcase.

'Is it your old man?' he said, looking at her sceptically, anxiously. 'You said you didn't have a bloke.'

'It's not a bloke,' Anne said, and got up, still holding the sheet, trying in vain to wrap it around her as she stumbled out towards the hall.

**READ THE COMPLETE BOOK –
AVAILABLE SPRING 2013**

VANISHED

LIZA MARKLUND

People can't just disappear . . . or can they?

At a derelict port in Stockholm, two brutally murdered men are found by a security guard. In the same area a young woman, Aida, is on the run from a deranged gunman.

Meanwhile, journalist Annika Bengtzon is approached by a woman wanting her story published in the *Evening Post*. She claims to have founded an organization to erase people's pasts – giving vulnerable individuals a completely new identity.

Annika helps Aida to get in touch with the foundation. But as she begins to investigate this woman's story, more bodies turn up and she finds herself getting dangerously close to the truth – that all is not as it seems . . .

'One of the most popular crime writers of our time'
Patricia Cornwell

THE BOMBER

LIZA MARKLUND

SEVEN DAYS. THREE KILLINGS. ONE WOMAN WHO KNOWS TOO MUCH . . .

Crime reporter **Annika Bengtzon** is woken by a phonecall in the early hours of a wintry morning. An explosion has ripped apart the Olympic Stadium. And a victim has been blow to pieces.

As Annika delves into the details of the bombing and the background of the victim, there is a second explosion.

When her police source reveals they are hot on the heels of the bomber, Annika is guaranteed an exclusive with her name on it. But it soon becomes clear that she has uncovered too much, as she finds herself the target of a deranged serial killer . . .

'Edge-of-your-seat suspense'
Harlan Coben

'Nail-biting action and excitement'
Daily Express

The number one international bestseller